P9-CFY-322

SIDE BY SIDE

ALSO BY JENNI L. WALSH

Becoming Bonnie

JENNI L. WALSH

A TOM DOHERTY ASSOCIATES BOOK
NEW YORK

This is a work of fiction. All of the characters, organizations, and events portrayed in this novel are either products of the author's imagination or are used fictitiously.

SIDE BY SIDE

A Forge Book
Published by Tom Doherty Associates
175 Fifth Avenue
New York, NY 10010

www.tor-forge.com

Forge® is a registered trademark of Macmillan Publishing Group, LLC.

The Library of Congress Cataloging-in-Publication Data is available upon request.

ISBN 978-0-7653-9845-1 (hardcover)
ISBN 978-0-7653-9846-8 (ebook)

Our books may be purchased in bulk for promotional, educational, or business use. Please contact your local bookseller or the Macmillan Corporate and Premium Sales Department at 1-800-221-7945, extension 5442, or by email at MacmillanSpecialMarkets@macmillan.com.

First Edition: June 2018

Printed in the United States of America

0 9 8 7 6 5 4 3 2 1

SIDE
BY
SIDE

PART ONE

BONNIE PARKER

1

I'M A FOOL FOR BUSTING CLYDE OUT OF MCCLELLAND COUNTY jail.

My fingers rest on the typewriter keys. It's my own fault "Bonnie and Clyde" only exists in my head. That's the way it's been for nearly two years, ever since Clyde got caught again.

I breathe in, a cigarette clenched between my teeth, and the tip glows red. The smoke swirls 'round my mouth, escaping between my lips. I can right my wrong. We can be *us* again, if I can convince the governor of an early parole.

I snuff out my cigarette, glance 'cross the Barrows' living room at Clyde's daddy with a newspaper, and get down to business. I jab my fingers into the typewriter keys.

Dear Governor Sterling:

Letters ago, I searched for that colon. It took practice to remember to also hold down the shift key, or else a semicolon would blot onto the paper and I'd have to start again. Now both my pinkies know where to go. I press the carriage-return lever. The paper turns up and the typewriter screeches as it shifts to start a new line.

With my back ramrod straight, I begin.

I am writing on behalf of Clyde Champion Barrow, prisoner number 63527, to ask that his seven, two-year sentences be served concurrently, concluding at two years—

Ding!

I press the carriage-return lever. The paper feeds up. The typewriter screeches.

—as opposed to the mandated fourteen years.

Tears well up in my eyes, and I sniffle. The winter air feels too cold, even indoors, even with the fire crackling beside me. Mr. Barrow sets his newspaper aside to stoke it, a distant look masking his features.

On his behalf, I have secured a paying position.

I don't feel even a lick of shame over that fib. If ya want a parole, a job is a necessity—and a challenge to find nowadays.

More words fill the page.

Profoundly remorseful.

Even if that's not particularly true. I'd say Clyde's more profoundly resourceful, 'specially with his quick hands—on cars, on safes, and on me.

Clyde's daddy ain't more than a few feet away, yet I can't help trailing a finger up my thigh, pretending it's Clyde's touch. Eyes closed, through my dress, I cross the seam of my chemise, imagining Clyde working his palm beneath. He'd smirk. That boy is always quick to smirk. My lips quiver, fighting to keep my face from showing the fantasy running through my head.

I open my eyes, and the reality of where I am—and who I'm without—crashes into me. With renewed focus, I keep typing, line after line, trying to persuade the governor to let Clyde come home to me. Then I can start living again. Then Clyde can, after all he's been through.

V—

I hold down the key, biting my lip, composing myself. I let up, and continue.

Viciously brutalized.

Buck, being Clyde's older brother, struggled to relay that to me. His teeth grit and his breath held as he explained how guards are swift to beat Clyde. I cringed, imagining the guard patrolling on horseback around the grounds, smacking the butt of his rifle into Clyde's back. A demand to work harder, faster. Clyde referred to life at the prison farm as slave labor.

"Stay in Dallas, darling," he wrote to me, the letter typed. "I can't have you seeing me like this."

This.

What in God's name does it mean? I've seen Clyde purple and blue, the aftermath of him stepping in when my deadbeat husband came back for me. What makes these bruises different?

I shake the thought from my head and focus on my letter.

I implore you to see Clyde as worthy of reconsideration, compassion, and clemency.

In closing, I add:

Respectfully,

Cumie Barrow

Clyde won't let me sign my name, not wanting those guards who read our letters to utter it. His letters to me are addressed to *Darling*. Mine to him are signed *Honey*. Pardon letters are from his ma. She's able to read and write just fine, but with both Clyde and Buck locked away, the poor woman's heart is too heavy to find the right words.

The typewriter whines as I rip the paper free.

In her kitchen, I find Mrs. Barrow elbow-deep in a bird. After a quick wipe on her apron, she scribbles her signature with a pen. Clyde's mama gives me the letter and a hug, her thick arms pulling me to her. "Thank you, sweet Bonnie."

Then it's off to the post office.

I ain't more than two steps out of the Barrows' apartment, tacked on to the back of their service shop, when I'm face-to-chest with my much leggier best friend.

"What're you doing here?" Blanche asks.

By the looks of her, she's seconds from plopping down her bag, changing from her beauty shop uniform, and crashing into her borrowed bed at her in-laws. Her daddy only lives a few miles away, but Blanche would rather be with Buck's, being she hasn't seen her own daddy in months on account of the new lady in his life. And her mama, she's long gone. Over-a-decade gone.

I hold up the letter.

She nods, understanding. The way from here to the post office practically has a *Bonnie* path worn into it.

Blanche offers, "My dogs are tired as sin, but I'll keep ya company if ya want."

A little white something pops from the bag hung over her shoulder.

A little white head, to be more exact. "I'm more interested in *that* dog," I say. "Where'd she come from?"

"He," Blanche corrects. "I checked. And I named him Snow Ball."

"Ah, 'cause he's all white." For once, Blanche has a perfectly reasonable rationale for one of her decisions.

She scrunches her brows. "No, 'cause this here dog is the start of something good. And more good will stick to him, accumulating more and more. I can feel it. I found him on my way home. No tag or anything, so he's mine."

"And Buck's mama, she going to be all right with you keeping him?"

Blanche shrugs, a typical Blanche response. "Cumie can have some of Snow Ball's good, too." She nods to my letter. "Maybe he'll help get Clyde home."

'Cross the street, Old Jed whistles from his stoop, saving me from pointing out how that doesn't make a lick of sense. Both laces of Old Jed's ratty boots are undone. Really, it looks like Old Jed himself has come undone. But he's still a permanent fixture in West Dallas. Always there, always hooting at the gals who scoot by.

I shake my head, taking one more peek at Old Jed as we head down the cracked sidewalk toward Elm Street. "Somehow, I bet ya that man outlives us all."

Blanche loops her arm through mine. "As long as he's got enough teeth for whistlin', that's fine by me."

We both laugh, but quickly cough away our giggles as we pass a man curled up against a building. A *Hoover blanket* covers his midsection, leaving feet, arms, and a head exposed. I squirm out of my jacket and lay it over the newspaper that's doing little to serve as an actual blanket.

Blanche clucks. "Bonn, that heart of yours is going to land you on the streets, too."

I raise a brow in Snow Ball's direction, then shrug. Maybe both our hearts are too big, but fortunately, working at the diner's been kind to me after the stock market crumbled and the bank stole all I entrusted to them. Since, I've been squirreling away tips when I can, and I've got some clams in my pocket. Not a lot, but enough.

Too many others aren't as lucky. President Hoover may claim the economy is fundamentally sound, and this depression is merely a passing incident in our national life, but I'm calling his bluff.

There. And there. Blanche and I pass one building after another that's boarded up.

A pang of sadness hits me as we approach what used to be Victor's, the soda shop Blanche and I used to frequent after school let out. I swallow, afraid to look 'cross the street from Victor's to Doc's. I'll look at the three-story building, though. I always do, as if pressing on a bruise to make sure it still hurts.

It throbs: setting my eyes on the physician's office, knowing that Dr. Peterson still practices inside those walls, but beneath the office is nothin' but empty bathtubs and a dusty bar. Blanche and I used to secretly spend our nights there, serving bootlegs. I stood on the stage, feeling the heat of eyes and lights on me. In those moments, I allowed myself to think I could be somebody. That a *somebody* would see me up there and put me on a real stage on Broadway. Or maybe in a film, instead of my always watching from the crowd. I'd be somebody who was more than poor, somebody who would've made my daddy proud if he were alive to see it.

But no, our country went to hell, Doc's and Victor's crashing along with the banks. Everyone's dreams are stuck in the mud, not just mine. Once in a blue moon, a gal gets discovered at a diner, but none of the fellas I've shown my pearly whites to have fancied making me a star. I reckon I should simply be happy to have a regular shift to work. Many can't say the same thing. Took Blanche a while to find new work, grudgingly charming her way into the Cinderella Beauty Shoppe.

So yes, I'm calling your bluff, Mr. President.

Blanche's gaze is higher up, on a third-story window where she once lived.

I ask her, "Miss it, don't ya?"

"I miss him more."

Buck.

The wind carries the faint sound of a bell and a *ping* of a coin into a kettle, and blows Blanche's short hair 'cross her face. She tucks a strand behind her ear. Her wedding band, still shiny and new, catches the sunlight.

Blanche is someone who'll always surprise me. Selfish yet caring. Impulsive yet levelheaded. She once threw caution to the wind, the one who dragged me into Doc's in the first place. "But the wind'll change directions on ya, Bonn," she told me a few days ago. "It can all come back and hit ya square in the face."

That's why she sent her husband off to jail. "Buck," she told him, "you got to go."

While she once saw his arrests as scandalous and delicious, she now sees the police's eyes on him as restrictive. Mostly for herself.

"Do your time," she told him. "Get rid of those warrants out on you. Then no one will be after us no more."

Two years ago, I should've let Clyde do his time after the law came for him.

But no, I couldn't stomach him being away for five years, so I taped a gun to my upper thigh and smuggled it into the prison's visitors' room. Clyde's expression was priceless. *Astonished* would be a word for it. He chuckled, dimples showing. "My God, Bonnie, what am I going to do with you?"

I wanted to beam at impressing my man, but I shrugged, and mostly feigned bravado at what I'd done. "Someone once told me that big things await us. But not in here."

Goodness me, he did it. He escaped. We were going to run away together, hide out on a plot of farmland. He knows a bit 'bout tending one since he came from one. But Clyde, fresh out of jail, said it was too dangerous for me to go with him right away. He'd come back for me. The law stomped on that promise when they caught him two weeks later. Then there he was, facing fourteen years instead of five. Clyde would've been nearly halfway done if it weren't for me.

I squeeze Blanche's hand, as much for her as for myself. She jars out of her own memory and drops her gaze from the window of her onetime home.

"I hope you're right about Buck finishing his time," I say, "and having that fresh start."

She says, "When is Blanche ever wrong?" I open my mouth. She adds, "Don't answer that." Snow Ball barks sharply. "Would you look at that; Snow Ball agrees."

Really, I hope the same will apply to Clyde, and no one will be after him once he gets out. Then there won't be a need to hide out on a big stretch of land. We'll start anew in Dallas. But fourteen years . . . That's a lot different than Buck's year and a half. I'll be thirty-five. I ain't going to think where I'll be or even who I could be with—'cause this here letter will work. I hug the envelope against my chest.

Clyde and I will have our chance at being free. Even if Clyde doesn't believe it himself. "I'd leave all the stealing behind for ya, Bonnie," he told me once. "But ain't much I can do 'bout the name *Clyde Barrow*. You know I'm more likely to find a door in my face than a handshake."

Maybe that's how it's gone in the past, but—for our future—I want to believe Blanche—and her dog. I kiss Snow Ball's furry head, and then set my sights on the post office down the block. Outside, a man from the Salvation Army collects money. I finger a coin in my pocket. I'll drop it in, for good luck.

This will be the letter to get Clyde pardoned. This letter will breathe life into the word *free*. He'll come home to me. My life will no longer be stagnant. I'll be moving forward, with Clyde.

2

THE MORNING'S BEEN SLOW AT MARCO'S, WITH FEW PATRONS and even fewer tips. I shouldn't complain; there *have* been tips. But now the diner's lunch hour has come and gone, taking its chatter and commotion with it. I make my rounds, checking on the dawdlers, my heels tapping against the tiled floor. One woman asks for buttermilk pie. Then, coffee in hand, I refill and refill.

Ain't life grand.

Blanche thunders in at half past one. She often comes in on her days off, and the sight of her makes my day a touch grander. I'm behind the counter. She slaps a palm down, bent over at the waist, with Snow Ball tucked under her other arm. Blanche ain't out of breath, but I reckon she rushed here to beat the cold and is now letting her dramatic side show.

I restrain from rolling my eyes. "Blanche?"

Head down, she holds up a gloved finger.

I tap my foot.

"Stitch. In my side. Better now." Blanche lifts her head. Her nose and cheeks are rosy. "Clyde."

It's only one word. Yet that one word is all it takes to send my heart beating like hummingbird wings. Problem is, I don't know if I'm 'bout to soar or fall to the ground. So much can happen in prison.

All I say is, "Tell me."

"He's gettin' out."

My Lord, my knees buckle from a wave of relief.

Blanche fishes out an envelope from her coat. "Got it here in black-and-white. Cumie asked me to take it to you. Wants you to be the one to greet Clyde at the bus after all you've done."

It's the fastest a letter has ever exchanged hands. Excitement has my eyes jumping from spot to spot, unable to put more than a few words together at a time. But I see what I need to see.

Clyde Barrow.

Conditional pardon.

To be released February 2, 1932.

"That's—"

"Today," Blanche finishes. "Letter's dated a few days ago, but Cumie only just got it. I raced it here, 'cause I'm a good friend like that."

I squeal loud enough for the woman taking too long with her pie to look down her long nose at me. Not like I care.

She says, "I'll even take the couch tonight so you two can have my room. That's how good of a friend I am." Blanche shakes her head. "It's been a while for you two. My goodness, it'll be nearly as long for Buck and me by the time he's paroled. What've I done?"

I roll my eyes. This ain't 'bout her and Buck. It's 'bout me and Clyde. "He's getting out," I repeat, and then a second time at barely more than a whisper. Clock says it's nearly two. I scan the letter, but, "What time?"

Blanche shrugs. "Buck said it took him five hours last trip."

"Five hours. So if Clyde got the nine o'clock bus"—I yank at the bow at the back of my apron—"he'll be here any minute now."

I grab my hat and coat from beneath the counter. Marco isn't anywhere in sight, and I'm not going to take the time to find my boss. Pie Woman startles as I race toward the door.

"You've got Snow Ball to thank, ya know," Blanche calls at my back. "The good's going to keep rolling and growing bigger and bigger. You watch."

I won't say it aloud, but *God bless you, Snow Ball.* My new life with Clyde starts today. I only pray he doesn't get off—or has gotten off that bus already—with no one to throw their arms 'round him. I run 'cross town, rubbing a hole into the heels of my stockings, and my skin.

The bus station has others waiting, a sign the nine o'clock bus hasn't arrived. I lick my lips, breathing the cold air in and out through my nose, trying to collect myself. I hope Clyde didn't leave Huntsville earlier. Surely he'd have surprised me at the diner, though. Blanche found me at Marco's easy enough.

I turn up my collar against the wind and clench my hands together, anticipating our reunion. Only me, Clyde . . . and the army of homeless fellas 'cross the street. To pass the time, I watch 'em. Their cardboard and scrap-wood shelters are a sight to cause sore eyes, haphazardly filling what was once a park. Now it's a community of displaced souls unable to make ends meet.

Hoovervilles, that's what I've heard these areas called. And that armadillo roasting on a spit, I believe that's known as a *Hoover hog.*

President Hoover ain't a popular man.

But that man won't get a second more of my thoughts. A bus is approaching down the street, kicking up dust. I smooth my hands over my new secondhand coat, then down my long dress. My hat gets a quick adjustment, too, before I wring my hands together. And wait. I wait to see the man I haven't set eyes on in almost two years. I haven't heard his voice. I only know Clyde in the stiff letters of a typewriter and through Buck's deeper tone.

Clyde will be different. I know it. I just need to look deeply into his hazel eyes to know if everything will be okay. If we'll be okay.

The five-hour ride from the town of Huntsville shows differently on everyone who exits the bus. A man stretches. Another has ruffled clothing. A woman exhales, a red-faced child in her arms. I chuckle as one fella stomps his boot at the top of the bus's stairs, shaking life back into his numb foot.

Reunions happen at the mouth of the steps. I wait impatiently for my own, praying for my own. A man exits, then it's like the bus is out of more. I stare at the opening, my spirits darkening as the seconds go by, before surveying the small group that's formed.

Then another fella appears at the top of the bus's stairs, slicked-back hair, a face that appears to be freshly shaven, a full bottom lip I'm aching to kiss.

Clyde.

My smile and my fluttering heart compete to be the first to respond to the sight of him after so long.

I rush closer, saying *excuse me* as I angle my body left and right.

Clyde chucks a bag and a long stick down the bus's steps, and I don't realize 'til I'm standing over them that the second is a crutch. He shuffles forward, then hops down the three stairs. Each thud he makes against the steps pounds in my head.

All his weight is on his right foot, his left foot hovering above the dirt. The laces of his boot are undone, the shoe's tongue hanging to one side. I'm a statue, my mind rattling with too many fears of why Clyde Barrow stands before me—lame—to think of what to do next.

"Bonnie," Clyde breathes.

Then I'm in his arms. Clyde wobbles, steadying himself against the bus. At first, his arms are stiff. He softens. Our eyes meet, and it aches how badly I want him to crash his lips to mine. Clyde's too slow, and I cup the back of his neck, pulling him to me. Our kiss is clumsy, as if we're trying to remember how the other's lips move. I help him remember, taking the lead. Then Clyde deepens the kiss. Boy, does he kiss me, like he's got something to prove.

I stay in his embrace, my forehead tucked beneath his chin, and we both breathe in, like we're trying to recapture each other's scent. I don't recognize Clyde's.

He pulls back, raising his hands. Clyde hesitates before framing my face. His own features, 'specially his jawline, are tense. Then there it is: I recognize the intensity of his eyes. My heart expands and my breath catches, a wonderful tightness seizing my chest.

A line of poetry flitters into my head, as it so often does when Clyde sets his gaze on me.

Love comes in at the eye.

Thank you, William Butler Yeats. I know with certainty that Clyde's love for me knows no ends. But I also can't miss the darkness lurking behind those eyes. I should ask Clyde why part of his body weight rests on me, but I ain't eager to learn the answer to how the guards hurt him this time. The bus's engine fires to life. I lean toward Clyde's good ear, the one the malaria he got as a boy didn't steal the life from, and a lie tumbles out above the engine's rumble: "I've good news."

Clyde's head cocks. "I could use a heaping of that."

I push on, desperate for our reunion to be a happy one. But even more, I'm desperate for Clyde not to break the terms of his parole and be sent back to a place that's made him unable to walk on his own. "I've gone and found you a job."

Clyde's voice comes out unhurried, unsure, as he says, "Did ya now?"

No, but I nod eagerly. The bus pulls away. Clyde bends to pick up his crutch. I ignore the sight of it. "I was leaving the theater the other day and the owner—Mr. Johnson, his name is—joked he should put me on his payroll, since I'm there so much." This much is true. With each step, my shoes rub my heel raw a bit more. Clyde moves beside me, all his weight to one side. "But Mr. Johnson really does need an usher. His last one—this big, burly fella—just landed himself in the big house. So this morning," I say, transitioning from fact to fiction, "I marched over to the theater and demanded for you to get the job."

"Did ya now?"

"I did. And when Mr. Johnson said no, I threatened to take my patronage elsewhere. I told him Clyde Champion Barrow could keep things in line better than most. No one would dare slip past *you* with a five-finger discount."

Clyde's on the verge of a smirk, but it's not quite there. I lean in to kiss him, but ain't it strange, he turns away. "Truly, Bonnie, I'm flattered you think I could do the work of a big, burly fella. But—"

"Just say thank you"—I force a smile—"and show up tomorrow for the matinees. *Shanghai Express* opened today and the line stretched 'round the block to see Marlene Dietrich. Tomorrow is sure to be just as busy. You'll show 'em how burly you are, honey."

He stares at the cracked sidewalk. For a few unbearable seconds, it's just the thunk of his crutch followed by the quick movement of his good side to catch up with his bad. Finally, with those eyes of his still trained down, he says, "Thank you. I'll do good by you, Bonnie."

Excitement over Clyde's return fills me again, and this time my smile is genuine. Now, I got to exit stage left to get Clyde that job. I ramble some more, telling Clyde to go on home to see his family, then I say, "I'll come by tonight."

I expect a kiss good-bye, but Clyde's head must be elsewhere, and I have no problem taking matters into my own hands.

I'm halfway to the theater, my blisters screaming at me, when I remember I ran out of the diner with hours to go. I curse at my foolishness; another gal would gladly snatch up my future shifts. By the time I reach Marco's, I got my excuse on the tip of my tongue.

"Feminine problems," I tell my boss, and promptly hold my breath.

He mumbles something incoherent before, "Don't do it again."

"I won't, sir," but it's as if Marco is reading my mind, as all I want to do is get to the theater. I busy my hands with pouring coffee, and I busy my mind with how Clyde's hands are going to relearn my every curve tonight.

When it's finally quitting time and I escape outside, the crisp air is a rush to my senses. I hightail it down the street, and in between breaths, I practice my conversation with Mr. Johnson.

"Clyde's a hard worker." I pass Doc's, not looking at it. "Wonderful attention to detail." Up ahead, a crowd is already lined up outside the Palace Theater to see Marlene Dietrich on the silver screen. That'll work in my favor, as Mr. Johnson may be eager to make me smile and get me on my way. "Committed to his work."

I find Mr. Johnson inside, rushing here then there, that way then this way. Frankly, it's baffling his midsection resembles a spare tire with all the running he does. I tap him on the shoulder, his round face lighting up as it does when he sees me.

Chin raised, I spout off my idea and Clyde's better qualities.

Mr. Johnson says he won't hire him, not a fella like Clyde, known for robbing all over Dallas. "I ain't keen on swapping one convict for another, Bonnie," he says, not making me smile one bit. In fact, it boils my blood.

Clyde tried before at an honest life, going so far as to ink *USN* on his upper arm before trying to enlist in the United States Navy. 'Cept, it didn't go as planned, not with him having malaria as a boy. The navy didn't want a lad who had trouble hearing out of one ear.

I ain't going to accept Mr. Johnson being someone else who doesn't want Clyde. My chin goes up more to deliver my rebuttal.

"I ain't keen on finding a new theater to go to. I rather like it here."

Despite the depression, Mr. Johnson ain't hurting for patrons. I'm a dime a dozen, but there's something to say 'bout loyalty in these times, and he exhales, louder than his already abnormally loud breathing. Mr. Johnson fetches me the previous burly man's uniform. "Bonnie, don't make me regret this."

"Won't be nothin' to regret," I say. "Clyde did his time. He's straight now."

Later, I tell the same thing to my ma as she purses her lips at me. She sighs and stitches into the sleeve of the uniform's red jacket. Clyde'll need it shorter. I could sew it myself, but the new cuffs on his matching pants will take me long enough and Ma's spent decades working as a seamstress. She'll have the jacket fitting Clyde in no time, which will get me over to the Barrows' in half the time. My foot's already tapping with the need to see him.

What I don't need is my ma mumbling under her breath 'bout Clyde getting out sooner than she thought he would. Or should. Then, loud and clear, she says, "Your brother made manager at the cement plant."

We make eye contact. The single lamp in our living room casts shadows 'cross her face. Ma pokes her needle through the fabric. I nod and glance at the clock. It's getting late. "That's wonderful for Buster. Daddy would be proud."

My ma pokes again. "Did Billie tell ya she's going to be a nurse? Of course, she still has a year of senior high to go, but she's got her heart set on it."

"I'm glad they're both building futures for themselves." I say it 'cause I am, but also 'cause I know what my ma's getting after with her not-so-subtle updates. I focus on Clyde's pants, restraining from pointing out how I dropped out of school after Ma got sick to work extra hours, all to keep a roof over my little sister's head. It's not as if I wanted to say goodbye to one of my dreams, of standing in front of my own classroom, all those eyes on me.

She says, "Ever think 'bout going back for your degree?"

"Some," I say, but it's been hard to pull myself from the "life's on hold" feeling that swept over me when Clyde was sent away. But now he's back, with a second chance at an honest life. No reason for me not to get another shot, too.

Ma rips the thread with her teeth. "Ya know," she says, and I brace myself for whatever she's throwing at me next, "I heard over the party line that Roy's back in prison."

"Sounds 'bout right," I deadpan. "What'd my charming husband do this time?"

"Roughed up a fella. Mrs. Malone told Mrs. Davis that Roy was three sheets to the wind at the time."

I'd be redundant to say *sounds 'bout right* again, so I settle for a slow headshake.

"Sometimes ya think ya know a boy . . ." Ma shakes her own head.

I smile tautly, not giving in to her taunts. *Sorry, Ma, but my heart's set on Clyde, and there's a future waiting for us.* Clyde believes it so much that a few years ago he wrote it into a song. I complete the stitches of Clyde's pants, our chorus filling my mind's ear. *Bonnie and Clyde*—sung one after the other. Four quick beats, followed by three slower ones—*Meant to be*—I pause, then think—*a-live*—I dip my chin once, twice, before the two final notes of our melody—*and free.*

A free man is what Clyde is now, even if earlier it seemed like chains were still wearing him down. It'll take time, I'm sure. But tonight, it'll be the two of us: Bonnie and Clyde. Boy, am I ready to feel alive.

3

MA SEWED AT A SNAIL'S PACE, DELAYING MY REUNION WITH Clyde as long as she could. But here I am, the moon high in the sky, twisting the knob of the Barrows' apartment door. Each time I come here, I'm impressed with Clyde and his family. They didn't end up in Dallas 'til after the Great War, when life fell apart for farmers. Cities promised more. Still, Clyde's family lived under their wagon, then a tent, 'til they opened this here Star Service Station.

It's almost as if our relationship started under a tent, too. But now we've got a chance for more.

The door's unlocked, Clyde no doubt expecting me. I smirk at Blanche asleep on the couch, like she said she'd be, and tiptoe toward the second of the two bedrooms with his uniform slung over my shoulder.

The door's ajar, the room dark on the other side. On a twin-sized bed, Clyde lies on his side, his back to the door. I lay down his uniform and shed my coat. With each step toward him, my anticipation grows. My foot connects with something hard, and I nearly stumble. The noise startles Clyde, and he rolls over. What I kicked gives me a start. His crutch. I step over it, not sure I'm ready to know what caused his broken bones. All I know, they'll heal, given enough time.

"Sorry for waking you," I say. I'm not. This is Clyde's first night home, and what I have planned doesn't allow for much sleeping.

Clyde rubs his eyes. "What time is it?"

"Late," I say. "Sorry I couldn't get here sooner. I've got your uniform for tomorrow."

I kick off my shoes. Clyde's now slouched in bed, darkness hiding his features. He pats the space beside him, and it's all the invitation I need. There ain't much room, but I have what I need to lie facing him. Something—a hesitation I feel—stops me from draping my arm 'cross his body. Maybe it's 'cause we haven't been intimate in years. Or maybe it's from how I had to kiss him first back at the bus station.

"Bonnie," he says, and I'm glad he spoke next, as I'm at a loss for words, besides asking for another kiss. "I'm mighty thankful for you."

"Oh yeah?" I stretch out my arm now. His stomach is hard beneath my touch.

He nods. "Aye."

I'm encouraged and rock into him. "How thankful? Want to show me?"

Clyde clears his throat. The roughness of it vibrates through my arm. He scratches his neck. He sniffs. The boy does everything besides move to touch me.

"Some other time."

Some other time? I prop myself up. My heart thumps in my ears, no longer from anticipation but from the fact this is going all wrong. "Not now? It's your first night home."

He nods. "That's right. First of many nights, Bonnie. Reckon we'd be better off when my parents aren't on the other side of the wall. Go on and lay your head down. Let's get some sleep."

I glance at the shared wall, then back at Clyde. His rejection has me stuck between thoughts. "You want me to stay?"

Clyde mimics my position and runs the back of his fingers 'cross my cheek. "More than anything, darling." He settles back down. "Tomorrow's a big day. I don't want to misstep."

"Okay."

I slowly shift to my back, as if I got to move at a snail's pace myself, uncertain of how to act. By now, I thought Clyde's hands and mouth would be running all over me. That's certainly not the case, and I can't help wondering if his parents were an excuse. Or if being home, and all I threw at him, is too much after what he faced in jail. I glance again at the crutch and decide it ain't fair of me to be impatient. And Clyde's right, tomorrow's a big day. There will be another one after that. There will be plenty of time for us to discover each other once again.

• • •

The next afternoon at Marco's, I glance at the clock every two minutes. My shift fell later in the day, keeping me from overcompensating with one smile after another as Clyde worked the matinees. I can imagine his smirk in reaction to my grins. I can hear him say, *Bonnie, you can do better than undressing me with your eyes.*

'Cept, I haven't seen that smirk of his since he's been home, and last night makes me feel like those words aren't ones I would've heard.

It's nearly dark by the time I'm headed toward the Barrows'. Down the block, in front of a boardinghouse, Clyde sits on the stoop with a boy I've never seen before. The kid's looking at Clyde like whatever Clyde's saying is going to be on his next exam.

Clyde sees me, whistles. The boy mimics Clyde, earning the kid a hoot from Clyde. The whistle is odd enough, but coupled with Clyde's animation, it's like he's putting on a show. He edges himself off the steps.

"Quite the greeting," I call and point at the boardinghouse. "Ya getting us a room?"

"Nah." Clyde tucks the crutch under his arm. "Just here talking to an old friend."

That there strikes me funny, being the kid looks to be teen-aged. I wave to the young'un, resembling Clyde in his dark hair and narrow shoulders. Clyde totters toward me, I walk toward him. He says, "Reckoned you and I could find a spot of our own, though." He nods to his family's service station down the road, their apartment tacked on to the back. "That place is feeling a bit cozy."

I smile, which will be the complete opposite of my ma's reaction. In fact, it's a bit of a relief Clyde's thinking 'bout us getting a place that doesn't share a wall with his parents. "How'd your first day go at the Palace?"

Clyde says flatly, "Po-lice came by."

We stop, face-to-face; a streetlight flickers above us.

"What on earth for?"

"Johnson did me good and called the laws to let 'em know I was employed. They came down to see for themselves."

"Good," I say, still not sure why his voice has an edge.

He raises a brow. "Would be good if they didn't take me in."

"In where?"

"'Cross town to the station. Sat me down. Questioned me—"

"'Bout what?" I shake my head. "Clyde, tell me you didn't go and steal something within hours of getting out of prison."

Clyde turns away. "That's great, Bonnie. Thought you'd have more faith in me. In us."

I curse myself and grab his arm, keeping him from going any farther from me. He tenses. "I do," I say. "I'm sorry. It got me nervous, that's all, at hearing they took you downtown."

"Well, I didn't do nothin'. They only wanted to shake me up, let me know they have their eyes on me. I'll tell ya what, I didn't enjoy the twenty-block walk home."

I flicker my gaze to where the crutch meets his arm, imagining the skin rubbed raw, even beneath his coat, uniform jacket, and shirt.

"Bonnie," he says, "ya didn't tell Johnson I'm crippled."

I hadn't. Mr. Johnson needs an able body. But that's Clyde. "You ain't crippled."

He starts to limp toward home, as if proving his point, and I've no choice but to finally acknowledge it. "I'm sure you don't need that ol' pole. Not for long, anyway." I raise the pitch of my voice at the end of the sentence, indicating a question. A large part of me hopes it goes unanswered. I'm terrified of the happenings of the prison farm.

Clyde stares straight ahead, but it looks like he rolls the words 'round his mouth until he says, "I cut off two of my toes."

"*You* cut . . . You did it to yourself?"

"I had no choice, if I wanted to survive. I ain't exactly a big, burly fella, Bonnie. It was hard out in them fields. But with two less toes, they assigned me to the kitchen."

Clyde's clever, horrifyingly clever. But the more I think 'bout it, Clyde's willingness to forever handicap himself is every bit horrifying. And also limiting, being Clyde will need work that doesn't require manual labor. I restrain from wringing my hands, not wanting Clyde to see my unease, and also my worry that ushering at the theater may qualify as a job unfit for him. I swallow, refocusing, 'cause one thing's for sure: "I'll take that limp if it meant saving your life."

"Me, too," he says. "I'll be damned if I didn't wish that pardon came a few toes earlier, though."

"Me, too," I mumble. Yet now he's out. We're living the straight and narrow. Clyde'll make ushering work, and the law will grow bored with him.

"But Bonnie?"

I look over at Clyde, and, golly, I'm taken aback by how much I missed being next to him. I only wish pain wasn't etched 'cross his face.

"I need ya to know something," he says. "I ain't never going back."

"To the theater?" I lick my lips. "Clyde, you got to."

"No, Bonnie. I meant to prison."

I scrunch my brows and reassert the thought I just had. "The police are going to move on and find a new fella to harass."

He slowly shakes his head.

"Clyde," I say firmly. "They've no reason to take you back to prison."

"It'll break me."

He packs so much emotion and conviction into those words. I count my heartbeats, suspecting there's more to Clyde's survival at the prison farm than I've been told. I'm at twenty heartbeats before I muster the courage to say, "Whatever it takes, we'll keep you out."

Clyde turns to me. He kisses my forehead. "That, we will."

4

THE PALACE LOOMS AHEAD. I LOWER MY HEAD AND LEAN INTO the wind. The first week of Clyde's job, all went well. I convinced myself the law only came on Day One to set the stage, almost as if saying, *Now be on your best behavior.*

Which Clyde has been, I note, and tuck an escaped strand of hair beneath my hat. As the days went on, his foot healed enough where he left his crutch at home. He limped, but that teeter gave him an edge, one the theater's patrons didn't seem like they wanted to cross. My man had that theater orderly, running like a well-oiled machine. Mr. Johnson had no reason to work himself into a sweat. 'Til the police started coming in again, their fingers pointed at Clyde, their hands gripping his arm as they took him away—for no good reason.

I sigh, hoping today will be one of the good days, with Clyde ushering people to their seats instead of him sitting on a wooden seat down at the police station. After the first handful of times he got picked up, I practically had to drop to my knees for Mr. Johnson to keep Clyde on his payroll. *We'll keep you out,* once spoken with such positivity, became a battle cry.

Each day, I donned my hat, my gloves, my coat, and marched to the theater. Each night, I lay beside Clyde at his parents' and spoke those words aloud. Mostly, Clyde stared at the ceiling, only ever holding my hand in his.

Today's matinees are 'bout to start, and a crowd's got their dimes ready to get in the doors. I wait my turn, the wind nipping at my face, and rub two nickels together between gloved fingers. Inside the building, I blink to adjust my eyes to the darker lobby. My coat's only half shrugged off when I see Clyde.

I exhale. He's here. His red uniform is pressed. His dark shoes shine. His black bow tie is slightly askew. The poor boy's put together well enough, but I see the tightness of his shoulders. I've offered to massage his muscles at night, but his answer is always no. I can't help being hurt by that, still aching for Clyde to do more than rub a thumb over my hand or press his lips to my forehead.

I take a step toward him, planning to level the bow tie. Maybe I'll even try for a kiss. But then, a man shoves him. My mouth drops open. Clyde rocks on his heels, taking a cluster of steps backward.

"Clyde," I call, just as he shifts his balance forward. He charges the man. *No, don't,* I finish in my head. Clyde bowls over the man, along with an innocent couple standing nearby.

I wince; nothin' will save Clyde's job now.

"Filthy cop," Clyde growls. A cop? The man's in plainclothes. Clyde's got him by the shirt collar, pressing him down.

I run over the patterned carpet toward Clyde, watching his arm cock back in anticipation and his fist take aim.

"Clyde, no!"

Mr. Johnson, wheezing, grabs Clyde by the shoulders and yanks him back. He yells at Clyde—not at the undercover cop who started this whole scene. I can't believe it, 'cept I can. With both hands, I tug my hat lower, clenching the brim so tightly my knuckles might burst. And I watch. I watch as two ushers take Clyde by the arms, forcing him through the double glass doors and onto the street.

"Sorry, Bonnie." That's all Mr. Johnson says to me. "I'll be sad not to see you anymore. But I can't have this in my establishment."

My hands drop from my hat, thumping against my thighs. I don't even bother responding.

Outside the theater, Clyde paces like a lion in a cage. Most of the crowd is inside by now, but those remaining stay out of his path.

"I made it a month for ya, darling," he says.

I take in a mouthful of cool air and touch his back. He startles.

I snap, "Why you keep doing that?" I breathe deeply and focus on this right here . . . the fact Clyde's conditional pardon is currently going to hell. "We'll find you another job."

He turns quickly, facing me. "For what? To be hounded again?" Clyde shakes his head. He takes a step backward, out of my reach. "That won't do."

"Stop that," I say, to the distance he keeps creating, to him giving up, to this whole mess we're in now.

His head still shakes. "You know that won't do. That cop could come out right now and haul me off."

"You'll get a new job. You have to try, honey. Please," I plead.

He comes back to me and takes my hands. "We can't be out here. Let's go." His jaw is tight. His next word comes out silent, one syllable, a profanity spoken only to himself. Then: "Bonnie, I'm sorry. We'll talk 'bout it more tonight. A nice supper. What do ya say?"

I agree, but I reckon I won't have much of an appetite. How can I when Clyde's tight as a drum? But we'll figure it all out. We'll talk it through at a table for two, instead of on a sidewalk of rubbernecks.

Blanche is more than happy to help me prepare.

"I'll get ya all gussied up for that dinner of yours," she says.

Soon, air rollers dangle from my head. As I wait for Blanche to take 'em out, I twirl my wedding band from Roy 'round my finger, a habit I do when I'm nervous. Can't seem to quit it. Lord knows I twirled the damn thing plenty when Roy and I were together.

Blanche is helping a woman settle underneath what resembles an upside-down trough, maybe ten feet long. Two other women are already positioned under it, their hair trapped under hairnets. One woman is also receiving a manicure in Look-at-Me Pink. *The full treatment,* as Blanche calls it. Off in the corner is a scary-looking device I'll scratch and claw to avoid. From the bottom of the saucer-like contraption hang two dozen tentacles, little clips dangling at the end of each. I reckon it resembles a medieval torture device more than anything else. One designed by Medusa herself.

Blanche chuckles, walking toward me. "By the looks of your expression, you're making up stories 'bout the Scary Hair Machine in your head."

My eyes bulge. "It's really called that?"

Blanche reaches for a roller. "You got a better name for it?"

She's got me there.

Blanche removes another roller from my head. "Last week, one lady asked me to perm her dog. Actually wanted me to hook her little pooch up to that thing." She bends and talks in a baby voice to Snow Ball, who's curled up on a fluffy bed beneath Blanche's counter. "Don't worry, my li'l love. I'd never do such a thing to you."

I think I see relief pass over her little love's face.

"Now, just relax, Bonn. When I did this for a woman the other day, I had her shut her eyes. Didn't want her knowing how to do a finger wave for herself. She'll start doing it on her own, and I'll be out a customer. But I'll let ya keep them eyes of yours open. The perks of being Blanche's nearest and dearest."

I smile at her and clasp my hands together, waiting for whatever a *finger wave* entails. Being there aren't any devices 'round us besides a few clips, a spray bottle, hair spray, and a comb, I let my shoulders relax.

Blanche wiggles off her wedding band. "I hate taking this here off, but I don't want to get any goop on it, you see."

This time I really smile at her. Blanche and Buck tied the knot in July, then drove her Ford, lovingly named Big Bertha, to Florida for their honeymoon. Blanche said it was a glorious week of sand, sun, and sex.

Plus, "Icing on the wedding cake," Blanche said, waving 'round her marriage license. "I finally know Buck's real name."

All Blanche had known for years was that it's six letters long. Drove the girl crazy Buck kept it to himself.

I'd be lying if I said I'm not jealous. Not of her knowing Buck's name; I only feigned interest 'cause she prides herself in knowing. I'm green with envy 'cause I didn't get a honeymoon or cross-country trip of my own. My marriage to Roy only gave me heartache, his name inked on my upper thigh, and a hunk of silver on my finger. But divorce doesn't make sense. Ain't worth the distress or time. One party has to be at fault, and Roy wouldn't ever let that be him, despite his wandering eyes. Our marriage is long over in my mind, even if I still got his ring. I could easily take it off, but I keep it as a reminder of my past mistakes.

Not thinking for myself.

Lettin' someone steamroll my dreams.

Trying to keep up with the Joneses.

Blanche says, *Fuck the Joneses*. But not the comic strip. We both enjoy reading that, find it funny. And maybe that's 'cause ya got to find the humor in life.

Blanche is my humor. Without her, there'd have been little laughter this past month. Also, without her on the couch, little time for Clyde and me to be alone. Not that it has done us much good. I'll admit, Clyde being home isn't what I imagined it to be. Nothin' 'bout our day-to-day is feeling free, and I let out a sigh.

She says, "Hey, this'll be painless. Mostly." Blanche winks and keeps removing rollers from my head, curls springing to life, and runs her fingers through my hair. "Wish I could say the same 'bout some thoughts I've been having."

I try to meet her eyes in the mirror, but she's concentrating extra hard on my hair. "'Bout what?"

"My ma. After Buck gets out and all, I was thinkin' of finding Lillian. Just to see her. What's it been . . . ten years?" She uses her shoulder to scratch her nose. "Don't know if I want to know her. Who knows, I could change my mind by the time Buck gets out, but for now, that's what I'm going to do. I'm going to knock on her door, then, I don't know. Feels like something I should do, right?"

Now she looks at me. My head involuntarily tilts to the side, as if pity pulled me by a string. "You certainly didn't get your spirit from your daddy. May be nice seeing who gave it to ya."

"Yeah," she says, drawing out the word, still thinking it all through. She shakes her head. "Say, did my brother-in-law hint to what this dinner of yours is all 'bout?"

I bite my lip as Blanche styles my hair, cinching it between her fingers until it creates a wave. She sprays it with the goop, then clamps the wave in place with a clip.

"These'll come out once your head's all dry. And voilà, you'll have the perfect look for a fancy night out with your fella. He won't be able to keep his paws off ya."

Blanche starts on another wave. She adds another clip.

"That'll be a change," I say.

The tip of Blanche's tongue sticks out, one eye closed. Clips another. "Huh?"

"Clyde," I say, "hasn't had his paws on me. Even said he was going to find us a place but never did."

Blanche laughs. "Wish he would." Then she stops, cocks her head, seeing me in the mirror. "Bonn, Buck don't know all the particulars, but he said that prison took Clyde to hell and back. He's adjusting, that's all. But ya know what, that tilt works for him. It pushes all his smarts toward his good ear, so he'll be back to his old—dare I say—charming self soon. In the meantime, let's give him something pretty to look at." She slides in another clip. "There you go, baby. Nice and smooth."

"Blanche, don't talk to my hair. That's nutty."

She sprays more goop from the bottle and speaks in that same baby voice. "This'll keep you in place. Yes, it will."

"Blanche."

She laughs. "Go on and answer me, then. What's tonight all 'bout?"

I bite my lip.

• • •

I'm at a loss for the meaning of Clyde's expression. Besides how his tongue pokes out. That means he's thinking. I fidget with my napkin, laying it over my lap. His eyes ain't giving anything away, and that jaw of his has been tight since he stepped off the bus over a month ago.

Clyde shakes his head and reaches 'cross the table, pushing aside the butter plate to take my hands. I lean forward, sinking into his touch. "It ain't working," he says. "I tried to give life on the outside an honest try, but . . ." His words hammer in my head, and all I want to do is hook up Snow Ball to the Scary Hair Machine for letting me believe Clyde could ever be free. "Bonnie, I appreciate you doing all this for me, writing those letters, finding me a job—"

"There's others out there," I insist. "What 'bout your daddy's service shop? You've worked there before."

Clyde nods, even as he says, "Not a chance. I won't bring that type of attention to my mama's door." He eyes the other restaurant folk 'round us. "It ain't going to happen. No job in Dallas is going to happen."

I sip my water, wishing it were gin. As much as Clyde feels cornered, I do, too.

"Ya know," I say, "I once had this silly daydream that one day you'd play your guitar and I'd sing. We'd be stars."

"Darling, we can still do that." He strokes my hand with his thumb. "Not for all eyes and ears to see, but for you and me. I have every intention of writing the next verse in our song, you hear?"

I'm not so sure I do, or see how, with what Clyde's saying. Another verse in our song is another chapter in our story, a story he's saying is done in Dallas. So far, we've written two verses here. Clyde wrote the first one after I saved his life. During a bootleg trip gone wrong, Clyde found brick walls on either side of him and a gun pointed his way. But I had a gun, too. Took all my faculties to pull the trigger. Of course, my aim wasn't at the man. I only wanted to scare him off with the noise.

That man wasn't the only one who left the alleyway spooked. The intensity of Clyde's gaze seared into me. His eyes unnerved me; I couldn't stop wondering what else those eyes had seen, where else Clyde Barrow had been. His name started to bounce 'round my head. Then his name caught in my throat. I didn't want to admit my budding feelings for him, not when I was trying so hard to make Roy and me work.

Roy ruined that plenty well on his own. In stepped Clyde, with his guitar and some fancy words.

"Death is a five-letter word, with a five-finger clutch," he said more than sang, his jaw relaxed, eyes closed. *"It cornered him, pitting him against the bigger man . . . By the throat, edging closer, nearing Death's final touch."*

The rhythm of Clyde's guitar quickened, the beat an unexpected surprise. *"Then there she was, light in the dark, defying Death's plan . . . She stared it down, held on tight, fired off a shot all her own . . . Ohh"*—he drew out the word, as if taunting Death—*"Oh, oh, oh, death for the boy has been postponed."*

Clyde's fingers shifted to a higher pitch on the guitar. He smirked and sang our chorus—what he hoped to be our chorus—from the corner of his mouth, *"'Cause lean closer, listen close . . . How the story ends, no one knows . . . But one thing's clear, you'll see . . . Bonnie and Clyde, meant to be, alive and free."*

After that he asked me a simple question: *You and me. What do you say?*

Wasn't long before the boy took up residence in my heart.

And now, Clyde's making my heart race 'cause I know what's going to happen next. If Clyde is without a job . . . if he ain't willing to look for another . . . I let out a long breath, laced with sadness but also, I'll admit, aggravation.

"You're giving up," I state. "You want to leave town, don't you?"

He nods. "I don't have a choice."

I'm stuck between agreeing and disagreeing. But that ain't what's important right now. My next question catches in my throat before I ask, "Without me?"

Clyde closes his eyes, exhales. "I don't ever want to be without you, Bonnie. I'm trying to give us a future. That farmland we talked 'bout years ago. I'm going to find some and get it ready for us."

"But Clyde," I say, "you left last time thinkin' you were protecting me." I pause, swallow. "It took two years for you to come back."

Clyde comes as close to rolling his eyes as I've ever seen. "Be fair. I didn't have a choice. Ain't like I asked to be locked up, and"—his eyes flick to the side, back again—"for all that followed."

I whisper, "I'm sorry."

He squeezes my hand. "Dallas doesn't want me here. They chewed me up and are ready to spit me out. No one is going to be looking for me. Certainly not on all that land. It'll be safe for all of us, our families, too."

I free my hand and take a bite of my chicken. I chew, slowly. Getting a stretch of farmland was a dream for a prison escapee and his lovesick fool. I thought that was all behind us, yet I ain't done loving the man sitting 'cross from me—and he's still a wanted fella.

Problem is, life for a farmer is even harder after the stock market crash. I've read the headlines and the words beneath. The average household brings in less than fifteen hundred clams. But farming—farming is much less, the underside of two hundred. And that's for an able-bodied man working eighteen-hour days. How'll Clyde manage limping 'cross all our acres? He's got blinders on 'bout having the farm, and I know why.

Dallas equals nothin' but heartbreak for his family—ever since they lost his little sister. Mrs. Barrow still spends her Saturdays down by the tracks that reduced their family by one. The farm, any farm, is a place prior to all of that. And while I connected those dots, Clyde's been sucking on his tooth.

"What ain't you telling me?" I ask.

"I ran into Raymond—"

"Raymond?" I hadn't heard that name in forever. Last I did was when Buck told me Raymond got locked up. Last I'd seen him was when Doc's closed, and, like me, Raymond was out of a job.

"Ray got out the other week. We got to talking and decided to help each other get back on our feet." He stabs a piece of chicken. "So, he's going out on the road with me."

"You're leaving with Raymond? What 'bout me?"

"Bonnie, I got to go." Clyde drops his chin to his chest, shakes his head slowly. Then he meets my eye. "And you're making this hard as sin 'cause you look so pretty. But you know I can't stay here. There ain't a future for us here. But I'll be—"

I shake my head briskly. No, Clyde ain't understanding what I'm saying. I've just spent two years without him. Even if I don't have all of him back, I ain't willing to let any of him go. Hell, I've waited twenty-one years, six months, and fourteen days to start living. If Dallas won't allow us to add verses in our song, we'll do it elsewhere. "Clyde, honey, I ain't going to stop you. I'm going with you."

What I really want to add: *I'm going to get you all of the way back, too.*

His shoulders relax an inch. "I was hoping you'd say that." He snorts. "Selfish of me, ain't it?"

No, I want to say. What's selfish is how I needed that reaction from him after all he's been through.

"The thought of leaving you behind—again," he says, "was eating a hole through my stomach. I needed you to say it, though, without me putting the words there. But here, on your finger, I was hoping to put this." Clyde produces a ring and takes my right hand instead of my left.

"I can take Roy's off if—"

"I know you have your reasons. He can have one li'l finger. I get the rest of you. I made this while I was gone. See here"—he twists the ring—"it's a serpent. That means power. You and me, Bonnie, we're a force to reckon with. You hear?"

I nod. I'm too touched to do more.

"And this here number three, I etched that in 'cause I learned once it's for good fortune."

I swallow to find my voice. "We could use a heap of that."

He slides the ring onto my finger.

"A perfect fit. Do I know my lass or what?" Then, he exhales. "Bonnie, I'm relieved this ain't a parting gift."

On my left hand, I wear a reminder of my mistakes. But on my right, that ring's a promise of a future. I smile at Clyde's relief. I say, for both of us, "You and me, Clyde. It's always going to be you and me."

5

THE OPEN ROAD PLAYS TUG-OF-WAR WITH MY HEAD AND heart. For starters, we're in a stolen car, and I try not to think about the person we took it from. Years ago, I found myself in one for the first time, and I said, "I want out. I want out this very second."

But now I accept our borrowed car as a means to an end, to get us where we need to go. Beside us, the MKT train races out of Dallas. Headed for Kansas, then Missouri. We're set for Kansas ourselves. I wanted to be moving forward, and Clyde is putting a seemingly endless amount of road ahead of us. But it meant a tear-filled good-bye with my family.

"Ma," I said. Sitting in her favorite chair, she twisted her lips. "It'll only be a few months. Once we find land, we'll settle down. We'll call for you. You can quit sewing at the factory and rest your fingers and live with us on the farm."

I held on to those words with such conviction. To the word *us.* To the way Clyde and I used to be together.

I didn't want to take on Clyde's dreams of the farm as my own a second time, but they snuck inside my head and planted themselves deep, as a way for Clyde and me to continue to grow together. The farm will be a foundation for all that's to come.

My ma shook her head. "What 'bout Clyde breaking parole? They're going to come after him. I don't want you anywhere near him when that happens."

"They won't, Ma. They want him out of Dallas. Once he's gone, he's someone else's problem."

"Yours." Ma's words even startled her, as if she never meant to say 'em aloud.

I pressed my lips together, saving myself from a response.

Ma sighed. "How do you two kids expect to buy land? With what money?"

Easy. The boys are planning to rob a bank.

'Cept I didn't actually say that.

'Cept I actually hate the sound of that. I didn't realize that's what the boys meant to do. If I'm being honest, I didn't think beyond not getting left behind.

On the way to the car, our bags packed, Clyde said, "I ain't aiming to hurt anybody, Bonnie, and I'm only taking what the bank took from me, from you. Plus a few clams more. Think of it as interest."

I twisted my lips, just like my ma did to me. Clyde's words gave me mixed feelings. Robbing ain't right. Like, how the banks robbed me blind during the crash. "One bank," Clyde said. Then we'd be even. So I had climbed into the passenger seat, consoling myself with the fact I'd only be taking back what's mine.

Not long after, Raymond climbed into the back. Now, he pulls out a syringe and a bottle. I stare at Clyde, open-mouthed, my brain screaming 'bout how we're saps to rely on a dopehead.

Clyde shakes his head, but doesn't say a word 'bout Raymond's newfound addiction. Or at least I assume it's new. It's been over a year since

I'd seen him manning the door at Doc's or keeping the peace at the poker tables. Time—and I'm guessing morphine—hasn't been kind to him. He's pale, gaunt, enhancing the size and color of the mole on his forehead. The name *Mary* tickles my lips.

I haven't seen his girl, either, since Doc's closed down. Mary's uncle, Dr. Peterson, owned the joint, but it was Mary's through and through. She put all of herself into it, always quick to remind me she was in charge. Now Mary is God knows where, doing God knows what. But the rumors haven't been kind, saying she went from one kind of illegal establishment to another.

I wonder how Raymond feels 'bout that, and if those two are still wrapped up in each other. Is she the reason he keeps a syringe in his pocket like someone would a pen? I can't reason if mentioning Mary will bring him pleasure or pain. So any thoughts of that snarky broad stay in my head and memories.

I light a cigarette, take a drag, and study Raymond in the rearview mirror. His head is propped against the window; he's asleep. Moments ago he was wide awake. Beyond his head, the twin smokestacks of the Dallas Power and Light Company peek out from above the trees. And in front, a sign: LEAVING DALLAS, TEXAS. POPULATION 260,475.

Without bothering to ask or look, I pass my cigarette to Clyde.

You couldn't pay—or drug—me to sleep. Not with us looming closer to the First National Bank of Lawrence.

Robbing a bank was Raymond's idea. "You scratch my back in Lawrence, and I'll scratch yours," he said to Clyde. I ain't exactly sure what Clyde's got in mind, but it's all making me itchy.

Clyde said the trip to Kansas will take all of seven hours. I wonder, though: "Why are we going all the way to Kansas?"

"Almost was Minnesota," Clyde replies. "So many banks are closed nowadays, so slim pickings. But all the big bucks are up north. So are the icy roads, though. Makes a getaway a wee bit harder if we got to run. Kansas cuts the distance, and the danger, in half."

Splendid. I get to thinking more. "How'd Raymond end up in prison before?"

Clyde glances at me, and would you look at that, there's a hint of amusement in his eyes. Out here on the road, it's like he shed a layer of worry. He asks, "You really want to know?"

"I asked, didn't I?"

"He got caught robbing a bank."

My jaw drops.

Clyde frees a hand from the steering wheel and nudges the underside of my chin. "Go on and close that mouth of yours. We're going to be fine. I'm calling the shots this here time."

I shake my head, 'cause Clyde's is 'bout as thick as the cattle outside our window. He's got to know he could be caught the same way. He's held up filling stations, but they only got one register and maybe a small safe to clean out. What's Clyde know 'bout robbing banks? It's not like he'll waltz in, declare *Open Sesame,* and the bank will reveal all its hidden treasure.

But look at him now, tapping the wheel. Could be he's nervous, but there's a beat to it, like he's got a song playing in his head.

I smile, and silence settles between us as Lawrence settles 'round us. We drive down a wide street. MASSACHUSETTS STREET, I read. The brick and stone buildings on either side of us connect, creating walls. Or at least it feels like walls, confining us, 'specially when we slow outside the bank.

"There she be," Clyde says. He pulls the car over, putting the parking brake into place.

"What ya doin'?" I panic, sitting straighter. "You ain't robbing it right now, are ya?"

Clyde chuckles. "'Course not, darling." He points to a building 'cross the street. "We'll be getting a room at the Eldridge Hotel for a few days."

In our room, Clyde unpacks his guns. I'll be honest; the sight of 'em is jarring. It's not like I've got much experience with guns. Buster taught me to fire a shotgun at a bird just fine, and my aim ain't bad. But *pointing* 'em straight at a person isn't something I've done before. Clyde has, I'd imagine, with his arrests being all burglaries and auto thefts, but he's never shot a man.

"You going to use them?" I ask.

"How else will we rob the place?" Clyde retorts, then grins—all sweet-like. "Would ya rather I ask 'em nicely to give me all their money? I may need some pointers."

I put a hand on my hip. "You going to fire them?"

His face changes from casual to serious, his dimples melting away. He knows I'm good and spooked. "Not unless I have to. I won't shoot unless I have to, Bonnie."

"When would you have to?"

"When someone's shooting at me first. Or," he says, "if I don't have a choice."

I swallow, not liking the sound of that. I wish Clyde *could* nicely ask for their money, or use a silly magic word. To busy myself, I peek through a slit in our hotel room's draperies, watching the goings-on of the bank.

It's a bustling joint. Throughout our first day scouting, the door to the lobby has people coming and going on a regular basis. The second day doesn't offer much of a change.

I don't think 'bout those men in suits, or the ladies with children's hands in theirs, as our targets. It's the institution. The bank that had no problem stealing from me—and others.

"Too busy," Raymond says on day three, pacing, his speech slightly slurred. Clyde sits on the bed, cleaning a gun, something that seems taboo on a floral bedcover. "There's no consistent lull. And I ain't hankering to handle no crowd."

Meaning, there ain't a conducive time to hold her up, with so many people inside. But, "I noticed something," I say.

Raymond keeps pacing. Clyde keeps cleaning.

"The same man opened the bank the past two days in a row. Noticed his cane both days. Thing is," I say, feeling my heart quicken at the excitement of it all, "no one else arrived for another ten minutes, the past two days, at least."

Raymond stops, and Clyde's hands go still. In the vanity mirror beside the window, I watch the boys look at each other and nod. They've got a ten-minute window to get in and out. The plan's been set.

And I'm more than okay with the fact I've got little to do with it. Clyde doesn't want me sitting in the getaway car, waiting for them, so I'll stay here, amidst the floral wallpaper, the floral bedcover, and the floral carpet. I'll wait.

If they got to run, they'll take the car and come back for me later.

If the coast is clear, they'll move the car and come back to retrieve me.

If they can't both make it to the car, they'll separate. Clyde calls it his 'heat rule.' His "every man for himself" rule, when things get a little hot. That way, if someone gets caught, it's not both of 'em.

That night, side by side with Clyde, my stomach is in knots, and sleep only comes in small bursts. The sun is barely glowing behind the draperies when Clyde presses up behind me. It's an intimacy that surprises me—not only 'cause Raymond is 'cross the room—and I welcome how he pulls me against him, whispering in my ear, "Bonnie and Clyde, meant to be."

I smile, rolling over to face him in bed. "Alive and free."

"You and me, darling."

"And Raymond. I don't like that there's morphine racing through his body."

Clyde nods to him, asleep in an armchair. "Ain't sure he could've slept in that thing without it." Clyde rubs his neck with a sour look on his face.

"Not funny," I say.

Clyde kisses the tip of my nose. "We'll be fine as long as it ain't me who touches that dope. I'm the one in control. You hear me?"

I nod.

"You trust me?"

I nod again. My nose gets kissed again.

I wish he had another question in him so I could get another kiss, but Clyde throws Raymond's shirt at him, and he stirs. The boys ready themselves for the bank robbery, and I pack our things.

When Clyde walks out of the bathroom, my hands still and my eyes widen. His usual tee and baggy trousers have been replaced by a three-piece suit, the jacket still unbuttoned. He runs his hands down the striped vest. "Think this'll make me look like I got money to invest?"

Lordy, I can't help myself. I say, "Raymond, I may need a minute or two alone with Clyde."

"Saint Bonnelyn." Raymond gasps, then laughs. "No such luck, you'll wrinkle his suit."

The nickname from Doc's triggers a bout of nostalgia, back to when Blanche first dragged me, as saintly as they come, into the juice joint. Me, the honor student, the spelling bee champion, the girl who pressed her shoulders back and belted out a hymn on Sunday mornings. Then life changed me. Then I became Bonnie, thanks to Clyde.

He wraps his hands 'round my waist, talking into my neck, "Raymond, dear friend. I think what Bonnie has in mind has me wearing a different kind of suit."

I blush, Clyde putting it so plainly, but also 'cause I ain't sure if Clyde's saying all that for Raymond's ears or 'cause he's starting to come back to me.

Raymond laughs again, peeks out the window. "Sorry, Bonn, but I see our man with the cane down the block, coming this way."

Suddenly, everything seems to be moving too fast. Fortunately, too fast for Raymond to pull out his trusty syringe. Time slowed to a crawl the past few days, but now Clyde buttons his jacket, pops a tan fedora on his head, and checks his gun. Raymond slides his own into the waistband of his pants. And Clyde is kissing my forehead, saying words I don't hear through the pounding of my heart in my ears.

They grab our few belongings, packed away in bags, then they're gone. The click of the door, sounding too much like a gun, brings me back. I trip over myself to get to the window. Bank Man is only steps from the bank's front door. Like the past two days, he fiddles with the keys, his lips pursed together as if he's whistling a tune.

I look straight down, 'til Clyde and Raymond appear as they lower the car's trunk door, bags gone. I'd recognize Clyde forward, backward, upside down, or four stories up. But now he stands out even more. While

Raymond walks straight ahead 'cross Massachusetts Street, Clyde rocks to the side with each step. That limp is a constant reminder of why Clyde and I need the farmland for him to hide out on. Why, frankly, robbing this bank is something I can stomach. It's my nerves, not guilt, that's getting the best of me.

Bank Man now fiddles with the lock, his cane stuck under his arm.

Clyde's arm raises to the right, directing Raymond, who cuts in front of Clyde and veers off that way. Down the block, two men approach the bank. Bank Man waves at them.

They're not supposed to be here yet. I hold my breath.

Clyde approaches Bank Man. Then he's got his front against Bank Man's back. Raymond brings the other two men over. The three bank employees are escorted inside.

I imagine the guns at their back. I imagine Clyde, in his deep, confident voice, instructing Bank Man to open the vault.

No reason for anyone to get hurt, Clyde will say. He'll even apologize on his way out for any inconveniences.

Yes, this is how it'll all go.

Seconds pass.

Then minutes.

Two men burst from the bank, hooting and hollering. I reposition and feel a touch of nausea after standing so still, my knees no longer locked. Raymond's got a sack in his arms. Clyde's got one slung over his shoulder, moving as fast as his limp will allow.

Both men got smiles on their face, mirroring the one on my own.

Butter my butt and call me a biscuit. Clyde just robbed a bank.

6

I RUSH FROM THE HOTEL ROOM, NOT FOLLOWING OUR PLAN for me to wait for Clyde to fetch me. But I didn't hear any alarm bells, didn't see anyone after the boys, and, Lord help me, adrenaline carries me to Clyde.

He's in the driver's seat, ready to go. His frown at seeing me on the sidewalk is short-lived. He grins, but motions for me to hurry into the passenger seat. And we're off, Raymond falling into the rear seat at Clyde's quick acceleration.

Once back there, Raymond hollers, banging his fists against the ceiling of the car. He takes a swig from a dark bottle. "Saint Bonnelyn"—Raymond hangs over the front seat—"Mr. Clyde Barrow, that was our first successful bank robbery. April eighteenth will go down in history."

"And stay there," Clyde says, chewing on a toothpick. "Once is enough for me. My underclothes are going to be wet for a week."

"Come on, now. We pulled it off without a hitch." Raymond knocks my shoulder with the back of his hand, as if he's expecting me to encourage Clyde to rob more vaults. But I know Clyde. Neither money nor greed motivates him. Clyde only wants to be free, with me.

"You should've seen him." Raymond pauses, drinks. "On our way out of the vault, that fella of yours lowered his voice all deep-like and said, 'Best not go telling no one now. Imagine how that'd make the bank look, 'specially to others who have the thought to rob ya.' Then he dipped his hat, like he was saying *good day* or something. Genius."

Clyde smirks. For the first time, he smirks. Sure, he's smiled. He's even grinned. But neither of those are linked with Clyde's pride. And at his core, Clyde Champion Barrow is a proud man.

I'm feeling a little smug myself. "You said that?" I ask him.

He reaches over, rubbing my arm. "Something along those lines."

Raymond hoots. "Well, it worked. Didn't see no coppers in front of the bank, did ya? And you'd know, since you were out there."

"Whoops," I say, and Raymond, laughing, passes up his bottle.

Clyde shakes his head at my offer of a sip. "Want to keep my wits 'bout me in case I'm not as suave as Ray here made me out to be. And Ray? How 'bout you start counting that dough."

"Don't got to ask me twice. But, Clyde, man, these bills are large. My guess is ten large."

I widen my eyes. "Ten thousand dollars?"

Raymond waggles his brow. "Each."

"Clyde, honey, is that enough for some land?"

Clyde laughs. "Hell, Bonnie, we could get us three hundred acres."

He winks, and a smile spreads 'cross my face. "They make farms that big?"

"Bigger, Bonnie. You're looking at over three hundred for most farms. I can't imagine any po-lice trudging 'cross all that land to track me down, 'specially with us keeping quiet, living off it."

I stare out the windshield at the open road, my knee bouncing with excitement. "Then we'll get your ma and daddy, my ma, Little Billie, maybe Buster can come, too, though he had his eye on this gal, Edith, before we left town, and—"

Clyde laughs again. "Got to find the right land first. But we'll get there, Bonnie. We'll get there."

Yes, we will.

I take another sip of whiskey, my chest filling with warmth, and hand the bottle back to Ray, who's 'bout as happy as a hog in mud. Some whiskey and some clams. What more could a fella want, save maybe a gal? Again, I've the mind to ask him how Mary's doing, but, again, I think better of it. I'm too tired anyway, after my eyes were held open by nerves all the way to Kansas and practically three nights thereafter.

Smiling, I rest my head against the car's window and close my eyes. Clyde takes my hand. Before sleep claims me, I think of our song. The second verse—the one I wrote after Roy left me in pieces—comes back to me, and warms me further.

Dreams can be forgiving, with second chances to strive.

But only if—she says from the heart—all is truly lost.

Love has failed, hope is gone, feeling no need to survive.

Then there he was, after all this time, saving her, no matter the cost . . . He looked into her eyes, held on tight, told her he'd never let go . . . Ohh—I draw out the word in my head—*oh, oh, oh, hope for her future has been restored.*

When I open my eyes again, Clyde whispers my name. Rain pings on the windshield. The landscape hasn't changed much, just miles and miles of fields.

"Bonnie," he says.

Clyde's face is serious, the joy after robbing the bank gone. I sit up straighter. Nothin' seems amiss, but I feel as if I've missed something. Something big. "What's wrong?"

"Well, Bonnie . . . there are some things you should know. Some things I've kept from you."

"You've what?" I cock my head. "Clyde, what's going on?"

He stares straight ahead, his knuckles white on the wheel.

I press, "Clyde."

We bump off the road. My hands flies to the door handle for something to hold on to. Clyde yanks on the parking brake. He sits there, not moving. I look all 'round, confused. His gaze flicks to the rearview mirror. Raymond still sleeps behind us. "Let's get out."

I ask, "In the rain?"

Clyde opens his door, steps out. I rub my eyes, put on a hat, then do the same. He waits for me under a tree, the canopy helping to mostly shield us from the rain.

"What is it?" I ask him. "You're making me nervous."

"In prison"—Clyde licks his lips, averts his eyes—"I was targeted."

"I know."

"No, ya don't. No one does. There was this lad." Clyde's chest rises, falls. He still won't look me in the eye. He wipes rain and also what may be tears from his face. I want to reach for him, touch him, but I ain't sure if I should. He says, "Ed Crowder. I won't ever forget the name. Called me a punk. Took a liking to me. He took the wrong kind of liking to me."

My hand's in the air, stopping him, before I even know I moved. "I don't need to know the specifics."

Clyde's face shows one thing: mercy.

He tells me he had to stop it, no matter the cost. He tells me 'bout a fella named Skelley, another inmate, a "heavy," not ever going to see the light of day outside the prison farm.

"I was a 'short-timer,' you see, and Skelley didn't want me getting caught with Crowder's blood on my hands. He knew I had you waiting at home for me."

He and Skelley worked it all out. Clyde slipped a galvanized pipe in his pants. After he was done doing his business at the urinals, he waited for the others to leave. By himself, his back turned, Clyde knew it was only a matter of time before Crowder crept up behind him.

"Bonnie." After all he's said, hearing my name makes me jump, as if I were at the prison with him. Being here, hearing it secondhand, seeing how every feature on his face is tilted down, is torture enough. He swallows. "Bonnie, I cracked his head wide open. Then Skelley stood over the body for me."

I hug myself, glad in that moment that Clyde and I aren't touching. I feel too many emotions for one to rise to the top. I'm numb. I'm cold. Then, I realize, there is something I feel above all else. Relief.

"So, he's dead?" I ask.

"I've done some bad stuff," Clyde says, "but I ain't never killed a man before. You got to understand, though. It was either kill or risk a part of me being killed."

"I understand," I say, barely more than a whisper. And I do. Not only why Clyde did what he did in prison, but why he's been acting distant with me since. I uncross my arms. I reach out. I touch him. He lets me, looking down to where my palm rests on his arm. Clyde covers my hand.

He says, "You see me differently now."

"No." The truth is, I do see him differently. I see a twenty-three-year-old man who almost lost himself. Who lost some of himself. A man who's still healing. I step forward and kiss him, wanting this kiss to chase Ed Crowder's contact further from Clyde's mind. Our noses, our faces, our lips, are wet. But here we are, standing together on the other side of what happened to Clyde in prison.

I'm thankful he told me, but with the heaviness of his story, I try to lighten things. "Couldn't have been sunny when you told me all that, huh?"

He clears his throat, his eyes flicking away from me again. "Bonnie, with this bank money, we got a shot at a life now."

"We do. We'll—"

"But—"

My breath hitches. "Honey, I ain't ready for a *but*."

"But," he says. "I can't settle down into a life before making things right. I couldn't wait for the sun to tell you all this."

I blink, keeping my eyes closed. I'm sympathetic to what Clyde went through—how could I not be?—but he just turned a corner from his past to our future, and my chest is tight as hell. "Clyde Barrow, if there's more, you better spit it all out now."

He says, "I got to get Skelley out."

I go to run my fingers through my hair, forgetting my hat's on. I knock it off. "Jesus, Clyde, you want to bust him out, don't you?"

Clyde dips on his good leg to retrieve my hat. He places it back on my head, keeping his hands there. "You've always been smart, darling." He licks his lips. "I also want to get back at that place, badly, for all it's done to me."

"When?" But my Lord, I know the answer. Rain is pelting me, after all. This conversation couldn't wait.

Clyde nods to the car. "I told you Ray and I were scratching each other's backs."

I shake my head. "But you left out how. I thought it was a bank. One bank. That's all. Now we're raiding a prison right after?" I say again, "Jesus, Clyde. How could you keep this from me?"

"Bonnie," he says, and his voice is eerily calm. So calm that I startle. "I told you something I've never uttered to a single person before." He takes my hands. "If it weren't for Skelley, I wouldn't be telling you at all."

I'm not sure if he meant them to, but Clyde's words hit me two times. Ed Crowder would've killed Clyde's insides if it weren't for Skelly. And, if Clyde weren't busting out Skelley, I may've never known the truth 'bout why Clyde's been pushing me away. I rub my lips together. "I owe Skelly a thank-you after we get him out."

Clyde tries for a smile. "Let's get you dry."

In the car, the engine allows hot air to shoot from the vents. The outside air's warm, so I don't feel particularly cold, but I don't particularly like being damp.

Clyde says, "There's a town up ahead. If my memory hasn't failed me, there's a hardware store, and that's what I'm after, for some more guns and ammunition. I'll need that to bust open the prison farm."

Even while knowing the *why* behind all of this, it still leaves me feeling like I swallowed a rock and the darn thing is sitting in my belly. "After the prison farm, it's our farm, right?"

He nods. "Then it's our farm."

I exhale and eyeball the open fields outside my window. "How do you plan to raid it?" I look back at Clyde. "I know you've got a plan."

"Aye, our part ain't much more than setting it up. Ray will go in and visit with Skelley to tell him how it's happening, and I'll hide the guns out by this ol' sewer. Skelley's earned himself a bit of freedom to move about, so he'll retrieve 'em. Rest is up to him to get out. I ain't going in."

"Then we're even," Ray says from the rear seat. I didn't even know he woke up. "I got my money. You got your prison raid. Unless you want to do more banks together."

"Then we're even," Clyde says.

But first, they need the guns to plant. We arrive in Mabank, Texas. Population: 967.

It ain't much, but halfway down Market Street is a hardware store. We park down an alley. When I open the passenger door, Clyde rushes 'round the car to meet me. "Oh no, you ain't coming in with us."

I scrunch my brows, cross my arms. "I've been in the car for hours."

Raymond laughs. "Let her come. She's Saint Bonnelyn, remember. No one will think she's up to no good."

I scoop up a discarded newspaper from the ground and shield my head from the rain. Clyde exhales, turns on his heel, and walks toward Market Street.

It's not 'til Clyde's got his hand on the hardware store's doorknob and Raymond makes a comment 'bout going two for two that I glean the boys mean to *steal* the guns and ammunition. I'm on my heels, but the owner's looking at us through the storefront window, and if I backpedal now, red flags may pop up all 'round him. I grit my teeth, cursing to myself, and step inside the store. There, I plaster a friendly smile on my face.

"Easy now," Clyde whispers to me. "Stay by the door. You don't know us if push comes to shove."

It's Clyde I want to be shoving, for once again not telling me what's going on. The boys approach the counter, and I reach for the nearest doodad, fiddling with it. It brings back memories of Roy and our many trips to the hardware store as we were fixing up our godforsaken house. Funny, I'd rather be here, feet away from Clyde, even as I'm huffy with him, and even as he waves 'round a gun and starts barking commands at the storekeeper. 'Cause even though Clyde's breaking the law, he won't break his promises to me. That means something in my book.

Raymond, with his back to the counter, swings his gun from side to side, keeping an eye out for any movement. But we've got the place to ourselves.

I peer out the window. No one there either.

"And some ammunition," I hear Clyde say. "Put it in a bag. Aye, now fold it over."

I startle at the touch on the small of my back. "All ready," Clyde says with an alarming amount of firearms tucked under his arm. He nods to Raymond, who joins us.

Clyde leaves first, Raymond walking backward, keeping his gun aimed on the storeowner. Sandwiched between, I start shaking my head at the unnecessary risk the boys just took. We've got money. Why not pay for the guns? All five of 'em. I can only imagine the tongue-lashing Blanche would give Buck if he did such a thing. She'd probably say—

"Run!" Clyde pushes me toward the alley. "Now, now, go!"

I go, Clyde's hand connecting with my back with each hobbled step he takes. Raymond's first to the car.

I scurry to the passenger side, slipping against the wet gravel, and into my seat. I ain't laughing no more. My breath comes ragged, too ragged to ask Clyde what's going on. He's got the car moving already, barreling down the alley.

He looks over his shoulder. Rain drips from his long lashes. "Shit!"

"What?" I manage.

"Po-lice, just turned after us. They were down the block when we came out. I don't know how we spooked 'em"—he takes a breath—"but we did."

I look, too, and sure enough, another car is following us.

"Better outrun 'em," Raymond says. In the rear seat, he starts shoving bills and coins down his shirt. He tucks his pants into his socks. More coins and bills disappear into his pants.

I'm in complete disbelief at all that's going on; my cheeks are feeling too hot, my heart beating too fast.

"Clyde."

"Bonnie, I got you. One more turn and we're outta town. I'll get 'er going on that open road."

I hold my breath 'til we've put Mabank in our rearview window. Problem is, the copper's reflection shows up too soon in that glass.

"Let's see how fast she'll go," Clyde says.

I grab the door's handle, pressing back into my seat. We thump over the road, part rock, part dirt, and I pray we don't get a flat tire.

"Shit!" Clyde yells again as we round a tight bend.

We're stuck in the mud.

I should've been praying for that instead.

Clyde scurries out of the car. Raymond next. I sit, hands tucked between my knees, pressing the fabric of my dress between my legs. In the side mirror, I see Clyde and Raymond trying to push the car.

It's rocking, but not enough.

Clyde slams his fist down on the trunk. His head flies side to side, and I know the wheels are turning inside his mind. He pops the trunk open, blocking my view of him—and also the copper, who can't be more than a half-mile back now. I panic, reaching for the door, but it opens on its own. Clyde's head appears, his hair matted against his forehead, our sack of money at his feet.

"Let's go," he says. "I found us a new ride."

He pulls me toward a fence, three rungs high. Picking me up, he drops me over, then climbs over himself. I catch sight of a gun tucked into the back of his pants. Raymond hands Clyde our sack, his coins clinking against one another as he hurdles the fence.

I survey the field. Rain pelts me. My eyes land on mules. My jaw drops open to speak, but Clyde beats me to it: "Bonnie, darling, did I ever tell you I once did rodeo over in Fort Worth?"

"Clyde, honey, that ain't a horse!"

"Well, its daddy was. Now, get on."

The police car slides to a stop behind ours. Two officers hop out, guns drawn, and scream for us to stop.

Raymond pulls himself up on the mule. Cursing under my breath, I put my foot in Clyde's hands to give myself a boost up in front of Raymond. The mule's back is slick with wetness, and I slip to one side. I hold on to its mane with all I've got, finally straddling the ridge of its backbone.

Clyde gets his mule going and thankfully ours follow. I close my eyes, not wanting to know where this rodeo is headed, this situation too ridiculous for the pages of any of my beloved books.

"He ain't following us," Raymond says.

"Can't in his car," Clyde's voice chimes in. "We'll ride 'til we find us another car."

I open my eyes, seething. "So you can steal something else?"

"What'd you rather I do, Bonnie?" Clyde says.

"Not steal!" I risk letting go of the mule's mane to wipe wet hair from my face. "Why couldn't you pay for those guns like a normal human being?"

Clyde waits one, two, three beats before he says, "I'm sorry, Bonnie, but I can't take ya seriously when you're bouncing on the back of a mule, both of ya dripping wet."

Raymond laughs behind me, and I elbow him in the gut, right into a wad of thick bills. He laughs harder. Clyde, too.

From the pocket of my dress, I free a box of cigarettes. Naturally, they're soaked through from all the rain. I toss the soggy pack at Clyde, but hit the mule instead.

• • •

I've had just enough of riding a fake horse 'cross a field in the rain, without the comfort of a smoke, when Clyde spots a house, its lights blazing. The sun's nearly gone.

Under the cover of a tree, we all dismount. My rear end aches. My thighs are chafed raw. My dress is plenty wet.

"I reckoned this will be a story for the grandkids one day," Raymond whispers. "That's an hour more than I ever wanted to spend on the back of a mule."

"You and me both," Clyde says.

Blanche would've named our mule, cooing at him the whole ride.

Me, I can't get away from him fast enough. Clyde kisses my wet cheek. "Sorry 'bout all of this, Bonnie."

"It's fine," I say. But is it? I shake my head. "It ain't fine. Why'd you have to steal?"

Clyde sweeps his arm, pointing out where we are, as if saying, *You want to discuss this now, while we're on the run?*

I cross my arms.

He throws up that arm, says, "Folks are beginning to take a look at who they're selling guns to." He motions between him and Ray. "And here we are, two cons asking for a whole lot of 'em. That reason enough for you?"

I don't like it, but I get it. So I take a deep breath and say, "No more surprises. You hear?"

Raymond steps in. "If you two are done discussing right and wrong, I'd like to get out of here."

I flippantly point to the car. "Best go steal it."

Clyde opens his mouth, must think wiser of it, and runs at a crouch past a two-story house, pillars out front of it, and toward a black car.

Soon, we're backing out of a long driveway and onto a main road. Thankfully, the rain is nothin' more than drizzle now.

I wring out my dress, not caring an ounce that a puddle of muddy water is going to ruin this fancy car.

Clyde bobs his knee. "This here road is too long, been on it too long. Keep your eyes peeled for a new one."

It's nearly dark, but I don't point out that small detail.

We find a road branching off to the right, and I let out a sigh of relief we're moving in a new direction.

"Clyde," Raymond says, his back to us, looking out the back windshield.

Then we hear it, the sirens. Lights beam behind us.

"How'd they find us?" I ask.

Clyde raises a brow. "My guess is someone saw us bickering from inside that house and called it in. Po-lice put two and two together."

I ain't going to apologize for questioning him. I'm out here risking my future. Better believe I want to know what's going on. Besides, we don't know that's for sure why the law caught our scent. What I do know is, Clyde is pressing down on the gas pedal, hard, but we ain't going any faster. In fact, we're doing the opposite. "Why are we slowing down?"

Clyde slams his hand against the steering wheel. "She's out of gas."

Raymond spits profanities, then says, "Ain't that rich. You two are cursed."

"What now?" I ask. My heart's back to pounding.

"We run," Clyde says. "Into the trees."

My car door slams the same time as the police car's door.

Clyde pushes me toward an embankment. He tries to lead me, yanking me up the small hill, but I slip once, twice. I need both my hands and shake him free. On all fours, I crawl, tears already falling, blinding me.

I follow Clyde's voice.

Next to me, a bang rings in the air. I slip again. "Holy hell," I breathe, and realize that shot came from Raymond. He fires again at the police. The sound vibrates in my ears, through my body, holding me in place with my face against the mud.

"Stop!" the police yell. "Or we'll shoot!"

I ain't moving, I want to scream. I'm still laying, hands over my head, wondering how the hell I got here.

"Bonnie." Clyde's muddy hands turn me over, frame my face. "Bonnie, we need to move. Now."

His eyes broadcast one thing and one thing only: *We can't get caught.*

Move. Yes. I crawl feverishly, my fingernails digging into the mud 'til I'm at the top of the hill. Raymond is behind me, literally pushing my behind. His breathing is shallow, sounding almost unnatural compared with how hard I'm huffing. I fall forward.

I hear another gunshot. This time it wasn't from Raymond. He clutches his arm and screams, "I've been shot!"

Clyde yanks the gun from his pants and fires. With his eyes focused on the cops, he says to me, "Go, Bonnie, run!"

I do. Raymond, too.

The boys alternate taking shots at the police to hold them off.

We run as fast as our legs will carry us.

My breath is coming ragged now. Raymond's breath rushes out of him as he hits the ground, tripping. Instinctually, I stop to help him. I ain't sure where to grab. When I try, I get a fistful of dough beneath his shirt instead of his body to pull. Clyde keeps running, one arm 'cross his stomach to hold our money in place. He keeps telling me to hurry, as if I'm right behind him. But I'm not.

"Raymond, get up!" I scream.

His eyes are unfocused, blood dripping between his fingers, off his fingertips. But he starts moving, and I exhale.

I don't make it more than two steps before unfamiliar arms are 'round me, pulling me to the slick grass.

Raymond's running.

Clyde's running.

A second officer goes running after them.

"Honey!" I yell, not wanting to use Clyde's real name.

He stops so quick he rolls. He aims his gun, but doesn't fire. How can he when I'm standing between him and the police? The copper chasing him drops to his stomach, not knowing Clyde ain't going to shoot.

Tears sting my eyes as my heels drag against the ground back toward the hill, as I keep my eyes trained on Clyde.

Raymond grabs him. He's bigger than Clyde, stronger than him. Clyde's got no choice but to be pulled into the trees, leaving me in another man's arms.

7

THE LAW AND I DON'T DRIVE FAR, AND THEN AN OFFICER escorts me, in a matter of forced steps, through a miniscule town. It's dark, but I feel eyes on me. Judging me. Curious 'bout me, the gal coated in mud, her shoulders shaking from tears. Never, in my wildest dreams, did I think I'd be that girl.

In a small clearing, the outline of an even smaller building sits smack dab in the middle of the grass. A skeletal branch of a tree extends over the building, like it's grasping at it, ready to snatch it. Ready to snatch me.

My feet are heavy—from my rain-soaked shoes, from the mud, from my nerves. But my hands aren't confined behind my back. The officer's hold on my arm is tight but not overbearing, and the second officer's gun isn't aimed at me. In fact, he's whistling a jovial tune. I'll count those as wins, 'cept for the whistling. That's only putting more attention on me.

The building's brick, I realize, and, oddly, there's no pitch to the roof.

It's just as flat as the four walls keeping it up. The second officer pulls a key ring from his belt, and I realize something else: They mean to put me inside that thing, nothin' more than a box. I stiffen and crane my neck to the side, looking through my blurry eyes for Clyde.

But I didn't see him as the coppers drove me to town or as we paraded down this so-called main street. A row of trees is nestled behind the clearing. Could Clyde be hiding in that tree line? Surely he hasn't put miles between us.

Surely his 'heat rule' didn't apply to me. Years ago, he once told me it never would. But had he run without me? No, he thought I was right behind him. But where is he now?

"Miss," the officer says. I startle. "In you go."

My lips part.

"Just for tonight," he says.

A night? I shake my head vehemently.

"Tomorrow"—he yawns—"you'll be taken to the county jail. We'll figure out what to do with ya then."

I clutch myself, feeling as if there's cow dung no matter which way I turn. 'Specially straight ahead, straight into this brick box.

The officer shoves me, his hand damn near my rear end, and I shuffle forward. The box is dark, even darker when the door slams closed, sounding as if it's made of metal. Or iron. Or something equally heavy.

I don't bother pounding on the door. I don't bother screaming bloody murder.

It's not as if I don't want to. My hands and throat itch to react, but I know it won't do me any good.

Two small windows, three bars running 'cross each of 'em, are my only sources of light. And even that's barely more than a glow. I stand on my tiptoes, trying to balance to see out. I tip forward, my hands almost touching the wall, but I throw my weight back.

The walls are brick, but they look slick, and I can only imagine the many hands and bodies that have rubbed against them, smoothing the surface.

I want no part of that. Instead, I take special care in finding the exact middle of the room. I slowly stretch out my arms, careful of my progress so as not to touch the walls. My fingertips stop with mere inches to go.

I sigh, then sit on the dirt ground. Standing all night would be ridiculous, though it does cross my mind. Horses sleep standing. Most likely mules, too. I read 'bout it once. They're prey animals, and if they lie down to sleep and a predator comes 'round, their chances of getting away aren't in their favor; it takes 'em too long to get up. So they stay on their feet, ready to open their eyes and run at a moment's notice.

But I don't have it in me. This morning, we successfully robbed a bank. We were one step closer to getting the farm. But at the moment, there's no *we,* it's only me, alone in here. I can't help wondering, is Clyde coming for me? Surely he won't let me rot in here all night.

• • •

Clyde never came. I listened. I waited for his familiar voice. The branch scratched at the roof, sending shivers down my spine. Unknown voices floated through the two small windows, replacing my nerves with irritation. The townsfolk hazarded guesses 'bout what I'd done. The guards don't know. A Mr. Fred Adams, the sheriff, doesn't know. I haven't said a thing 'bout how I ended up covered in mud, caught in the crossfire.

But the town's speculation was all a bunch of malarkey, as if Blanche temporarily possessed their brains, putting hooey into their heads. Somehow, after all their blubbering, there was no mention of mules, which I personally find the most ridiculous portion of my day prior to coming to this godforsaken place. The townsfolk surmised I was arrested 'cause of vagrancy.

"Has to be why," someone said. "Get a look at her? I reckon she hasn't seen hot water in weeks."

I twist my mud-crusted hair, the strands stuck together in clumps. My dress is stiff and heavy. But homeless? Ain't that rich.

"Does she have a name?" a different voice asked.

"Betty Thornton," the officer told them, 'cause that was what I told him last night on my way here.

Bonnie had begun to leave my lips, but I changed direction after the *B*. And as far as my last name . . . what do I care if spending a night in this box tarnishes Roy's last name of Thornton? It's better than those pigs knowing I go by Parker, my maiden name.

No one knew the name Betty Thornton—no surprise there—'cept one fella who proclaimed his friend had a cousin by that name. He wanted a look at me to see. "A quick peek," he said. "I'll recognize that vixen. Spent a few hours with her one time, if ya know what I mean."

The officer laughed, so I reckon he did.

But the officer said no, a sliver of decency left in his body.

"Betty Thornton," I hear now. There're three taps, as if he's knocking on my bedroom door, then the jingle of keys. Morning fills the tiny room.

"Rise 'n' shine!"

I get to my feet and tug at my dress, having to break a crust of dirt to get a crease out of the fabric.

Outside, another guard waits. I scan the trees, the buildings, the other faces, but none of 'em belong to Clyde. It's only a few lingering people biting at the bit to get a glimpse of the vagrant who spent the night in their tiny town.

"Get a job," I snap at a man. Then he'd be off somewhere else, not eyeing me like he's above me. "I ain't homeless," I add. But my foot misses a step, like my head was too consumed with my next thought: *Or am I?* It's not as if Clyde and I have a place to call our own yet. It's not as if either of us has a job.

I left a home and a job behind.

Those thoughts stay with me as I'm taken to Kaufman County Jail, as I'm questioned again, as I take a shower, as I'm given clean clothes.

The shirt is baggy, swimming on my hundred-pound frame. The black-and-white stripes go 'cross my chest horizontally. The pleats of my black skirt cut vertically, stopping a few inches above my ankles. The bars of my cell are both horizontal and vertical.

Inside my cage, I rotate my ankle in a circle, listening each time for the cracking noise the movement makes. My foot always creaks at the same place. I never noticed it before. However, I've never turned my ankle an indeterminable amount of times before, either.

But I've nothin' else to do right now.

A pack of cigarettes lands at my feet.

"Keep yourself busy, will ya?"

I almost laugh, pleased with myself for annoying the guard stationed outside my cell.

"Got anyone you need to telegram?" he asks.

"No," I say. Telling my ma I'm in here is out of the question. It'll break her heart. I snatch the cigarettes. The pack is half empty but, stretched out on a hard bed in the corner, I help myself to a ciggy, then another, and another. Each drag on the cigarettes pulls a thought with it—'bout trust, 'bout unknowns, 'bout where I want my life to go, 'bout Clyde.

"Hey!" I shout. "Can I get some paper and a pen?"

Feet up on his desk, the guard doesn't do much more than shrug. But when my lunch shows up through the slot, there's a pen and paper on the tray.

I sip a spoonful of chicken stew. Veal stew, I correct myself, after swallowing the cheaper meat. And I get to thinking.

No one's mentioned Clyde yet. Or Raymond. They ain't in a cell beside me, so I got to imagine they got away. And that begs the question: Is Clyde still carrying on, off planting guns at the prison? Is he doing that instead of coming for me?

I can't help the doubt that wiggles its way into my thoughts. All 'cause of Roy. Childhood friends. High school sweethearts. Husband and wife. Then, nothin' more than the man who abandoned me when the going got rough, who got caught with another woman on his arm. He was a man I thought I knew.

Just like I thought I knew Clyde, thorns and all. Then he goes and tells me he killed a man. Clyde's capable of such a thing. A murderer . . . the first time I've attached that description to him. Clyde's confession is still fresh; it was barely spoken before the robbery went wrong and I landed in here. Now I can think 'bout it, really let it sink in. It scares me. What else is Clyde capable of when desperation stares him in the face?

Desertion? Allowing me to rot in here to save himself? Clyde won't go back to prison. No, he can't go back to prison. He won't give himself up—I begin turning my ankle again, it creaking each time—even for me.

I'll get out, eventually—even Buck only got a year and a half—but what will come of Clyde and me after I'm back on the outside? I could leave him and his demons behind. I could be with a man whose soul hasn't been marred by murder. I could live out in the open, not hiding on three hundred acres of land.

I could be onstage.

I could go home. Makes me wonder, does anyone even know I'm stuck behind these bars?

I bite into an Irish potato, the thing half cooked.

Days pass—twenty-three more than I thought possible—and, while they figure out what to do with me, I'm moved to a more permanent location with the other gals. They're in for theft, bootlegging, soliciting, but mostly theft. I don't see them as dangerous but desperate. One girl, Annie, broke into a department store late at night with her eye on a fur coat. When the police came looking, she posed as one of the mannequins, wearing the fur coat. She even wore the thing while they took her mug shot.

They never took mine, nor my fingerprints. As far as I know, they're still looking into what exactly I'd done wrong—what happened that night, who I was with, and how I was involved, something made harder to determine by the fact my lips stay sealed.

Progress is slow. Real slow. Each interrogation ends the same way, with me not saying a thing and my cell door slamming closed.

Another month passes. My visitor log stays empty. So do the sheets of paper one of the guards gave me. I'm unsure how to put my feelings into words, besides the fact I feel hot. It's stifling in here. Instead, I ask the guards if there was anything to read, and I busy myself with other people's prose. Agatha Christie, William Faulkner, Virginia Woolf.

What is the meaning of life? That was all—a simple question; one that tended to close in on one with years, the great revelation had never come.

Footsteps thump down the hall. I instinctively look up, peel my damp blouse away from my skin, then concentrate again on the page:

Instead there were little daily miracles, illuminations, matches struck unexpectedly in the dark; here was one.

Feet stop outside my cell. "Betty Thornton. You have a visitor."

8

MY HEART LEAPS, AND IN THAT MOMENT, ALL QUESTIONS 'BOUT Clyde's character dissolve. If he's willing to pull up a chair in the visitors' room, he's willing to risk it all for me.

The gals, not many of them receiving their own guests, shout their encouragement. But when I walk into the room, I stop dead in my tracks.

"*Betty* Thornton," Blanche says, standing behind a small table. "Stripes agree with you."

My cheeks burn, and I can't seem to get my feet to move. She's not who I was expecting. She's not who I want to see me this way.

"It's okay," she says. "Remember how I once had intercourse," she says plainly, then lowers her voice, "in a church? I ain't one to judge."

I shake off my disappointment. It only takes a few steps before my arms are 'round her. My eyes sting with tears. I hug Blanche harder.

"Enough of that," she says. We both sit, and while Blanche's eyes shine with excitement, like she's stuck between right and wrong, her back is stiff, like it gives her the heebie-jeebies to actually step foot in a jail. She lowers her voice. "You okay? I'm surprised you ain't panting with how hot it is in here."

I nod. I am fine—physically, at least.

"He said they had ya in a calaboose overnight."

I'm quick to say, "You spoke to him?"

"How else would I know where to find you? He was watching from the trees. Said it took all he had not to open fire on the coppers and townsfolk alike." She shakes her head, as if unbelieving he'd ever do such a thing. But there's no denying: Clyde walked into jail a petty thief and limped out a murderer. I shake the thought away.

"Where's he now? Blanche, I've been in here for nearly two months."

Blanche's hands are in her lap, not even willing to touch the table. "He's working on it." She leans closer, holding her clean blouse against her. "He's run into some trouble."

My heart races, 'specially as Blanche is slow to divulge more. "Well, out with it."

"He got some men together to help him *get to you*. But they needed things." She discreetly mimics a gun with her hand and pointer finger.

I widen my eyes. He wasn't out raiding the prison farm. Clyde has the mind to raid this prison. For me.

"But things went south," Blanche says. "A job went bad, and the fella behind the counter died."

"Did Clyde do it?"

"Not Clyde," she says, and Lord, I'm relieved it wasn't Clyde. Him taking a life to save his own is one thing, but to shoot an innocent . . . That's another. "One of his guys did the killing, but eyes are on *him*. They made camp by some lake, and the police found it. Took everything." One of the guards looks over, and Blanche bats her lashes at him. She then takes my hand, whispering, "Everything from Kansas is gone, which, *Betty*"—she squeezes my hand too tightly—"was a mighty foolish thing to do."

I close my eyes. The fact our money's gone is a dagger to my heart, and to our plans. Everything unraveled, quicker than I ever could've imagined.

"Bonn," she whispers. "That ain't all." I almost beg her to stop, but I open my eyes.

"His group got picked off." She dips her head closer to say, "Raymond," then leans back again, "left. He said too much has gone wrong. I figure him being shot didn't help, 'specially after he used up all his supply. I didn't know he was a dopehead, did you? Anyway, now he says he doesn't care 'bout no cons or no farm. Though he was kind enough to find Lillian's place for me in Wilmer."

I let out a long exhale through my nose, not caring where Blanche's ma lives.

"Right," she says. "After all that, Raymond poofed, probably before you-know-who could throttle his neck."

I shake my head. Raymond double-crossed Clyde. We helped him, but now he's abandoning Clyde. And me. Probably so he can go find his next fix.

But Clyde never abandoned me. Clyde's been working for me this whole time. A man died while he tried to get to me. I ask, "Where's he now?"

"Won't tell me. After his original plan went to hell, he came and got me, all sweaty and panicky. Didn't want you thinking he up and left. But he won't tell me where he is. Just said to tell you that he's coming soon." She shakes her head. "I told him to let you be. They've got nothin' on you, and you'll be out soon enough. I don't see the point in him getting caught, you getting more time. How am I supposed to explain that to Buck when he gets out? All I want is the four of us together again, Bonn. Is that so much to ask?" She shakes her head again, then keeps on hearing her own voice as she says, "But that boy of yours is stubborn and insists you being in here even another second is too long. He said to keep your wits 'bout you."

I could do that. I could also stay on my feet.

• • •

The guard's keys jangle outside my cell. He doesn't have to tell me to get on my feet. I'm already there.

"This way, Betty Thornton. It's your lucky day."

As we walk down a hall, I got ears like a dog, eyes like a hawk, nose like a shark—all keen to whatever Clyde has planned.

I'm giddy with excitement, and I try not to let my smile show.

I'm given a chance to change back into my clothes—laundered, no more mud—and given a bag for the few items I've acquired: cigarettes, paper, a pen. Then, I'm taken to a desk, riddled with stacks of folders. An overweight man sits behind it, a mustard stain on his uniform. "This her?"

The guard escorting me nods. I look 'round, expecting to see Clyde or at least someone I recognize. But I don't see a soul.

"Well, Ms. Thornton. It's your lucky day." So I've heard. I keep my expression neutral. "It appears we don't have enough to keep you any longer." That neutral expression is even harder to maintain, given the length of time they've already kept me. "People saw ya with those fellas," he says, "but can't say for certain if you were or weren't in cahoots with 'em. Unless you want to finally answer that one for us?"

"No, sir."

That's what saved me. I didn't do the robbing, I didn't ride my own mule, and I didn't fire any shots. I've got three for three in my favor, and that must've been enough for them to let me go. I thought Clyde's fingerprints were all over my release, but they aren't. He's not the reason I'm standing here.

"Very well, Ms. Thornton." The chubby man taps his fingers on a folder. "But we'll be keeping an eye out for ya. You, being a pretty li'l thing, won't be hard to miss. You hear?"

I'm disgusted, that's what I am, but I heard him. I nod, doing my best to train my features into a sorrowful expression, my lips slightly pouting.

"There's a bus stop 'bout half a mile down the road." He puts a few bills in my hand. "We suggest you get on that bus, alone."

I offer 'em a tight-lipped smile, then step outside, where it's 'bout ten degrees cooler, and that's saying something since it's 'round ninety out here. Texas is showing its true colors. What it ain't showing is Clyde. Or anybody else, for that matter. There's just a field and a whole bunch of trees on either side of a long dirt road.

I start walking.

The sun beats down on me. The whole time it's like I'm chasing my shadow. But no matter how fast I walk, no matter how far I leap, my shadow always stays ahead of me. I sigh; of course now's the time the good Lord throws a metaphor at me, making me question: If I stay with Clyde, will I only ever be chasing our dreams?

The bus-stop sign and a rickety bench come into view, almost like a mirage, twinkling in the sunlight. At the stop, I sit, letting it all sink in. Clyde isn't here. I've got enough money for this bus. Nothin' more. My future ain't looking grand.

I think it again: *I could go home.*

I cup my eyes, shielding 'em from the sun, and peer down the road. There's no sign of the bus, or Clyde.

Even if he is coming for me, that'll mean scrambling to survive. Getting enough for the farm won't come easy. My head falls back, and I let out a guttural noise, still in dismay how I got here.

From my bag, I pull out my sheaf of paper and tap my pen against it, hoping my thoughts will finally come pouring out. It's a sad truth; life's been giving me plenty to work with. In fact . . .

Sometimes, life's got a fork in the road, with two ways to go.

The good Lord says: Girl, go on, take the straight and narrow home.

It's as if the good Lord chose that exact moment to send the bus my way. Within another few heartbeats, it stops in front of me. The door opens, and my heart thumps some more. A trail of sweat slips down my spine.

The driver leans down, making eye contact with me. "You coming?"

I gulp in the humid air, and another line forms in my head, as if the words are out of my control. I got to get it down on paper, right now.

But her heart, it beat, beat, beats for a fella with a different path to sow.

"Miss?" the driver prods. "I ain't got all day. You getting on?"

I lick my lips and, Lord help me, I shake my head. The driver shrugs.

The door closes. And it's just me again. It's both horrifying and exhilarating, but I know it. I know . . .

He's coming for her, off they'll go, a new life to build and roam.

They'll take life one day at a time, always an eye on the road.

Ohh, oh, oh, oh, their story will be the best the good Lord's ever told.

I smile, not realizing 'til I was done, I just wrote the third verse in our song. And I believe every word, 'cause when I'm with Clyde, having air in my lungs is enough.

That boy is coming for me.

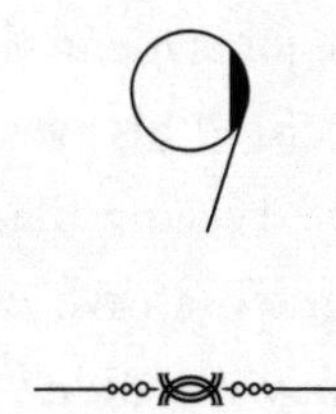

A RUMBLING NOISE APPROACHES. A CAR, GOING FASTER THAN it should. The brakes screech. Through the dust, the door flies open.

Clyde nearly falls out. I stand from the bench, my heart leaping. He runs toward me, favoring his good foot. In front of me, he drops to his knees and rests his forehead against my belly. Wetness from my dress, soaked with sweat, presses against my skin.

"Forgive me, Bonnie."

His voice is muffled.

I slide my fingers into his damp hair. "I'm here, aren't I?"

Clyde tilts his head back, one eye squinting against the sun. "You are. I'm so sorry they got their hands on you. I thought you were right behind me."

"Well, I wasn't." And I spent nearly two months behind bars. I lick my lips. "But here I am, right in front of ya."

He drops his head again, his voice too hoarse to make out. My eye catches on the *USN* tattoo peeking out from his shirtsleeve. Clyde stands, putting our faces in near alignment. I've always liked that it only took a slight roll onto my toes to see Clyde Barrow eye-to-eye.

"Let me get a look at you," he says.

Clyde runs his hands up and down my arm. His thumb caresses my cheek. Each touch is like dipping into a cool lake on a hot day, raising goose bumps on my skin.

"They didn't hurt me, Clyde. Didn't lay a finger on me."

He nods, and it's as if Clyde joins me in that lake, the tightness of his jaw easing. Darkness lingers behind his eyes, though.

He says, "I take it you enjoyed seeing Blanche?"

I smile. "That girl can brighten a cave. She wasn't too keen on you breaking me out. She'll be happy you didn't bust in with guns blazing."

I say it lightly. We need light. But I'm relieved more shots weren't fired.

He taps his temple. "That'd be an insult to my abilities."

Yet, I think, one of Clyde's men killed a man.

"As of ten minutes ago," Clyde says, going on, not sensing my unease, "you're looking at the son of the Honorable Thomas Bradford, mayor of Dallas."

I scrunch my brows, intrigued. "Am I, now?"

"That reaction of yours has already outdone those small-town folk. They didn't want to insult my father by second-guessing I was who I said I was. Didn't even ask for identification. Then they lapped up what I had to say like a kitten with a saucer of milk."

"Which is what, Mr. Bradford?"

"Oh, the other day I was passing through their town—one I said I'd report back to my father as being quite charming—and I saw this young woman in the company of two young men. She seemed to be in duress. The hair was raised enough on my arms that guilt set in that I didn't do more, so I thought to check up on her. Imagine my surprise when I found out she'd been put behind bars without any real evidence against her. I insisted that anything she may've done was against her will. Coercion, you see. I was sure my father would agree."

"I like it when you use that head of yours." I run my hand down Clyde's tie, letting my pointer finger slowly trail behind. I'm encouraged when he doesn't stiffen, like he would before he revealed his secret. "I'm going to have to find the proper way to thank this Thomas fella."

Clyde chuckles. "I may know where you can find the lad. Though I think he's going to be hiding out for a bit."

My hand goes still. "Are we talking 'bout you now?"

"Afraid so. Funny thing, when I turned 'round to leave the precinct—"

"You went inside the jail?"

"Of course, how else was I going to talk with them? When I was done, I turned and almost walked right into myself. Clyde, that is. Not Thomas." He pulls a paper from his pocket, folded up into a smaller square. Unfolded, the left side of the paper is devoted to Raymond, with two photos of him. In one, he stares straight into the camera. In the other, he's turned to the side. The right side of the paper has Clyde in the same positions.

He's been fingered for the bank robbery. Clyde's a wanted man, even outside of Dallas. Yet the scariest thing is how, 'cross the top of the poster, it reads $250 REWARD.

That could get someone over a year of rent at a nice place.

That could get someone thousands and thousands of loaves of bread to feed their family.

That could get someone a lot.

It feels like the earth is moving right under my feet, even though the last time an earthquake struck Texas was nearly ten years ago, all the way over in El Paso. It ain't nothin' new for coppers to have it out for Clyde. But with this poster, anybody could.

Lord help me, I can't shake another thought. After Clyde escaped prison, the manhunt lasted only two weeks. It only took two weeks before the law caught up with him, and that was over in Ohio, a thousand miles away.

Has the countdown begun again? Do we only got ourselves fourteen more days to be free, to be Bonnie and Clyde? Out here on the road, with miles and miles of openness 'round us, we're exposed. Are there folks looking for Clyde *right now*? Since leaving Dallas, that ain't a feeling I've had. Like I told my ma, Dallas was happy to get rid of us. But now, I ask Clyde, "How're we going to evade the law?"

He rests his forehead against mine. "I got to say, I like that you said *we,* Bonnie. You could leave. You could've left a few times by now."

I wrote in my verse how I had the option to take the straight and narrow. But it's true my heart beats for a fella with a different path to sow. I meet his eyes. "Would you quit trying to shake me? I want the farm, too, whatever it takes. But Clyde?" I let my next sentence work its way 'round my mouth before saying, "I'll admit fear's got me, with all those eyes looking for you. Your track record ain't too great."

Clyde lets out a belly laugh, catching me by surprise. He kisses the tip of my nose. "Two weeks shouldn't be too hard to beat."

• • •

"First thing's first," Clyde says. "We got to dress the part." We pass a store that sells furniture, coffins, and stoves—all under the same roof. "I reckon part of my mistake before was that I looked like I just escaped from prison. But you and me, Bonnie, we'll play the part of a young couple off exploring the country."

Honeymooning. I smile at that. We park outside of a drugstore, and I cock my head. "Am I to decorate myself in bandages and bottles?"

"No, I'm to rob it. We need us some money for our new life, wouldn't you say?"

I'm itchy again. "I'd say, last time you robbed, I ended up in jail."

Clyde shrugs. "Fine, we won't rob. We won't have money to eat, no money for gas. Well, we may have enough gas for me to get you back to Dallas."

I let out a long breath. "Don't be an ass."

"What? I'll bring you back, but I ain't staying there. It'll sting like a hornet to drive away from you, though."

"You done?"

He's got the nerve to laugh at me.

I say, "I'm being serious. Robbing is what got us into this mess. In fact"—my voice grows louder—"it all dates back to you stealing those turkeys."

"Bonnie, darling, are you really bringing up something from when I was fifteen?" Clyde scratches his brow. "Or maybe I was sixteen, can't remember. But that was all Buck's doing. It was his idea to steal 'em and sell 'em for a profit. We made us some clams that day."

"Then you got arrested."

"Water under the bridge, no? Here we are. And unless you got a better idea of how to save for the farm . . ."

I don't. But it feels wrong to save by stealing. Feels dangerous, too.

"Don't look so worried, Bonnie, I've got a trick up my sleeve for the drugstore." He pulls out a ten-dollar bill.

My jaw drops. That's more than some people make in a week, and Clyde's got it all in one bill. "Where'd you get that from?"

"The po-lice may've found our stash, but I had this one on me. Now watch," he says. "The owner will need to open his safe for me."

Before I can question what he means by all of that, Clyde kisses me hard, then slips from the car. I'm left touching my lips and bouncing my knee from the passenger seat, staring through the large storefront window.

Inside, Clyde puts a thing or two on the counter and presents the proprietor with the ten-dollar bill. Clyde's reaction is agreeable when the owner points to a safe. And I get what Clyde's up to: The owner will need smaller bills to break such a large one.

I cringe; the boy's ingenious.

The man turns his back. Clyde pulls a gun. The pistol is pressed between the man's shoulder blades a moment later, and the man's quick to empty the contents of the safe into a bag.

I read Clyde's lips, and if I got it right, that boy wishes the man a good day. I can't help myself, I laugh at how cavalier he is. I'm still laughing when Clyde's back beside me.

He removes the parking brake. "What?"

"I shouldn't praise you."

"You should. Go on."

Fine, I will, but only 'cause I want more of the carefree Clyde. "I made myself a mental note to tell your ma what nice manners you have."

Clyde grins. "I'd be obliged. Say, I just doubled our money."

I'll be damned, but excitement laces the air as we pull away and as Clyde gets to driving, getting the car moving good, 'round fifty miles per hour.

Ain't long before a single, fat raindrop lands on our windshield.

The wind pushes the raindrop up and up 'til it streaks off the glass. Then, Mother Nature tilts her wrist and dumps a whole bucket on us. Clyde flicks on the single wiper. It struggles to keep up.

The rainfall is invigorating, the sheer power of it. Clyde feels it, too, leaning closer to the windshield to get a better vantage point of the sky.

"Where'd that come from?" he asks. The barrage of rain nearly drowns out his voice.

I shrug, not minding. The road is straight, lined with trees, leading toward a covered bridge. And I haven't seen such awe on Clyde's face since before he was locked away. He adjusts his leg, pressing harder on the accelerator. I let out a gleeful noise, exaggerating the force of the movement pushing me against my seat.

The rain pounds. The rain roars.

We drive into the covered bridge, and it's quiet. Just like that. Abrupt. Sudden. Powerful.

Freeze.

It's a moment I commit to memory, feeling as if, right now, Clyde and I already live in our own little world, where nothin' can touch us, not even Mother Nature. His body faces straight ahead. Both of his hands grip the wheel. But his head turns toward me. His dimples appear.

We pass by one, two, three openings in the bridge's walls; each time light blinks onto Clyde's face, illuminating his cheekbones and eyes.

Then we pop through the other side of the bridge.

The rain assaults us once more.

It only took one breath—held in my lungs—and a few beats of our hearts, but it was magical, a moment made for us, after months of being ripped apart. Now we're together again, nothin' but opportunity ahead of us. Which, Clyde says, begins with us getting those new clothes.

We stop at a boutique to get another suit and shirts for Clyde and a few dresses, blouses, and skirts for me. Red lipstick, too. I twirl and curtsy and swish my hemline in front of the mirror. Then Clyde goes and pays for 'em. No stealing this time, even if the money is dirty. But it won't always be, not after we get our farm and start working our land. Makes me wonder, does Clyde still want to raid the first farm?

That night, I check into a hotel under my given name, being no one's looking for Bonnie Parker. The storm washed a layer of jail off me. A warm bath melts off even more. I slip in bed behind Clyde and drape my arms over his bare skin. He's quick to pin my arm to him. Nothin' more. It hurts, 'specially after seeing him lighter today, and I bite my lip to feel pain other than Clyde not wanting to be intimate with me, even after I know his truth.

"Say, you still thinkin' 'bout the other farm. Eastham?" I ask him.

He stays on his side, his back to me, my arm tucked under his. "Aye. Got an idea to send a telegram to a lad tomorrow who could help with that."

"Who?"

"Pretty Boy Floyd."

I repeat the name. Then others pop into my head. Bugs Moran, Legs Diamond, Lucky Luciano. "Pretty Boy's a gangster, ain't he?"

Clyde snorts.

I sigh and say, "I'm already uncomfortable with robbing and now you want to be in cahoots with a gangster?"

"He can help, always has a finger on the pulse. Has to, since he's been running for over two years."

I say, "Sounds dreadful."

"Yeah, well, he's resourceful, and I need some information."

I wait, expecting Clyde to go on. "You going to make me drag it out of ya?"

Clyde rolls a little toward me, but not quite seeing me. I spy his smile, though. "You and Pretty Boy may get along better than you think."

I push him back to his side. "How do ya expect him to help us?"

"Want to see if he knows of anyone who can help me with the raid. Problem is," he says, "I ain't sure there are too many I'm willing to trust." *After what happened with Raymond,* I finish in my head. "I want Buck."

"Buck?"

"My brother. I believe you've met him a time or two."

"Clyde," I say. "Doesn't he have . . ." I think the timing through. Buck's been in prison since 'round Christmas of last year. "Are you telling me you ain't going to do the first farm for another year?" I drop my forehead into his back.

"He could get out sooner, Bonnie. Buck's well behaved."

I'm itchy again. I start with my collarbone.

Somewhere Blanche is saying, *Leave my man alone.*

Sorry, Blanche, I'd say back. *It's selfish of me, but I won't lie: If Clyde wants Buck to help him with Farm Number One, then I hope Buck gets out early. Tomorrow, even.* I rub my hand over Clyde's chest, wishing he'd react. But he doesn't, and if raiding Eastham is going to help Clyde move on from what happened there, then . . .

"Clyde, working with Pretty Boy sounds like a grand idea."

• • •

In the morning, we stop at a Western Union, then, telegram sent, go to a café for a bite to eat. While the waitress puts in two orders of cheese grits—something Blanche would surely approve of, as they're her favorite—I eye the public phone by the counter. It's been months since I've spoken to my ma. She's crossed my mind plenty, but I surely wasn't going to write her from jail.

With his back to the phone, Clyde twists, following my gaze.

"I need to call my ma," I say. "She'll be worrying that she hasn't heard from me."

Clyde answers by pushing a bill 'cross the enamel tabletop. "Let me know if this ain't enough."

To use the phone, I prepay at the counter, giving the woman my five dollars. I'm expecting change, but the woman only says, "You've got three minutes once it connects. You want longer, go fetch some more from your fella."

I glance at Clyde, feeling guilty a phone call is costing us so much. We could get ourselves sixteen bowls of cheese grits for that price. Exhaling, I settle myself in front of the phone. Before I pick it up, I slide some red lipstick over my lips, as if my ma will even be able to see it.

The operator asks who I'm after, and I give her my ma's party line. I imagine the phone ringing in my ma's house, along with the houses of three of our neighbors that all share the number, and I pray it's my ma's voice I hear on the other end.

Thank the Lord, I do. Tears spring to my eyes.

"Ma, it's me," I say.

I got to pull the phone from my ear as my ma replies, shouting my name like a question. I smile so hard, so happy to finally be talking to her.

"Where are you?" she asks.

Being the operator knows where the call originates, there's no point lying. Takes me a moment, though, to remember where we are. "Oklahoma."

"That where you're settling?" she asks.

I bite my lip. "No, ma, not yet. But I wanted to let you know I'm doing well. Safe and sound." I force a smile and finger-comb my hair.

"They're after him, you know that, don't you?"

"Ma." I stiffen. A neighbor—or even the law—could be listening in on the line. "Let's not talk 'bout that. How's Billie?"

"Your sister's good. You eating enough?"

"Yeah, just waiting for a waitress to bring us some food. Funny to have someone waiting on me for a change." I try to infuse happiness into my voice, but hearing hers is making me nothin' but homesick. And that ain't good, not with us staring down another year, at least, without a home. Of course, I can't tell my ma that. Or how we've got less than ten dollars to our name, nowhere close to what we'd need to buy a farm. None of my news would make my ma—or my daddy—proud.

Time goes too fast, and my three minutes slip by in the blink of an eye.

We both cry.

Back at the table, our food arrives, and Clyde and I continue to play the part of a young couple, well to do, off exploring the country. I force a smile and eat my food, but each bite tastes bland.

On our way out, Clyde gives me a nod and says, "Go on, Bonnie, wait in the car," and he heads into a small general store.

I'm too down to put up a fuss 'bout him robbing again. Next time, I'll feel bad.

Clyde comes out in a hurry. "Couldn't steal." He starts the car, peering over his shoulder as we pull away, wheels squealing.

I look 'round, but I ain't following what's got him spooked.

"Walked in," he says, "and saw my face on the wall."

"No," I say, and rub my forehead. Only yesterday, I worried 'bout us lasting more than two weeks and we're already feeling the heat. I wish I could make all the posters go away.

Being I can't, we got to stay out of sight for a while. After talking to my ma, I've got family on my mind, and I've an idea where we can go. My daddy has a sister over in New Mexico. I haven't seen my aunt in a long while, which makes visiting her perfect. Anyone looking for Clyde—or us, if they've put two and two together I've run off with him—wouldn't think to look there.

I have to shake the memories loose to remember how to find Aunt Nellie's. Couple hundred miles later, we drive through a whole lot of dirt to a stucco house with a row of cacti out front. My aunt walks out through an arched opening, her brows raised. Clyde makes a noise, like the world now makes sense. "You look a bit like your daddy, do ya?" he says. "'Cept you've got your mama's light hair."

I grin at that, seeing myself in Aunt Nellie's sharp cheekbones and thin nose. She doesn't share the warm personality my daddy had, though. I get a rigid hug, Clyde gets a firm handshake, and with a stiff voice, she ushers us inside.

My aunt's eyes jump from me to Clyde, back to me. "Will you be staying for supper?"

I nod and smile meekly.

She asks, "Longer?"

"Few days?"

"All right." With a surprisingly soft touch of her hand, she leads us into her family room. Where, she adds sternly, "Your fella will stay on that there couch. Your daddy, God rest his soul, would never forgive me if I let you share a room."

Her nod is curt, then that's that. My aunt's never been one for chit-chat, and she's quick to excuse herself to make coffee.

Clyde leans into the aging furniture, crosses his legs at the ankles. It's early afternoon, yet the white blinds are drawn shut and a single lamp lights the room.

Aunt Nellie doesn't have much, but everything has its place, right on down to the antique plates aligned on the wall. I reckon it all resembles a museum more than a homey place to be. But at the moment, I'm relieved to have any place to be, 'specially with family. "Comfortable?" I ask Clyde.

"I wouldn't say no to another pillow."

There's a knock at the door, and while Clyde retains his position, his head ticks to the side to listen, being we can't see what's going on from here.

Aunt Nellie's feet click against the tile. She mumbles 'bout more unexpected visitors before opening the door. "Gladys?" we hear.

Clyde lips to me, *Know her?*

I shake my head.

"Where's my brother?" The sternness of the woman's voice is a match for my aunt's, who says, "Frank's in town."

I lip to Clyde, *My aunt's sister-in-law,* then whisper, "I can't hear *Gladys* without thinkin' 'bout Blanche. She did this thing with the name. Gladys sounds like *glad ass,* yeah?"

"I suppose," he says; his eyes flick to the wall as if he can see through it.

"Blanche says that *glad ass* may as well be *happy heinie*. That's how she refers to a poor gal back home." I shrug.

"Ya tell me all that, then shrug? Sometimes I wonder what Buck sees in the lass."

I chuckle, then startle at the voices, growing louder.

"Quiet, now," my aunt snaps.

"I will not. Guns," Gladys growls, not a stich of her sounding happy. "I see 'em all over their rear seat. Who you got in there, Nellie? Frank wouldn't stand for no ruffians in his home."

I gasp, insulted by the term. Clyde leans forward, his hand on my knee, fingers splayed.

Aunt Nellie says, "I won't have you speaking 'bout my niece that way. I think it's best if you're on your way."

"Oh, I'm leaving," Gladys proclaims. "But I'll be back with Frank."

The door slams and a few footsteps later Aunt Nellie comes into the room.

Clyde gets to his feet. "We don't mean you any trouble, ma'am. We'll be on our way."

My heart's heavy, but as I turn to leave, my aunt grabs my wrist. "Try back tomorrow."

We spend the night off in the woods, sleeping stomach-to-back on our rear seat, guns now on the floor beneath a blanket. It was careless of us to leave 'em out, a mistake we won't make again.

In the morning, we debate what to do. Clyde says, "If ya can't trust family, who can ya trust?"

Dirt kicks up 'round us as we approach the house again. My uncle's old beater is parked out front next to a big ol' water tank. Besides that, it ain't nothin' but cacti and barren trees.

"I don't see any sign of her," I say of my aunt's hoity-toity sister-in-law.

My aunt doesn't come out to greet us this time, maybe expecting us to come straight in. We park behind my uncle's car. Clyde's door and my door slam one after another. I'm two steps toward the house when I hear, "Stop right there."

A man in blue steps out from behind the water tank. He ain't more than an arm away from Clyde, a gun at the end of that there arm. My chest seizes. Panicked, I look left and right, but there isn't anyone else in sight. Just the officer and Clyde, staring eye-to-eye, both faces shadowed from their hats. Clyde's got both hands up. With a flick of his wrist, his hat flies off to the right, along with the copper's attention.

That's all it takes for Clyde to swipe the officer's gun. The man's in the back of our car after that.

"We're taking him?" I ask. "Whatever for?"

Clyde drives. He taps his temple. "Lad can't tell anyone 'bout us if he's here with us. Now, keep his gun on him."

"On him?" I ask.

Clyde raises my arm, gun in hand. "On him." I readjust, facing backward in my seat, pistol on the man, doing my best to keep my hand from shaking. Over his head, I watch as a curtain is pulled aside within my aunt's house.

Now I'm really shaking, and the flames of Hades may as well be coursing through my veins. My daddy would be livid with his sister for sitting by as the police came for Clyde, and maybe even me. It all makes my stomach pang for real family, the ones who'd never put us in harm's way for the bounty of the equivalent of half a new car.

"Focus, darling," Clyde says, as if he feels my anger 'cross the bench seat. Then he brings his finger to his lips, indicating, *Now no more talking out of us.*

We drive 'round for a bit. A while, actually. Maybe seven hours or so, in complete silence. My hand tires from gripping the gun. I switch hands, the pistol feeling foreign in my left hand, and I wonder where we're going or when we're going to stop. Then, after we do, what's to come of this fella.

I still don't say a word. Clyde doesn't either, not to me, not to the fella. It's probably making the copper's mind turn even faster than our wheels.

In San Antonio, a town we end up in just 'cause, Clyde pulls off the road. He looks over at me, his voice a bit rough since he hasn't used it in so long, and says, "Well, what should we do with the lad?"

The lad, who is no doubt older than us, goes white as a sheet. But we've got no reason to hurt him. He ain't the one who double-crossed us.

He gets left on the side of the road, nearly five hundred miles from his home.

I sigh and ask Clyde, "What now?"

10

THE DAYS GO BY, RUNNING TOGETHER 'TIL WE'RE BEYOND TWO weeks. I relax a hair, as if that number's magic. But it ain't, not with Clyde's face showing up in Texas, Oklahoma, New Mexico, and Lord knows where else.

After slinking from one hotel or tourist camp to the next, our money's wearing thin. So are our clothes, worn multiple times over. We drop everything at a dry cleaner, save what's on us.

"We'll swing back in a few weeks for 'em," Clyde says. "Now, darling, you ain't going to glare at me if I say I need to hold up a store, will ya?"

Glare? No. "I've progressed to a stiff-lipped frown."

"That'll do."

He robs. By now, we've exchanged cars so often I've lost count, only keeping each one for a handful of days. Our travels—'cause it sounds better saying it that way—bring us to Oklahoma, and we stop into the

Western Union there. Clyde retrieves a private message from Pretty Boy Floyd.

"Got a direct phone number to contact him," Clyde says. "No news on Buck, though. So that means—"

I pop my lips. "We've got ourselves a whole year. Twelve long months."

"To save, remember?" There's a mixture of tension and lightness to his voice, if such a thing exists. I reckon it does when we're caught in between feeling free and looking over our shoulders.

Before long, we've got ourselves a routine. We drive, we sleep, we rob. Not always in that order. Not always all in one day. But we try to add more, week by week, into our piggy bank for the farm.

Sometimes we'll splurge on a cabin and sleep all day, the shades drawn shut, Clyde holding me. It's almost become taboo, me wishing for us to do more.

Sometimes Clyde will drive all day. He'll take off his shoe and sock, getting a better feel for the pedal with his bad foot, and just go and go. I think he likes the rumble of the engine 'round him. Personally, I like the dirt our wheels kick up. It's like we're invisible inside, just a cloud of dust.

There are days I think 'bout writing, but then the day doesn't bring anything different than the last—and I reckon it ain't bringing anything new tomorrow—so I shrug the idea away.

Clyde buys a bunch of maps, figuring it's better to know where a road goes. Can't argue with that. One day, a road takes us to this big ol' cotton gin, and out of all God's creatures, there are mules out front pulling wagons. There's also a shiny new car ripe for the picking, 'cept for the fact it's locked.

Clyde lets out a low, appreciative whistle. "Cotton must be king in these parts. This here is a 1932 Ford Model B two-door coupe. I won't mind driving her one bit."

I reckon Clyde stares at the car the same way I did at the Silver Jubilee Hoover electric cleaner I saw in a storefront the other day. The signage propped up next to the machine claimed it had a unique, patented cleaning technique known as Position Agitation that'd vibrate the rug as you ran the machine over it. It'd shake out and suck up all the dirt. I made a mental note to buy one of 'em once Clyde and I get the farmhouse and he starts tracking mud all over the place. Only four dollars and fifty cents down and a few small payments seems worth it to me to save myself the agitation of shaking out rugs on my own.

Outside the gin, I ask Clyde, "You going to stand there? Or are you going to pick the lock?"

"Neither. I'm going to ask the owner to open her up for us." Clyde eyes the gin. "Bet he's inside. Come on in with me, I could use some of your Saint Bonnelyn charm."

It's rare for Clyde to ask me to get involved, but in we go, and at the office, Clyde makes his voice silky as he says, "Excuse me, sir. Is that your fine automobile out front?"

I put my best smile on my face, my hands folded 'cross my front.

The man, hidden behind a mustache and beard, looks from me to Clyde. "Why, yes, she is."

Clyde's grin shows his teeth. "I was eyeing up that exact model last week. I hate to trouble you, but would you be willing to let me see the interior?"

"Honey." I run a hand down Clyde's suit jacket. "Don't bother the nice man that way. He clearly has a business to run."

It's no sweat off the man's back, or so he says. He follows us right outside, and as soon as the Ford's door clicks open, Clyde has a gun at its owner's back.

"Watch your head," Clyde says, putting yet another man in our rear seat. From one Ford to the other, I move over our robbery winnings and anything else we own: clothes and some sandwiches we picked up earlier.

Again, my job is to keep the pistol trained on him, in case he does any funny business. Not that he looks like he will, with how his mustache is twitching from nerves, and not like I want to use the gun on him. I feel bad 'bout taking him, being he ain't like the cop. But this here man and his car were a package deal.

After driving for hours with nothin' but the engine's purr, the silence must get to Clyde. "Tell us a joke," he says to the man.

Our hostage hesitates; maybe he's not sure if Clyde's the one who's joking. Or 'cause of the gun I have on him. Finally, in a shaky voice, he says, "Why's it so hard to keep a secret"—he swallows—"when it's rip-roaring cold?"

I raise an eyebrow.

"'Cause your teeth won't stop chattering."

Clyde busts up laughing.

"I got another," the man says. I offer him a sandwich with my free hand and he takes it. "Read it one time in a book."

"I like reading," I encourage him.

Our hostage almost smiles, and I nod for him to go on.

"There was this young fella, a laywer," he says. "He had a sign out front with his name on it. 'A. Swindler,' it said. So, a man comes in, looking for help, and says something along the lines of, 'My goodness, don't you know how that sign looks? Spell out your first name. Ambrose. Alexander. Whatever your name is.' The lawyer's got this defeated look on his face and says how it won't make the sign any better. 'Why not?' the client asks? The lawyer sighs and says, 'My name's Adam.'"

I work the joke 'round my head. It comes to me. "A damn swindler!"

I laugh. Our hostage laughs. Finally, Clyde laughs.

"Hey, what's your name?" Clyde asks him.

The man takes a big bite of his ham and cheese, mumbling, "Pistol Pete."

Clyde and I laugh again, being I'm the one with the pistol trained on poor Pete, who stops chewing when he gets our joke.

Not like we're going to hurt him. There's no reason to. Plus, we learn, we're of like minds. Pete has *pistol* in front of his name because he's not afraid to wave one 'round.

"Times are hard," he tells us. "Desperation is likely to perch on your shoulder and whisper in your ear. Hell, sometimes you got to do things you ain't proud of to get by. Try growing cotton in a drought, man." He laughs then, and adds, "And I don't got a pretty doll by my side. Partners through thick and thin, right? That'll get you two far."

I hope so. Right now, I ain't sure how robbing mom-and-pop stores is going to add up to a farm.

In the end, we tie Pistol Pete loosely to a tree, put some bills in his shirt pocket so he can get home, and Clyde assures Pistol Pete we'll send a telegram to let him know where we leave his car.

"Are we really going to return his car?" I ask Clyde as we drive away.

Clyde shrugs. "Why not? I sort of liked that Pistol Pete."

I did, too. I even considered writing a poem 'bout him, but lost my interest before I even began.

We let a few months pass, the weather growing cooler, our piggy bank slowly growing bigger, and sure enough, Clyde stops by a Western Union to send Pistol Pete an address of where his Ford was left weeks ago. Actually, it's depressing to think it's been weeks. Even more so to think we first left Dallas eight months ago. It's been six since I've spoken to my ma.

When Clyde's back in the car, I tell him, "I'm glad ya did that for Pistol Pete."

"A Christmas present for the lad."

Soon, we're driving again. I'm antsy in my seat. Antsy for a lot, but right now, the word *Christmas* is stuck in my head. "Clyde?"

"Bonnie?" He glances at me again. "Darling, what's wrong?"

"Can we go home?" I ask, adding, "For the holidays?"

Clyde reaches over, takes my hand and kisses it.

"It ain't smart. But," he says, before I can refute how none of what we're doing is smart, "we'll be careful."

• • •

I don't know why I thought Dallas would look different. It's not as if the homeless would suddenly have homes. Shops would suddenly be reopened. Folks in glad rags would suddenly, but discreetly, sneak to the basement of a physician's office once more.

President Hoover's had years to get us moving again in the right direction. People sure as hell don't have a chicken in every pot or a car in every garage, like he promised they would, and that's probably why Franklin D. Roosevelt won last month in a landslide. I read in the papers the electoral vote was 472 to 59, in favor of FDR. Only six states voted Republican.

If Clyde and I could've shown our faces, we would've walked into a voting station and handed over our ballots, too. Roosevelt had confidence. Roosevelt confidently pledged himself to a "New Deal" for the American people. The unemployed. The homeless. Our new president wants to help them both. He also wants to help the farmers. Clyde and I, perched on diner stools, listened to it all on the radio. We kept our heads down, but we wanted to lift them and applaud right alongside the others.

I wonder what those people would've done if they knew they were sitting beside a wanted man. Now, even as we drive down Elm Street, I can't help worrying there'll be big ol' billboards with Clyde's handsome face on it. But there aren't, and I'm too excited to see Ma's face to give it another thought. She doesn't know we're coming. I could walk right into the house, but I want to knock. She'll scrunch her brows and wonder who's at the door. And there I'll be, almost like a Christmas present. We'll invite over Blanche, put on some carols, and all sit 'round playing cards. Billie, Blanche, Buster, that girl of his, Clyde, and me.

We decided to wait until the cover of night before we slinked back into Dallas. And apparently, Clyde has a plan on how to keep our cover, which is probably why we didn't go straight to Cement City, my humble town on the other side of the railroad tracks.

I look over at Clyde, breaking my gaze from the glitter of Dallas at night. The darkness covers the dirt and debris, and the lights pull my attention up to the buildings, shooting into the sky, making Dallas seem bigger than it really is. Clyde spins the wheel left, pointing us toward West Dallas.

"Remember what to do when you're behind a wheel, Bonnie?"

Being Clyde's normally the one to grip it, I narrow an eye at him. But . . .

The left lever sets the parking brake. One on the right does the throttle. Other one on the left does the ignition timing. The right pedal is the brake. The middle pedal is reverse. I say, "The left pedal means go."

"That's my lass. I'm going to swipe us a new car while you stay in this here one. Then you'll follow me down to the river, where we'll make our new car nice and cozy. If eyes start poking 'round this one, we'll have a backup ride and—" Clyde honks the horn. "I just got myself a better idea."

Clyde pulls the car over, twisting in his seat to see behind him. There's a boy walking down the sidewalk. "That there was Jones."

The name's familiar. "Kid from the boardinghouse?"

"That's him. I've known him for"—he sucks on his tooth—"got to be ten years now. His family lived next to ours under that ol' bridge when we first got to Dallas."

That's all fine and dandy, but I ain't sure why we're stopped here instead of getting done what needs to be done so I can get to my ma. "Are you going to keep driving? Or get out to say hello?"

Jones loiters on the sidewalk, like he's not sure how to respond to that honk.

"The lad's got quick fingers." Clyde presses that middle pedal and the car reverses. "I've got a mind to do more than say hello. If Jones nabs the car, there'd be no way it can track back to us."

"You're going to ask that boy to steal for us?"

Clyde rolls down his window, Jones now standing right outside. With the streetlight broken, it's hard to get a good eyeful of him, but I remember him looking more like a boy than a man, small like a pup. He glances over at us. But he does it in a way where he's trying not to look, his head barely moving.

Clyde laughs. "He doesn't know it's me."

"Clyde," I say between my teeth. "Leave him be. It's Christmas Eve. He's got to be on his way home. Besides, he can't be more than fifteen." Not much younger than Billie. I'm shaking my head like Clyde's lost his sense, probably 'cause he has.

"I reckon he's sixteen. Same age my sister would be. She used to have a crush on Jones, if her red cheeks spoke any truth." His eyes sadden a moment, then his cool façade returns. "Bootlegs. Stealing Cars. Picking lots. The lad ain't green 'round the gills, Bonnie."

I sigh inwardly; if Jones ain't a stranger to it, then maybe it'll save us some trouble. But the whole thing makes me uneasy, relying on someone else, trusting someone else. To Clyde, I shrug.

"Jones," Clyde calls, his elbow propped on his open window. "It's me. Clyde."

If I were Jones, I'd have half a mind to run. The boy takes a hesitant step forward. "Clyde Barrow?"

The one and only, I think to myself.

"Want to make some spending money?" Clyde asks.

Doesn't everyone?

But I wish for the kid to say no.

Jones grins widely, then he's climbing into our rear seat, Clyde twisting to give him a *welcome* pat on the back.

Introductions are made before we drive a ways, ending up in a more remote section of town, where people have lawns and driveways, along with a false sense of security, often leaving their keys in the ignition. They often have nosy neighbors, too.

Clyde slows our car and nods toward a car tucked in for the night in front of a two-story house. "I wouldn't mind that Model A Roadster. What do you think, Jones, she's from nineteen twenty—"

"Nineteen twenty-eight," I say feigning confidence.

Really, I don't have a damn clue, but I'm 'bout to bust out of our own Ford 'cause of my anxiety, and my mouth opened on its own.

"Clyde, you lucky dog," Jones says. "Your lady knows 'bout cars and looks like that?"

I scrunch my brows, assuming that's a compliment from the kid.

Clyde laughs. "My Bonnie's something special."

And my Clyde's a sweet talker.

"Just get her going," Clyde adds, 'bout the car. "Be as quiet as a cat with the dogs close, you hear?"

Jones bobs his head and hops out, leaving us idling on the other side of Thirteenth Street, our engine still purring. The house is dark, 'cept for a big ol' twinkling Christmas tree in their front window. I hold my bottom lip between my teeth, watching for any movement.

The driver's door opens, unlocked, and Jones is in. From where we are, Clyde and I squint, trying to make out his movements. He's in the seat, but the car's not starting.

"Maybe the key isn't there?" I say. "Can he start it otherwise?"

"He'd be running this way if the key wasn't there. I'm concerned 'bout her being cold." Clyde licks his lips, his foot tapping. "Maybe Jones forgot something. Spark up. Key on. Gas down," he mumbles to himself. "Shouldn't need to choke her more than once unless she's been sitting there awhile." He runs his hands through his hair.

Something catches my eye inside the house. I spit out, "They're home."

"Shit, I got to go help, Bonnie."

My heart's in my mouth, and I don't have time to protest before he's gone. It's dark, but not dark enough to hide him as he runs up the driveway. The porch light flashes on. And now Clyde's on full display; bent low, one hand on the driver-side door, his head poking in the open window.

I panic, touching my throat, my leg, the door handle, the whole time my eyes jumping between Clyde and the front door. No one's coming out. Clyde disappears into the car, Jones's shadow moving over to the passenger seat.

It jolts me into action, moving over into the seat Clyde just vacated. I put my hands on the wheel.

Come on.

God sends the wrong person coming; the front door swings open. A man runs out, the long barrel of a gun swinging at his hip.

"Clyde!"

I roll my window down, catching the tail end of the man saying, ". . . my boy's car. Get out!" His woman runs out of the house, too, hollering.

Get out, Clyde. *Get out and we'll go. No harm, no foul.*

'Cept, no, Clyde shouts, "Stand back now, both of you, and no one will get hurt."

Listen to him, I silently plead to the man with the shotgun. I can barely watch, not wanting that gun pointed at Clyde.

Suddenly, two becomes three as another man rushes from the house. "Call the police!" he yells. He grabs the man and woman, forcing them back. Pushing them back toward the house. The man takes his shotgun with him, and I exhale.

Then, the second man goes and does something stupid, lunging through the window, his hands leading the way. I sit here shocked, picturing the man half in, half out of the car, wringing Clyde's neck. There's a flurry of movement, and it's as if the window spits him out. Clyde's voice rises to say, "Stop, man, or I'll have to shoot."

The man doesn't stop; half his body goes through the window again, his feet scuffing the driveway.

I breathe through my fingers—watching, praying, waiting to see if Clyde makes good on his threat.

There's a gunshot.

And another.

I jump in my seat.

The man slumps to the ground.

The woman, outside again, screams. I didn't see her return. She collapses on top of the fallen man. The first man aims his gun, but no shots sound. I ain't sure why, and as luck has it, the car picks that time to come to life.

Before I know it, Clyde has the car down the driveway, down the street. I can't bring myself to look at the figures in the driveway. I've never seen a person get shot and not get up.

I can't be sitting here—in a stolen car, no less. I go after Clyde, my hands shaking on the wheel.

When they stop, I stop, not even close to the river like we planned, and I fill my lungs with air.

The boys run toward me, and I drag myself 'cross the bench seat, back to the passenger's side. First thing Clyde does, he kisses me. Hard. I find myself sobbing, and Lord help me, it's not for the man, it's for the image of the man's hands 'round Clyde's neck. Still, I whisper, "The man's dead. He's got to be."

Clyde already has our Ford going as fast as the city blocks will allow. He glances toward the rear seat, toward Jones, who says, "I ain't sure which one of us got him."

I sob again, filled with pity; this time it's for Jones.

"Don't matter," Clyde says. "We can't stay in Dallas. You can't, either." Clyde nods at Jones. "You know that, don't you, lad? You got murder on you, just like me. You can't go home right now."

It's silent, save the engine, and I can't bring myself to see Jones's reaction. It's bad enough I hear the hitching of his breath and feel the way he punches the back of my seat. Soon, Clyde stops the car, nodding to Jones again. "Lad, shinny up that pole and cut them phone wires. We don't want the law calling ahead."

Smart. But I can't help staring at Jones, climbing up the pole like a lost bear cub, and feeling like we're 'bout to be cut off from a hell of a lot more. Now we're truly in our own little world, and Clyde's truly a murderer.

11

I STARE AT THE WOOD SLATS OF THE CABIN'S PITCHED CEILING. Jones snores lightly on a pallet on the wooden floor. Clyde's quiet beside me on our twin-sized bed, my right side touching all of his left, fitting together. And I let my mind roam and remember.

I could've left, snuck away. A passerby would've picked me up. I technically didn't have blood on my hands. But I felt like I did, having wished for Clyde to do whatever he had to do to get away. He did, and the bruises on Clyde's neck slowly shift my thoughts from him taking a life to saving his own—and to us carrying on, together, so we can eventually leave this life behind.

Two weeks after we fled Dallas, we were out of money. Bone dry.

"We need a quick hit of dough," Clyde said and rubbed his brow. "A big quick hit."

Clyde hated holding up the Home Bank of Grapevine, with the risk of getting caught so high, but he and Jones did it, successfully. Two thousand eight hundred and fifty clams have helped us lay low, 'specially with another mouth to feed—one I feel responsible for.

How low we need to lie? Clyde's not sure. Knowing if he's been named—or the boy's been named—for the murder would help. The papers haven't said yet, but that doesn't mean there hasn't been talk. Clyde keeps debating a meet-up with a pal, Odell Chambless, who often makes a nest at Raymond's sister's place. Problem is, that's in West Dallas, and Clyde himself said we can't be there.

I also can't let myself leave Dallas behind, not fully. Even now, we're only thirty minutes outside the town limits at a tourist camp, skirting 'round our childhood homes. The first time we left Dallas, it felt like a solution to Clyde getting pinched for breaking parole, a way to get the law to forget Clyde's scent.

But this time, we all have our hands in our hair. Clyde's wanted for motor theft, bank theft, probably theft I haven't heard of yet, kidnapping, and maybe even murder. I can feel us all becoming reckless. Hell, it's more than a feeling; we *are* being reckless. Just this morning, while I was putting dresses and trousers on the counter of the dry cleaner, the woman working the place looked at me too long, and I sneered at her, stopping short of baring my teeth. That ain't like me to try to intimidate a gal, but I knew it'd make her end her scrutiny of me. It also could've sent her to squeal on me: the young woman with bags under her eyes, who had two men, one fitting the description of a known fugitive, waiting for her in the car outside.

Wouldn't that take the cake? Fingered by a Nosey Parker. No relation to my family, of course.

My next breath is deep, the air in the cabin never seeming enough. What I wouldn't give to be in a place that felt even a fraction like being in a home.

"Bonnie?" Clyde whispers, not 'cause he doesn't want to disturb Jones. Well, maybe, but in general, we always whisper. The cabin is one of many, all lined up down a dirt road. You drive in, you hand over some bills, you stay the night, you leave. You also don't know your neighbor from Adam. Our conversations aren't ones we want heard. I roll onto my side and run my hand over Clyde's forehead, pushing aside his tousled hair. It's one of those nights where the moon takes up the Texas sky, and it's brighter outside the window than inside our tiny cabin.

"I've had Doyle Johnson clogging up my head," he says.

The man we killed only hours into Christmas Day. I read an article 'bout it. The man wasn't much older than us, only twenty-seven. He worked as a grocery clerk, an honest job. Doyle had a wife and infant son. Now that son doesn't have a daddy.

I know a little something 'bout that. My chest still tightens when I remember my ma's cries at learning my daddy died in the Great War. Much changed after that, with only four of the five chairs occupied at supper each night, my ma refusing to take my daddy's away. With my ma working her fingers to the bones, and still the electric company coming after us. With wondering if the choices I was making would've made my daddy smile or brought out those creases between his eyes.

I want none of that for Doyle's li'l boy.

"You know why he died, right?" Clyde asks.

A bullet.

"You can't go back to prison," I say.

Clyde nods and kisses the back of my hand. He's silent, then says, "But it's weighing on me. I'm guessing Doyle barely made ends meet for his family, and now they won't meet at all. If that car would've come to life seconds earlier, that family wouldn't be suffering now. I wouldn't be suffering now. Sounds selfish, don't it?"

"Some," I admit. "But, Clyde, you were only out to get the car, not the family or Doyle himself."

I believe it, and leave it at that, letting Clyde say more if he's got an itch to do so. He doesn't. I roll onto my back and slide a leg out from under the quilt; the electric stove, our makeshift heater for the night, is too stifling for my liking. My daddy never liked the heat either.

Jones is the closest to the warmth, nearly pressed up against the stove, being this room is barely bigger than that calaboose, but sound asleep, he doesn't seem to mind. Me, I'm the one always counting sheep.

"Bonnie?" Clyde whispers again. "I feel responsible for the lad."

"We'll take care of Jones like our own." The pillow rustles in my ear as I turn my head. My question sticks on my tongue, with us still not being intimate, but I manage to ask, "Think we will, though—ever have one of our own?"

One side of Clyde's mouth turns up. "God willing."

That may've been the first time Clyde's mentioned Him. I smile back.

"'Til then," Clyde says. "I want to tell the family we do have that we're okay, and have that chat with Odell."

"How we going to do that?"

Now those dimples appear. "I've an idea."

• • •

"Jones, let's see if that aim of yours has improved since you threw a ball through Ms. Myers' window. That is, if Bonnie ever finishes our letter."

I narrow an eye at Clyde. Playfully, of course. He's got a way of adding enough amusement to his voice to never ruffle my feathers. From the rear seat of our latest Ford, Jones lowers the Coca-Cola bottle from his lips to say, "My aim's just fine."

"Don't sign it," Clyde says to me, "your ma'll know your handwriting, right?"

"Right." I cross a *t*. "Ya know, this would go faster if you didn't keep telling me how to write it."

"Wanted it worded a certain way. And, like I said, we'll see 'bout that aim, lad. You done with that drink yet?"

Jones lets out a carbonated belch, and I give him a *have some manners* look. "Then you could've written it," I say to Clyde. "And watch those potholes."

He shrugs, and turns us down a new block.

"Well"—I swallow, knowing the Star Service Station is only a few blocks away—"letter's done."

Now his parents will know 'bout our failed Christmas surprise, that we're getting enough food, that we miss them and want to know the second Buck's out of jail. We leave out that Clyde wants his brother for Farm Number One.

They're to plant flowers—yellow ones so there's no confusion—out front of my ma's house once Buck's back home. Then we'll come for them—Buck and Blanche. We'll all be together again. We'll be moving again.

I can imagine Mrs. Barrow going to Ma's door, and the smoker lines on my ma's upper lip becoming more pronounced when she purses them. She ain't the biggest fan of Clyde's ma, holding her responsible for the antics of her son. But I know my ma. She'll invite Mrs. Barrow in and she'll hang on her every word as she tells Ma we're okay. If I weren't so excited, I'd be more jittery 'bout being back in Dallas, 'specially with us 'bout to drive past the Barrows' service shop.

Clyde takes the letter, keeping one eye on the road, and passes it back to Jones. "Roll her up. Put her inside."

Jones does, creating our own message in a bottle.

We pass the service station once—go 'round the block—pass it again a second time. I fidget, absently tapping my fingernails against a pistol nestled on the bench seat between Clyde and me, but my mouth stays quiet, knowing Clyde will only risk one more circle of the block. The first two times, a customer was in the shop. We need it empty.

Halfway down Eagle Ford Road a third time, I let out a breath. A car pulls out of the station.

"Go on," Clyde says to Jones. He slows our Ford. Jones rolls down his window. The winter air seeps in. "Show me that arm of yours, boy."

Jones whips the bottle from our car, the glass shattering against a barrel by the station's door.

Clyde's heavy on the gas, and I rock in my seat as I twist to see Mr. Barrow emerge from the store, dropping to a knee to retrieve our note.

I smile at Jones.

"Told ya," he says to Clyde, to which Clyde removes his tan hat, using it like a disc to fling into the rear seat.

We laugh, a sound I could hear for days.

Don't have time for that, though. Our next stop is tracking down Odell Chambless, to see if Clyde—or Jones—has been named for

Doyle's death. Facing forward again, I wring my hands, not willing this renegade lifestyle on anyone, 'specially not a sixteen-year-old kid.

The house is so close we nearly passed it while staking out the service station. There are double doors, the house split in two, with bars on all the windows.

We park out front.

"How well you know this fella?" I ask Clyde.

"Well enough where he won't pull a shotgun on me when I'm at his door, but not well enough where the law will think I'll show up here."

I suck my bottom lip. *All right.* "And what makes him somebody who'd know things?"

"He's Mary's brother, which got him introduced to Raymond, which is how he got friendly with Ray's sister Lilly. And Lilly is friendly with even more." Clyde leaves it at that, then says, "There shouldn't be any trouble. But I'll run if I need to. You take the car and the lad. I'll find ya."

Before I can object to such a loose plan, Clyde taps his lips. I kiss him. I start to pull back, then kiss him again.

I feel Clyde slide the pistol toward me, pressing it against my leg.

"You remember how to use this, right?"

I stare at the hunk of metal. "The gun?" It's a dumb question; nothin' else Clyde could be referring to.

"Bonnie," Clyde says softly, "we live in a world where it's either kill or be killed."

I nod.

He says, "I don't want you using it. But if things go south"—he places it in my hand—"fire at the sky. It'll spook whoever it needs to spook."

Jones leans over the front seat. "I can do it."

"No," I say quickly. "I can." Jones has already done enough, and I've fired off a shot to save Clyde's life before.

Clyde flicks his collar up, shielding his face from lookie-loos and the bite in the air. His hobble is less pronounced as he walks 'cross the street and toward the house. I don't reckon it's cause his foot's any better; can't regrow toes. His smoother gait is Clyde trying mighty hard to stay straight, making himself seem like the old Clyde Barrow.

One thing's for sure, either version of Clyde's got enough pride to fill the ocean.

Like so many times in the past few weeks and months, I scan 'round me, looking for signs of danger.

I crack open the passenger door. If I need to, I'll kick it open and get to firing at the clouds.

Using the back of his knuckle, Clyde casually raps the front door. He stays nonchalant, looking down the street as if he doesn't have a care in the world, his face shaded under the brim of his hat.

The door opens on the porch, and the leather seat creaks behind me.

"That ain't Odell," Jones says to me.

Clyde retreats a step. The fingers on his right hand twitch, no doubt ready to pull the gun from beneath his dark trench coat if it comes to that. I lift my foot, ready. The gun's heavy in my hands.

"How you know that ain't Odell?" I ask Jones. Clyde's talking to the man at the door. The fella's tall with a smart look to him. He put himself together, maybe too well. We know something 'bout dressing up to play a part.

"I've seen Odell. He's done a few banks. His face ain't unknown."

Panic seizes me.

"Shit, Bonnie," he says, and that panic is for good reason. Another figure moves inside the house, passing by the barred window. "This here's a trap."

"For us?" I practically scream.

The man at the door has his own twitch

"For Odell," Jones says—to my back. I've got the car door open and I let a bullet fly at the sky. Clyde's eyes fill his face. He draws his gun a heartbeat later. So does the copper, nearly salivating at his dumb luck that Clyde Barrow stands in front of him.

It's either kill or be killed, I think.

I'll be the hero, he must think.

Not as long as I can help it. I round the car, pistol leading the way.

We all fire.

PART TWO

THE BARROW GANG

12

THE UNDERCOVER COP FALLS. HE TUMBLES DOWN THE THREE porch steps. He doesn't get up. The shots still echo in my ears. I stand and stare, my own gunfire too reckless to know if I've caused the bloom of red on the man's gut.

Clyde runs toward me, away from the house, and I eye him for any wounds. None, but still a pang of worry nearly folds me in half. To the law, his back is a coward's target. An opportunity that ain't beneath them these days. Clyde may not know it, but I do: There are more men inside.

Glass shatters and the long barrel of a gun appears on the windowsill.

I close one eye, raise my hand, doing my best to keep the gun straight and level. Clyde's life is in my hands, and I can't afford for the gun to shake. I fire again, imagining the bullet spiraling past Clyde. Wood splinters on the porch's post, and the barrel withdraws.

Clyde runs into me, picking me up as he goes. He wears me 'round his middle, my feet no longer on the ground, carrying me toward the car. I keep the gun free, aimed. I got two bullets, maybe one. I ain't sure how many times desperation pushed on my trigger finger when I first rounded the car.

I let one more shot fly before yanking my hand back, dipping my head and squeezing past the wheel. On the passenger side of the car, I drop the gun, my fingers shaking, it landing at a thud at my feet. Jones curses. Clyde's already got us moving. My breath comes fast, my chest tight, rising high then low, up and down, fast, but not nearly as fast as my heart.

"Clyde?" I ask, not recognizing the sound of my own voice. "Did I kill a man today?"

"I did, Bonnie."

My vision's blurry. "But I fired bullets, too."

"I don't miss. It was me, you hear?"

I nod, but I ain't sure it's better it was Clyde. He's already got enough dark spots on his soul.

Clyde drives like the devil himself is after us, right out of Dallas, right out of Texas.

He barely lets up for days. I need those days for my hand to stop trembling. I remind myself firing those shots gave Clyde a fighting chance. That the copper died in front of that house 'cause he wanted to take Clyde's life away. Even if they didn't kill Clyde right then and there, they would've locked him up. Either scenario equals death.

We're in Missouri or Kansas now, can't be sure, but I'm thinking Missouri. Either way, it's rip-roaring cold. Up ahead, there's a big lake, frozen solid, a bridge stretching 'cross it.

Clyde's got a thing 'bout bridges, doesn't like 'em, likes to get off of 'em as fast as possible so he's not trapped. I glance over at him.

He's staring in the rearview mirror.

I turn to look out the back of our car. Jones is fast asleep. A motorcycle is coming up behind us.

The bridge rumbles beneath us.

The motorcycle pulls up alongside our car, motions for us to pull over. Clyde and I curse in unison, believing—and at the same time not believing—it's the law again, so soon. By looking at him, it's hard to tell if this fella is an officer; he's so bundled up, his uniform covered, but there on his helmet is the insignia that gives him away. Clyde does his own motioning to me, silently asking me to scoot closer to him. I slide down the bench seat, using part of my long coat to cover the gun that's always between us. I can't help wondering if this officer is after us 'cause of what happened only days ago, but I got to imagine if he was, there'd be more than just him.

Clyde rolls down his window, still cruising along, the icy air flooding our car. He smiles, shouts, "Just a minute, sir," which reassures me that I'm right. This copper coming after us is a lousy coincidence.

The officer, a young fella, gets nasty, hollering at us to pull over, but Clyde keeps driving to get off the bridge. On stable ground, Clyde stops the car and slips on the charm like it's his favorite shirt. "Something wrong, Officer? I got a taillight out?"

The officer's eyes flick to me. "Long way from home."

I search my memory for what plates are on this car, but I can't seem to remember. Clyde nods, slowly, as if he's trying to remember, too.

The copper's breath comes out in puffs. His eyes flick to me again. "Any reason why you're moving so fast?"

Clyde smiles. "Didn't think there was anyone 'round to stop me."

I could smack him upside the head for saying that. Jones, now awake, stays quiet in the back. I keep my own mouth shut.

The officer's eyes flick to me a third time. Clyde responds with our shotgun.

The fella becomes yet another unfortunate soul who finds himself in our rear seat, sitting on bags of money, trying to find space for his feet between our things. This time, Jones is the one to keep a gun on him as we give the copper a thrill ride, a short one. Our battery dies after an hour or so, taking with it our source of heat.

Clyde sucks a tooth 'til he decides Jones and the copper will go fetch us a new one. He runs a finger over a map. "It's your lucky day; looks like there should be some folks not far off. Maybe a mile or so up ahead."

The officer's already bundled up from his motorcycle patrol. Clyde gives his coat to Jones, our Texas boy now wearing two. Off he goes with the patrolman, on foot, Clyde saying to me, "They'll be the best of friends by the time they get back."

I eye the stretch of road. It dips and disappears beyond a small hill. On either side of the road are clusters of barren trees. "If they aren't frozen stiff."

"What 'bout me, Bonnie? I'm the one without a coat."

"Poor Clyde," I say in a mocking voice. "Come here, honey. I'll keep ya warm." At first I think I conjured it, but no, Clyde has a glimmer in his eye. He only reaches for me, though, to hold me close. He whispers in my ear, "Can't get it out of my head how you rounded that car for me. My very own Annie Oakley."

I laugh at that. "Anything for my Billy the Kid."

Minutes, then an hour ticks by before Jones and the copper appear again over the hill. Jones passes the car battery to the patrolman. After another thirty seconds or so, he passes it back. I imagine both their arms are quaking after hauling the thing. I can't help wondering why the young officer didn't run off, but I reckon Clyde's got a way 'bout himself that makes ya want to listen.

It's not long before our engine's purring again, glorious heat filling the car. I sit in the passenger seat, letting it warm my bones.

Clyde drops the hood. Jones scrambles into the car. The officer stands there, his knees practically knocking together. He's got to be in his early twenties like us. Any of that bravado he had while shouting at us from his motorcycle is gone.

"End of the road for ya," Clyde says to him. "With us, anyway."

The patrolman says, "Please."

Spare me, that's what he's asking for.

Clyde points to the gravel road. "Have a seat." Down the fella goes. "We'll be on our way now. You stay right there."

"Thank you," he mutters.

I snort at that.

As fast as we can, we cross the state line into Kansas, which is plenty fast. It's only a handful of miles, and it's like that line is magic. The officer can't follow us for two reasons. The obvious one is he's without his motorcycle. But the second one is 'cause Kansas is out of his jurisdiction. He ain't allowed.

Jones is the first to speak: "Clyde, I saw an apartment while getting the battery, in Joplin. Had a rental sign out front. Think we could ever stay in a place like that?"

I was facing forward when Jones said it, but there was such desperation in his voice I'm compelled to get a look at him. Ain't a surprise there's desperation on his face, too.

"What was it like?" I ask.

"Signage said it had a bathroom, kitchen, and two bedrooms. Fully furnished. Thirty-three forty-seven and a half Oak Ridge Drive is where it's at."

The idea of playing house has me saying, "I could sure use a dose of that. Clyde, why don't we rent it? We got us some money saved up."

"For the farms," he counters.

"Which," I point out, "we ain't doing until Buck gets out. We've got ourselves nothin' but time that we could spend sitting on a couch, with electricity and running water, where coppers can't pull up beside us."

Clyde taps his fingers on the wheel.

"Honey, what's to think 'bout? The boy and I need this."

Jones adds, "Rental comes with a garage, too. It'll hold a Ford plenty well."

A small chuckle comes out as Clyde shakes his head. "Quiet, both of ya. I *am* trying to think. We can't rent it straight off, not with us fleeing the area only seconds ago. We'll wait a stretch. Better yet, if we wait for Buck to get the place, he can stay with us. It'll give me some time to work on him, convince him to do Eastham with me."

I fight the urge to point out how Buck isn't supposed to be released for another five months. Five more months of hopping from place to place and from car to car. Each of 'em is an opportunity for the law to spot us. I sigh but agree, then promptly cross my fingers Buck is pardoned early.

We fall into that familiar routine: drive, sleep, rob. Plus, now we'll also check for those yellow flowers, once a month, we decide. But it's not as if we can simply drive by my ma's house; Cement City is short on people and even shorter on folks with automobiles.

We park a ways off and Jones goes by foot. I imagine him passing the library nestled next to Ma's house. Next, the cemetery will be on his right. There ain't much more before he's at the church, general store, and telephone connections building. Then that's that, my hometown.

The days are starting to warm, enough where the nights don't leave me shivering no more, and on Jones's second trip to my ma's house he walks at a clip back to us, a blessed flower behind one ear.

Clyde hoots.

I say, "You went and picked one!"

"Didn't want Clyde doubting me," he jabs, then mocks Clyde's deep voice: "You sure it was yellow, lad? Not green?"

At least Clyde's laughing as he puts Jones in a chokehold. The boy surprises me, twisting out of it. Moment later, they're both fixing their hair.

That night, three blessed months earlier than I was expecting, Clyde makes a call to 3347½ Oak Ridge Drive and reserves the apartment under the alias William Callihan.

"Now," Clyde says. "It's time to have a chat with Buck."

"Nope." I shake my head. "Blanche."

• • •

She sure doesn't make it easy to have that chat, which heightens all the emotions I'm having 'bout asking to borrow Buck. Guilt, shame, and ya might as well throw jitters into the mix. Her and Buck have up and left town, or so my ma says when we sent Jones to her door. I wish it were me, knocking, hearing her voice, seeing the inside of my childhood home. I wonder if Ma's had a chance to stitch the tear in her favorite chair. For months before I left with Clyde, she kept saying how she'd get 'round to it one of these days.

"That lass," Clyde says, referring to Blanche. His voice pulls me back to the here and now: some road outside of Dallas. His head drops to the wheel. "Where could they have gone? Ain't like she knows anybody outside of town."

It dawns on me. "Her mama's house," I say mostly to myself. "She said that once, after Buck got out, she was going to track her down. Truth be told, didn't think she would. I forgot she even said it 'til now."

"Where's that?" Clyde says.

I close my eyes, search my memory. "Honey, I can feel you looking at me." It comes to me, despite feeling like I'm on a witness stand. "Wilmer."

Clyde snorts. "First stroke of luck we've had. That's a stone's throw away."

We get lucky once more that Wilmer ain't a big town. Population: 247. It takes all of five minutes 'til I see her, Big Bertha. I spent enough time with Blanche in that car growing up to recognize her dents and marks anywhere.

Of course, when Blanche comes storming out of the house, Buck on her heels, we know for certain we're in the right place.

Even with Blanche originally in the lead, Buck overtakes her and reaches us first. Rather, he reaches his brother first. Buck goes for a hug; Clyde resists, but Buck persists, not releasing him 'til Clyde shakes him off. Buck still doesn't let go. He takes Clyde's head between his hands and bends 'til their foreheads touch. The words they exchange are private.

All of it is a punch to the gut, seeing their reunion, but also seeing how small Clyde looks next to his brother. Clyde's always been two heads shorter, but Buck's emerged from prison seemingly taller. And whole.

Now I sit beside Blanche on a big ol' rock, her ma's house off behind us. She stares out at a river and the flowered fields beyond.

It's so good to see her; all I want to do is give her my own hug. But she's holding back tears, and if I embrace her too tightly I may squeeze 'em right out.

She says, "Confronting my so-called Ma didn't go so well. The woman had no answers, couldn't give me a sound reason for her disappearing act. Just up and left." Blanche swings her arm into the air, disturbing Snow Ball. "Poof!"

I let her talk; I know she's got more to say. "All these years and she's been a handful of miles away. Can you believe it, Bonn? I even called her Lillian to her face, thinking she'd flinch. Not even a li'l. I didn't bother to bring up my pa, how he hasn't been there for me, either. What's the point? But you know what, I feel like I've won. The way she looked at Buck, when she's living all alone. That could've been me; didn't think marriage was for me, with Lillian and Freddy for parents. But I showed her. Showed her my backside, too, as I stormed out of the house."

"I'm sorry." It's all I can say.

"It's fine. All I need is you and Buck."

"In that order," I say, hoping for a smile. I get one.

"Speaking of you. What on earth are you doing here? Don't get me wrong, I'm happy to see your face. It's your other half that's giving me the heebie-jeebies right 'bout now. Buck still has the stench of jail on him, then up pops Clyde."

I sigh and try to think of the best way to appeal to Blanche. "Remember my blouse with the ruffles?" I wave my hand down my chest. "And with the bow 'cross here?" I run a hand over my navel.

"Yes, unfortunately."

"Well, it's gone." Blanche scrunches her brow, and I'm not sure why I expected a monumental response from her at that moment, like *now* it's crystal clear why I'm here. "I dropped it off at the cleaners a few weeks ago. The woman eyed me funny, and when we went back, my gut said, don't go inside." I remember trembling, the fear of another shoot-out almost too much to bear. I let out a slow breath. "I'll never see that blouse again, Blanche."

"And you want me to take you shopping?"

"No. I want to stand still for a moment, with you. Clyde's got an apartment reserved. Come live with us for a few weeks. It's not like you and Buck have a place of your own, right?"

"Right," Blanche says slowly. Her eyes are glued on Snow Ball. "Listen, Bonn, me telling Buck to go back to prison . . . *prison*," she repeats.

"Well, that was the hardest thing I ever had to do. But now he's out. He didn't have a conditional pardon like Clyde did, Bonn. He was flat-out pardoned. There's a difference."

"No one's going to come after him," I whisper and pick at a thread on my dress.

Blanche shakes her head. "'Cept maybe his brother and that boy he's with."

"That's Jones," I offer.

"Where'd he come from?"

I regret offering.

"Bonn?"

"We've been keeping him safe," I half lie.

"'Cause you two got him in trouble. Am I right? There was the time I envied your pants off, but now, I want nothin' to do with your pants. And frankly, if you guys keep both feet on the ground like you're doing, you won't ever be able to get your own pants off."

I say, "I ain't even wearing pants."

That gets a light chuckle from Blanche. I miss her throaty laugh.

"I saw it in a book. Stop," she says, before I can react to her newfound pastime. "It was a proverb. Basically, you keep doing what you're doing and nothin' will change."

"And that's exactly why we want to get off the road for a bit. Clyde needs time to plan without having to always look over his shoulder."

She runs her hand from the dog's snout up over his ears, stretching Snow Ball's eyes with each pull. "Is that where Buck comes in?"

"You'll have to ask Clyde that one." It's a coward's response, but how can I ask her to let Clyde borrow Buck? All I can ask is, "Will you consider living with us?"

"I don't know, Bonn."

I should walk away. I want to slug myself for not walking away, but I don't. I won't. "You'll like this, Blanche. You'll get to make the place our own with whatever furnishings you want. *Then,*" I say, emphasizing the word, "when you and Buck go back to Dallas, you can take it all with you. Think of it as our gift for helping us feel human again." I realize that's what it all comes down to for me. Clyde may want Blanche to get to Buck. But I want Blanche for me. Getting the first farm out of the way is an added bonus. A big one, I admit. It means being closer to the second farm, and not having to run anymore, and no more police traps, and a litter of kids with Clyde. I sigh. "It's been so long, Blanche. Give me just a few weeks of you and me."

Blanche twists her lips. She dangles the dog in front of her face, their noses nearly touching. "We miss Bonn, don't we?" she asks the dog in her baby voice. Her attention's back on me. "How 'bout this. I'm going to let Snow Ball decide."

"The dog?"

"It's March, in Texas. So, yes, the dog." Blanche settles Snow Ball in her lap and tilts her head at me, as if saying, *Are you really questioning me?* But she actually says, "He's brought me nothin' but good fortune since I've scooped him up. Haven't you, my li'l fur ball?"

I stare at the dog, not sure what I'm waiting for. Then Snow Ball, bless his heart, chooses that moment to lick my hand. I could kiss him right back.

13

I PEEK OUT THE CABIN'S WINDOW. NO BLANCHE, NOT YET. But soon, after her and Buck get here, we'll be saying sayonara to this tourist camp. It's the nicest one the boys and I have been in yet, with a brick exterior, a separate bedroom, and an attached garage. It'll be nothin' compared to the garage apartment we're headed to in Joplin, Missouri.

I almost feel like I should be marking my whereabouts on an actual map, but a spiderweb comes to mind, with all that we've been moving around. That's 'bout to change, for a few weeks anyway.

I pull on a dress, tug free my hair and finger-comb it. I pull aside the curtain again. I'm supposed to be packing. There are guns, ammunition, clothing, and random odds and ends strewn about. I'm still a bit shy of those guns. Still find it alarming how quickly I fired at a living, breathing man—and how I'd do it again for Clyde.

I squeeze the back of my neck and change the direction of my thoughts. With the mess, our cabin may as well be a college dorm. It's certainly small enough. It's fun to imagine: me at a university. In a different lifetime, I don't think getting a higher education would be too far off, 'specially since teaching and nursing are the top two fields for women. But standing in front of a classroom isn't the path I'm on, hasn't been for a while. And I'm okay with that, 'cause of the fella 'cross the room, studying a map.

Clyde does that often, familiarizing himself with how the roads bend and curve, how they intersect, and the ones that dead-end.

I often track for him as we drive. I like being a team, working toward a life together where the sun will beat down on our tanned skin while we shoo our chickens into their roost and get our milk straight from a cow. At night, our kids will chase the fireflies between the trees. Clyde once said he wanted a simple life, away from the rules and the people telling him that he's doing wrong. My Lord, I want that, too. You hear me up there?

I smile to myself and push aside the curtain again. Well, lookie here, Blanche climbs out of a car. Strange, though, it's not Big Bertha. There must be a story behind that, and also the frown she's wearing. Though her resistance to joining us may easily explain the latter. Blanche reaches into the car, Snow Ball appearing in her arms. I love that dog.

After shoving my belongings into my luggage, I throw my arms 'round Blanche, then we're off to our new home. Clyde asks me to ride with Blanche and Buck into town to get some breakfast. Him and Jones are going to stay a few miles off in the countryside, where fewer eyes can spot 'em.

I climb into their sedan, pausing on the way when my eye catches on the president's face on the car's radiator. From the rear seat I ask, "Do y'all know Roosevelt is on the front of your car?"

Buck's laugh booms, deep and low, and my insides warm. Clyde's veins are still thawing from prison, but Buck is Buck, his snicker that of a man ready to scheme. "Blanche's been calling her Teddy."

I pull a pack of cigarettes from my dress pocket. Only got one cigarette left, I realize. I light it and drop the box at my feet. "What happened to Big—"

"I don't want to talk 'bout it," Blanche says, holding, yet not petting Snow Ball.

"She was showing her age," Buck says, "and it would've been more expensive to fix her than to get this here Marmon. Teddy's bigger than Bertha, too, despite having *Big* in her name."

"Big Bertha was perfect, and Buck went and traded her for a newer model. Is that what you're going do to me when my ladies are touching my knees?" Blanche stares out the window.

I blow out some smoke and hide a smile behind a new draw.

"If you put it that way." Buck shrugs.

Blanche responds, falling into their familiar routine of playful bickering, but I'm looking over my shoulder, not listening no more. Clyde and Jones are only a few car lengths behind us. It feels like miles. Clyde and I are always in arm's reach of one another, 'cept when one of us slips from the car to pick up food or clothing or to use the John. It's been that way for nearly a year. I want it to be that way forever.

Clyde's car veers into the grass to park, as close as they'll go to town. I inhale, long and hard, on my cigarette, calming myself. A bend in the road steals him from me right as a flash brings my free hand flying to my chest.

Blanche lowers her camera.

"That'll help, blinding the driver," Buck says.

They both laugh, and I try to let the melody soothe my unease. But as we pass a sign for MUSKOGEE, OKLAHOMA. POPULATION: 32,026. I slink lower into my seat. It's what I do when I'm with the boys. I slink. Jones stops yapping. And Clyde's hands stiffen on the wheel. Then he mutters a landmark with each turn we make through town. Bread crumbs, like Hansel and Gretel. "Fire hydrant," he said one time. We whipped back 'round that hydrant when we were being followed. All it took was three turns for Clyde to shake the unmarked car. By the drugstore, we lost 'em.

"You okay back there?" Blanche asks.

"Our girl thinks highly of herself," Buck jokes.

I narrow my eyes at them, but they've got a point. Why am I slouched when no one's looking for me? I'm over three hundred miles from Kaufman jail, and the newspapers that reported on the death of Deputy Sheriff Malcolm Davis during our shoot-out outside Odell's house only mentioned a female. Clyde Barrow and a female. No one noticed Jones in the car either. Nevertheless, Clyde likes to keep him hidden away whenever possible.

I think I'll stay slouched. We pass a Gulf station and a storefront where, in each window, a different letter appears to advertise SALARY LOANS $5-$50, then we pass a theater. My gaze lingers on the building, my head slowly turning with our progress. Two oversized posters create a triangle over the awning, promoting *King Kong* and *Scarface.*

In the gangster flick, there's a gal in red glad rags. Nostalgia hits me. What I wouldn't give for a fancy dress, afternoons in the cinema's dark, and evenings in a stage's spotlight. Singing at Doc's was a high unlike anything a dopehead could ever feel.

Buck parks Teddy, its nose pointed toward the sidewalk like all the other cars. We're out front of the Jefferson Hotel. Blanche waits for a streetcar to pass, then runs 'cross the street to a café. I'm left to chew on my lip. I pat the pocket of my dress—empty.

Telling Buck I'll be right back, I lift my chin and parade down the sidewalk toward a tobacco stand. Clyde says that when we do mingle with the public, act like ya belong. I do, giving the attendant a meek smile. Clyde also says never to put on my best performance. Memorable isn't something we want to be.

Back inside Teddy, my cigarette tip flares. I exhale the smoke and some of my unease. The cigarette lasts 'til Blanche returns, and we drive down the road to meet Clyde's car. I quickly give up one comfort for another, lodging myself under Clyde's arms.

I plan to stay that way during every second of our running-board picnic. It's not glamorous like a real picnic, where legs are stretched out and time is lost. We eat quickly, before anyone comes by wondering why we're on the side of the road.

With mouths full, Buck and Clyde scheme 'bout our apartment and how we'll make sure Clyde stays under the radar.

Jones pipes in with suggestions.

Blanche nitpicks, grumbles, and protests the need for a plan. "It's ridiculous we're even in a situation where we need to take these precautions," she says.

"Baby," Buck says, then yadda, yadda, yadda.

I only pay attention to each glorious bite of chocolate, graham cracker, and marshmallow I shove into my mouth, happy to focus on my MoonPie and be left out of the planning for the first time in a while. As long as I've got Clyde's arm 'round me, I'll be okay. That may be the confection talking, but for the moment, I'll take it.

The moment's over too soon, and once we're headed toward Joplin, my sugar rush runs out right 'round the time Clyde pulls over and asks me to ride in Teddy again. I hate leaving him a second time, like chopping off a limb, but with Blanche already on edge, I don't want my restlessness to add to hers.

Joplin's green, with parks and trees and grass. Street after street, there are tiny homes, all well kept, with owners who must take pride in 'em. The area has a nice feel to it, somewhere I'd be happy to spend my time. Halfway up a hill, Buck points off to the right. "There she be, 3347½ Oak Ridge Drive."

Blanche sighs. "Home sweet home."

I smile. *Home sweet home*. For a little while, at least, before it's on to the farms.

We park in front of the garage apartment, and Buck goes to the main house to check in as William Callihan and get our keys.

Blanche says, "You know I love you, Bonn, but I still ain't jazzed 'bout this setup."

"Blanche." I eye the two garage doors, with a door off to the left. Above the garage is our two-bedroom apartment, a row of five windows inviting me inside. "You once said all you wanted was the four of us together again. I believe you even said, 'Is that too much to ask?' It's not. Here we are. But Clyde was run out of town. The only way for it to be the four of us again is if you run *with* us."

At that moment, Buck unlocks the front door. I'm skipping toward him, never giving Blanche a chance to respond.

I could cry happy tears as I enter our new home, albeit a temporary one. Off to the right is the inside entrance to the garage, and up a flight of stairs, overtop, is the apartment. The kitchen's immediately off to the left; straight ahead is the sun-drenched living room.

Blanche opens a closet. "All the guns go in there. And stay there."

Bucks nods like one of those marionette dolls. It's funny, seeing a man who towers over Blanche, who herself has gams for days, doing whatever she says. Reckon he's that way with Clyde, too. Buck was the one who first made Clyde a criminal, after all. But Clyde took it from there, the mastermind behind their jobs. Buck's happy-go-lucky, making him happy to go along.

I keep walking toward the two bedrooms, one facing the front of the house, the other facing the back, with the glorious bathroom in between.

I call out, "Clyde's going to want the bedroom in the back."

Buck laughs. "He already put in his request."

Mid-yawn, I check my watch. "You better keep an eye out for him."

That's another bonus of this place: its many windows to keep a lookout from. Soon, Clyde and Jones will drive by 'em, which is Buck's cue to start walking down the hill. Clyde's to pick him up, and if Buck gets the sense that everything's okay, Clyde will park our stolen car in our half of the garage. The other side is rented out to a fella we don't know. That leaves the Marmon out front, but that's fine and dandy, being she's been bought and paid for. No one's going to be looking for Teddy.

Buck holds the curtain back, sees the boys drive by, and leaves to head down the hill.

While waiting for them, I sit properly in a chair, purposely not fidgeting with the hemline of my dress, not bouncing my knee, not itching the back of my neck, not twisting my wedding band. Blanche is the one twisting her ring 'round her finger.

She's worried 'bout Buck.

I know that feeling. Right now, though, excitement edges out my nerves, fear, and exhaustion. The door opens below, and I'm on my feet. Clyde's barely had the chance to thank Blanche again for coming before I drag him through the apartment. It's not big, but big enough for me to point out the eating nook in the kitchen, the antique dresser in our bedroom, and the cast-iron tub in the bathroom.

"My God, you're beautiful, Bonnie," Clyde says, leaning against the bathroom's pedestal sink, ankles crossed, that lazy smile on his face. When's the last time I truly saw that smile?

In the mirror behind Clyde, I see my own grin. It belongs to a more confident girl from long ago, before all this, before what happened to Clyde. I'm learning the future ain't something I can count on, but this night can be something special. Then, I watch myself bite my bottom lip. I slide my blouse down one shoulder.

Clyde's body tenses, in the way I was hoping for, something else I haven't witnessed for far too long. He licks his lips. "Bonnie, you better get over here."

"Yeah?"

"Aye."

I breathe out a laugh. Within two steps, Clyde's hands are on me, pulling me against him. Blanche, Buck, and Jones are only a few feet away, but the door muffles their voices. Let's hope it does the same to all the noise we're 'bout to make, finally.

Clyde nips at my neck, his lips still next to my ear. "Thank you."

I turn on the tub. "Show me."

Oh, how I need to know he desires me.

He does, with every clutch and grasp, every caress, every stroke, every second he relearns my curves.

14

I EMERGE FROM THE BATHROOM A NEW WOMAN, MY SKIN pink from the heat of the water and Clyde's touch. I'd like to also think Clyde's a new man.

Blanche meets me with a knowing smile. She doesn't know it's Clyde's and my first time since before he got sent away. Nor that I'll have a bruise or two, as if Clyde couldn't hold on to me tight enough, and in my mind, he couldn't. But she knows Clyde and I christened the apartment, beating her and Buck to the punch. I return her devilish grin, then in customary Blanche fashion, she takes charge and demands we go buy linens and things so we can keep house.

We take Teddy, and maybe it's 'cause he's bought and paid for or 'cause we're doing something so normal as shopping for sheets or 'cause I have a place to come home to—not just tonight but for the foreseeable future while Clyde's planning Farm Number One—that I don't duck my head at every stranger's glance in the department store. I laugh. I enthusiastically point out a quilt I hate. I joke with Blanche, 'specially when she picks up a dog bowl with rhinestones.

"Don't think that fits Buck's style much," I say.

She whacks me with a dish towel.

On the way home, we stop by the market for food. The grocer said he'd be happy to deliver our bags for us, and before I can stop her, Blanche rattles off that new address of ours.

"Why'd ya go and do that for?" I hiss when we're out of earshot.

Her eyes are huge. "You assured me we're safe."

I avoid a real answer to that by saying, "Teddy's too packed anyway to fit in all that food."

When Jones meets us at the garage, his eyes—all big and wide—reaffirm we bought too much. Funny how Blanche hemmed and hawed 'bout coming to Joplin, but she's got no problem spending our dirty money.

In fact, she's eager to spend more of it. Tomorrow she's got our afternoon planned at the theater. Not like I'm going to say no to that. Nor 'bout spending the money, if it's going to make my best friend stick 'round longer. All that does is give Clyde whatever time he needs with Buck, and gives me the time I need with her.

Jones starts unloading Teddy, the boy getting a kick out of how many we bought of each item. Eight large feather pillows, a feather bed, four sets of sheets and pillowcases, fourteen quilts and blankets, four bedspreads, dishes for eight, silverware for twelve, two towels for us each, three dish towels, and six bags of other odds and ends.

Blanche nods along with Jones, as if she's also counting.

Once we get it all inside, Clyde uses a few empty bags to bring in his guns. He's barely up the stairs when we hear a knock. Blanche skips to the door to answer, smothering the grocery man with thank-yous for bringing by our food. But when he insists on carrying the bags upstairs, Blanche's voice tenses, even more so when their conversation volleys back and forth.

"I've got it," she says.

By the abrupt rustle of bags, I picture her yanking 'em out of the man's hands. She thanks him once more, adding her usual Blanche-like melody back into her voice, and the door closes. At the top of the stairs, Blanche's eyes immediately jump to the bag of guns propped against the couch, then to Clyde, his own shoulders tense.

He says, "They're on their way to the closet."

"Good. Now, no one goes into my kitchen, you hear?"

Buck laughs 'til Blanche cocks her head at him. He quiets right up.

I gladly stay out of her way, making up our house. I walk from room to room; all the blinds are drawn tightly shut, but every lamp is on, feigning daytime. Then, once all the beds are made, I curl up on the couch, tucking my legs under me, and simply watch the fellas as they carry on with a poker game on the table they dragged out from the kitchen, making Jones go in to fetch it. The boy's a quick study, even though he claims he's never played before and even with a quarter of his whiskey gone. Drinking ain't something new to him, 'specially with how he helped to run bootlegs since he was twelve. He's got a youthful look to him, almost a younger version of Clyde's own baby face, but I get the sense Jones has seen a lot in his sixteen years. Not as much as Clyde in his twenty-four, though.

Clyde pushes back from the table, his own whiskey barely touched. Come to think of it, he hasn't gone near the bottle much since we've been on the run. He's said it's to keep his wits 'bout him, but we're good and safe here. He nuzzles next to me on the couch, and just by the shape of his lips—not a smile, but not a frown—I can tell he's 'bout to say something sly. "I can't even call the lad a cheat. He's just whooping me on skill alone."

I raise a brow. "Or maybe your lack of skill?"

Clyde's lips are now clearly a smile, and his eyes broadcast he's 'bout to throw me into the pillows.

"Off my table," Blanche says to the boys, saving me. She's carrying two plates. The girl even has on an apron.

Before I know it, we've got five chairs pulled up to the table.

Buck's plate and mine both have pickled pig's feet and olives.

Clyde and Jones got French-fried potatoes and English peas, smothered in cream and pepper.

Blanche made herself some cheese grits, her own heavy-handed dusting of pepper on top.

We all have our favorites—Snow Ball, too, with boiled chicken in his rhinestone bowl.

"Dig in, folks," Blanche says, proud of the meal she fashioned for us all. Somebody has been spending lots of time with Mrs. Barrow in the kitchen. I reckon Blanche didn't have much else to keep her busy when she wasn't at the beauty shop. I was gone. Buck was gone. Now we're all back together.

With a brand spankin' new utensil in each hand, I pause. It's not 'cause my pickled pig's feet don't look tasty. They do. It's also not 'cause I'm not hungry. It's quite the opposite, actually, considering it's well past suppertime. I pause 'cause I can. Normally we're shoving food in our mouths, getting it down before any surprises sneak up on us.

But anyone who knows where we are is sitting 'round this here table. I cut into my pig, slowly, and take the time to chew thirty times, for optimal digestion. In this moment, no one's chasing us. We can stand still. Ain't that beautiful.

• • •

"This should do the trick," Blanche says, wagging a pair of scissors behind me. I'm glad the mirror I'm holding up ain't any larger. It's best not to fully see what Blanche is doing to my head. She flicks some water onto my hair, getting me in the eye. "I got to say, though, for living out of a car, you don't look half bad. But now you've got Blanche, so you'll look better than half bad. Fully good, in fact."

I wipe my face. "Thanks?"

I've been trying, though, to keep myself put together as best I can. Sure, Clyde and I were playing the part of a young well-to-do couple out exploring the country. But I also wanted to look good for Clyde, and for myself. We spent so much time in a car, and it wasn't rare to catch myself in the sideview mirror. I'd much rather catch a glimpse of a face with red lips and rosy cheeks, the face I used to show to a crowded dance floor, than my otherwise washed out skin.

For a couple days now, Blanche and I both have put extra effort into gussying up. We saw a show the past three afternoons, just like old times, while Clyde and Jones went off looking for potential land or scheming what store's register to empty once the first farm's done. That'll mean no longer keeping house with Blanche and Buck. Something I don't like thinking 'bout.

Even with nothin' illegal going on at the moment, Mr. Blanche Barrow always stays behind in the apartment or tinkers with Teddy. Neither Clyde nor Buck wants to make Blanche's nostrils flare, being she's got a flair for dramatics.

She does another snip of my hair, then hops to the kitchen sink to pull the drain. Our clothes have been soaking all morning. We'll wring 'em out once the water's all gone, then string our dresses, skirts, shirts, and pants 'cross the kitchen, while trying not to trip over Snow Ball. Normally I'd be mortified by our drying methods, but with the blinds pulled tight, it's not like the neighbors can see how we're living, and Clyde doesn't want us to hang our things outside, inviting small talk from anyone passing by.

It'd sure be nice to get a lungful of fresh air. More than we get going from Teddy to the theater.

"Hey," I say. "How 'bout we do a picnic?" I flap my hand. "Somewhere off the beaten track."

I tilt the mirror to catch Blanche's face. She's smiling. The fellas are going to have to do as she says.

Doesn't take long before all five of us are packed in and then out of Teddy. To catch sight of anyone coming, Clyde found us a spot where a crest of rocks hides us on one side, a row of bushes shields us from behind, and there's nothin' but open land on the other sides.

Our biggest worry, in my mind at least, will be retracing our way out without giving Teddy a flat. I surely thought one of her tires would blow on the way here as we cut 'cross the field.

I cast a blanket up, then down, settling it over the grass. We all stretch out our legs, my Mary Janes clanking against Blanche's, and we pass a bottle of whiskey and a bucket of chicken legs in a circle. Buck and Jones light cigars, puffing out smoke between laughs. Clyde barely lets any brown pass his lips, and even with us being hidden away I catch his eyes darting left and right and toward Teddy, where Clyde insisted on bringing a stash of guns. Blanche doesn't know it, but that boy even slyly slid a shotgun beneath his side of the blanket.

It's a shame; Clyde always has an eye and ear out for trouble. Along with keeping the blinds closed at all times, the other day he brought home a Missouri plate for Buck to put on Teddy. Clyde didn't want people seeing the Texas plate, even if Teddy ain't hot. Decisions like that make Blanche nervous, which I can understand.

She licks chicken grease from her fingers, not nervous at the moment, and disappears behind her camera.

It gives me an idea on how to loosen up Clyde: I'll put a gun in his hands.

"Blanche, will you take some photos of Clyde and me?"

Buck hoots, no doubt remembering all the times Blanche has used him as a prop. Before Clyde protests, I drag him to his feet, then wink, revealing his gun from beneath the blanket.

"Here you go," I whisper to him. "Looks like you've been missing her in your arms." I nod for Clyde to take a seat on Teddy's front bumper. In my most sultry voice, play-acting I'm onstage, I say to him, "Show me how bad you really are."

Clyde's smirk is to die for. He goes and props the shotgun 'cross his leg and tilts his head like he means business. That look of his is smart, accented by his slicked-back hair, suit, and tie. I'll pretend I don't see the dirt mucking up his black shoes.

Blanche clicks, capturing his devil-may-care pose.

"Move over, baby brother," Buck says. He joins Clyde on the car's bumper, shoulder to shoulder. Neither of 'em smile, but not for lack of enjoying themselves.

Blanche clicks. Jones gets a nod from Clyde. He's added to the picture: Clyde in the middle, sandwiched between his older brother and Jones, who may as well be his younger one.

"Our tough guys," Blanche says to me with a laugh.

The photo's taken, the three boys. Jones and Buck with their cigars. Clyde with his gun.

"I reckon it's your turn, Bonnie," Clyde says in his smooth voice, standing and popping on his hat.

"I reckon it is." Slowly, I wipe any grass and stray dirt from my dark dress, running my palms over my rear end, down my sleeves, 'cross my belly. Then, in a heartbeat, I got the shotgun out of Clyde's hands. I turn it 'round on him. Jones and Buck both jump back. Clyde's arms shoot out in surprise, his fingers splayed, but his face is calm, cool, collected, accented by those gosh-darn dimples.

My left hand dances against his chest, my fingertips brushing aside his tie. Clyde ain't soft, but it comes at a surprise his chest is unnaturally hard. Chuckling, I ask, "Are you wearing a vest? All the way out here?"

He nods at the gun I've got pointed at him. "Darling, clearly there's danger everywhere."

He licks his lips, and I trace my tongue 'cross my own. Then, Clyde whips the gun away, even faster than I pulled it on him. He tosses it aside. He steps toward me, his hat blowing off. He's against me, his whole body, but most important, those lips. The intensity of his kiss arches my back and Clyde's hands—one between my shoulders, one 'round my waist—are all that keeps me on my feet.

Not one part of me minds.

Too soon, he breaks our kiss, his breath trailing over my ear. "Bonnie, I'd rather have you in my arms than a shotgun any ol' day."

I swallow, still feeling every inch of him pressed against me, and adjust my crochet hat.

"Better believe I captured that on film," Blanche says. "Anyone got a cigarette after that?"

Buck laughs. "Come here, baby. I'll give ya a puff of my cigar."

She scrunches her nose. "I ain't touchin' that thing."

Jones motions for Blanche's camera. "Give me a turn with that."

Clyde lifts me into his arms, bouncing me up higher so I'm a head taller than him, perched so I'm sitting on his arm. "Here's your star. Let me sit out a few."

I kiss his temple before I'm back on my feet.

Jones puffs on his cigar between his teeth, trying to line up his shot. Without Clyde—and no microphone in front of me to place my hands—I ain't sure what to do with myself. Of course, Blanche knows. I become her doll, my elbow propped on top of Teddy's headlight, my other hand on my hip.

"Hmm, something's missing. Ain't a bad shot, but also ain't great," she says.

She returns with a revolver, holding it between the tips of her fingers, not looking directly at it. "Put it on your hip. And push your hip out. More. Li'l more."

Jones coughs on the cigar's smoke, the cigar still between his teeth and both hands on the camera. I break my pose to snatch it from his mouth, put it between my lips, then I'm back in my position.

It feels scandalous. Not long ago, seeing a woman smoke in public was considered vulgar. A cigar—a man's vice—makes it doubly so.

Clyde's gawking at me, so I reckon he likes what he sees. And I want to up the ante even more. My foot goes on Teddy's bumper. I lean into my arm, resting on the headlight, pushing out my hip even farther.

I remove the cigar to say, "Now, these pictures are just for us?"

"Bonnie, darling," Clyde says. "They're going to be just for me."

I put the cigar back in my mouth and puff out my chest.

Jones snaps the shot.

15

BLANCHE STANDS AT ONE OF THE APARTMENT WINDOWS, peeking out between the drapes. A car rumbles outside.

"Clyde home?" I ask, surrounded by too many jigsaw pieces.

"Nah, it's the fella using the other side of the garage. Must be headed out, but I don't like how he lingers, like he's got the volume of his ears turned to the far right."

"You're paranoid, baby," Buck says from the couch, without looking up from his magazine.

Blanche settles next to me on the floor, side by side on our knees, and proceeds to twist her lips. I'm not sure if it's 'bout the fella outside or the three-hundred-piece puzzle. I softly sing the tune I heard in *42nd Street* the other day.

"Do you think this could be a teat?" she asks.

I chuckle, the question catching me off guard.

She slaps my hand. "And don't go cheating by looking at the photo on the box."

"I wasn't going to," I say. But I was. In fact, I was a second away from flipping over the top of the jigsaw puzzle's box to give my memory a jolt of what this thing was going to look like with all the pieces in place. "I reckon it could be a dog's teat," I say. "Either that, or one of the bullfrog's eyes." I shrug.

"It's the teat," Blanche says matter-of-factly.

Buck groans. "Stop saying *teat.*" He shakes his head. "I should've gone with Clyde."

Blanche throws the teat at him. "No sirree. And don't think I didn't hear you whispering 'bout that prison job with him last night."

I raise an eyebrow, but I don't ask any questions and risk the wrath of Blanche. Besides, that girl will ask her own.

She shakes her head. "The two of you are thick as thieves."

Buck flips a page in his magazine, casual as can be. "We were only talking."

"And those guns. What were you doing with 'em?"

"Cleaning 'em, that's all."

Blanche stands, no doubt feeling more clout that way. Her hand goes onto her hip. "Funny how you're cleaning guns you won't ever use again, 'specially when it was agreed upon those things would stay in that there closet." She points 'cross the room.

I study the jigsaw pieces.

"Come on, baby. I wasn't doing any harm, ya know."

"Why you cleaning guns you ain't going to use?"

"Why you doing a puzzle you ain't going to finish?"

Something between a roar and a scream comes out of Blanche. She dives toward Buck. Snow Ball materializes and goes into a fit of barking. Blanche and Buck's wrestling match turns into tickles and squeals, and some dirty talk I'd rather not hear. Back and forth, Snow Ball hops, keeping a semicircle 'round his masters. Each time, his little paws scratch the discarded teat puzzle piece.

I save it.

Clyde appears at the top of the stairs, his eyes crazed, his revolver grasped between both hands. He sees me, doing something so ordinary as a jigsaw puzzle, clearly not in any danger, and I imagine the sound of his exhale, matching the release of his shoulders. I can't actually hear it with all the Blanche-related commotion in the room.

Clyde removes his hat and walks over to the couch to whack Buck with it. Snow Ball scurries back to Blanche's room, always weary of Clyde when he's on his feet, as if the dog doesn't trust Clyde's limp.

Jones appears at the top of the stairs, a big ol' crate in his arms, a big ol' grin on his face. If I were to rank who's enjoying our new carefree lifestyle the most, I'd put me first, no doubt 'bout it. But Jones would be second. Behind the eagerness to get a pat on the back from Clyde, I can see his longing to be back in Dallas, no longer a fugitive.

"What ya got there?" I call to him.

His grin doesn't waver as he holds up the crate. "Some suds."

Clyde adds, "As of a few days ago, beer is officially back on the market."

Buck quits his wrestling with Blanche. "Did Uncle Sam deep-six Prohibition?"

"Not fully, he didn't. Only beer," Clyde says. "Roosevelt said, 'How can I partially remove the stick from Blanche Barrow's bum?' and he decided on making one less thing we're doing illegal."

Blanche rolls her eyes. Buck laughs. That earns him an elbow to the gut.

Soon, we've all got a beer in hand, enjoying our evening. The boys got a poker game going, Blanche is on the carpet, halfway through her puzzle, and I'm stretched out on the couch with a book. Clyde pushes back from the table, a look of disgust on his face. "I ain't ever been good at cards."

I smile at him and turn my book at him, as if saying, *Want to read?*

He shakes his head and inches closer to Blanche. There's a Clyde-sized shadow covering the puzzle pieces, him standing perfectly in front of the lamp.

Blanche doesn't bother looking up at him, but says, "Don't go thinkin' you're going to work this here puzzle with me after that comment earlier. There ain't nothin' up my bum, thank you very much."

Clyde slides his hands in his trouser pockets and rocks back on his heels. One eyebrow arches. "Is that a teat?"

Blanche smirks and pats the carpet beside her. It ain't long, though, before she's on her feet and using the tip of her finger to push aside the drapes. Her feet reposition, and I know something's going on she doesn't like.

"What?" I say, over the noise of the boys. Clyde, on his knees, shifts his attention from me to Blanche.

She says, "Heard that fella drive in. But didn't hear him pull down the garage door. He's still out there."

Blanche's implication, 'specially this late, is that he's nosing 'round, looking at Clyde's stolen Ford he keeps on the other side of the garage. I don't think she's wrong, and that's making me feel as dark as the night.

• • •

I decide, after not having the urge for so long, to write 'bout all I'm feeling. While I hunt for the next word in my poem, I study Blanche's completed masterpiece. The puzzle piece did indeed belong to a dog. The pooch lies on its back, tall stalks of grass surrounding her. Or him. Both male and female dogs have teats, for whatever reason. Water is only inches away from the pooch, with five bullfrogs perched on five lily pads. The sun beats down on them all, glistening in the pond. Doesn't look like a bad place to be, if ya ask me. Better than hiding out. But the alternate to hiding out is running. I don't want that either.

Blanche and Clyde worked the puzzle to the wee hours of the morning. Clyde didn't want to come to bed 'til they had it done. Bet ya Blanche only stayed up that late to supervise, complaining 'bout her beauty sleep with each piece she put down. Lack of sleep didn't show on her this morning, though. Ain't sure how that's fair. She came prancing out of her bedroom in a blue crepe dress that had once been an evening gown. Few days ago, Blanche hemmed it at the bottom to make it into a housedress. I still got on my kimono nightgown and slippers. I yawn. I haven't bothered to put on hose or my housedress yet. Maybe after this poem.

I tap the pencil against my bottom lip as I think, as I ponder if we'll ever stop running.

Clyde comes up the stairs, then crosses the living room, going 'round the jigsaw puzzle on the floor like it's a piece of furniture. He pulls open the closet and deposits a few guns he had stashed in a bag.

"Where'd those come from?" I ask him.

Clyde peers over his shoulder at the bathroom door. "She still in there?"

He's referring to Blanche, who wouldn't be too pleased with the closet being turned into a full-blown gun arsenal. Quite frankly, I ain't too pleased she turned the bathroom into a darkroom, banning me from the room before I had a chance to make up my face. I nod to Clyde.

"Jones and I picked up some new toys," he says. "Had 'em in the back of the Ford."

I twist my lips. "But now that man's snooping 'round the garage." Which can mean one thing: Clyde's restless, and this hideout won't be ours much longer.

Clyde unbuttons then buttons his blue suit jacket and tilts his head toward the stairs. "Got a few more to bring up."

"Better make it quick. She's been in there a while." I glance at the bathroom door. Snow Ball is scratching at the bottom of it, his claws scraping off little bits of the towel that Blanche shoved underneath to keep out any light.

"What ya got there?" Clyde kisses my forehead, and I quickly cover the paper. My poem's dark. Ain't sure Clyde needs dark when he's already on edge.

"It ain't finished," I say.

He winks. "Caught a glimpse of my last name."

Billy said to the Barrow boy . . .

I smile, holding it 'til Clyde leaves, then I'm alone with my poem again. I tap my pencil over Clyde's name. Billy the Kid's in here, too, as if him and Clyde are swapping stories.

I only had my pinto horse
And my six-gun tried and true.
I could shoot but they got me
And someday they will get you!

Depressing, that's what this poem is.

The living man who can know no peace
And the dead who can know no rest.

But it's where my head's leading me, and with Jones downstairs with Clyde, Buck washing Teddy 'round back, and Blanche busy with her photos, it leaves me alone to explore my fears.

I enjoy the near-quiet to work through 'em, even if I keep getting distracted, my self-consciousness maybe not wanting to accept we could end up like Billy the Kid instead of sippin' lemonade on our farm. The dog is making the only noise. Blanche ain't making a peep, which surprises me. I've been convinced I'd hear her cackling 'bout the photos we took last week, 'specially the one where I put Jones's stogie in my mouth.

Lookie here, she'll say when she emerges, waving the photo 'round. *Proof of my very own cigar-smoking gun moll.*

I practice my fake, sarcastic laugh. Outside, shouting cuts my snigger short. I startle toward the window. Lots of shouting. I get to my feet, all else forgotten, but I've made it no more than two steps toward the window when gunfire erupts.

Instinctively I duck, my hands going over my head. My eyes fall on the stairs and my mind screams for Clyde, downstairs, possibly in the line of fire.

The *rat-a-tat-tat* pulls Blanche out of the bathroom, her eyes wide. Snow Ball's barking adds to the commotion; so does his jumping. Before I know it, those feet of mine lead me to the closet, then to the window:

pulling back the drapes, smashing the glass, the barrel of my rifle poking through.

I've a moment of clarity, realizing those may've been the longest and quickest ten seconds of my life.

There's four men. Five, I correct, but the fifth is lying facedown next to a police car in the driveway. The other men are running to a second car 'cross the street, firing a haphazard shot over their shoulders as they go. I line up my eye, staring down the gun. Outside the garage, there's Clyde, but he's not firing anymore. My finger dances over the trigger, resolved to what I may have to do, ready to pull the trigger if it'll keep Clyde alive.

"Blanche!" Buck yells.

He thumps up the steps, half bent over, fighting for breath. Blanche, hysterical, rushes into his arms. Buck's voice comes out ragged as he says, "Hurry, we got to get out of here. Clyde will hold 'em off."

As if those two brothers are connected by the brain, Clyde fires off warning shots at the officers hiding behind the car 'cross the street. They don't return fire.

"What?" Blanche says. She rubs her forehead. Her eyes are even wider than before, and now also unfocused. "Why do we have to go? We didn't do nothin' wrong."

Buck says, "Don't matter, baby. Let's go."

"But our stuff . . ." Blanche staggers toward the kitchen, with Snow Ball on her heels. She picks him up, puts him on the table, wraps her hands 'round her stomach. Blanche turns toward the bedrooms. "Our marriage license." She stops, steps toward the kitchen again. Snow Ball hops down from the table, and he's back on her heels. "My watch." Blanche had taken it off earlier to develop the photos. Ain't a second more before Blanche changes directions again, back toward her bedroom. "Your pardon papers, baby."

I've heard the expression of a chicken with its head chopped off, but this here is the first time I've seen it with my own two eyes. Buck goes to her. Their foreheads press together.

Gunfire erupts. Too much of it to only be coming from one gun. I look down, but I can no longer see Clyde. I tell myself he's in the garage, using the car to shield himself. It's what the coppers are doing, their heads popping over their car to volley a shot. 'Cept there's four of them.

"Buck," I yell. "He's outnumbered. He won't be able to hold them—"

A bloody hand appears on the top step, then dark hair, and finally Jones's face, etched with pain.

I'm halfway on my way to hell for letting out an exhale that it's not Clyde.

Jones half stands, falling forward, his arms folding 'round Blanche's neck. "Help me," he pleads. Blanche looks like she'd like to drop him right then and there, but her arm's wound 'round him.

It dawns on me it's quiet. No one's firing.

"Clyde," Buck says under his breath, then he practically falls down the stairs. I'm sobbing by the time I rush by Blanche, still holding up Jones, that blasted dog still bouncing at her feet, whining nonstop. My sob turns to a wail when I see a body in a blue suit lying in the garage, a circle of red expanding on all sides of his head.

"No, no, no, no," I cry.

"Bonnie," I hear.

At first I'm certain it's in my head, a voice I'll be hearing 'til I take my own last breath. Then, Clyde steps out from behind the Ford. Blood's splattered on his face. He lunges for me, catching me as my knees give way from relief. Somewhere along the way I lost my slippers. Clyde's lips are against my ear. "Get in the car," he says. "Get her started."

"But," I say, not even sure how I'm going to finish, yet needing a moment to fully appreciate that it's not Clyde's head leaking all over the cement.

He says, "I got to cover you all."

With that, Clyde steps through the open garage door and over the second dead officer in the driveway, spraying bullets.

I fumble to the car just as Jones appears in the garage, flanked on either side, Blanche doing half the work of Buck. He takes all of Jones's weight, dragging him to the rear seat.

Through the windshield I realize we got nowhere to go, unless we drive straight through the officers' car in the driveway.

Clyde's firing stops and I call to him. I rev the engine and point to the abandoned car. His mouth forms a profanity. I hold my breath as he hobbles to the police car's driver's seat, then to the front bumper. I curse, too, and flick my attention 'cross the street for any movement, then back to Clyde, whose gun hangs from a strap 'round his neck. He uses both hands to push the car. Being Blanche is one second from losing her mind, I can barely believe when she puts her own hands on the bumper, the back of her ball-gown-turned housedress cut low, lace cap sleeves trailing over each shoulder.

Together, they push, the wheels turning achingly slow. Too slow, and I wait for the law to fire again. I search the front seat for a gun, realizing I must've dropped my rifle upstairs when I thought Clyde had been shot.

I curse, then watch as the police cruiser Clyde and Blanche are moving starts rolling down the hill on its own accord. They're left standing there.

An officer fires a shot. Clyde uses his body to shield Blanche, fumbling to gain control of the gun dangling from his neck.

The other officers' heads poke up like gophers, their guns trained on Clyde and Blanche. He shoves her toward the garage and returns fire, meeting their revolvers with his automatic shotgun. They duck.

"Baby!" Buck calls. "Hurry!"

But no, Blanche doesn't start running back to us. The girl's running down the street, her arms flailing on either side, only steps behind the driverless police car.

A flash of white fur escapes from the garage. But once Snow Ball gets to Blanche, he doesn't stop at her heels. That dog keeps on runnin'.

CLYDE STANDS DUMBFOUNDED FOR A MOMENT, STARING. AT Blanche? At Snow Ball? I don't know which. Maybe both.

Then, his body rocks. Once. He folds in half, clutching his chest, and staggers to the ground.

My mind screams *no* faster than any bullet that's ever left a gun.

The quickest way I can think to get to him is in this here Ford. I press on the pedal, putting every ounce of my hundred pounds into the motion.

The officers take aim at us.

In the rear seat, Buck's already got his door open to retrieve Clyde.

I'm dizzy, barely breathing. Clyde's form in the driveway shimmers, like he's part of a mirage. I slam on the brakes, getting the car as close as possible without clipping his foot. The car blocks my view of him.

"No," Buck says. "Keep 'er moving. Slow."

I feel the ridges of the accelerator under my bare foot again. My stomach is hot, the sensation traveling up my throat. A shot cracks the passenger side of the windshield. The car lurches forward. I swear I can hear Blanche screaming even though she's not even here.

"Got him!" Buck yells. "Go!"

He does. He's got Clyde, his feet still sticking out of the car. I realize I've been gripping my throat, my nails digging into my skin. With both hands, I clutch the wheel, and I go, gunfire trailing us.

"Clyde," I call over the engine, the gunshots, Jones's moans. I forgot all 'bout the poor boy.

"I ain't dead, Bonnie."

My breath comes out with a hiccup in the middle. The car door slams. We pass the officers' abandoned car, now nose-deep in thick shrubs.

"Just shook me, that's all," Clyde says. He crawls into the passenger seat, his hands bloody, his face bloody, a bullet hole in his chest.

"We got to find Blanche," Buck says from the rear seat. "And a doctor for Jones. Fast."

Clyde frees himself from his suit jacket and rips open his shirt, crying out with each movement. "I've got a mind to go right on by her like that dog of hers."

Buck ain't pleased with Clyde's remark. But I ain't listening, I'm gawking at Clyde's chest, at the damage of a bullet to his ballistic vest, directly over his heart. I shake my head in disbelief, in relief, in thankfulness that Clyde's paranoia had him putting on that extra layer.

At the bottom of the hill I slow and look for Blanche, ignoring the bickering of the boys. Jones is the one who says, "There she is."

When I look back to see which way he's pointing, I wish I hadn't. I ain't even sure what color his shirt was before, but now it's red. All red.

"Enough!" I scream. "We're getting Blanche, and we're getting our boy some help."

Both brothers wise up and shut their traps. The firing's stopped, too, with us being at the bottom of the hill, out of their range.

When Blanche sees the Ford, I'm surprised she runs toward us. But when the door opens and she flings herself onto Buck's lap, it's clear she didn't come back for the rest of us. It's also clear she's a blubbering mess.

Blanche yanks at her hair, going on and on 'bout how all her dreams have gone to hell, and all in the span of thirteen days.

"It's okay, baby," Buck says, trying to comfort her.

I make a turn, my hands trembling.

I shouldn't be cross at her. Hell, I know the feeling of losing it all, but the noise she's making is irritating as sin. And there's Jones, of all people, also soothing her, also telling her it's going to be okay. I make another turn, onto some country road.

"Tend to Jones," I say to her between my teeth.

Then I glance at Clyde. With the way his knuckles are ghost white on the door's handle, he's trying to keep his anger in check.

When I look in the rearview mirror again, I only see the back of Blanche, and let my eyes fall closed for a moment in relief that she listened, even if she's still wailing like a banshee.

"I can't . . ." she starts. "The buttons are too slick."

"Pull over the car," Clyde says, just as Jones pleads, "Just yank it off. Please."

Blanche tears Jones's shirt, and my boy cries out.

I've barely pulled the park lever and let out a shaky breath before Clyde's out of the car. For a moment, I think he's the next to lose his mind when he starts jumping up and down under an elm. He reaches for the tree and lands with a branch in his hand. He snaps off a length of it. Back at the car, he tears his shirt and winds the strip 'round the stick.

To some, his face may appear cold and blank, but I see Clyde differently. I know he's battling with himself—over something he's 'bout to do—but he doesn't want the world to know he's struggling.

He nods for Jones to get out of the car. Buck and Blanche help him, propping him up, his shirt dangling open. On Jones's right side, his flesh has been blown wide open.

"First things first," Clyde says, talking low, like he's trying not to scare Jones off. "We got to see if that bullet's still inside ya, lad, or if it fired through ya."

It takes my brain a spell to catch up to Clyde's words, and by then, he's already got the stick pointed at the wound. I may lose my egg breakfast when Clyde's torn shirt appears from Jones's back.

• • •

"Here you go, honey, take this."

Jones's eyes flutter open, and I push the aspirin between his cracked lips. I try to keep my eyes on his face, but my gaze flickers to the bandage 'round his stomach, a spot of red bleeding through. His skin's covered in goose bumps. I reckon from the fact he's only wearing Clyde's torn suit jacket, his chest exposed, and also from the loss of blood.

Ain't fair our boy is suffering like this.

"Sorry," I say, for so many things, but in this moment 'cause he's got to swallow the tablet dry. "This place doesn't have any runnin' water."

The cabin doesn't have much space either, and Clyde and Buck are filling up every available inch with hot air, arguing the way brothers do, 'cept this argument is more backbiting than bickering.

Sitting here, perched on the side of the twin bed, it feels like I'm in the eye of the storm.

In our wake, we left a hell of a mess at 3347½ Oak Ridge Drive. All our clothes and belongings. I mean, all of 'em. From my poems to Buck's parole papers to Blanche and Buck's wedding license to all those photos Blanche developed, right on down to our five toothbrushes sitting in a cup on the bathroom sink. We brought nothin' with us, save what was on our bodies and the gun in Clyde's hands.

It curdles my stomach to think of the wreckage that gun left in the driveway. Two bodies, the officers' names still unknown to me, and it'll stay that way 'til I read 'em in the paper, in the aftermath of everything we've done.

After our escape, we left a trail everywhere we went.

A tire with a puncture wound, probably nicked by a bullet.

A broken storefront window of a pharmacy.

A gas station trash can with Jones's bloody shirt.

Muddy tracks, when the rain hit, leading away from our deserted car.

Clyde drove all night in the new Ford he stole—always a Ford—not stopping 'til daybreak, when all of our eyes were bloodshot, our stomachs growling, our nerves shot.

No one slept, not even Jones. That poor boy was afraid if he closed his lids for longer than a blink, he'd never open 'em again.

At daybreak, Clyde stopped driving. The SHAMROCK TOURIST CAMP sign told us we were in Shamrock, Texas. My best guess, based on how fast Clyde got the Ford going, is that we covered nearly five hundred miles since hightailing it out of Joplin, Missouri.

When we got here, Buck had to wake the owner to rent our two cabins. Blanche's scowl would put that man's to shame, though, and after Buck checked us in, she immediately slammed the door on her cabin. Buck helped carry Jones into ours, then stood there with his hands in his pocket, as if he were digging for gold.

"What is it?" Clyde asked him.

"Well, it's just that I wasn't thinkin', ya know, and when I wrote down a name on the register, I put William Callihan."

I bit my lip. No one in the room stated the very obvious mistake of Buck using the same name as from Joplin.

That started the argument. I slipped out for a minute to catch my breath, breathing deeply on the community John. I wasn't gone long, but here we are, the boys still going strong.

"You didn't hear those coppers yapping outside the garage," Clyde says. "I did. And they thought we were bootleggers from Chicago."

"Well, how'd they get that idea?"

Clyde throws up his hands, but his words are more pointed as he says, "I wager it didn't help that Blanche—"

"Blanche?" Buck all but growls.

"Yeah, that lass of yours had a laundry list of items she needed to develop those photos of hers."

"So!"

"So," Clyde says, slowing the cadence of his voice, "our lad"—he nods toward Jones—"says paint thinner is used in bootlegging. And it's not like anyone ever saw Blanche with her camera. Eyebrows were raised, Buck."

"You did the raising, too, Clyde."

I stand on the bed. "I don't care who raised whose brows. We're in this mess together."

And what a mess it is. The cops may've been chasing us for the past year, but they were chasing a name. Clyde's. Now, the law may know my name too. They certainly know Blanche's and Buck's. They'll know we had chicken and beans for dinner last night, if they go snooping through our trash. They've got my poems. Those photos, the ones that were supposed to be just for us, are now in their hands. Hell, they'll know my bra size is a 34A.

I've never felt so exposed. I've never felt so sick, knowing those officers will be yanking out our drawers, pawing through our things, discussing our personal items, making opinions and judgments about who we are, what we think, what we do, how we act, where we're going next. And really, all they've got to do is follow that trail, a trail where our scent's going to linger a lot longer, after our names and those photos appear in the papers. We killed two cops. A double murder. People are going to take notice of us, really take notice of us. Seeing us, telling the law which way we've gone.

I roll my neck, feeling the tightness reaching into my shoulders and back.

"I'm going to go talk to Blanche," I say, needing to move. "You two be civil and go fetch us some water." Hands on my hip, I add, "Put it on the stove, we'll need it rip-roaring hot to get Jones's wounds cleaned up and the blood out of our clothes. You hear?"

The boys grow some sense and don't object. Rightfully so; my stern words should alarm them. But there's no mistaking, Blanche is the queen of stern when she's been crossed, and I second-guess knocking on her door. She was silent the whole car ride after her wailing sputtered out, never getting out to stretch her legs. Then she went straight from the car to her cabin, with a thud of her door. One thing's for sure, that girl's bladder may be the only thing stronger than her will.

I lightly knock, then head inside her cabin, quickly closing the door. I'll be honest, partly worried she's going to chuck something at my head, I raise my arms to shield my face.

"I ain't got nothin' to throw," Blanche says dryly. "It's all back at Oak Ridge, all 'cept for this polka-dot dress."

Being she had a blue housedress on earlier, I lower my arms to see what she's talking 'bout. Blanche's face is dead serious, her knees are pulled to her chest, and she ain't lying, her dress may as well be polka-dotted from all of Jones's blood.

"The boys are getting water so we can clean ourselves up."

"Wonderful." She scratches at one of the red splotches, now dry. "That'll solve all our problems."

I wring my hands but keep my feet planted exactly where they are. "I'm sorry, Blanche."

Her head shakes slowly, her lips quivering before she says, "You two couldn't leave us be, could you?" Blanche shifts her head toward the plastered wall, talks to it. "Ain't life a son of a bitch. I get my act together. Buck gets his act together. We're happy. Then poof"—she looks me in the eye—"it all goes to shit."

"We're going to be all right."

That right there . . . that may be a lie.

Blanche straightens her legs quick as a wink. "The hell we are. You don't think I put the pieces together, Bonn? Buck's pardon papers are ripped up by now. They've got my marriage license. Our names—all of ours—are going to be as familiar to the law as their goddamn kids' now that we're cop killers. *Cop killers*!"

I've had these same thoughts, but it stings to hear it verbalized. I risk taking a step closer, but Blanche opens her mouth again and I stop.

"I had dreams, Bonn. You should know something 'bout that. Being with Buck, starting a home and a family, being happy, being free. And you know what those dreams are doing now? After only thirteen days with you and Clyde, they're tumbling down 'round me."

"Clyde and I have a plan." It sounds flimsy and quite frankly, not enough, even as I say it, but I push on, needing to hear it myself. "He's got to take care of some personal business at a prison farm, getting back at the people who hurt him. Then we're getting a farm of our own. It can be all of ours, that plan." I inch forward and sit on the other side of the tiny bed, which means I'm close enough for her to swat. "Buck, a family, happiness. Being free. We can do that there."

"Ya got me in a corner, Bonn. Where else do I got to go?" She scratches once more at Jones's blood, then drops her hand. "Snow Ball's gone."

"Yeah, that dog was the fastest out of all of us, it seems."

Tears well up in her eyes. "Don't be smart." She sniffles once, then blows out a long breath. "How's everyone else?"

"Our boy's hanging in there. His bleeding has mostly stopped." I hesitate, not sure if Blanche wants to hear 'bout Clyde, but I selfishly need to say it aloud. "And Clyde's fine. Got a wicked bruise over his heart where the bullet got him, but the vest . . . I'm mighty thankful he thought to put on that vest."

"We're in deep, aren't we?"

I bite my lip. "The law won't catch us."

There's a hint of a smile on Blanche's face, but it's one ya really got to look for. "I meant with the Barrow boys. I'd do anything for that fool."

I nod. But her words make me wonder. "Blanche, why'd you run from us at Oak Ridge?"

"Besides losing my mind?" She squirms. "Guess I wanted to see if Buck would follow. Couldn't help feeling like he chose Clyde over me by wanting to join you two. It was weighin' on me, 'specially after Lillian up and left when I was a child, then my daddy was always putting his women before me. I mean, holy hell, even my dog left me in his dust."

"That dog has a brain the size of a pea."

"No kidding. He chose to play house with you and Clyde."

I ignore that part and say, "Well, all I know is that Buck is bewitched by you. He ain't going anywhere." I lean forward, squeeze her hand. "We're in this together, okay? All of us."

She lets out a huff, a few strands of her hair wafting. A few other strands don't move at all, plastered to her head from all sorts of grime. Blanche grimaces. "I need to get clean. Now."

Soon, we've all bathed the best we could with a pot. Took couple rounds back and forth to the pump, but we finally scrubbed most of the blood out of our clothes.

Then we all stand there, save Jones, who'll be horizontal for quite some time, assessing each other, trying to figure out who's going to go to the camp's grocer for food. Clyde immediately says I ain't going, and I'm immediately thankful. Sitting 'round the apartment in my nightgown is one thing. Prancing into a store is another. I counter that Clyde can't go; too risky. Blanche offers, catching us all off guard.

"What?" she says. "These two jackasses look too much alike. If anyone would overlook Clyde's height, they may confuse Buck for him."

One glance at Clyde tells me he's letting the jab go. From his pocket he pulls the last of our money, and off Blanche goes in her housedress, still damp, still a trace of red polka dots.

She comes back with a bag full of food and a mouth full of worry. "I don't like how people were looking at me."

"Well, you ain't wearing a coat, maybe they were wondering why? It's cold this morning," I say.

"Maybe." She takes a deep breath. "My sorry appearance is sure to make anybody wonder what I'm up to, but the storekeeper said something 'bout us taking so many trips for water this morning."

Clyde uses his a finger and thumb to squeeze his tired eyes, then the bridge of his nose. "That's that, then. We got to go."

I glance at Jones, who finally fell asleep. I certainly don't want to wake him; the boy needs his rest. But we also can't stick 'round to find out if someone followed our trail. When Buck and Clyde lift Jones, his moan and bloodshot eyes are worse than I imagined.

"You're going to have to try to walk on your own, you hear? In case anyone is watching," Clyde says to him. "But we'll be right next to you."

Blanche scurries in the rear seat first, and guides Jones's head onto her lap. With his feet on Buck's lap and Clyde and me in the front seat, we skip out the back entrance of the tourist camp.

Clyde drives for hours, avoiding large towns, keeping to the backcountry roads, driving in a pattern that'd make anyone cross-eyed. I try not to think. Thinking means realizing that we've left the cabin where, if even for a few hours, time stood still. Now, we're no longer in the eye of the storm, we're off to take our chances in the unknown, beginning with Clyde pulling over the car.

"What's that there sign say, Bonnie?"

"Ten miles to Amarillo."

His gun sits between us on the bench seat. He pulls it into his lap "Okay, we'll wait 'til dark."

I don't much like not moving, and I will for darkness to come. At least I can count on the sun always dippin' beneath the horizon, and when she does, Clyde gets our Ford going again.

No one's said much since leaving Shamrock. Still, no one says anything as we near Amarillo and Clyde parks along a curb in town. I know my man well enough to know what he's got up his sleeve. He's going to find some place to rob. We need new clothes. We need food. Being our current car's been seen 'round the camp, we'll need a new one of those, too.

Thing is, Clyde doesn't like doing jobs alone. Never has. He had Raymond. He had Jones. And now, his voice is level as he says, "Buck?" and gets out of the car.

There's total silence, all of us stealing each other's air. I stare straight ahead, avoiding any mirrors that'll give me a glimpse of Blanche's face.

There's a whisper, presumably passing from Buck to Blanche, being the tone had a deep hum. Then, Buck's door opens and closes.

Blanche's sobs fill the car.

17

WITH IT BEING NIGHTTIME, IT'S HARD TO KNOW HOW MUCH time passes while Clyde and Buck are off robbing somewhere. Jones is in the back, the chills overtaking his body. He's wrapped in a blanket and, thank goodness, asleep. Blanche is back there with him, staring off into Amarillo.

It's too dark for us to see much of anything. All I know 'bout the town is that its claim to fame is a helium plant. I remember reading 'bout it in the paper a few years ago after the natural gas was discovered here. But from where we're parked, I don't see anything resembling the cement plant we got back home. Though, if I squint, the building off to my right may be an opera house.

If I were a different girl, in a different world, I'd breeze inside, letting my hand stroke each red upholstered seat 'til I reached the stage. There, I'd find my mark, smack dab in the middle, and I'd look out at the vast room. I'd have to tilt my head back slightly to see the very top balconies. I imagine the cries of my fans, demanding an encore.

Blanche was right, I do know a little something 'bout having dreams. I also know something 'bout them crumbling 'round me, clunking me on the head, and leaving me with a black eye. And not just standing front and center on a stage. I wanted to stand at the front of a classroom, too. Only finishing school wasn't in the cards. Not for me. Not with my ma's bills to be paid. Not with the crash of '29. Not with a husband who left me high and dry.

I feel like we should talk more, Blanche and I. But with the way she's staring out the Ford's window, barely blinking, her jaw clenched, I'm going to give her some more time.

What we had going at Oak Ridge was a good thing. More than good; it allowed me to feel like me again. But now what choice is there but to focus on the farms? And now, with Buck helping Clyde, just as Clyde wanted, it'll get us back on track. Soon we'll have our land, and a way for both Buck and Clyde to help their parents escape the memories of Dallas. Blanche'll understand that once her blood cools.

She straightens. "Buck's coming back."

"Only Buck?" I squint harder now, a flash of panic settling over me. But there's also a Clyde-shaped figure running our way.

From the moment they get in the car, running becomes our new normal. We drive, and drive like mad, going no place in particular, as long as it's ahead of the cops. I grit my teeth at how we're nothin' but aimless, but Jones isn't well enough to be on his feet, and Clyde wants 'em both for his next step in his plan to raid Farm Number One: stealing firearms from a weapons armory.

"May be the easiest way to get us a bundle of guns, and fast."

I let out an exasperated sigh. "Easiest? Clyde." I can't think of more to say than his name, in a disapproving tone.

He only shrugs. "Mind's already set on it, Bonnie."

I throw up my hands.

As Jones heals, each state blends into the next. Texas becomes New Mexico becomes Oklahoma becomes Kansas becomes Nebraska becomes

Iowa becomes Illinois. Along the way, we buy new clothes, we tend to Jones from a medical kit Clyde swiped from a physician's car, and Clyde—sometimes Buck—drives day and night, sleeping only a few hours at a time. When money runs out, the boys rob, usually a filling station, grocery store, or drugstore. *Low-risk hits*, as Clyde refers to 'em, since there's so much heat on us right now. Even with the so-called low risk, Clyde likes to put three hundred or four hundred miles behind us after each one. He calls it *jumping*.

From Illinois, we go to Missouri, then Arkansas, then Oklahoma, then Louisiana. There, we pause, and pull into the parking lot of a café. It's been two weeks, five cars, and only three nights in an actual bed. Otherwise, we sleep in the car. Jones can sit straight up now, no longer needing to stretch 'cross Blanche and Buck.

Better yet, his chills have passed, so now we can use our blanket to cover the few guns we have on the car's floor instead of him. The boy hasn't smiled much, though. Breaks my heart to see the sides of his lips turned down.

Too many miles ago, Blanche's dismissive frown wasn't any better when I suggested she name our first replacement car.

Now, the five of us head into the café, and Clyde leads us 'cross the black-and-white checkered flooring to a corner table. We haven't risked too many trips like this, all together. Normally one person slinks into a store, with the rest waiting down the street in our car.

But after runnin' all this time, we need a dose of not being on the run. Doesn't mean the boys don't got guns hidden under their jackets, though. And Blanche still has that sour look on her face, wholly out of place with the lively chatter going on 'round us and with the cheery, floral wallpaper behind her head. Being none of us is talking, I get up for a newspaper. We've been pulling them from each town we go through, and so far, we haven't seen anything too damning. Meaning, no one knows where we are.

Even now, no one takes much notice of me, besides a man with a cordial smile. "How do ya do?" I say, and grab a newspaper from the rack beside his table. I'm halfway back to my own table when my gaze lands on a picture of myself in black-and-white. My hand shoots out on its own, my pinkie finding the corner of someone's pecan pie. I mumble an apology and, head spinning, I concentrate on Clyde 'cross the room, my beacon.

He's on his feet, taking me by my elbow to get me safely into my chair. "Bonnie, what is it?"

"Me."

This, right here, is the first time I've ever seen myself in a newspaper. I drop it, my gaze unmoving as Blanche snatches it off the table, where my gaze falls on a burned spot, like someone put out a cigarette on the enamel tabletop.

Blanche barely has the newspaper in front of her eyes before she's laughing. The unusual sound, something I haven't heard for fourteen days, pulls my attention away from the dark spot on the table and to my best friend.

"'Clyde Barrow and his cigar-smoking gun moll murder two,'" she says and turns the paper 'round, displaying the headline, along with the photo of me: gun on my hip, elbow propped on the car, foot up on the fender, cigar between my teeth. "Oh, Bonn, ain't this rich?"

Ain't it cruel, is more like it. I take a deep breath. Clyde's thumb rubs circles on my knee. That photo, that was supposed to be just for us, that paints me in a horrible light, is now plastered for all of the country to see.

"You're mortified," Blanche says. "And rightly so." She shrugs and turns the newspaper back to herself. "But," she continues, "doesn't appear they got your name. No mention of Buck or me. Nor you, honey," she says to Jones with a wink. "Just Clyde, no surprise there."

Jones sighs so audibly I think the whole café heard him. Not that I'm blaming him.

Blanche tosses the paper onto our empty table. "Where's our waitress?"

Buck laughs, saying, "You're horrible, ya know that, baby?" as Clyde begins tearing the photo of me from the paper.

I ignore Blanche. "Clyde, you going to rip me out of all of 'em?"

"If I could, Bonnie, I would. But"—he finishes tearing out my picture, putting me in front of himself on the table—"this here will keep me company on the nights I can't sleep. Look at you." He whistles.

I chuckle, thanking my lucky stars I got someone like Clyde to turn lemons into lemonade. Or at least sprinkle some sugar on top of those lemons.

A gasp pulls my attention up, to an open-mouthed waitress, both hands grasping a pad of paper. Clyde stiffens beside me.

"You're Clyde Barrow, ain't you? That fugitive," she whispers. The woman looks over one shoulder, then another. When she moves, her hand dropping into the pocket of her apron, Clyde's hand shifts inside his jacket. She pulls out a silver certificate dollar bill. "My mama is going to roll over in her grave, but would you sign this?" The poor gal's hand is shaking as she extends a pen and the bill.

I reckon Clyde's smirk steadies her a bit, or at least her voice is a bit steadier as she says to me, "And you, you're his girl, right? Could you sign it, too?"

Clyde slides the dollar in front of me. "You go first, Bonnie. Your name should always go first."

"Would you look at that, Bonn," Blanche says. "You're finally famous, just like you've always wanted."

The waitress licks her lips. "I won't tell—that you all are here."

Blanche waves her off. "Ain't me they're after. I'll have your finest grits, extra cheese."

• • •

The waitress doesn't draw any more notice to us and no one else bothers to scrutinize our group in the corner. Bellies full and—I can't lie—my ego stroked at the waitress's attention, we head back out on the road. Where to? I can't be sure. But Blanche is chatty in the rear seat. She's making Jones laugh, though I worry 'bout the boy. His laugh sounds like it's lost some of its youth.

"What town we in now?" I ask Clyde, slinked down in my seat.

We pass a sign for RUSTON HARDWARE before Clyde can answer, and I read the sign aloud. This town doesn't look much different than the others we've driven through, and I guess Clyde doesn't see anyplace he wants to rob, maybe on account of how many people are out and about for a midday meal. The more we drive, the fewer the people and houses we see, and the more trees that span the spacious lawns.

"Hey, lad," Clyde says. He tilts his chin up, giving him a better vantage point of Jones in the rearview mirror. Our car slows. "You see that there Chevrolet?"

"Yeah."

"You want it?"

"I guess so."

Clyde stops the car, turns in his seat. "Either you do or you don't."

His words aren't aggressive, but I know what he's doing. He heard Jones laughing earlier, probably music to Clyde's ears, and Clyde wants to see if he has Jones all the way back. He misses the boy. Two peas in a pod, they are. Or at least they were before Jones got shot.

"I do," Jones says.

Clyde grins. "Then off you go. Highway is a few blocks ahead. Go on and take her straight there. We'll catch up."

Jones pauses. He swallows. From Clyde to me to Buck to Blanche, he looks.

"The choice is yours, honey," Blanche says. "No one's making you go."

Clyde doesn't say a word.

"I'll be okay," Jones says. His eyes find Clyde's but only for a breath, then Jones is out the door and walking at a crouch toward the car.

The boy looks guilty as sin, but fortunately the car's only a few paces up the driveway. The house is dark, and being it's midday, it's likely the mister ain't home. I imagine him working at one of the shops in town—it's walking distance, after all—or maybe the university that's down the road. A professor, perhaps. That'd make for a nice life. The house is two stories, enough room for a few bedrooms and perhaps a parlor off the entry. Not a bad life, at all.

Jones peeks over his shoulder at us, and the apprehension on his face triggers a flashback of Jones struggling to steal the car on Christmas. But this here is different. It's April. It's warmer.

Still, I hold my breath.

Jones opens the door, and maybe he gives his own exhale, because this time, when he looks at us, his expression is more confident. He slides into the car like he owns it, gets her started, then waves as if to say, *All's good here.*

Clyde laughs, saying under his breath. "That's my lad."

We don't leave right away. Clyde watches the house, making sure we don't have any trouble on our hands, then we go after Jones.

Once we're on the highway, one minute passes of us driving. Then two, and three. But there's no sign of the Chevrolet. I know we're all wondering the same thing: When's the boy going to pull over?

After ten minutes, Clyde makes a wide turn right there in the middle of the highway, back the way we came. He winds on and off the highway, going down each country road we pass.

Fear is etched 'cross Blanche's face with the reckless way Clyde's driving, and Buck tells her to get down on the floorboards. "It's better if you don't got to see the world whizzing by, baby," he says.

I'm half tempted to crawl back there with her, not wanting to see the pain on Clyde's face. He knows it. I know it. Our boy took off. He's gone.

18

CLYDE'S GOT A HEAVY FOOT ALL THE WAY TO DALLAS, THINKING that's where Jones has gone. But we don't spot him along the way and we don't go into town, not with us being the talk of it.

"Leave the kid alone," Buck says. "He left for a reason."

Clyde doesn't respond to that. He grits his teeth like he wants to but, his jaw still tight, he heads us back into Louisiana. I ain't sure why we're headed that way, or where we're headed after that. Our next stop was going to be an armory, and now we're without Jones again. Now, our plans are cloudy again. I've got a cigarette lit for Clyde and me before he can ask for one.

And we drive. Through rain, through hailstorms, through mud that takes the weight of our car and doesn't let it go. We leave the car behind, we've got no choice, and trudge over the soft ground, each of us cursing like sailors, 'til we reach some town. Clyde spots a Ford roadster, and he wants it.

"No way," Buck says under his breath. We already stand out like sore thumbs, legs plastered with mud and faces plastered in the papers. "Stupidest thing I've ever heard to get a ride that small. We'll be sittin' on top of each other."

I reckon that's precisely why Clyde wants it, besides having an eye for the model. That way, every time he looks in the rearview mirror, there won't be a gap where Jones's dark head of hair should be.

We end up stealing two cars, one for them, one for us. A little distance from Buck and Blanche will do us some good. After we move our belongings from the abandoned car into our practical sedans, we're going nowhere again. So many times the question's on the tip of my tongue: *Clyde, what we doing to get to the farms?* But Clyde's Jones-sized wound is still too large, and I let him drive. Just drive.

Buck and Blanche trail us, and as we approach a bend in the road, I hold my breath. My mind skips twenty seconds into the future, where I can imagine us hitting the straightaway but Buck and Blanche never doing the same. I may be happy to do without the bickering with them for a few hours, but that doesn't mean I want them to vanish, too.

I stare into the sideview mirror, watching and watching, hoping that vision doesn't come true. We come out of the bend. My breath's just 'bout gone. Then there they are, still behind us.

Clyde's eyes are hidden behind his shades, and I can't be sure, but I think his shoulders let down, as if he thought someone else he cared 'bout would up and leave him, too. For the past few days, his fear's been coming out as anger, his fuse short as can be. Really, I don't know what's been worse, Clyde's temper or the angry storms that have been sweeping 'cross the South. But I do know I'm tired of being tired, to the point where I feel fevered. Endless hours in a car will do that to ya, hour after hour of a thick silence, only broken when Buck bickered with Clyde or Clyde bickered with Buck.

Now we've got some peace and quiet, almost too quiet. I hum, trying to up my own spirits, then louder when Clyde doesn't object, even gives me a small smile. He's trying, for me. That sliver of a smile reminds me he'll always try for me, even when others let him down.

I hope he knows that won't ever be me. I squeeze his hand, wishing I had more to give him, wishing I had more to give myself. I want to laugh, good and hearty, a sound that feels foreign to me. Clyde's laugh does, too. His best ones always slip out when I least expect it, also catching him off guard. But neither of us got a reason to laugh at the moment. And if I start hooting out of nowhere, that can only mean one thing: I've lost my damn mind.

Some time later, we're in some town in some state, and Clyde pulls over. He dips his sunglasses, looking over them at a grocery store.

"Pretty nice town," he says. "Probably a decent haul inside."

I roll my head in a circle, my neck giving me a satisfying crack. "I'm coming, too."

He drops his sunglasses back into place, hiding his eyes. The tip of his tongue pokes out of his mouth.

"Stop your thinkin', Clyde. I need out of this car."

I need something concrete to do. I want to feel something, a rush of anything besides the tingling in my rear end from sitting here for so long—and the scrunching feeling in my tummy that our boy Jones had enough of being with us. It's a thought I don't allow myself to have too often. Clyde's probably having it enough for us both.

Clyde gives me a nod. It's cute of him, thinking that tilt of his head—saying it's okay for me to come along—would've led to a different response than if his head moved side to side. Almost makes me chuckle.

By the time I've hidden a small gun on me and I get to Buck's car window, Clyde's already there.

Blanche throws up her hands. "Well, I want no part of this. Bad enough Buck is involved."

"No one's making you join us," Clyde says. "Better you ain't."

Wrinkles appear between Blanche's eyes. "What's that supposed to mean?"

"Baby," Buck says, shaking his head. "You can't have it both ways."

She crosses her arms, and Clyde leans in through Buck's window, lowering his voice. "Drive her out 'bout two miles, Blanche. We'll meet ya there when the deed's done."

Clyde raps on Buck's door, his way of saying, *Come on, Buck, get out so Blanche can get the hell out of here.* He lights a cigarette and stares through his exhaled smoke at the grocery store, formulating a plan in his head.

Moving in sync, Clyde offers and I'm taking our shared cigarette.

"Let's make this easy. Bonnie, stay by the door. Once we pull our guns, pull yours, slowly scanning the store for any funny business. Fire if ya need to, but I'd rather we keep this outing quiet. Buck, you know the drill."

With that, we head 'cross the street. To the right of Jim's Grocer is a watchmaker. To the left, an insurance company. Coca-Cola signs cover Jim's storefront. I wouldn't mind a bottle, now that it's in my head.

Jim's door jingles as we walk in. It ain't a big place. A counter stretches down the left side, and shelving stacked with bottles, cans, and boxes fills the wall behind it. Almost in a haphazard mess, crates and sacks are grouped on the tiled floor to make up the rest of the small store.

Clyde and Buck weave 'round the produce, grains, and oversized cans, assessing the store. Jim, behind the counter in his white apron, a tie tucked neatly underneath, doesn't take much notice of the boys. His head's down, reading a newspaper. It'd be our dumb luck if it was an article 'bout us. Besides Jim, there's only one other man I see, looking as if he's trying to decide between red or black beans. I bet his wife sent him 'cause she forgot an ingredient she needs for supper.

Clyde catches my eye, holds up a single finger. Looks like I only got to watch the one man, as he decides which beans his wife needs. He stumbles to the side, and I snort. Bet ya he also got assigned this errand after he put back a few beers.

A cat, black on top, white on the bottom, winds itself between Clyde's legs. Buck shoos it away. Then, their pistols are out from beneath their suit jackets.

Quick, I yank my blouse from my skirt and pull my gun free from the waistband.

The man looks up, red beans in his left hand, black beans in his right. I wink at him, my arms stretched out, a pistol at the end.

"Jim?" he calls.

"Don't be a hero," Jim responds. I flick my gaze to the owner. His hands are up.

"No need for anyone to get hurt," Clyde says, his voice a purr. "Empty the register, and we'll be on our way. If your hands go anywhere 'cept into that there drawer"—he nods toward the register—"my brother here will make ya sorry."

The cat meows, and my eyes are back on the man with the beans, the cat now at his feet. He's a step closer than he was before. I cock my head at him, and get the bright idea to say, "Put those cans down."

We don't need him lobbing them at Clyde's or Buck's head, now do we?

It doesn't take more than thirty seconds for Jim to empty his register. Clyde stuffs the bills into the interior pockets of his jacket.

It ain't much, but it never is from these small stores. Jim's probably got a safe somewhere with more, probably a gun or two tucked beneath his counter as well. But Clyde wants to keep this quick and quiet. He's already backing away from Jim and, for some reason, toward the man, who no longer holds those beans. I keep my pistol on him. Then Clyde's got him by the arm, the gun pressed to his back.

"Let's take a quick walk, shall we?" Clyde says.

The man's lower jaw shifts back and forth as his legs move him toward the door.

Buck backpedals, his attention on Jim, in case he makes any quick movements below his counter. Not like he will, not when he's outnumbered three to one and we've got us a hostage.

The door jingles as I kick it open, stretching out my leg to keep it that way. Clyde steers the man through, pecking my cheek. "Thanks, sweetie."

The *sweetie* makes me chuckle; not something Clyde's called me before, but I reckon he didn't want to use my real name or even call me *darling* like he usually does.

Once Buck is out, he hovers outside the door and nods to me that I can let the door close. That bell jingles again, the sound trailing me as

I start running to the driver's seat to get her started. I feel eyes on me, but only a few. And the heaviness of their gaze is fleeting, as if they know something wrong is going on, but it ain't something they want to get tangled up with. That's how folks are nowadays, slow to intervene, as if part of them wishes they had the guts to also take what they want in a time where so much has been taken from them.

"See," I overhear Clyde saying to the man, "no one's getting hurt here today. Run on, now."

The engine purrs. The man Clyde released is down the block, running into another building. Buck's still got his pistol aimed at Jim's door.

"You think you're driving, do ya, Bonnie?" Clyde calls with a grin, no doubt fueled by the adrenaline of our successful robbery. I'm fine with that, being one of his dimples has come out to play, and is distracting me from a smart comeback.

I lick my lips, then open my mouth, hoping the words will come, when instead, I scream, "Clyde!"

Out of the corner of my eye, our hostage is running back up the block, with a shotgun leading his way.

Clyde's curses are jumbled, mixing with his shouts for Buck to get back to the car. The man fires, at Clyde, at Buck, I ain't sure, but both react to the sound, dropping to the ground. From his stomach, Clyde bangs on the outside of the car. "Go, Bonnie, drive!"

With both him and Buck outside?

A bullet fires, close by, probably from Clyde's gun, and the man down the street takes cover behind a newspaper stand.

I drive—right as Clyde starts to round the front of the car to get to the passenger side. He ends up splayed 'cross the fender. I switch my foot to the brake and Clyde lashes with the sudden stop. Somehow, he's still plastered to the front of the car. "Drive!"

My head's all over the place, turning every which way. Buck's runnin' toward us, now trailing us, being I'm picking up speed. Clyde's propped on the front of the car, his gun pressed against his hip so he can hold it with one arm. I will for Buck to hurry.

Gunshots have me dipping in my seat, barely able to see over the wheel, and when I do, there's Clyde, his body blocking most of my view of Main Street. I use the wheel to pull myself up and let out a relieved breath when, in the rearview mirror, there's Buck hanging onto the back of the sedan. At least I've got him, even if he ain't quite inside the car.

Not like Clyde is either, but I'm moving, getting us the hell out of here before one of those bullets knocks either of the boys off the car.

I look again at Clyde; it's hard not to. Then, I'm laughing. Clyde clinging onto the front of a car like a monkey shouldn't be funny, but—Jesus, Mary, and Joseph—I can't keep myself together. That is, 'til his hand slides 'cross the windshield, leaving behind a streak of red.

My laughter trails off.

I risk slowing the car to make a turn out of town. On a country road, I push the speedometer up to fifty, sixty, sixty-five, praying the boys can hold on. In the rearview, I look beyond Buck and see no one's following us, and I steer onto the road's bank.

Clyde immediately jumps off the fender, using both hands to brace himself after his feet hit solid ground. He makes for the driver's side, not the passenger's, and I slide over, gladly letting him have the wheel.

Two doors slam, and once more, the trees whiz by.

"Buck?" Clyde says, his voice even, cool. Now our speedometer climbs to seventy, eighty, almost ninety.

"In the legs, some buckshots made a home there," Buck says. "Took a shot to the hand, too, but it ricocheted off my wedding band. Can ya imagine that? Wait 'til Blanche hears 'bout it."

Clyde snorts. "Dear brother, don't be so cavalier when you tell the missus."

Buck laughs, and I'm happy I ain't the only one who's gone a touch loopy.

"And you, Clyde?" I say. "What ya got to tell me 'bout dangling from our car?"

"That you're a horrendous driver."

I cross my arms, but I'm smirking.

"Few slugs in my hip, and"—he frees the wheel to rip back his left sleeve, speckled with blood—"yep, got me in the arm."

The sight of Clyde's blood corks my adrenaline, and the fact he survived a shoot-out—again—finally sinks in. I rub my crossed arms, warming away the layer of goose bumps. Worries me, it does . . . how many lives could a cat like Clyde possibly have?

• • •

It's my turn to keep watch, and I gladly climb on top of our car, letting the others sleep below me as the pine trees stretch high above me, only showing a sliver of the moon. I'm glad for the light, even if it's only a little. Being in pitch blackness wouldn't do a damn thing for my nerves or for my growing unease that our plans are stuck in some void.

After escaping and meeting up with Blanche, we stopped to tend to the boys' wounds. It took us hours to dig the buckshot from Buck's limbs. Rather, it took Blanche hours. The idea of digging into his flesh with a knife turned my stomach upside down.

It's bad of me, but I didn't offer any insistence 'bout removing Clyde's after he said to leave 'em be.

"They don't hurt much," he said. "And they're likely to work themselves out."

The most I did was bandage his arm, while keeping an eye on the wind howling through the trees. It got strong, too strong, and an honest-to-God twister practically chased us north before Blanche could get the slugs out of Buck.

Those storms are no good, popping up out of nowhere. Unpredictable. As if we need something else on our tails, keeping our shoulders tense and our eyes red. We drove for a whole day, Buck and Clyde trading off behind the wheel, to get up near the top of Indiana.

At least the weather competes with us for headlines.

EIGHTY-NINE PEOPLE KILLED, ANOTHER THOUSAND INJURED BY TORNADOES

BARROW CLEANS OUT FIRST STATE BANK OF ST. PAUL, 'cept that wasn't us.

INDIANA FLOODING, WORST IN TWENTY YEARS

BARROW AND POSSE FLEE AFTER ROBBERY, GUNFIRE EXCHANGED

One would think we'd use our noggins, and not set up camp next to a lake.

"Fool," Buck said.

But Clyde argued the flooding was miles and miles away in central Indiana. We're practically in Michigan, based on his map.

Buck argued right back, "If that water so much as raises an inch, Blanche and I are gone."

Tensions are high.

Up here on the roof of the car, I stare into the near darkness, a shotgun in my lap, and I take in mouthfuls of the pinewood air. With queasiness wreaking havoc on my head, I need this, even if the nighttime unknowns give me the jitters. Who knows what creepy-crawly things slither 'round below me? I turn my gun toward every sound I hear. My muscles are beginning to ache with all the twisting and turning.

When morning comes, it marks a few days we've camped here, the boys licking their wounds, and we're back on some road. I can't recall what day it is, but it's no longer April, and May is ticking by.

"We can't go on like this," Blanche says from the rear seat. Her voice is muffled, with her two hands on the back of Clyde's seat, her head dropped between 'em. "Blanche is losing her mind."

Clyde veers off the road. Her head snaps up.

"Settle down, Clyde," Buck yells, steadying Blanche.

I reach over the gun that's always between us on the bench seat, and squeeze Clyde's knee.

"This ain't a dictatorship," Clyde says.

Buck snorts. "Could've fool—"

"What do ya have in mind, Blanche?" I ask.

"I just don't see how driving in circles is getting us any closer to getting off the road. You two want the farm, right?"

"Farms," Clyde says. "Both of 'em."

Blanche waves her hand. "Right. And what are we doing to make that happen?"

"*We*?" Clyde retorts.

"We're still here, ain't we?" she says. "You want to bust a bunch of convicts out of jail, by all means. I don't give a flying bung-hole anymore. I just want all this runnin' to stop so Buck and I can get on with our lives."

"Okay?" I say, the most amused I've been in quite some time.

"Okay, so go rob a bank or something," Blanche suggests. "We're already being blamed for ones we ain't even holding up. Might as well do it for real. Make it a big one and be done with all these games."

Clyde shakes his head. "Banks are trouble."

"Blanche's right," Buck says. Her chest poofs up like a peacock. "The loot's better. We won't have to rob something every day or two. We hit a bank, we bust open the prison," he says, not looking at his wife, "then with our winnings we'll have the means to hide away right away, ya know."

I like the idea. After we robbed the bank with Raymond, we had enough money to get ourselves a nice parcel of land. That is, before the law stole our stash back. After the bank robbery with Jones, we had enough to lay low for a few weeks. I can see Clyde working the idea through his head as well, his fingers tappin' against the wheel.

"All right," he says, "but it needs to be big-time." He leans his head back, facing the roof, but talking to Blanche behind him. "And I'll need Buck's help."

She doesn't miss a beat. "Fine. One and done."

19

A FEW AFTERNOONS LATER, I PICTURE CLYDE AND BUCK DRIVING a coupe into some small Minnesota town and waltzing into its bank. They'll hide, and when it's the bank's quitting time, the boys will be locked in 'til a banker opens shop in the morning. Clyde will be waiting with a *Good morning* and an *Empty the vault.* It's another of his clever plans that sounds gravy on paper, but I worry 'bout another fella thinking himself a hero.

Blanche and I stay behind, parked deep in the woods of Minnesota. I eye the trees all 'round us, ones that could come down on us any second. Lightning streaks ignite the night, and I pull my knees to my chest, taking up only a quarter of the sedan's front bench. Fat raindrops splatter against the windshield, and my goodness . . . "I've just 'bout had enough of these storms."

"I've just 'bout had enough of this life," Blanche says, her tone snarky.

I match it. "So you've said."

Last I checked, she was lying on her back, arms behind her head, her cheeks rosy, Buck's trench coat draped over her, the flash of each bolt illuminating her scowl.

Thunder cracks, and I press my hands over my ears as hard as I can, counting to ten before I release them.

"Just go to sleep," Blanche says. "I'm tired. I'm always tired, and dusty and hungry and cold and scared, and if Clyde picks one more fight with Buck . . ."

I sit up, the second coat I wear draped over my chest slipping off of me. "Clyde?"

"Yes, Clyde. I don't know who died and put him in charge, but last time I checked, Buck's the older of the two."

The rain turns to hail, how nice, and I shout over the pinging noise, "Age don't make you more mature."

"Sure it does," Blanche yells back.

"Fine, then. I'm older than you, Blanche. Guess you better do as I say."

"By three months. Spare me, *Bonnie*."

The storm screams at us, probably to stop bickering. Holy hell, I wouldn't be shocked if the wind tilted us onto two tires. I crawl to the driver side of the car, as if my weight will help keep the car down. The sky cracks again, and I let out a small yelp before I can stop myself.

"How is it that you've got the nerve to shoot at a real-life, living and breathing human being, but you're scared of a li'l rain?"

This ain't a little rain, but that's beside the point. God's work isn't something to mess with, and He is the one behind this storm. Not like I expect Blanche to understand that. Or really, anything 'bout who I've become or what I believe. When I pull a gun's trigger, I do so without thinking, because if I stop to think, it may be too late for Clyde or me.

Blanche won't touch a gun. She'd never pull a trigger. Lord help her, I hope a bullet—that she could've stopped from being fired—never takes out Buck.

I could say as much to her, but it won't get us anywhere besides into another disagreement. So we're quiet, the storm raging 'round us, 'til it grows tired and gives up. I fall asleep and wake to a new day, as if the sun chased away any signs of a storm. Apparently, it has chased away Blanche as well.

I take my time finding her. The grass slushes under my feet as I approach the lake's bank. She's crouched, her hands bright red. Blanche splashes water on her face and lets out a whooping sound.

"This water's cold enough to freeze the balls off a brass monkey," she says without turning 'round.

She splashes herself again.

"Maybe stop doing that, then."

"I may fall in face-first, otherwise. I'm so tired from that storm and worrying something went wrong at the bank."

At least we've got solidarity on both those points, along with how cold it is this far north. Going nine hundred miles straight down to Dallas would mean 'bout thirty degrees warmer this time of year. I miss it there, and for more than just its warmth. For my ma, and sister and brother—and 'cause Dallas is where Blanche and I grew up together. Sure, we bickered, like sisters do, but we always reconciled.

"Blanche," I say. "I'm sorry 'bout all of this. I really am."

She throws a twig into the water. It ripples. "This has been hard on me."

"I know. This ain't exactly how I planned things to go."

"I'd hope not." She shakes her head. "I ain't mad at you, ya know. Not you directly, at least. I should be, but I ain't."

"You should be," I agree.

"Anger's like burning the roof of your mouth. It hurts and hurts, then ya forget 'bout the pain and the next time ya think about it, the pain's gone. At that point, why worry 'bout it anymore?"

"This'll all be behind us soon, you'll see."

I say it for her as much as for me.

Tires crunch, and Blanche is on her feet, our conversation forgotten. But not our friendship. She pulls me by the hand as we run to meet Clyde and Buck. It doesn't take long before I notice the fact all the windows have been blown out of the car, and the temperature feels like it's dropped to below freezing.

Blanche veers to the right, me to the left, crossing paths, each of us trying to get to our man. Clyde steps out and my eyes move so fast over his body I nearly make myself dizzy. But I don't see any red, and I fling my arms 'round his neck.

"You scared me," I whisper into his ear.

"I'm all here," he whispers back.

On the other side of the car I hear Buck say, "Ow, baby, why you hitting me?"

I ignore Blanche's antics. "So," I say to Clyde. "How much ya get before they chased ya?"

Clyde sucks a tooth. "My guess is 'round twenty-five hundred."

I rest my head against his chest, so he can't see my disappointment. It's a lump sum, that's for sure. Equal, I'd say, to two years' worth of an average salary. Yet, it's not enough to get the kind of land we want so we can truly hide away. It's not the "one and done" Blanche—and I—hoped for.

"What now?" I ask. It all seems a mess. Farm Number One looms over us and Farm Number Two ain't within our reach. Not yet.

Clyde curses. "Reckon there's bigger out there, Bonnie."

I look up. "Banks, you mean?"

"Yeah, but"—he motions to the shot-out windows—"I ain't eager to do that again so soon. We should've stuck to our original plan and done the armory."

"But I thought you said you needed—"

"Jones. Aye, I want him for it. That's why I want to see if he's turned up in Dallas."

"But Clyde." I bite my lip. "He left us for a reason, just like Buck said."

"Fine," he said. "But I want to hear him say it with my own two ears."

• • •

My stomach flips and flops being back in Dallas; I want to be here, but I know it's not safe to be here. We drive in, just Clyde and I, under the cover of night and avoid the main streets with the flashing lights and billboards.

That ain't where Jones would be anyhow. He can't be living a flashy life out in the open. For all we know—and for all Jones knows—the law may be keeping an eye out for him. He's got us to blame for that.

I say, "Maybe we should let him go."

"Maybe." But Clyde doesn't stop driving. We go to West Dallas, driving down the same street where we first picked up Jones. He ain't on that one. Part of me hopes he won't be on the next one either. Not 'cause I don't miss the boy, but he can do better than us. Unless we pull off the farms. I hate my doubt, but here we are, back where we started. That land's never felt farther away.

"He'll be here," Clyde says to himself. "Old habits die hard. He worked these streets ever since he was a pup. Had to after his old man died from the flu. Younger sister and older brother, too."

"That's terrible."

"I can give the lad more than this. I got to."

Sure enough, Jones is 'round the next block. He huddles with another fella, exchanging something between the two of 'em. Clyde, with a hat on and his collar up despite the humidity, gets out to talk to him. The other fella scurries away as Clyde moseys up. Clyde and Jones exchange words, words I can't hear. Clyde leaves Jones standing there. He hasn't gone more than four steps before Jones is on his heels.

I smile.

With the three of us together again, Clyde hightails it out of Dallas, straight toward the state line. We hug the border between Texas and Oklahoma, Clyde ready to yank the steering wheel to the left or to the right, depending which side of the line we're on and which side danger is coming from.

The poor boy is taut as a bowstring in the back. When Clyde stops to do his business by a tree, Jones whispers to me, "Mrs. Barrow said Clyde and Buck are living on borrowed time." He swallows. "Clyde just used that phrase on me. Said the law was likely to pin me for murder, and if they did, I'd be a goner in Dallas. Said I'd be safer with you folks."

My heart goes out to him, 'specially with that being true. And also 'cause a slice of wanting Jones back was so I could get what I wanted.

I sigh and give Jones what I think he needs: assurance. "All mamas lose sleep over their kids. But not all mamas have two schemers like Buck and Clyde. We'll keep ya safe." Sure, they fumble, and luck's been on their side a time or two, but those Barrow brothers are crafty. I can be, too. "I've an idea," I say.

That night, in a rented cabin, I convince the boys we all need darker hair. Fresh starts. And, maybe even a bit of relief for Jones that he won't be running 'round with Clyde's blonde-haired moll. So on goes the product and on go the towels, on all of our heads. We sleep that way, and boy do we sleep, probably the latest in a long while, straight into the afternoon.

Clyde and Jones already had brown hair, so theirs comes out dark as coal. Mine wasn't as dark, but it's still a shock to see a brunette staring back at me in the mirror. Bet Blanche will have a thing or two to say about that when we meet up with them again, starting with how she can't believe she wasn't the one to dye it, her spending all that time in a beauty shop and all.

But as we return to the car and return to the road, putting miles and hours behind us, I've got other things on my mind. Bigger things. Happier things. Like how I haven't bought napkins since before Oak Ridge. And I did the math. It's been two months, nine days since Clyde and I splashed 'round in that tub.

It dawned on me last night.

I was running my fingers through Clyde's hair, stroking the hair color through each strand. We were close, me standing, him in a chair, my body rubbing here and there against Clyde's as I circled him. At one moment, when I was crossing in front of him, he nuzzled his face into my chest, and his hands gave the backs of my thighs a squeeze. It sent a spark of heat right up my legs and into my belly, igniting all the areas in between.

I smirked, leaning closer. I felt his nose press between my breasts and his teeth snap at the fabric of my blouse. My goodness, I wish Jones wasn't there, done up in a towel 'cross the room, cleaning his gun. But it was like something clicked, remembering one of the last times we were alone—and how we made the most of it. How we made a baby.

We made a baby.

I still find it unreal. Just the other day I was wishing I had more to give Clyde, wishing I had more to give myself. And for the past two months, my body's been hard at work, making it possible. God's work, is more like it. No wonder I've been tired and my stomach's been upside down, besides on account of all our criminal activities.

I glance over at my baby's daddy. I got to tell Clyde. I haven't yet. I want to tell him when it's just the two of us, alone with our little bean. He'll be excited. I think he'll be excited. He wants a family, too. This here timeline just wasn't one we discussed. But that doesn't matter, our baby will surely put more wind behind our sails to put acres of land 'round us.

I sigh, a happy sigh. My mind's been replaying it for hours.

Clyde's one eye is narrowed. Maybe it's the setting sun hitting his face, causing him to squint. "Jones," he says. The boy yawns, all the time in the car already wearing on him, I'd guess. "I do believe Bonnie's got something she ain't telling us."

Nope, that ain't a squint, Clyde's narrowing his eye at me in the playful way he does.

Jones laughs. And, I wonder, *Are we going to add another boy to our brood? Or will it be a li'l lady?* Throughout the years, I've had so much practice caring for Little Billie that it'd be like hopping back onto a bike.

Of course, Little Billie ain't so young now. She'd snap at me for still using that nickname. Last I heard, from one of our phone calls on the party line, she's been volunteering at a hospital. It's good for her. I'm glad she's got goals for herself that don't involve a life resembling my own.

Now we've got Jones back, we'll rejoin with Buck and Blanche, and Clyde'll hightail it to that armory. By the time the baby comes, we'll be on the straight and narrow, and folks will forget all the bad stuff we've done. Or at least they won't be able to find us to lead us to the 'chair.' My sins will be between God and me.

We're on our way, fast as our newest Ford can take us. A bridge is up ahead, one I believe will take us from Texas into Oklahoma, where Buck and Blanche are waiting for us.

I do a double take, my eyes skimming over the sign by the bridge. CLOSED, it says, and we're still moving like a bat out of hell.

"Clyde." He senses the urgency in my voice, his head jumping 'round like he missed something vital. He did.

I point at the bridge, at the sign, and scream, "Stop!"

Clyde yanks the wheel, not far before the mouth of the bridge. Just beyond, I catch a glimpse of missing planks. Then we're rumbling off the road. Down. Down a steep embankment, toward a dry riverbed below. I scream.

The world flashes 'round me, and next thing I know, I'm staring back up the bank where we came from, the car facing the wrong way, while we continue to fall.

20

WE CRASHED. WE MUST HAVE. BUT THERE'S ONLY STATIC 'round me, like a radio stuck between stations. And pain, like I've stepped into hell, escorted by the devil himself. I flutter open my eyes. I glimpse a face, all eyebrows and beard. A face I don't recognize. Not Clyde's. My eyes flutter some more. The bearded man is still there.

"Miss?" he says. He pulls on my arm, and I swat at him. He's not Clyde. But I ain't anything more than a rag doll. The devil steals me away.

I wake, and instantly wish I hadn't. I can barely breathe, my chest feeling half its size. My body's on fire, the worst of it in my right leg. Am I burning from the inside out?

I try to sit up, needing to touch the pain, to see it with my own two eyes, but my body won't let me. A hand also pushes me down, gently.

"Shh, child," a woman says.

But I wasn't talking. Was I?

Her face, tan and worn, replaces my view of a cracked white ceiling. A soft glow, emphasizing the sharp planes of her face, flickers from a lamp-light on the bedside table. I'm in a house, wood slotting on the walls. A baby wails. Other voices slip through the walls, too far away for my mind to fully grasp.

"Honey?" I whisper, finishing in my head, *Where's Clyde?*

"The battery, from the car"—the woman shakes her head, her face radiating sympathy with the creases between her eyes—"it exploded and got you good. I only got this to put on the burns." She holds up a tube. I struggle to focus on it; instead I hear myself repeating random words I've just heard.

"This is going to hurt. Is that okay?"

"Okay," I mumble, the motion hurting my jaw. "Honey?"

She says, "The other two fellas you were with are just fine."

Then there's the devil again, beckoning me with a curl of his bony finger.

• • •

I'm in and out of sleep, that much I know. Days pass, they must, from how it turns light to dark, with how the scenario changes from house to car, car to house, and back again. Faces hover over me, with some I recognize—Clyde, Blanche, Buck, Jones—and with some faces I've never seen before.

I hear singing, offbeat but soothing nevertheless. I have moments of clarity, at least I think I do, but they feel more like dreams, almost too flimsy for my mind to hold on to for long.

Like leaving the farmhouse. There was a ruckus, the law showing up. Clyde and Jones got the better of the two men, who ended up in the rear of our car. Then the woman, the one who put the salve on my burns, stood by the farmhouse's door, watching us leave. She reached for the top of the doorframe—for what I don't know—but Jones shouted 'bout her going after a gun. He shot at her. Instinctively. I know it was only his instinct to survive that made him do such a thing. His shot went wide into the doorjamb, but he crumbled in on himself; the woman held a baby in her arms.

A baby.

I push it away, that thought, that word: *baby*.

There are other moments that linger off to the side, a dark cloud that'll smother me if it gets too close.

"Bonn," I hear, from my darkness.

I open my eyes and an angel stares down at me, in the form of my sister. Dark hair, with soft waves. Pale skin. Thin lips.

"Billie?" I whisper. I have to swallow. It feels like my mouth is full of cotton, picked straight from Pistol Pete's land. I wonder how that fool is doing and if he has any new jokes.

"I'm here." Tears fill her eyes, stream down her cheeks.

"You're here?"

Her eyes drift to my legs, to my midsection, to my chest, back to my face. Everywhere she looks throbs and aches, as if an elephant is stretched 'cross me. She nods. "Clyde got me."

I was wondering. I look beyond her, then to either side of my sister, only moving my eyes. "Where is he?"

She sighs and picks up a bowl. "He's close by. He is."

And Little Billie's here. My eyes swell with a new 'round of tears. "You can't be here."

"Of course I—"

"No, I don't want you mixed up in this life."

"I'm not going anywhere," she insists. Billie dips a spoon into the bowl. Her hand shakes as she brings it to me. "Drink it."

I do, the liquid's hot, spicy. Then I roll my head to the right, needing to see something other than my sister's innocent face. I breathe sharply from the pain of moving my stiff neck. The room's nicer than a cabin, but less homey than the farmhouse from before. "We in a motel?"

I turn back, another spoonful of soup waiting for me. I eat, mostly to make my sister happy. She nods 'bout us being in a motel. "In Arkansas." She shakes her head, as if that was a stupid detail to add, then takes a deep breath and spoons me more soup. "I'm so glad you're okay. Mama don't know. Not yet. I've been dressing your wounds, keeping you clean. Clyde brought a doctor to you right away because one side of your chest sunk in. But the doctor said you didn't have any broken ribs that he could tell. He wanted to take you into a hospital but Clyde said no. The doctor wasn't happy, but he grumbled that it'd take time, but you'd heal. You'll heal." She sniffles. The spoon clanks against the bowl. "You're already looking so much better. This here is the first time you called me by name and it's been nearly a week since the accident."

"That long?"

Yet I still feel so tired.

Billie presses her lips together, the bottom one quivering. "I know you only just woke up again, but"—she reaches for a small bottle—"you got to drink some of this, too, before the pain comes back too strong. Morphine. The sleep's good for you."

"No." I ignore the shooting pain in my neck to turn my head away. "You can't be giving that to me. It'll hurt my—"

"Bonn . . ." She squeezes my hand. "You and Clyde can try again, when you're better."

Then, I remember the sticky feeling between my legs. A pain so intense—more than the screaming sensation in my leg, more than the pain I now compartmentalize as coming from my stomach—hits me like a freight train. I don't want to be awake a second longer.

"Give me the drugs."

When I wake, I insist for more, and more. The days lump together, 'til one day I wake to find Clyde bending over my motel bed. He's on his knees, his hands pressed together under his chest, his forehead resting on my "good" leg, the leg the battery acid mostly spared. My other leg is wrapped in bandages, more than my leg, really. From my hip to my toes, those burns make their presence known.

I stretch my fingers, noticing scrapes, scabbed over, on my knuckles. My fingertips barely skim Clyde's hair. He startles, and it breaks my heart to see the red in his eyes, the dark circles underneath, the sheen on his unwashed hair, a new shiny scar marring his face.

"Bonnie," he breathes. "I'm sorry I've been away."

I ain't sure where he's been, or how much time passes between each time I wake and before I'm drugged again, but this man looks like he's been torturing himself plenty.

I smile, or try to at least, with one side of my mouth turning up. It feels stiff, my whole mouth does. And dry. "I reckon you didn't miss much when it comes to my happenings."

Clyde shuffles, still on his knees, and brings a glass of water to my lips.

"Better?" he says. His hand finds the side of my head. "Oh, Bonnie, I was so worried 'bout you. I'm so sorry for missing that sign. The bridge . . ." He clenches, unclenches my bedsheets with his free hand. "Jones, he was mostly okay after he came to. I'm the one who should be in this bed, and I didn't even lose consciousness. I bet God did that on purpose. He kept me awake, let me walk out of that car, so I could see everything I'd done."

"What happened"—I pause—"after the crash?"

"These farmers were out on their porch, and they came running. We got you out of the car." He closes his eyes. "You were burned, bad. Down to the bone in some places. Your jawbone was showing, your chest uneven. My God, Bonnie, I thought I was going to lose you. So many times." He opens his eyes, his breath held. Clyde exhales. "Jack, the man's name was, he tried to carry you, and you went hog wild on him. But we got you inside. His wife was caring for you the best she could with what she had on hand, and Jack went into town to get a doctor. Jones warned me, though, that Jack had seen our guns. When he came back, he didn't come back alone. Jones and I got the jump on them. Guess the whole situation got our lad keyed up 'cause he ended up shooting at the missus, Jack's wife, thinkin' she was going to pull a gun on us."

"I remember that." And I bet the boy's still beating himself up over an impulse that could've taken a life, or two of 'em.

"Surprised you remember; you were barely there. But guess I ain't too surprised, either. You had the brains to call the lad Buck instead of his real name."

That part I don't recall.

"You're a good one, Bonnie, protecting Jones when your own life was the one needing protecting." He licks his lips. "From there, we had you stretched 'cross the coppers' laps in the rear seat. They did good by you, holding your head still. Didn't matter, though, not at first. I was mad, so mad at everything going on that when it came time to let them go, I almost didn't. I wanted to make someone else hurt as badly as you were hurting. But it dawned on me that it should be me, not those men. They didn't do anything wrong. I left 'em tied to a tree."

"I'm glad you didn't hurt 'em." I shift, and I'm in pain, but not like before. The devil's decided to let me be. "Tell me something happy."

Clyde clucks, like he's 'bout to question me or object or say he's got nothin' happy to tell me, but then his hands are 'round mine. "The farm. I reckon you don't remember much of it. The house wasn't grand or anything, didn't even have electricity."

"No electricity?" Now that ain't something I had in mind for our one-day farm.

"Nope. An icebox, though."

"Well, hallelujah for that."

He squeezes my hand. "A porch, too, that stretched right on 'round it. Ya know, for some rocking chairs. All white. The house, the porch, those chairs. They had themselves hogs, cows, and chickens. I put two and two together, figuring they sold milk and eggs to keep themselves afloat. They didn't even rely on the land, only had a small vegetable garden. But it looked like they were doing just fine, tucked away in their own li'l paradise."

I say, "Sounds grand to me." More than grand, considering Clyde will always be without those toes. "That farm is exactly the kind of place we'll have, but maybe with some lights."

He kisses my hand, resting his chin on the spot his lips touched when he's done. "And on that farm, Bonnie, we're going to make a baby." He swallows, his chin pressing into me. "Another one."

I lose my breath. "You knew?"

"I was blind as a bat to it, 'til your body let go of our bairn. But you kept mumbling 'bout him . . ." He turns his head away. "Or her. Then I knew."

"Come here."

Clyde practically crawls closer and rests his head on my chest. It hurts, but the pain Clyde and I share is worse.

"I had to put it into words," he says into my breast. "It ain't a happy one, but I wrote another verse in our song if you want to hear it."

I bite my lip, dragging the words out of myself to say, "Of course I do."

With my eyes closed, I hear him breathe out. Slow. Steady. "It won't sound as good without a guitar so bear with me, Bonnie."

Then, *"Death came for them, out of nowhere, quick as can be . . . It scratched, it clawed, it burned, right down to her bone."*

His voice cracks, but he goes on, his tone raw.

"But that girl's stronger, much stronger, with a fight to survive, you see . . . So, Death took what it could: the life they'd hoped to call their own."

I quit breathing. Clyde looks up at me, tears in his eyes. *"That could break them, if they let it, it'd be easy, it'd be fair. But, ohh"*—he draws out the word, not a second of it steady—*"Oh, oh, oh, they still got each other, forever and always, to hold on to."*

The tears in Clyde's eyes fall. Mine join his. Together, we cry for what could've been, and 'cause, at the end of the day, we're both still here to see another one of those.

21

BLANCHE IS NEXT TO VISIT ME. LATER THAT DAY, THE NEXT morning? I ain't sure, but everything hurts a bit less, my heart included.

Blanche has changed. She's thinner than I remember. Wearing pants?

"You know," she says, not quite trotting into the room. Her gait is slower. Heavier? "That boy ain't the only one who can sing."

"Was that you? When I was sleeping?"

Dear Blanche tried to carry a tune. She kept dropping it, though. I sit up. I can do that now: sit up, even if I do moan, and even if my leg won't fully straighten out. But if the stack of newspapers on the bedside table equates to a number of days, it's been nearly two weeks since I've been out of commission. One of the headlines peeks out.

DESPERADOS TIE KIDNAPPED OFFICERS TO A TREE

So I've heard.

"Girl," Blanche says, and I refocus on her, "you were doing more than sleeping; might as well call it a coma."

"That bad, huh?"

She sighs, gingerly sits down next to my bum leg. "Bonn, you scared me. Really scared me. All of this does. And just when I think things can't get any worse, Buck acts a fool."

"Dare I ask what—"

"The last few weeks have been expensive with us staying in cabins and motels and giving you all those drugs. That stuff doesn't come cheap, Bonn. All our money is almost all gone."

I scrunch one eye. "Sorry?"

She tugs on the ends of her hair. "I know, not like you wanted any of this. But Buck decided to be some hero and rob a grocery store. He took the boy with him. The jamokes got too excited and crashed into a car—a parked one—on their way back here. The law came." She shakes her head, but behind her stiff upper lip, I see Blanche's fear. "Buck and Jones had to shoot their way out. Jones lost the tips of two fingers. And Buck—he shot one of the deputies dead. To make matters worse, their car wasn't going anywhere, so they stole the law's ride."

"Holy hell, is Jones okay? Is Buck?"

"Buck ain't the one who got shot."

"Blanche," I say slowly, and I can't help feeling lousy I took one pill after another, keeping us here longer than we needed to be. "Buck ain't ever killed a man before."

She says, "No, he hasn't."

But that's it, and her expression ain't giving me much to work with. Blanche doesn't look like Blanche. Her hair's dark, maybe darker than mine. Her cheeks are sunk in. And, "Blanche, you're wearing pants."

A snort comes out. "They're riding pants." She lifts a foot. "And boots."

"Did you get a horse?"

"No. And you better not tease me like the boys. Dresses are too hard to keep fit. Grime hides easier on pants. The boots are heavy, though. Harder to run in, which the boys say is all I'm good for after that time . . ."

I nod. We'll leave it at that. Though there's no denying she wanted to leave before. It hurts to think it, but maybe she should've. Maybe she should now. "Blanche, you can go, ya know. I don't want you to leave, but you can."

She laughs, but it ain't a real laugh. "I can't leave Buck, just like you can't leave Clyde. But, there's still hope for Billie."

My head twitches. "What you mean by that?"

"Your sister and Jones have been ogling each other for days. And ever since he lost the tiniest piece of his fingers, she's hardly left his side."

I could wring Blanche's neck for not leading with this news. Of course, she'd talk 'bout herself first and foremost. Seconds pass while I regain my composure. "Where is she?"

Blanche's eyes widen. "You going to go runnin' in there like her mama?"

I shrug, and fight to swing my legs off the motel bed. It's pathetic. I'm only twenty-two years old, and I move like I've got one foot in the grave. My right leg slips free of the sheets, and my eye catches on the mass of bandages.

"Have you seen it?" I ask. "What's under all that?"

"It ain't pretty, Bonn. I won't lie to you. But your face is healing well."

I touch my cheekbone. "My face?"

Blanche slides my hand lower, to my chin. There's an indentation there that wasn't there before. My skin's puckered as if it's been . . . "Stitched?"

She nods. "Your whole chin was busted open, but Billie sewed you back together."

And now my sister is canoodling with a boy who ain't right for her. It's not like Jones ain't sweet as sugar and good-natured. Funny, too. He's a fine boy, someone I'm pleased to have with Clyde and me. But the thought of Billie sitting in a jail cell, trying to figure out if she should follow her head or her heart, well, that would wreck me. Mostly 'cause that girl's a lot like me. Heart always wins.

"Help me up." I reach for Blanche. She pulls my arm, straightening it, but my leg won't do the same. I stare at it, like somehow my head is getting back at me for the thoughts I just had, and if I try a little harder, the directions I'm silently shouting will make it all the way down to my leg. But it stays crooked. Not bent, not like I'm sitting in a chair, but my leg's curved ever so slightly, like a sickle.

Neither of us know what to do to get me on my feet—I certainly don't—so we're stuck in between me standing and sitting.

Clyde walks into the room, and Blanche exhales.

I sink back into the bed, quickly rearranging the sheet to cover proof of the fact I ain't the same girl I was before the crash. That girl could stand on her own two feet.

Clyde's so intent at looking at my face, I can tell it's forced. Before he can say a thing, there's a parade into my motel room: Buck, Billie, then Jones on her heels.

"Gang's all here," Blanche says dryly.

Buck hooks an arm 'round her waist, kissing her temple. "Don't sound so enthused, baby."

I ask, "What's wrong?"

"We got to head out," Clyde says, "But with the extra heat on us . . ." It goes unspoken he's referring to Buck taking out that deputy, and his tone broadcasts he ain't pleased with his brother 'bout it. "Well, we can't risk staying here any longer or getting a cabin or anything where we got to check in."

That leaves sleeping under the stars, and I'm not even partly a fan of the woods. I sigh. "Can someone get me a smoke?" I ask the room.

They all leave. Billie's the one who comes back with a cigarette, along with a change of clothes.

She pulls my dress over my head. I keep my eyes closed, not wanting to see any parts of my body.

"Aren't you scared?" I hear. "Being around someone like Clyde?"

Scared? No. "He'd never hurt me." Not like Roy did, deserting me, berating me, deceiving me. I fell for Clyde with open eyes.

"Still"—Billie yanks a new dress over my head—"Clyde seems capable of hurting others plenty well."

I open my eyes to see Billie's doe-like ones. "Maybe it doesn't scare me 'cause I know the real him."

I think, *I knew him before all this.* I knew the man he was, the man he wanted to be. Commander Clyde Barrow of the United States Navy—that's who. Someone could easily think the *USN* letters inked on his upper arm are an ex-girlfriend's initials. Lord knows I've got Roy's name on my upper thigh. But those letters meant something bigger to Clyde.

"Clyde tried," I tell Billie. I think of how Dallas also rejected him after he was paroled. "He tried more than once. But life keeps dealing him a different hand. I'm not making excuses. It's wrong. Don't think I don't know that, Billie. But . . ."

She gently takes a brush to my hair. "But what?"

"But I'm in this with Clyde, no matter what. That makes me horrible, I know. You, though, Billie. You don't need to be like me. I want you to stay away from Jones, you hear?"

She startles, no longer brushing my hair. My sister apparently didn't know I knew 'bout their budding love affair.

"Billie," I say. "Jones is a nice boy, he is, but isn't there somebody at home more to your liking?"

She doesn't answer. Instead, Billie finishes with my hair, with not as much care as before. I let the topic of Jones go, for the time being.

• • •

The girls and I are stretched out on blankets. Being in the woods is bad enough, and now it's nighttime. I shudder.

When we got to our new makeshift campsite, Clyde carrying me through the trees, he set me down, then took extra care to clear the ground of any sticks or pine cones. He spread out sheets for me to lie on, ones he took from the motel. When he did, though—when he took those sheets—he dug into his pockets and left some bills behind.

That wasn't completely out of character. He's given money to our hostages before we've set them loose. But then, it was only enough to make a point-to-point phone call. This time, Clyde left behind a wad of bills, and based on my conversation with Blanche, I don't get the sense we have much to spare. I think Clyde's conscience is chasing him 'bout what happened to me—and to our baby.

He's off with the boys now, retrieving a few rifles they stashed somewhere and maybe trying to add to our piggy bank. Then it's back on the road.

"Tonight," Clyde said, "we need to put some distance between us and this town."

The sun left shortly after they did, though heat still lingers in the air. The humidity certainly doesn't make it easier to breathe. I'm uncomfortable all over, including a bladder that's too full. It'll have to stay that way; I ain't going to ask Billie or Blanche to carry me away from our camp and into the unknown. There's barely any moon in the sky, and the trees are thick. I reckon that's why Clyde chose this spot, those trees doing their job to keep us hidden, but it's dark. Too dark and—

"You hear that?" I whisper.

Billie's only a few feet away and she's barely more than an obscure bump on the ground. Blanche is on her other side, another bump in the night. "I don't hear anything," Billie says.

I say, "I do. Something's slithering."

"A snake, I'd guess." Blanche. "Or a lizard, one of those legless ones. Not sure why they don't just call it a snake and be done with it."

"'Cause it ain't a snake," I counter.

I can imagine Blanche shrugging.

"If it's a lizard, it's a lizard," I add, as if this distinction truly matters.

"Fine," Blanche says, drawing out the word. "It's a lizard. Unless it really was a snake."

Billie chuckles. "Both of you have always been so pigheaded."

Blanche says, "I prefer *headstrong*."

It's quiet, besides a faint rustling that I'm resolute 'bout ignoring, 'til Billie says, "Bonn, when's the last time you've sung?"

That came out of nowhere, and I'm immediately defensive. "What kind of question is that?"

'Cause I know it's been months—since the Oak Ridge apartment, maybe—and that ain't like me.

"Not sure how to word that question differently," Billie says.

I scrunch my nose, twist my lips back and forth, annoyed. It's hard to put into words exactly why my feathers are ruffled, but I know I don't like my younger sister seeing me as a different version of myself. And I ain't talking 'bout my body being disfigured, though that's a load of horse dung, too. But it's like Billie recognized, at the drop of a hat, that my soul's scarred. She hasn't even seen me awake long enough for me to sing, yet she knew, and that knowledge has been festering on her mind enough to ask me 'bout it.

It doesn't help that Blanche's shape now appears propped up, like she's waiting to hear what I've got to say as well.

But I'm afraid I don't have an answer for them, or for myself, besides not having a reason for wanting to sing.

Billie's voice almost startles me. "Remember," she says, softer this time, "when we used to fish down at the creek?"

I swallow a lump in my throat, already nostalgic, only a few words into her story, for the picture Billie's 'bout to paint. "Most Saturdays we'd go."

"When we were younger, yeah, life was slower then. But every time we went, it felt like the sun was shining, the birds were chirping, but you, Bonn, you were always shining the brightest and chirping the loudest."

I smile. "I don't remember you liking my songs at the time. You used to pick up your skirt and your pole and wade to the other side of the creek."

She laughs. "You were scaring away all my fish. And, I'll be honest, your shadow couldn't reach all the way 'cross the water. It wasn't always easy having you as an older sister. The perfect grades. The perfect boyfriend—well, at the time, before Roy turned sour. The perfect voice."

"The perfect best friend," Blanche says.

Billie laughs again.

"Quiet, child."

But I can tell, even without seeing Blanche's face, she's smiling. I am, too, at how Billie used to see me. I bite my lip, hard. The sharp pain adds to the dull ache in my leg. Too bad the smile can't last, not with all the "what could have beens" snaking their way into my head. Yet I'm still here. After all the crashes life has thrown at me, I've always found a way to pick myself up. I like the pain, both sharp and dull. It's something undeniable. I can still feel, which means there's still hope for me. So maybe, just maybe . . .

"I'll sing again one day."

"I hope so," Billie says.

22

SILENCE HANGS IN THE AIR AFTER BILLIE'S STORY OF OUR childhood. The hours tick by, well beyond midnight, or at least it feels that way. With clouds snuffing out the moon, the only source of light is the slight flicker of lightning bugs who have joined us in the night. Finally, the boys return, and we can get on with things. Whatever and wherever that may be, though, I know it can't be with Billie tagging along.

"Clyde," I say, "will ya help me?"

He scoops me into his arms and walks us, almost blindly, a distance away. He holds me in position so I can do my business, and I do my best for that business not to splatter us both.

Clyde says, "There's nothin' we can't share, is there?"

I chuckle and nestle my head into his neck as he carries me back to the gang, using their soft voices as a guide, taking care so we don't catch any branches.

"Thank you for getting Billie to take care of me. Never did thank you for that."

"But it's time for her to go home," he states, not a question.

"Blanche says she's been getting cozy with Jones."

Twigs break under his feet. "Yeah, I've been seeing them exchange sweetness."

"I just don't want her ending up like me, that's all."

With his next step, he dips lower to one side, almost as if my words caught him off guard. I squeeze my eyes shut, feeling bad, but Clyde's gait returns to normal and he doesn't respond. I open my eyes, unable to read his features in the dark.

Not far off, there's a sudden glow. I tense 'til I realize it's the interior light from the car. Blanche and Billie are folding our sheets and packing the car. Buck and Jones are straightening the guns to make room for us.

Clyde stops walking and lowers his voice. "Do you regret this life with me? I know there's a lot we could've done without . . . But you and me, do you wish you could turn back time and gone a different way in life?"

There are a lot—heaps—that I wish would've gone differently so far in my life. I probably won't ever have the chance to stand in front of my own classroom or climb on a stage again, the heat of the spotlight on my face. Those are big hits to the dreams I've had for myself.

But Clyde . . . do I wish for a life without him? Do I wish I got on that bus in Kaufman? Never. I grab his chin, focusing on the outline of his face. It's all I can see of him, but it's enough. I know the curves of his face and what those lines mean. Right now, his chin protrudes, like he's got his lower lip sucked in.

"Clyde Barrow, there's no one I'd rather pee with."

He laughs, exactly my intention. We need to do more of that if we ever want a shot at holding on to who we really are.

"Ya know, Bonnie?" he says, and shifts my weight in his arms.

We're still not walking, still standing still. I don't think either of us is quite ready to rejoin the group. So I lay my head back against his chest, the night all 'round us no longer scary when I've got Clyde's arms under me.

"Yeah?"

"After the crash and leaving the farm, we found a schoolhouse. It was empty, being it was a Saturday. I don't reckon you remember any of this, but I stretched you out on the desk at the front of the room. It was a big ol' one. Blanche and Buck stayed with you while the lad and I found a doctor to bring to ya. You should've seen the looks the whitehead gave me. Jones thought he was going to turn my own gun against me 'cause I wouldn't take you to a hospital. But the doctor did good by you, fixing you up the best he could." Clyde sighs. "Sorry, I'm rambling. What I want to say, Bonnie, is how it dawned on me—with you at the front of that classroom—how it's somewhere you've always wanted to be. And there you were, 'cept you didn't even know it. And I wish you had a different reason for being there. I wish *I* had put you there for another reason. But, Bonnie, I can't read."

I react, my head shifting, but I don't lift it from his chest. "I've seen you read maps."

"That's learning and remembering how lines fit together. Words," he says. "I can recognize certain ones. My name. Other words I've seen and heard plenty of times. But on that godforsaken road sign, *Closed* wasn't one of 'em."

His lips graze the top of my head, and I know this boy well enough to know his eyes are closed as he punishes himself.

"It's okay," I say. It is. But I still got to know. "Why didn't you ever learn to read?"

"I stopped going to school after I got sick. It was too hard when I had trouble hearing. I got behind, and it took a toll on my ego, I guess you could say. But I want to learn, and Bonnie, I was hoping you could teach me."

My chest warms. "I'd like that."

He exhales. "And I'd like to get you on that land. I got ahold of Pretty Boy, and he suggested an armory that's ripe for the picking. Would give us plenty to bust open the prison. I need that, to make it right after all I've made wrong recently."

He needs it, that's plain to see. "All right, but not with Billie 'round."

"We'll get her home," he says, "Then . . ."

I nod. Farm Number One.

We rejoin the others, and soon our little car is cramped with the six of us. We begin zigging and zagging our way on back roads toward Texas, so I can put Billie on a bus home. We decide on the town of Sherman, it being close but not too close to Dallas.

The moving is slow. The mountain terrain wreaks havoc on our tires, giving us one flat after another. We stop to rob. We stop to eat. I shift uncomfortably from my wounds. We stop to put ointment on my leg, and I get a good look at it for the first time. I gag, while the others look away, giving me a moment to come to terms with the large divots in my skin, shiny now, with fresh skin growing over where the battery acid had eaten away my flesh and bone.

I put my dark hose back on as fast as I can, the ointment soaking through. Maybe it'd be easier to wear riding habits like Blanche, but I don't want to give up my dresses and skirts.

Sometimes we camp in the forest in the afternoon, then drive at night. Sometimes we sleep at night and drive when the sun is blazing, now nearly July. There are times the boys rob in the thick of things, middle of the day, a time where they aren't noticed amongst the crowds. Other times, they slip in under the cover of night like cat burglars. Clyde likes to mix it up, be unpredictable.

I miss some of it, the drugs forcing my eyes closed for hours at a time.

Along the way, between doses, I decide there's no time better than the present to give Clyde lessons. His head whips toward me, all of us bracing when the wheel turns. He's embarrassed. But I shush him. The way I see it, he shouldn't be embarrassed to not know something he wasn't ever taught.

I smirk, too, when I get under way with my teaching and see Jones and Buck, their heads poking out from the rear seat, taking note of what I'm saying. It seems Blanche, Billie, and I are the only educated people in our one-car schoolhouse. Imagine that, in a world dominated by men.

One day, Clyde brings me a newspaper so I can spell out common words as I go. It's dated a few days ago. I shake open a page, start skimming aloud, then clamp my mouth shut before I can say a word.

ONE HALF OF CHRISTMAS DAY KILLERS IN JAIL

I read the article as fast as my heavy eyes will allow, confused how one of the killers is locked up when both of 'em are in this car.

A convict named Frank Hardy, a name I vaguely recognize, was fingered for a robbery in Missouri. That got his photo in the system. Later, mug shots were pulled into a lineup, so Johnson's mother could point to Clyde's accomplice. She fingered Frank. Which means Jones has never been implicated in anything we've done. I should tell him as much—right now. Jones could easily be a free man. Free, at least in the sense he doesn't have any murders to his name.

But if I do, he might get on that bus with Billie.

I can't have that. That boy has a piece of my heart, but he also has the taste of *fugitive* on his tongue. He'll find his way to trouble again. He'll take Billie with him.

"What is it?" Billie says, between Clyde and me on the front bench seat, as far from Jones as I could get her in our car.

I flip to a new page. "Nothin'. Brain's foggy, moving a bit slow." I rub my eyes, then read the next headline. "'SHARKEY LOSES TITLE IN SIXTH-ROUND KNOCKOUT TO CARNERA.'"

"What?" Buck says. "No way."

Clyde shrugs. "No surprise there."

While the boys hem and haw 'bout the boxing match, I hem and haw with my conscience 'bout keeping the first headline to myself. As much as I like having Billie close by, I let out a sigh of relief when it's time to let her go. I feel like I'm saving her from ever having to say, *I'm in this with Jones, no matter what*, when it comes to hurting other people.

I get out of the car at the bus stop and hop like a drunk rabbit to my sister. The rest of our gang stays in the car, giving us privacy.

"Don't tell Mama," I say. My new disability goes unspoken—even now, as I'm standing on one leg—but for me that plea for silence can apply to many a things.

Billie braces both my arms, under my elbows. "I wouldn't tell Mama, even if you didn't ask me not to. She paces the house at night, ya know, wondering if you're okay."

"I will be," I say. "You can tell her that."

Billie nods. Her chest rises, but doesn't fall again for a second or two. "Bonn, I want to see you again."

Suddenly, my throat is too thick to swallow, but I force the motion, and my emotions, down. This time, she's the one with an unspoken message: *Don't die on me.*

I wipe the corners of my eyes with the heel of my hand. It's one thing for me to have those fears, but I can't let them find their way to my little sister and to my mama. With the bus rumbling nearby, I give her the tightest hug I can muster, a silent thank-you for loving me despite how black my heart's become, then climb back into the car.

I turn my head away as Jones slinks from the car to say his good-bye. When he's back, when we're moving again, I keep my eyes off the rearview mirror so I don't see his face.

Guilt hits me from every angle, including how Jones could also be on that bus, headed home. 'Cept he's headed with us to Oklahoma, to an armory on a prim and proper university campus.

But before the boys go near the school, Blanche insists they need some cleaning up. She sits on the car's hood, cross-legged, scissors in hand. She snips at Jones's hair. The boy's still standing at the front of the car when Blanche yells, "Next." Buck takes his spot in the hot seat.

Through the windshield, I watch her work. I got the passenger door wide open, letting in the sticky air.

Her fingers move quickly, and I'm fearful for the tips of Buck's ears. At least with Clyde's, with how they stick out, they're easy to spot. He's pacing, waiting for his turn. I know he wants to get this charade over with so we aren't sitting here on the side of the road. Anyone could happen by, think we're stranded, and offer their help.

"Next!" Blanche calls. It's Clyde's turn.

If all goes according to plan, the boys will come back with a large haul of guns to bust open the prison. Then, we'll rob a big ol' bank to get our land. I'll tell Jones the truth after that, giving him the choice to stretch out on our land or go on home.

Clyde, now with his hair freshly cut, lifts me from the passenger seat and takes me past the tree line. I run my hand over his shorter hair. There's something addictive 'bout the feel of a man's hair right above the nape of his neck after it's been cut. I could run my hand back and forth 'til the cows come home.

Or 'til he places me on a blanket that Jones has out for me on the ground. Clyde hands me a sedative to dull that ache in my leg, and also my nerves. Then, he taps the underside of my chin, forcing me to meet his eyes. Clyde kisses me, short and sweet, an "I'll see you later" kiss.

It's another dark night, but Blanche and I don't risk talking too loud or even lighting cigarettes for fear of someone seeing the glowing tips. Soon, I'm drowsy, but despite the sedative, I can't fully fall asleep. I must, for short stretches of time, but then my eyes shoot open, blurry, with my head full of fuzzy uncertainties. The last time I wake, night still hovers over us, but the sky's beginning to glow red. Blanche's eyes are rimmed in a similar color.

She shakes me, her fingernails digging into my arm. Headlights peek through the trees.

"Is it them?" she whispers.

Voices float through the night, ones we recognize, and we both audibly exhale.

"Sorry, baby," Buck says, greeting Blanche, "but it ain't going to be a comfy ride from here."

Neither Blanche nor I know what he's talking 'bout 'til we get a glimpse of the backseat. Even in the lingering darkness, it's clear the seat is piled high.

Clyde laughs, patting Jones on the back. "There are actually so many guns I ain't sure what to do with 'em all." Then he says to me, "Did you muster any shut-eye?"

I rub the back of my neck, feeling a bit overwhelmed. "A li'l. How we all going to fit in the car?"

Buck puffs on a cigarette. "What it matter to you, Bonn, you'll be up front like always."

I scrunch my brows; I can't tell by his voice if he's cross or not, and I wonder if I missed something while the boys were gone. Must've 'cause Clyde moves fast, knocking the cigarette from Buck's hand. "Why ya got to be like that?" He stomps on the cigarette. "Let's go."

No one says anything. Based on Buck's scowl, Clyde's reaction left a sour taste in his mouth. After we've put a few miles behind us, Blanche is the first to speak, propped up on the guns next to Buck, the top of her head brushing the top of the car. "None of these are loaded, right? I ain't going to blast a hole in my derriere if I move?"

Between Clyde and me, Jones lets out a soft chuckle, his laughter growing when Clyde laughs, too. Buck doesn't. Not this time.

We make it to Iowa, far enough north where the temperature drops by a few merciful degrees. We make camp along a river, and while all Blanche and I want to do is sleep, the boys are eager to try out their new toys. Clyde assures us we're off somewhere remote, where no one will hear their gunshots. And when Blanche starts to complain, Buck is the one to quiet her, taking his brother's side. Those Barrow brothers can be hot and cold.

Tired of sitting, I'm simply happy to lie flat. I ain't happy, however, that each blast, followed by one of the boys' hoots or hollers, doesn't allow for much sleep. Neither do the mosquitos, who sure have a taste for my blood.

The day's excitement comes when Clyde's automatic rifle somehow gets stuck, firing bullets nonstop. The thing won't stop, not 'til he throws it in the river. Blanche is keyed up after that, convinced someone had to have heard the prolonged noise or noticed how every bird in a mile radius of us seemed to take flight all at once. She offers to keep watch that night, and the next two, while we wait to see if the headlines link us with the armory. I'm not sure how she stays awake when tiredness makes my eyes burn all day long.

"Rubbing alcohol," she tells me. "I dab it on my face. The sting and the smell keeps me awake."

I scratch a mosquito bite on my arm. "That's horrible, Blanche."

She shrugs. She's been doing a lot of that lately, shrugging, in between her scathing remarks 'bout one thing or another.

The fish is undercooked.

Buck's the one with brains, not Clyde.

And about me, how she has to pick up my slack.

If Clyde lets Blanche get to him, it doesn't show. I wish it didn't get to me. I wish Blanche and I were the same girls we once were, reading *Photoplay* magazine in my room.

I wish Clyde and me were the way we once were, too. We haven't had a repeat of Oak Ridge, after everything unraveled. For a while, I thought it was me—my injury and Clyde being careful how he touched me. But no, it must be the prison farm and the memories from there—ones he's got to put behind him.

On our third day by the lake, Clyde walks up to my blanket, where I'm struggling with writing a new poem, and he asks me, "What do you see?"

I scan the trees—so many trees, trees I've grown so sick of hiding behind—and the lake, where Buck, Blanche, and Jones are scrubbing their spare set of clothes.

"Sorry, Clyde, I ain't in the mood for riddles."

If Clyde's deterred by my response, he doesn't show it. Instead, he stands there in his suit and loosely knotted tie, his hands in his coat pockets, and says, "Boom." Quick as a rattler, a shotgun appears from under his coat. He's grinning like a goon. "That was fast, wasn't it?"

Despite it all, this boy has a way of making me smile. "Built yourself a li'l contraption, did ya now?"

"Sure did, and look here. I sawed off the end to make her shorter." Clyde flips the gun back under his jacket. "Easier to conceal. Then, you see, I cut a band from a car-tire tube and attached it to the cut-off stock." Animated as a clown, he shakes off his jacket, slips his arm through the band, then puts his coat back on, hiding the gun. His hand goes in his pocket, where he pats it. "I sliced my pocket open, so I'm touching the gun right now. I can hold it against my hip. Then, you see, when I snatch my arm up, the band releases, and I'm ready to fire." Clyde's smile drops a hair. "Bonnie, why you laughing at me?"

"I ain't," I say, but I am, inside, and Clyde can tell without me making any noise. I can't help it, though, Clyde's so gosh darn proud of his invention.

It dawns on me, it's a deadly one, but that ain't something I can get held up on. Not now, not after all we've done.

Finally, Clyde's convinced no one's looking for us as a result of the armory—only all the other places we've robbed—and we leave our makeshift camp behind to drive south.

I never thought I'd be so eager to bust a bunch of fellas I don't know out of jail. I apply fresh makeup, shake out the wrinkles of my dress, and put a tam hat on my head.

Before leaving, Clyde slapped a new license plate on our stolen car, one he found in a junkyard, and threw the one we've been using for the past week or so in the lake. It should keep heads from turning our way, at least for a little while, and Clyde drives us straight down the United States. As night falls, the lights of Kansas City twinkle in the distance.

Clyde blinks, yawns, noticeably so. "How's everyone feel 'bout sleeping in a real bed tonight?"

I perk up. We all do, 'cept for Buck. Blanche perks the most and says, "I won't say no to that, long as Buck and I get our own cabin."

"I don't like it," Buck says.

Blanche huffs. "Excuse me?"

"No, baby, not that. Clyde, this ain't smart. Kansas City is a hotbed for people like us. There's got to be eyes everywhere."

"That's right. There are eyes everywhere, not only in Kansas City."

"Think 'bout it," Buck says, "Stop now and you'll have hours to go tomorrow, ya know. Go hours now, and we'll be a hop from the farm. I'll drive if you can't."

"Neither of us," Clyde growls, "are driving anymore tonight."

Buck throws up a hand. "Clyde, come on, what ya doing?"

I can't help wondering it, too; Clyde's normally so careful, but I also don't like how Buck's going after him. It's enough to raise my hackles in

Clyde's defense. "Listen," I say. "I ain't in the mood to hear you two bicker. If Clyde's tired, we'll stop."

"What's going to stop is our luck," Buck says, his head shaking slowly. "It ain't going to last forever."

"It'll last one more night, all right?" Clyde says. And the way he says it, it's as if he warns *I dare you to keep fighting with me 'bout this.*

Of course, Buck, being a stubborn Barrow, does. "Someday, Clyde, you're going to meet someone who won't give you a chance to fire a shot, ya know?"

Buck's remark hangs in the air. It stays there, thick and heavy, as Clyde locates a tourist camp. We pass a place with two cabins, the brick façade darker in the night. Two attached garage doors separate the two cabins, the white doors reflecting the moonlight. And up top, running the length of one cabin, over the garages, and onto the top of the other cabin, is a white decorative fence.

"Look at that," Clyde whispers to me, leaning past Jones, "I've gone and given you a white picket fence."

I smile, but I'm distracted; behind us, Blanche and Buck are doing their own whispering. I can't be sure all they're saying, but I do hear Buck promise they'll get their own car as soon as possible. I won't put a stink up over that. Distance would do us some good, beyond tonight's cabins.

Clyde drives past the cabins, then turns down a side street. "I'm going to need Jones and Blanche to switch places. I want 'em to see Blanche during check-in since she'll be getting our food in the morning. And brother dear, would you mind covering yourself and Jones with blankets?"

I keep quiet. I don't even look in the mirror to see Buck's reaction. I can only imagine he's seething 'bout lying with another man on top of a pile of guns, suffocating under a layer of wool.

The next few minutes go without a hitch, and after we've paid our four dollars and we're all checked in, Clyde tucks our car into the garage for the night. Once I'm deposited into our cabin, I hop to the bed. I let out a soft moan as I fall onto it. I'm still nuzzling into the mattress as Clyde and Jones bring in armfuls of guns from the car to our bathtub. We nearly fill the thing. And here I was looking forward to soaking in something other than a river or lake or pond.

In the morning, after a night of blissful, sedative-induced sleep, I contemplate knocking on Blanche's door to use theirs, but she's knocking on ours first.

"Buck wants to know if you all want any food."

Clyde uncrosses his legs, sets aside a newspaper. He's been antsy so far this morning, mumbling and pacing, so I busied him with underlining words he recognized and circling ones he still needs to learn. "My brother couldn't come over here and ask us that himself?"

"It's too early for all that," I say, letting my eyes fall on everyone in the small living room, even Jones at the table with his deck of cards, in case he decides to chime in. Though he doesn't. Ever since my sister left, he's been quieter than usual. But now's not the time to dwell on that. "Chicken," I say. "You can't go wrong with chicken. Get us some of that to cook up."

On the way out of our cabin, Blanche pauses; she notices the newspaper covering our windows, even the small pane on the door. She licks her lips, as if she's got something to say 'bout it, but only goes on her way.

It ain't long before she's back. Blanche gets to cooking, but the chicken's not the only thing heating up.

"I don't like being here. Buck is right: too many eyes. And those eyes have tongues and brains. Found out the man who jotted down our license number last night ain't here anymore. He's gone into town."

"For what?" Clyde says, his weight forward.

Blanche uses her fingers to flip the chicken, shaking 'em after to relieve the heat. "Don't know. But I do know it was extra quiet when I was in that store, like everyone's words dried up. The girl helping me didn't talk at first either. She just stared at me like I was a goddamn ghost. Then she turned on the charm. Almost too nice, ya know? She even called me *deary*. And you three, you ain't helping matters with all the shades drawn *with* newspaper on top of that. I think we should go, now. Thought you were hell-bent on getting to that prison anyway."

I listen for his response, curious myself.

He only says, "Are you done?"

Blanche grinds her teeth. "Chicken is."

Clyde says, "We ain't leaving yet. The prison ain't going anywhere." His nose twitches at his own mention of the farm, and it shakes loose a thought, one made stronger by the careless way Clyde's been acting: He's putting off the farm. It ain't like I can blame him for dragging his feet. Ya can want something badly but be afraid of the emotions it stirs up, 'specially after working for it for so long.

He says, "Jones and I will go into town and get a feel."

"And," I improvise to give him the time he needs, "I'm out of medicine. Could you get me some more?"

Clyde's eyes flick to me, knowing full well I ain't out. I keep my face blank.

Blanche huffs and turns on her heel.

"Wait," Clyde says. His voice softens. "Will you sit out front, Blanche, and keep an eye on things?"

He asks 'cause of me, 'cause I'm stuck inside, unable to walk. And even if Buck ain't here at the moment, if Blanche hollers 'bout something, Buck will come running—to protect me.

Clyde and Jones head out, and Blanche makes herself comfortable on a swing out front, where she's got a view of the restaurant 'cross the street and the filling station and café down the road. I peel back a corner of newspaper from the door to catch a glimpse of her. In between bites of chicken, she's writing, not something she does much of, and I'm more than a little curious to know what's making its way from her head to that paper. I'd do some writing of my own, but I don't see another pen lying 'round. I'd do some reading, too, if there was a novel to be found.

Hours later, when I'm bored as sin, the boys return. Clyde insists it's safe to stay another night before heading to Eastham. Even I got to bite my tongue, but I don't want to put Clyde on the spot. I can only imagine the reaction that got from both Buck and Blanche next door. Their voices seep through the walls, not intelligible, but they probably don't mean for us to overhear.

As night falls, I get a feeling deep in my stomach, one that causes me to slip out of bed, crawl past Jones on the couch, turn off the floor lamp we kept on in the living room, as not to illuminate myself, and peel back that newspaper again.

'Cross the street, the light from a restaurant clear-as-day shows people standing by their cars, pointing directly our way.

I half crawl, half jump to the bedroom, fear jabbing at me. "Clyde."

A knocking noise, over at Blanche and Buck's cabin, is louder than my whisper.

I hold a finger to my lips as Clyde stirs, and count the beats of my heart. By eight, Blanche's voice is muffled, but it's there, responding to that knock.

Then, loud and clear, as if Blanche also wants us to hear, she says, "What do you want?" Few seconds later . . . "Wait 'til I get my clothes on and I will come out."

Clyde and I exchange nervous glances as he shoves one leg, then the other through his trousers. His shirt is halfway over his head, an outline of his face against the cotton, when there's a gunshot. My head whips toward Blanche and Buck's cabin, the shot sounding as if it came from there. From Buck; Blanche wouldn't ever touch a gun.

Another shot sounds, this time from outside.

Then there's a volley. The sounds overlap, and my heart seizes, praying those bullets aren't anywhere close to finding Blanche or Buck.

Clyde pulls his sawed-off shotgun from under the bed and barrels out of the room, telling me to get dressed. I can't move. Clyde and Jones thump 'round the living room. Glass breaks. Shots are fired.

It's all too similar to last time. But we got away. We'll get away now. The firing stops, but a horn blasts. Nonstop. Last time, I fled in a nightgown. With shaking hands, I change into a dress. I put on shoes, and realize I forgot to put my stockings on first. Suddenly, it feels like the cabin is shaking, and I splay my fingers on the bedspread.

Clyde yells, barely heard over the horn, "They're driving into the garage door."

I fist my hands, clenching the sheets, and pray this is all a bad dream. I'm half on, half off the bed, an invalid. A hindrance. That feeling only intensifies as Clyde takes me in his arms and carries me. My stockings dangle from my hand.

"They're retreating," Clyde says into my ear. "I got 'em good."

With both hands on me, he doesn't have any left for a gun, and even though he *got 'em good,* I'm still worried he'll be exposed. Then I feel the gun shaft pressing against my ribs, and I know Clyde's wearing it, hiding it beneath his coat. That gives me an ounce of relief. He could drop me and have it out in a heartbeat, if he needs to.

I dare ask, "Buck? Blanche?"

"We'll all be fine," he insists.

Clyde kicks open the front door. I wait for gunfire, wracking our bodies, but it doesn't come. Arms tight 'round me, Clyde hobbles to the now-broken-down garage door and inside. Blanche and Buck's cabin is on the other side, but there's no sign of 'em. After another few rapid breaths, I'm in the passenger seat, Clyde's lips on my forehead.

He straightens and screams, "Buck! Let's go!"

But it's not as if he'll hear him. I barely can over the horn. Earlier, Clyde's bullet must've hit it 'cause it's stuck, blaring. I cover my ears and watch as Clyde whips free his gun. His posture is fierce, one foot in front of the other, and he scans the night for any movement.

He hollers, "Buck! I've got you covered!"

Jones scurries into the backseat, then reaches forward to start our car—something I should've thought to do. There's a spark of light from a gun, then another. Clyde's return fire drowns out the horn. Then his head ticks to the left, toward where I pray Blanche and Buck will appear any second. Clyde's mouth opens, as if he's screaming. His gun drops, and my heart drops along with it.

Clyde wouldn't ever put down his gun unless it's for something more important than him dying. He disappears off to the left. He returns, dragging Buck's body.

Buck ain't moving. My stomach rolls at the blood pouring from his head, half his face dark and shiny.

Blanche is beside herself, pulling her hair, wailing, the noise drowned out by that damn horn, by the gunshots still firing at the people I love most in this world. It makes looking at Blanche even more heartbreaking as she reacts to the sight of the man she loves with blood pouring from his head.

Right when I expect her to crumple to the ground, she hurries to the rear door, rips it open, and climbs inside. Blanche pats her lap insistently, 'til Clyde gives her an unconscious Buck.

Next thing I know, Clyde's behind the wheel, his foot digging into the pedal. A hail of bullets are fired at us, hitting the doors, the hood, the windows. We all duck our heads. We all pray; I know we do, each and every one of us, even Blanche. I hope God hears her prayers the loudest.

THE FIRING HAS STOPPED. HEADLIGHTS DON'T TRAIL US, NOT right now, at least. Half-turned in the front seat, I see the front and back of our ravaged car. Blanche holds Buck as close to her as humanly possible. Her head is drooped. Her short hair, blowing in the breeze through the shattered window, masks both their faces. The little bit of Buck's skin that's showing on his hands and forearms is paler than usual. Too pale, lit up in the darkness. Blanche ain't crying. She's not moving. She ain't doing a thing.

"Blanche," I say sharply.

She doesn't react to her name. In her lap, Buck's body looks broken. He's bent, twisted, to fit all six foot of him in half the rear seat. On the other side of Blanche, Jones keeps swallowing, as if to keep his chicken dinner down.

"Tell me . . ." Clyde begins. Even in the dark, I can't miss how his knuckles threaten to break through his skin with how tight he grips the steering wheel. "Tell me he's alive."

I tap my foot, my fingers. "Blanche!"

Her head snaps up.

I gasp. "Your eye." Dark blood streams from it. Dark blood is pooled 'round Buck's head, soaking into Blanche's pants.

"Shut it," Blanche growls. "I can't hear him breathing with you two talking."

Breathing. She said the word *breathing*. I squeeze Clyde's arm, his shirt stained from his brother's gunshot wound. "He's alive." I lower my voice to say, "But they're both bleeding bad, we got to pull over."

Emotionless, Clyde says, "We got a flat anyway."

When the car stops, Buck stirs, as if his body instinctively knows we've arrived someplace. Blanche cries out, happy his eyes are fluttering.

"Baby," he whispers. "I need air."

Blanche moves her feet, blood audibly sloshing. A horrible noise. Somehow the sound is worse than Buck's moans as he's lifted out of the car and steadied on the running board. Clyde holds him there with one hand pushing on his shoulder to keep him upright. His other hand grips his chin. "Jones," he says. "Light a match. Hold it here."

I can't look at the boys examine Buck's head. Blanche paces outside the car, wiping at her eye.

"Come here," I say to her. I bunch the bottom of my dress, exposing myself, to reach her face with the fabric. Up close, I gasp when I see the glass there—in her eye. I do my best to dab each shard away, turning her head ever so slightly 'til the glass reflects the glow of the moon. "Does it hurt?"

"I'm numb."

"Yeah." It's all I can say.

"I got to get us back on the road, cross state lines," Clyde mumbles. Jones curses, shakes out his hand, lights a new match. "Iowa is only 'bout an hour or so north."

But will that help us? We're wanted in Iowa, too. Maybe for different reasons, but wanted all the same. At this point, is there a state 'round here where there ain't a price on our heads?

Clyde and Jones fix the flat. Progress is slow. Buck's in and out of consciousness, saying things that don't make sense. We stop outside a drugstore, and Jones runs in for a slew of supplies—ice, bandages, antiseptic, aspirin, and rubbing alcohol—to try to do what we can for the hole in Buck's head.

"Keep the ice on him," Clyde says to Blanche. "The cold'll slow the bleeding." He looks to me. "Billie taught me that."

Next Clyde pulls a sedative from his pocket, one he normally gives me to help me sleep.

"No," Blanche snaps. "He'll never wake up."

I start crying at that.

At a service station, the gas attendant mentally counts the bullet holes in our car; I can see it in how his head bobs fourteen times. He peers into our rear seat, right through the busted-up window. Blanche and Buck lay 'cross the seat, covered by a blanket. We all hide the blood on our clothes the best we can. I think Clyde may kill this man right here and now, but he keeps his gun between him and Jones. I can't help being surprised, 'specially since Blanche said it was the law who came knocking at her cabin door looking for "the men." This attendant is likely to call the law before the dust settles in our wake.

By daybreak, we'd only gone about fourteen miles. Not far enough. Not yet to Iowa. An hour or so later, I released a breath as we crossed the state line. We drive and drive, looking for a place to hide. At one point, we come upon an abandoned something. Clyde and Jones get out to investigate, running half bent. I lean forward in my seat, trying to make sense of our surroundings. There appears to be a carousel that somehow looks worse than we do. And there's a swimming pool, green water probably a few feet deep. It smells, even from a distance away.

Clyde and Jones return with a pamphlet.

Dexfield Park

65 Acres of Beautiful Shade

The brochure boasts of live bands, high-diving, baseball games, a roller-skating rink, evening fireworks, vaudeville shows, a merry-go-round, campsites, and concessions of all kinds.

Wouldn't that have been a sight to see? It saddens me, how it all turned out for this place. Broken. Dirty. Unwanted. A shell of what it's supposed to be.

We make camp on one of the unused campsites, in a small clearing surrounded by trees. We clean ourselves, wringing blood from our clothes, treating wounds—it all has become too common.

Clyde goes out for more bandages and morphine, posing as a veterinarian. When he returns, he rips the cushion from the car so Buck can lay on it in the shade of a tree.

Blanche says she can barely see out of her right eye. I don't want to tell her, but a shard of glass I couldn't get out is stuck in her pupil. I expect her to complain, but Buck is all she cares 'bout, always at his side. She often lays her hand on his chest, staring at the slow rise and fall of her fingertips.

I'm shocked when we wake on our second day and Buck's still alive.

I'm shocked on day three.

That afternoon, I hop on my good leg, trying to find Clyde. I'm out of breath by the time I do. He's on his hands and knees, pawing at the dirt. A hole is starting to form.

"What are you doing?" I ask his back.

His muscles go still, but they're still tight. "He ain't going to make it much longer."

"And what?" I demand. "You think we ain't going to bring him home to your ma?" My voice trembles as I add, "That we'd leave him here?"

I turn and hobble back to our campsite before he can reply. Though part of me wants to fling my arms 'round him and acknowledge the fact that Clyde's doing the best he can as his older brother slips away.

That night's the longest. A whippoorwill—or at least that's what Jones says it is—won't stop chirping, as if saying, *Here they are!*

A screech owl responds, the sound chilling. Twice, Clyde jumps up, gun in hand, only to settle beside me a few minutes later. Buck may be the only one who sleeps.

And to think, the first farm could've been done by now. I could be mad, but with all I'm feeling, there ain't room for it.

Once again, I'm shocked when on day four I find Buck's chest still rising and falling. Blanche is changing his bandages.

"Don't leave me," she says sternly. "You better not leave me, Buck."

His eyes are closed, but he's grinning at her. And I know that smile is undoubtedly for her. He's always given Blanche her very own look. I saw it that first night we went to Doc's—when he fiercely, passionately wrapped his arms 'round her.

Back then, 'cause of my own unease, I demanded we leave the speakeasy. Blanche did, at my persistence. Now, I wish I gave them more time to be together in those moments of first touches.

"Weiners will be ready soon," Jones says. He's got sticks through 'em, dangling over a fire. We had weenies last night, and I ain't looking forward to having 'em again. Hell, I ain't looking forward to spending another day out here in the woods. All the trees look the same, every place we go. I tap my pocket, thinking 'bout starting my day with a smoke.

"Look out!" Clyde yells. He scurries for his gun, his eyes trained off into the trees. I'm frozen in place on the blanket, too overwhelmed to know what to do. "We've got company," Clyde says evenly. His tone jars me, and I try to stand. "No, Bonnie, stay down. We got us some cowards, hiding behind trees. But I saw 'em."

My eyes flick to Blanche. She's sobbing, her body over Buck's. Jones pushes open the trunk and removes an automatic shotgun. He closes the trunk and—*bang*—I cover my ears. A gunshot reverberates through our campsite and the trees all 'round us. I jerk every which way 'til I see Jones. No longer standing, but on the ground, clutching his head, a wound eerily similar to Buck's.

I begin to crawl to him. Pine needles and dirt slip under my palms, but I'll get there. He's going to be okay. He has to be okay. Jones ain't sharing that sentiment; he's howling like an ol' hound does when a thunderstorm passes through.

"Blanche," Clyde says. There's panic in his voice, a rare thing. He's propped behind the hood, looking down the barrel of his gun. "Get Buck to the car."

I'm halfway to Jones, having dragged myself for only a handful of seconds, when there's a second shot.

Clyde goes down, and it rips all breath out of me.

By the time I'm breathing again, I see he is, too. His hand's over his shoulder, his mouth gulping in air. I change direction. Forest debris pokes beneath my fingernails as I pull and scratch and push and kick my way, frantically, toward Clyde.

There're more shots, and I cry out as if I'm the one who's been hit. But it's not me who is. It's the car. With a pop, a tire sinks, the car groaning as it leans toward the deflated corner. My lip quivers, not believing we'll ever get away now.

"Clyde," I call, nearly to him, desperation making his name sound like it came from someone else. The car blocks the men from us, but I know they're there, creeping closer. It's only a matter of time. "They're going to get us."

His hat fell off when he hit the ground. He licks his lips, puts his hat back on, adjusts it ever so. "Bonnie," he says. "We're going to have to run for it."

My mouth drops open. The tree line ain't far off; beyond it, plenty more trees.

"I'll carry you, Bonnie. You're mine. Always mine. You hear that?"

I nod, and swallow down the emotion—from Clyde being hit, from Jones being hit, from Blanche now staring at us like she don't know what to do.

"Baby." Blanche slaps Buck's cheeks. "Baby, I need you to run for me."

Buck's head lulls to the side, but he answers, "I ain't got any shoes on, ya know."

Blanche drops to the ground and reaches for a shoe, as if him wearing shoes is the most important thing in the world. Not the men scouting us. Not the fact that all three of our boys have bullets in their bodies.

No other shots are being fired, but do they even need to fire more? We're still lying in a clearing of trees, here for the taking. Jones crawls toward me.

"My head. I need you to look."

I shut my eyes, bracing myself for the white bone of his skull, like Buck's after you've wiped away the blood, before the blood comes right back. I've got my lip between my teeth when I open my eyes, and let out a sigh. "My God, I think you've only been grazed."

"Don't feel that way," he mumbles. "My head's all rattled."

"I know, honey," I say. "I know."

"Now," Clyde says. "All of us. We got to go." Clyde reaches for me, his face scrunching in pain. "I got you."

"No," I say. "You don't. You can't carry me with a busted arm."

"I got her," Jones says. "We both may fall over, though."

Somehow, I smile. This boy's always been earnest through and through. Earnest and good-hearted. I'm on his back, my arms and legs wrapped 'round him like a monkey. Clyde walks backward toward the tree line, cringing with the gun pressing against his busted shoulder. Buck's got his arms and body draped all over Blanche, and my heart breaks with each piece of encouragement she gives him to get to the trees.

We do, then they do, and I'm relieved we've made it this far.

We're broken. Dirty. Unwanted.

'Cept we've never been more wanted, just not in the right way. The scary thing—besides all the wounds and injuries and blood—is that whoever is pursuing us is playing a game of cat and mouse. They're out there, in the trees on the other side of the clearing, but they ain't in a hurry. They can take their time. Where do we got to go? Why do they have to hurry when a boy with a bullet mark on his head is carrying a crippled girl? Or when a ninety-pound girl is trying to support the weight of a six-foot man? The only one who has a chance—who truly has a chance—of getting away is Clyde.

Buck and Blanche are getting farther and farther behind.

"Clyde," I say. "They can't keep up."

He doesn't respond, doesn't react.

"Clyde," I shout.

"I know that," he states, his voice somehow calm. His eyes ain't, though; they're frenzied, looking between the trees. "Don't you think I know that? But Buck wouldn't want us to get caught to save him."

I glance over my shoulder at Blanche. She's on her knees, her arm 'round a thick trunk, using it to counter Buck's weight as she pulls his arm. "But—"

"Darling, there ain't time for that."

I bury my face in Jones's neck. His breath is ragged, his body leaning forward as he fights for every step up a small hill. I can't help it; I look back. Buck and Blanche are at the base of it, Buck on the ground, his eyes shut. Blanche's head is on his chest. Then she's pulling again on his arm.

Get up, I plead.

Clyde sprays a few seconds of bullets. Off in the distance, a group of men are visible between the trees. Or they were; now they're behind those trees. He says, "We need to hide. I ain't seeing how we're going to make it on foot. Not like this."

At the top of the hill, Jones steadies us against a tree. My left arm is soaked with his blood. I press my hand over his head wound.

"Thanks," he mumbles. Then we skid down the hill, using our body weight to get us to the bottom. Jones barely keeps his feet under him.

On the other side of the incline, now's our time to hide without the men seeing us. It also means we can't see Buck and Blanche anymore. It tugs at my heart, making me want to go back over the hill. I close my eyes, glad Jones is carrying me, giving me no choice but to move forward. The three of us cross a dry riverbed. What I'd give to palm some water in my mouth right 'bout now.

Jones puts me down so he can haul his body over a large log. I climb on it. Jones dips, and with a quick look over my shoulder, still no sight of Blanche or Buck, I fight back tears and resume my position on his back.

"That there may be our only chance," Clyde says, pointing. There's a den of sorts. My best guess is that it's the work of beavers, pulling together sticks and mud to make a dam. One the critters no longer need with the drought that's hit Iowa.

The space is tight, too small for two grown men and a girl, even if weight's been falling off me like leaves from a tree in the fall. We cram in, knees to our chests. My heart pounds into my leg. Peering through the thicket of branches, Blanche and Buck appear at the top of the hill, and I release a sob.

I'm 'bout to shout, *Over here!* when Clyde says, "No, Bonnie, we all can't fit."

I want to tell him he's wrong, that we'll figure out a way for all of us to be in here, but he ain't wrong.

With Blanche's first step down the hill, she ain't able to keep them upright. They're a mess of arms and legs 'til they hit the bottom.

I can't help myself and edge toward the dam's opening, and Clyde snaps, "No." More calmly he says, "No, Bonnie, we're goners if we go out there. The law will be showing their faces any second now."

I know Clyde's right, but I don't want him to be. Blanche is strong, though. I've never seen this type of strength in her before. She's already on her feet, running her hands down her pants. Then she's doing her damnedest to get Buck on his feet. They make it to the log, they cross over it, then there they stay. Blanche leans against it. Her chest heaves. Buck's head rests in her lap. She strokes his hair, her lips moving. I look away.

She could leave him. Blanche has run off before, with Blanche putting Blanche first. But she doesn't. She won't. Blanche would rather die than be without Buck.

As if on cue, the lawmen descend over the hill. They keep coming, one after another. Thirty of them, if that's possible. My heart jumps into my throat. Fingers point at Blanche's head sticking out over the log. She turns slightly, her face falling at the realization they're sitting ducks.

Clyde stiffens—we all do—when Buck springs to life, pulling a gun no one knew he had. He's on his knees, his stomach against the log, firing at the men, looking 'bout as steady as a cattail in the wind. The law returns fire, their automatic guns overpowering his Colt. He throws himself on top of Blanche. His body jolts, and I quake at the thought of a bullet finding its way through the log and into his side. Blanche struggles, trying to push him off, crying, "No, baby."

Buck's voice is indiscernible but fierce. Then, they kiss, maybe for the last time.

My nose stings with emotion. My eyes blur with tears.

Clyde's chin drops, touching his chest. His body trembles into mine.

All I can do is watch as the lawmen, so many of them, creep closer and closer, guns raised, an almost enraptured expression on their faces. They're 'bout to capture two from the Barrow Gang.

When I look back at Buck and Blanche, she's on her feet, arms raised.

No! I call out in my head. But all she's doing is speeding up the process of getting caught. Two men yank her over the log, each with a firm grip on one of her arms. She screams for Buck as she's separated from him, as men yank him to his feet.

"Don't die, Marvin," she pleads. "Don't die without me!"

That name is a punch to my gut. Buck's real name. Blanche has kept it to herself all this time, only to reveal it now when it may be her final words to him, ever.

I sob, turning into Clyde's chest. It's wet, hot from his wound. I don't care. I want to feel his warmth. I want to feel his heart beating. I don't want to live in a world where it's not beating in tune with my own.

"Bonnie," he whispers. He presses his lips against the side of my head harder than he's ever done before. "My brother . . ." His breath hitches. He blows out a steadying breath. "I don't want to die, but you know I ain't going back to jail." I nod into his chest. "I hope you know I ain't going to live without you, either. If they take you, I'm taking myself out. But I need to give us a chance." I meet his eyes. He runs a thumb down my cheek, spreading the wetness there. His blood. My tears. Jones is quiet next to us, 'cept for the shudder of his breath.

"I'm going to sneak off," he says, "and see 'bout finding us a way out of here."

My head whips back to where Blanche and Buck hid, not knowing how he intends to escape with a posse of officers only a stone's throw away. What was once thirty of 'em is now cut in half, a group of officers taking Buck and Blanche up the hill. Buck is all but limp. Blanche is all of a rabid animal. The rest of the men stand in a circle by the log, talking. Maybe they're figuring out their plan for tracking down the rest of the Barrow Gang.

"Clyde, if they catch you . . ." I whisper. "They ain't putting you back in jail. They're going to give you the chair."

Clyde considers it, exhales. "That sounds like something they'd do."

"Clyde." It feels important to keep saying his name, as if I may not have too many more chances left. And I make a decision: Clyde's name will be the last thing I utter, even if it's nothin' more than a breath. I reach behind him, knowing he's got a pistol tucked in the back of his pants. I put it in Jones's hand and raise it to my head. "If Clyde goes out there and he goes down, you pull this trigger. You hear?"

Jones swallows.

Clyde palms his own face, but I pull his hand down, needing to see his hazel eyes. And now . . . "Can I see that dimple of yours before you go?"

Clyde's cheek twitches more than anything 'til he forces a smile in place. There it is. Then he crashes his lips to mine. I taste earth and blood. I taste fear. I taste love.

He crawls backward from our den. With Jones pressing the gun to my temple, I utter, "I love you, Clyde."

PART THREE

BONNIE AND CLYDE

24

I'VE NEVER PRESSED MY EYES CLOSED MORE TIGHTLY. I'VE SEEN Clyde shot one too many times. I know what it's like to see the eruption of red on his skin, 'cept when it's fatal. I don't want to see that. Nor do I want to see my own death coming. If he goes, I go. That's our pact.

A twig snaps. Jones reacts to Clyde's movements, and the pistol he holds against my head slips to my ear.

I breathe a few more breaths, still alive. Emotion bubbles in my chest 'cause I know I deserve to die. Clyde and I both do. Even still, Texas has never given a woman the chair before, and I don't want to be their first.

I won't let that happen. Clyde won't, either. We're in this together, to our final breaths.

But it's utterly terrifying, hiding behind my lids, not knowing if death's coming for me this second or the next.

"Bonnie," Jones whispers. The metal against my skin, now warm, disappears, and my skin responds with goose bumps. "He made it. I can't see him no more."

I open my eyes, and all the tears I've been suppressing pour out. "He made it?"

"He crawled down the riverbed." His cadence is shaky. "Or at least I assumed he did. I couldn't see him in there."

Bless this drought. There's no doubt the officers would've heard him if he was splashing 'round in that river.

"So now what?" Jones eyes the gun. "Bonnie, I don't want to use this no more. Not on you."

I take the pistol from him. It was wrong of me to ask this boy to kill me. It was wrong of Clyde and me to bring Jones back into our games. Our games aren't for seventeen-year-old boys. I curse myself; there's a lot I've been doing wrong to Jones. I should've told him the truth, but I waited for selfish reasons. I can't be doing that no more. Not when life's shown us it can turn a corner in a heartbeat. I ain't sure how to tell him besides spitting it like poison.

"Jones," I whisper. It feels cowardly to confess so quietly, but I ain't got any other choice. "You ain't wanted for any murders. Doyle Johnson's was pinned on somebody else."

He pokes a finger in his ear, itches. It comes out bloody. The boy stares at it, calm, so much like Clyde. "You've known for a while, haven't you?"

I nod.

"And you kept it from me?"

"Only 'cause of Billie. I didn't want ya following her."

"'Cause I ain't good enough?"

"Not you, Jones. It's this life that ain't good enough for her." That ain't the whole truth. Jones was on his way to the slammer before we picked him up. But he needs to hear that he's got worth. Everyone does, even if they've done horrible things. "But you can have more than all of this, too."

Jones sniffs, his nose scrunching. "I could walk away. You really think so?"

"Not right this second." I try for a smile. It doesn't feel right. How could it? But the boy's a good kid, half his mouth's turning up. I say, "I reckon the law could find plenty to arrest you on, but they'll treat you differently than Clyde and me if they get their hands on you."

"Like they will with Blanche?"

I got to close my eyes at the sound of her name. I ain't ready to digest how I turned my best friend from a gal who, without me, wouldn't have done worse than table dance with some bootleg in her hand.

While she was with us, she never pulled a trigger, but she'll go to jail nevertheless—all 'cause she couldn't quit Clyde Barrow's woman and Clyde Barrow's brother. And to think there was a time that Blanche only ever thought 'bout Blanche. Turns out, I'm the one who only thinks of herself. And of Clyde. Always Clyde. I need to start thinking 'bout more, like how I'm going to get this boy out of here alive, then get the bleeding from his head to stop.

We haven't been hiding long, Clyde's only been gone a few minutes, but I don't trust that circle the officers are in. Their heads move ever so slightly. I know cunning when I see it—thanks to Clyde—and I'd bet money they're standing there for show, trying to give us false confidence to make a break for it. They pursued us slowly up 'til this point, knowing their bullets hit their mark with Clyde and Jones. They had to have seen I wasn't walking on my own. That adds up to one thing: we couldn't have gotten far. Clyde snuck out while commotion was still going on. But if we move now, they'll see it. If they see it, we're sunk. I'll be forced to use that gun on myself, and pray that after I do, Jones puts his hands high in the air.

Not as if he'd be able to do that from in here. Those beavers could've built something larger. My good leg is as stiff as my mangled one. I try to slide it straight, but I end up kicking the wall of the dam. Some of the mud and leaves fall, and I've done it. I've caused one of their discreet-moving heads to turn this way.

One man jostles another with his elbow. Another regrips his gun. One laughs, loudly. A distraction? No, it's a way to mask the words they're exchanging.

Gunfire erupts, a sound I've heard so frequently during my time on this earth that I'll hear it even after I'm buried deep. And maybe that's what's happening now: The sound has followed me into death to haunt me, 'cause surely if they are shooting at us, this shelter isn't doing a damn thing to block their bullets.

But no, it ain't the men. They take cover, behind the log, behind a tree, flat against the ground. They aren't the ones firing. Still firing. Then there's a touch on my arm. I jump and find a face covered in grime. "Clyde," I utter in relief, the gunfire swallowing his name. "Would you look at that," he hollers into my ear. "That gun of mine got stuck on again." Hysteria from the realization I ain't dead but saved bubbles up in me, and Clyde's quick to add, "Let's go."

Within a few feet, we're in the riverbed, Jones on our heels. We crawl. The bullets stop.

It all happened so fast, in the matter of seconds.

We drag ourselves all the way 'til the river winds into a farm. It couldn't have come any sooner. There, Clyde makes a car ours.

In that passenger seat, farmland—that ain't ours—passing us on either side, it all hits me, every moment of this final ambush. Final, 'cause that's what it is for us. Blanche is in cuffs. Buck is on his way to dying, if he hasn't already met our Maker. I turn my hands palm up, down, up. Doesn't matter which side I look at, it's all blood and filth.

I drop my hands and say, "Holy hell." And that's it. I don't got anything more, at least not to out-and-out verbalize. I could write it down, my deepest and darkest thoughts 'bout how I failed my best friend. Or 'bout how Buck took more shots than his body could handle to protect the woman he loves. But I'm too numb to move.

Clyde's only got one hand on the steering wheel. His other arm lays limp at his side. He taps the wheel, his cheek sucked into his mouth, gaining composure. I know his ticks.

I say, "You best not be blaming yourself."

He's slow to look at me. "Ya blame who's at fault, Bonnie. That's the way it works." Clyde shakes his head. I shake mine right back. I ain't surprised he changes the topic of our conversation as he says, "Got one of your poems. In my pocket."

It takes some work, but I retrieve the paper that's folded in a tight square.

"Found it laying 'round the camp site last night. Some of our money, I buried, in that hole I started for . . ." He licks his lips. "And some guns. We can go back for it, once things calm down. But we've lost everything that's not on us"—he pauses—"again."

I squeeze the paper in my palm. In a reality where it's hard to see beyond the straightaway we're flying down, it's even harder to know when we'll stumble upon that calm. But I nod again, and I'm appreciative of the small mercy: a poem with my innermost thoughts isn't in the hands of those lawmen.

All they'll do is feed our stories to the news reporters, who'll sip their illegal booze and smoke their imported cigars while writing tantalizing headlines 'bout *our* illegal goings-on.

Even now, I bet today's coppers will clink glasses with those dirty reporters, once they see how the newspapers paint them as heroes for dismantling the Barrow Gang. Maybe they'll count it as a victory that one of us didn't survive.

I hate having that thought, without knowing Buck's fate, and I hate the idea of a world without Buck's booming personality and voice. I can't imagine what Clyde must be feeling, and frankly, it'd be too painful to hear. I open the paper, to see which poem Clyde rescued. My throat's immediately too dry. It ain't my handwriting. It's Blanche's.

Sometimes
Across the fields of yesterday
She sometimes comes to me
A little girl just back from play the girl I used to be
And yet she smiles so wistfully once she has crept within.
I wonder if she hopes to see the woman I might have been—

Fuck.

It's all I've got to think. I close my eyes and blindly put away Blanche's poem.

• • •

We all do our best to heal. New scars mar our bodies and hearts. With little money, few days are spent in actual beds. Normally we sleep in the car, windows down and bugs feasting on our clammy skin, tucked away in some thick patch of trees. Each day I wake, expecting Jones to be gone. I think his head hurts too much to go off on his own. He should, though. We ain't doing more than fumbling, nothin' more than the same sad song stuck on the radio. I want to change that, but I ain't sure how—or where Clyde's head's at.

Some days I stir to find him walking—just plodding along—with hands in his pockets, his head tilted back, mumbling to the sky. He'll rub his forehead, then thrash his arm down, as if trying to rip a thought straight from his head.

On a Saturday, I catch him looking toward home, as if he's imaging his ma down by the railroad tracks, his daddy's arm cradling her to him.

North, south, east, west—our direction changes like the wind. Clyde's too paranoid to go in any one direction for long. Jones is restless when we stop, afraid we'll be caught if we stay in one place too long. Seems to be true.

Whenever Clyde can, he telephones Pretty Boy Floyd, my only inclination Clyde's still got an eye on our future. Jones and I wait in the car, awaiting whatever news he'll bring back to us.

We learn that Blanche was charged with assault with intent to kill, 'cause of how she delayed the law when they came knocking at the cabin's door so Buck could open fire. Her bail's been set at fifteen thousand dollars. That amount is staggering, more money than we've ever had. Pretty Boyd Floyd says not to bother trying to pay it; it'll only buy her a few months on the outside before she's brought back in for her trial.

On the next phone call, Clyde drops the phone. He sinks to his knees. He howls, punching the phone booth. I rush from the car, jumping and crawling my way to him, and shove the booth's door, barely opening it enough to slide through with Clyde on the ground, blocking the door. I find a way, and awkwardly drop to my knees beside him. Blood smears the glass from his fists. I put my arm 'round him, and Clyde tries to shake me off.

I won't let him. I won't lose him after he's come so far to be us again. I hold on tighter. His elbow jabs me, pushing me off, and my head knocks against the glass.

"You ain't doing this alone," I say. Then I'm leaning into him again. I whisper, "It's you and me, Clyde."

Finally, he turns into me, the weight of his body rocking me into the glass. There, I hold him. There, I learn what I've been afraid to hear: Buck died five days after the law got him.

I help pick up Clyde, get us back in the car, get us back out on the road. As the days go on, Buck's death ain't something Clyde wants to talk 'bout. Neither do I, and I'm scared to push too hard.

"Bloodsucking cops," Clyde says one time. He can't look at me as he says it. He just drives, eyes narrowed. "That's who was with him when he died. Not my ma. Not me. Not Blanche."

I clench my hands, my nails biting into my palms; all Blanche wanted was to be by Buck's side. That's all I can ask for, when it's my time to go, to be beside Clyde.

During the next call, Clyde laughs. All the way from the car, we hear the boom of his amusement. Jones and I exchange confused expressions, even more so when Clyde's laughter dries up. When he's back in the car, I say, "Out with it. What'd he say?"

He keeps me waiting a few long seconds 'til we're moving again. The wind twists my hair 'round. I put on my tam hat, hoping the breeze doesn't take it right back off, and prop my elbow on the open window, anxious to learn more.

"Seems our friend Ray," Clyde says, "robbed one too many banks. In fact, he was too high to remember he already robbed the bank before. They recognized him as soon as he walked in the door. Now guess where he is?"

"The joint?"

"Not just any prison." Clyde sticks a toothpick in his mouth. "He's at Eastham."

My jaw drops. Well, ain't that ironic, the exact place he was supposed to help us raid.

Jones, being he doesn't know Raymond, ain't all that interested in what we have to say. In the rear seat, he props his hat over his face, hiding the bullet scar near his left ear. But I'm eager to hear more, this being the first Clyde's mentioned Eastham after his delay in going there. A delay that cost him his brother's life.

"The thing is," Clyde says to me, "Raymond got word to Pretty Boy. Ray wants us to get him out."

I swallow, waiting to hear Clyde's next words. That'll mean getting the first farm done and allowing us to move forward. But Clyde doesn't say more. He only moves the toothpick from one side of his mouth to the other. I lick my lips. "Clyde, I got to know what you're thinkin'."

He clamps his teeth down, talking 'round the toothpick. "I'm thinkin' I ain't jumping at the chance to help the lad, but Ray knows people, people who say they'll turn their heads if we visit their armory."

I exhale, slowly, not to show my relief. Instead I ask, "Why would they do that?"

"Why do any of us do anything? Maybe Ray promised to line their pockets once he gets out."

All this sounds good. I'm ready to go like lightning to that armory. 'Cept for one thing. "But Ray . . . do you think we can trust him?"

Clyde flicks his toothpick out his window. Then he taps my chin, flicking his gaze to me before it's back on the open road. "Life's been nasty, hasn't she? We take two steps forward then we're yanked one step back."

"If you haven't noticed, I can't step no more."

He takes my hand, presses it to his lips. "Bonnie, I won't lie to you. I lay awake at night wondering how many more got to die before we can have the life we want. If only I didn't hesitate. I spooked myself 'bout being back at Eastham. Now Buck's dead."

"Clyde, honey, he's dead 'cause the law shot him, and the same thing is going to happen to us. We can only dodge a bullet for so long."

"We'll be off the road before that happens. I promise you. One damn thing." He bangs the wheel three times. "I got to do one damn thing right, and that's paying my debt."

I say what we're both thinking. "To Skelley." I bob my head. "Clyde, ya got to get that farm done."

"I will."

"No more delays. That prison's been haunting you for too long."

He nods.

"It needs to be in our past," I say. "Now."

"All right." Clyde peers into the rearview mirror. "Jones!"

The boy startles, his hat falling off his face.

"The missus gave me her blessing, so I got to ask one more thing of you."

"What's that?" he says.

"Get some guns with me."

I straighten. "Now, I didn't give my blessing for that part."

"Help me get those guns," Clyde says. "Then that's that. I want you to scram. You've seen enough blood and hell for one lifetime, at least 'cause of us."

"That," I say, "actually has my blessing."

I hope the blood and hell are coming to an end for us, too. We'll get the guns, we'll get out Raymond and Skelley, then we'll get the hell out of this life. So help me God.

THE BOYS RAID THE ARMORY WITHOUT A HITCH, THANK YOU Lord. In September, it's time to sit Jones down, the three of us on the side of some road. In a few moments, it'll only be the two of us.

"Now listen, lad," Clyde says. He holds Jones by the shoulder. "If the laws get their hands on you, I want ya to do something for me."

Jones cocks his head. "What's that?"

"Lie."

"Lie?"

"That's right. Now, repeat after me," Clyde says. "Clyde Barrow forced me to run with 'em."

Jones laughs.

Clyde grabs him by his collar. Not rough, but the boy knows without a doubt Clyde's serious as sin.

Jones mumbles, "Clyde Barrow forced me to run with 'em."

"You're a minor. Remind the po-lice of that. It was Buck, Bonnie, and me who did all the shooting and robbing. Never you."

"Oh?" I put a hand on my hip, but every part of it is playful. "You don't want the boy implicating himself, but he's free to throw 'round my name?"

"Darling, don't trick yourself into believing they'd go lenient on you."

"Shucks," I say.

Clyde kisses the back of my hand, then his attention's back on Jones. "Last thing, tell 'em we tied you up. Trees, car bumpers, whatever was 'round. You never had a chance to escape 'til now."

Jones asks, "How'd I get away?"

Clyde jabs at his ribs. "Don't tell me my wits haven't rubbed off on ya by now."

The boy chuckles, but he ain't looking overly confident, his hands going in and out of his pockets like he don't know what to do with 'em.

I pull him into a hug. But no tears. Jones will leave. Still, I see the way he's tethered to Clyde. Me crying won't help matters. I assure him, "We won't come for ya again." At arm's length, I remind him, "And you'll stay away from Billie."

He snorts. "I'll let her be."

"Reckon it's my turn," Clyde says. He's got Jones by the shoulders again. "First time I saw ya, you were nothin' but five. I hope you live to a hundred five, but—don't take this the wrong way—I hope I never see ya again. Go home to your mama, lad."

Then, Jones makes his break, his thumb in the air. I plant my rear end in the passenger seat before any of us change our minds.

Now just the two of us, the days and weeks start ticking by. Side by side, in our newest Ford.

Clyde exchanges telegrams and phone calls with Pretty Boy 'bout extra hands to help us plant guns at the prison farm. Clyde doesn't like it—relying on people who ain't Buck or Jones—but he doesn't have a choice if he wants to get Farm Number One done.

I remember his words: *I got to do one damn thing right.*

But then, "Bonnie," he says to me one random day in November. "I can't go to Eastham yet."

"Clyde . . ." With our pattern of two steps forward, I've been bracing myself for the inevitable one step back. And here it is, hitting me square in the face.

"No," he says. "I ain't hesitating like last time. It's just that I need to see my ma. It's been eating away at me. She deserves to know what happened to Buck. Not whatever cockamamie shit the law fed her."

"Are you saying you want to go home?"

"I want to go home—first—then, I swear to ya, Bonnie, we're going to Eastham. At home, we'll see your mama, too."

That does it, that gets me to agree, and Clyde points us toward Dallas. Like the first time we left home, the open road plays tug-of-war with my head and heart. My head's obviously sayin' it ain't smart to go near Dallas. My heart don't care. It's been too long—so long, in fact, that I ain't sure how many days and months have gone by since I've seen my ma. In my head, I've pictured her plenty, always pacing, fingering the blinds as if she'd see me walking up our front path. But we know I can't do that, and now she'll know it, too. There's too much to think 'bout.

I'm content staring out the window at the passing landscapes. My mind protects me better this way, from my ma, but also from Buck and Blanche. When my gaze catches the sideview mirror, glimpsing the rear seat, the void is obvious. There's a thin line between out-of-mind and top-of-mind. It's easy to force Buck's death and Blanche's incarceration into the recesses of my mind. But the truth is that those thoughts don't sink deep. They surface in a snap, like a rabbit from a hole.

Iowa becomes Nebraska becomes Missouri becomes Kansas. We rest. Kansas becomes Missouri becomes Oklahoma becomes Arkansas. We rest. It's not the quickest path, we could've cut out Nebraska, Kansas, and Arkansas, but the extra miles allow us to hug the state lines. At the first sign of danger, after a car seemingly follows us for too long or if we know there's a bridge up ahead, we cross back into the state we came from. Then over the line again.

All the back-and-forth ain't good for my nerves. We finally hit Texas.

Pretty Boy's been our eyes and ears and, this time, also our helping hand. The fella coordinated a secret rendezvous with our family outside the town of Sowers, only twenty minutes from Dallas.

"Why's he putting his neck out for us?" I ask Clyde. After all this time, I never thought to ask. "You two have history?"

"Guess you can say we got a lot in common. He came from a farming family. Dirt poor. And"—Clyde presses his lips together, bobs his head—"we're of like minds. Neither of us will go back to prison."

I've heard that a time or two.

"He's got news on Blanche," Clyde says.

My eyebrows rise in a flash.

"Can't say I expected it of her, but the lass pled guilty. Wouldn't testify against my brother." He swallows. "Even though he's gone."

I'm heavy all over. My head slumps forward, and the back of my neck feels tight. Too tight, every muscle all wound up. "How much time did they give her?"

"Ten years." Clyde cups my chin, bringing my eyes back to him. "Darling, say the word and I'll move heaven and earth to get her out."

"No." That's all I say. Clyde doesn't need me to explain further. This is Blanche's chance to start over. She'll show the little girl from her poem. Blanche will do her time, and then be free. Though I know she won't ever truly be free, not really.

Those aren't thoughts to be having now. Sowers is upon us. It's got a stretch of road where our car will meet nose to nose with another car. Pretty Boy Floyd said Clyde's parents, my ma, and Billie should be waiting for us, inside the parked car. Buster won't be there. He doesn't support our ragamuffin mode of living. That's okay; I don't support it either. Sure wish I could see my brother's face, though.

Night casts shadows over the dairy farms on either side of the road. All I see are hulking figures, cows that'll be called into their barn soon. Clyde slows our car. Blanche once said it's best to never look a cow in the eye. "They've got a direct way of looking at you. It's best to take a step back and not wonder what they're thinkin'."

To this day, I still ain't fully sure what Blanche meant by all of that.

"There they are," Clyde says. We decelerate a hair more. I slide on some cheery red lipstick. "At least I think it's a car," he adds.

Clyde flashes our headlights, like we've planned.

They signal back, and our speed picks up. My heart hammers in my chest.

"Don't help me out of the car, okay?" I say to Clyde. "I want my ma to see I'm all right, even if I'm down the use of one leg."

His smile's tight, as if he's remembering it's 'cause of him. But then it eases, as we roll closer to our families. I know he's dreading facing his ma 'bout Buck, but seeing family is a spark that lights a fire in both our hearts, more powerful than any dread that's darkened it.

The other car's headlights illuminate the inside of our car. We're just 'bout there. Ours does the same to theirs.

My heart swells at the faces of those I love. Then, "That ain't Buster behind the wheel, is it?"

Clyde cocks his head. "Don't think so. Sorry, Bonnie." He squints. "Fact is, I don't know who it is. Reckon we'll soon find out." He snorts. "I'm going to give 'em a small bump to say hello. Billie sure looks happy to see you."

"She does." I meet her grin, start to wave. Off to the side, in the ditch running parallel to the road, a shadow catches my eye. A line of shadows. Heads, if my eyes ain't playing tricks on me.

"Clyde," I breathe.

We've been set up.

THE GUNFIRE IS LOUD. IT'S TERRIFYING.

Bent in half, my chest pounds against my thighs. I turn my head toward Clyde. Glass shatters. Clyde's position mirrors mine, his head twisted to the side to avoid the wheel.

He screams in pain.

Pain radiates through my body, too, but it's hard to pinpoint where.

All I know is pain.

Our car goes dark. It takes me a moment to realize it's from the other car's headlights turning off.

Clyde screams out again. The firecracker of gunfire keeps coming.

My body jolts as the car flies backward with a jerk, and another.

"Hold tight, Bonnie," Clyde says, and I shudder at the fear in his voice.

We go back, back, 'til Clyde shifts his foot, moaning, and we fly forward again. Still hunched down below the dashboard, he drives blindly, only his arms and hands exposed. In between bullets, the sound of our car scraping against the other car sends chills down my spine. Then it stops. We go faster. Our back windshield shatters.

Clyde straightens, and I scream, "No!"

"I got to see. I got to drive."

I stay down, arms wrapped 'round my legs. That's when I realize the slickness of blood running down my good leg, starting from my knee. "I've been shot," I say, deadpan, as if realizing the truth of it. I've been shot at, I've been burned with acid, I've been unconscious, I've been cut by glass, but I've never had a bullet in my body before.

Dizziness washes over me.

"Stay with me, Bonnie. I ain't strong enough to do this without you."

I blink, and lean back in my seat, feeling an array of notches in the leather from bullet holes. Headlights flash in the rearview mirror. "Coppers," I say. "Behind us."

"Aye."

It's all Clyde says. His head is rolling 'round on his neck. I move closer, propping him up with my body. Our blood mixes on the floorboard.

"I need you to get my shoe off," he says. "My foot keeps slipping."

Head first, I rip off his shoe and sock. The car slows in the seconds it takes before his bare foot is back on the pedal.

"Quite the team, ain't we, Bonnie."

I wish his teeth didn't chatter as he said that. But he focuses on the road, his gaze flicking to the rearview mirror every second or so. We go faster. Clyde veers 'round a turn. We crash through a fence, rumble 'cross a field.

The next time we look back, there's nothin' but blackness with no headlights or bursts of red chasing us.

We end up with our own headlights beaming 'cross a river—and Clyde's body slumped against the wheel. I lean over, flick off the lights. I thank the Lord adrenaline pounds through me stronger than the pain. It's the only reason I'm able to get Clyde out of the car and both of us into the dark river. The river is the reason why he got us here; I know it. It's cold, the air itself only being a jump above freezing, but that coldness is what we need to staunch our wounds and to stay alive.

Submerged, I lean my head back against the bank and close my eyes.

• • •

I must've passed out. I wake shivering, the moon in the same spot in the sky. Clyde's slumped beside me, his head teetering on the water's surface, and I panic. Barely able to move from my injuries and the onset of what can only be hypothermia, I struggle to get myself, then Clyde out of the water.

My breath comes out in small poofs, then when Clyde moans, my breath's one big exhale.

We both strip. The movement brings some of our senses back, and we find our way to the rear seat and into each other's arms.

Clyde stutters, "We've really done it this time, haven't we?"

The air I breathe in and out into his neck is warm. I want to sink my whole body into it. "Clyde Barrow, you're going to be the death of me."

"Not today, darling."

And he means it. Clyde's got a resolve that could stretch 'round the world. With sheets that have traveled with us from car to car, we tear strips to wrap our wounds. Clyde's got four gunshots, in his left arm and leg. One of the bullets got past him, lodging into my knee. With our window blown out, it saved our lives that we both bent ourselves in half. But bullets still ripped through the car's metal door.

We use what's left of the sheets to wear 'em, creating holes for our head and arms. It's ridiculous how we look, how close we came to death, how close we still are to death, needing real medical attention. It's a miracle no one found us licking our wounds, and as soon as we can, we leave Sowers behind. The whole time we drive, Clyde grips my hand.

"Where we going?" I ask.

"My brain's still thinkin' that over. It's all clogged up, trying to figure how that mess back there happened. I could really use a smoke, but they got soaked when you threw me in that river." He tries for a smirk, but it's more of a grimace 'cause of how badly he's hurt.

"And saved your life."

He kisses my hand.

I say, "Ma and Billie ain't capable of double-crossing us. It had to be that fella driving."

"We'll find out who he is. And what the po-lice gave him for tattling 'bout where we'd be."

"From Pretty Boy Floyd?"

"Yeah . . . and that's where we'll go. His brother's up in Oklahoma, last I heard. Owes me a favor."

The thought of getting all the way up from Texas to Oklahoma is daunting. So is the thought of not finding the place or Pretty Boy's brother not being there anymore. I grip a map.

Each rattle of the car rattles my knee and my breath. The air's cold, colder with how fast we move. My sheet does nothin' but fill up with air, chilling my skin. Clyde ain't faring much better, and by the fifth hour I see him wavering. His skin has lost all color. When he veers, I right the wheel. I talk, with nothin' really to say, for the sake of him hearing my voice. I struggle to stay awake myself, the sun now creeping up over the horizon.

By the skin of our teeth, we make it to Carl Floyd's home, on the outskirts of town. Clyde has a rare lapse in judgment, laying on the horn. With how he falls against it, I realize it wasn't a lapse. It's all he's got left.

I've never met Carl before—or Pretty Boy Floyd, for that matter—but I reckon it's Carl who lumbers out of the house and hangs on our car door, poking his head in the window, careful not to touch the shattered edges of glass.

"I don't got to ask who you are," he says, taking in the sight of our bullet-riddled ride and blood-soaked sheets.

"Carry her in first," Clyde insists. And Carl does, into his three-story row home.

I'm put in a bed, and when Carl holds up a bottle of morphine, I all but rip it from his hands, elated for the release from pain and into sleep. I wake a number of times to a soft voice and soft hands. A woman tends to me by flashlight, and I never see her face. I reckon that's the point; she can't see mine either. She gently but swiftly removes the bullet fragments from my knee. My leg is put into a splint and hoisted into the air by a hanging device made from bedsheets. When the woman—an educated nurse, I've gathered by this point—insists I need surgery, Carl only responds with how that's not possible.

"She'll need therapy, at the very least. See her other leg? How it's bent?" the nurse says. I listen, my eyes closed. "Her tendons and ligaments restricted while they healed. This leg needs to be worked or this young lady will lose the use of this one, too."

I'm glad my face is hidden in the shadows, so my reaction can't be seen. Though I'm not sure my face can look any more downtrodden. I imagine my skin washed out, my hair disheveled, the scar on my chin.

I'm at a loss for words to explain all my body's been through. And Clyde . . . he was in worse shape than me, this time 'round.

I wait for the nurse to leave. Carl follows. When the door creaks open again and Carl steps in, light illuminating him from behind, I clear my throat and ask, "Clyde?"

Carl's got broad shoulders, a thick body, a square jaw—and he gets knocked aside a moment later. The door's wide open, light flooding into the room. On a crutch, Clyde hobbles toward me.

"There she is," he says.

I can't see the bandages under his clothing, but I know they are there, along with the many puckered scars 'cross his body from previous wounds. "You shouldn't be on your feet," I snap.

"You shouldn't be dangling from the ceiling."

Clyde stares 'til my smile starts, then his does, too.

I say, "We're a sorry pair." My mind slips to the bullets hitting our car, lodging into our bodies, whizzing over our heads. And I realize . . . those bullets were also fired at the other car as we escaped. "Our families?" I dare ask in a low voice.

"They're all fine, Bonnie."

I sigh, but my hands still ball into fists that the law would shoot in their direction. All 'cause of us. "We came close to dying, didn't we?"

He whistles. "The closest. Other two times, they came with warrants, knocking on our door. 'Course we responded with guns to save our hides. But that there in Sowers, they aimed to kill us. Straight off."

His crutch bangs against the ground—once, twice—the sound pounding in my head, before his fingertips touch mine. His grip is soft. His fingers tighten. My hand's shaking good under his. "Yet, here we are, and here's the thing, Bonnie. I'm done. I ain't going to hurt us no more." He sighs. "I don't need Eastham anymore."

I flip my hand to lace our fingers together. The prison farm always was important, a stepping-stone to our farmland, a way for Clyde to move on from his past. But now, I say, "Clyde, you need it. I do, too. Those lawmen didn't only fire at us." My voice bubbles with the threat of fresh tears, but is also ripe to yell my next words. "They shot at our family. They didn't care a lick if my ma or sister or your parents died while they came for us. That's sick. It's sick, Clyde."

"So, what do you want to do?"

I blow out a breath. "I know those officers at the prison ain't the same ones, but in my mind, they're all the law. I want to get 'em back. Let's boil their blood like they've done to ours."

"By busting out Skelley and the others?"

"That's right. And I want the law to know we're behind it."

"All right." Clyde squeezes my hand. "Let's get this leg workin', then."

Over the next few weeks, fury pushes me as Clyde bends and straightens my knee. I grit my teeth, knowing each movement is strengthening the muscles, ligaments, tendons, and anything else that needs to properly function inside my leg. It don't feel good. But I distract myself with teaching Clyde. In between moans and groans, I spell words, I read words. He says 'em back to me.

We talk 'bout what needs to get done, all starting with planting guns on the prison farm for Skelley to retrieve. For that, we need men to help us carry out the particulars.

In December, men start showing up at Carl's house. A fella, old enough to be my daddy, named Mullens. And Raymond's older brother, who goes by Hamilton. They ain't who Clyde wants helping us, but who Clyde wants is gone, shot down by the law.

That anger surrounding Buck's death only flares when Prohibition ends. I can't help thinking if that amendment was ratified seven months earlier—just seven months out of the thirteen years Prohibition was in effect—maybe we never would've been ambushed at the Oak Ridge apartment, the law thinking us bootleggers. Maybe Buck would still be alive. Seven godforsaken months.

By January, my knee's working enough to get myself 'round Floyd's house. I keep an eye on Mullens. He's a fidgety sort. Could be that he's a dopehead, looking for his next fix. He's frail enough, little more than skin and bones. Or could be that he's passing information back to the law, ready to lead us into another trap.

Clyde must have a similar thought. He straight out calls Mullens a stool pigeon. Mullens's feathers go up, putting on a tough-guy façade with his chin raised.

"Prove me wrong," Clyde says. "If you ain't an informant, you'll have no problem planting the guns."

I startle.

Mullens stiffens.

Clyde grins.

That only makes Mullens stiffen more.

But he agrees. At least someone does. I ain't happy 'bout putting our future on the line, yet again. But tomorrow, we'll see Mullens's true colors. For his sake, and for ours, they better not be blue. I ain't keen on the police putting us in their crosshairs again.

27

CLYDE'S JAW IS TIGHT AS HE DRIVES OUR GANG TOWARD THE prison farm. But he does. Not once does he look into the rearview mirror, and I wonder if it's 'cause he can't look back.

Clyde stops the car, and I'm quick to survey him. He gives me a look as if to say, *I'm fine*, but he can't be saying it aloud with our two companions in the back. Instead, he says, "Entrance is a mile ahead. The road dead-ends up there. But we don't got to go any closer."

Our Ford sits idle, our headlights off. At this time of night, even on a Saturday, all the inmates are tucked in their cells, probably exhausted, blistered, and bruised. Once, Clyde told me the farm is over twelve thousand acres, a lot of land for the prisoners to work. The prison began, after all, as a "convict leasing" program by people who used dollar bills to wipe their derrieres.

Clyde twists in his seat, his eyes on Mullens. "Time to plant some guns."

Way back when, it was supposed to be Clyde and Raymond planting the guns. Then, Clyde and Buck. Now, Clyde won't be the one to step onto the farm. Not yet, anyway. He could, he insists, but it's important to see where Mullens's allegiances lie.

"Planting the guns ain't the riskiest part," he told me. "It's what comes next."

That being, helping Skelley and the others escape. Then, Clyde'll go onto the land. He'll need Mullens at his shoulder, without worrying Mullens's gun will point his way.

But first, we need those guns in place for Skelley to get. I feign confidence and say, "Go get it done, fellas."

Clyde smirks and temporarily sidles out of the car, allowing Hamilton and Mullens to exit our two-door coupe. "You heard the lass."

The boys do as I say. The night's quiet, their movements stirring a bird or two, and also my nerves. Time and time again, we've been nothin' more than sitting ducks. This may not be the riskiest part of the plan, but it's a risk nevertheless, being this close to the prison, trapped on one side by a river and the other by the prison's chain-link fencing. There ain't nowhere to go to conceal our car if someone else happens down this road.

Hamilton strides off toward the prison's property, a bag filled with guns and ammunition over his shoulder. Mullens, on the other hand, has an unsteady gait, as if he's hit the bottle. He didn't. We haven't taken our eyes off him. I reckon he's drunk with worry.

Hamilton makes quick work of clipping the fence, and ducks through. Mullens hesitates, his finger tappin' against the chain link. Eventually, he creeps onto the prison's land, with another backward glance at us, as if saying: *Don't make me go.*

Back beside me, I ask Clyde, "What do you know 'bout him?"

"Mullens? Aye, he got out of this place a week ago." Clyde breathes in, out. "I reckon he ain't too keen on stepping foot on the grounds again."

I nod. "Why's he even here, helping us?"

"Raymond got to him, is what I hear. Ray knew Mullens was getting sprung. He told Mullens he'd give him a thousand clams if he went straight to Hamilton to get this raid rollin'. Can't be too careful, though, he could've cut a bigger deal with the po-lice."

Clyde's head jerks to the left, toward those many acres, now nothin' but shadows. I didn't hear nothin', but Clyde stares into the darkness—the seconds piling on top of each other—and I hope he ain't remembering his years spent in prison garb, working that land or cowering in the dark corners of the prison's buildings. His jaw protrudes in and out as he grinds his teeth. Then he turns back to me, the burrow between his brow smoothing. "Say, I think my reading's getting better."

I swallow the emotion at watching Clyde and follow him into a new conversation. "Yeah?"

"I know it says *Ford* on the outside of our car."

"Now don't look so smug, Clyde."

"Why not? Those letters are fancy, even."

I laugh. This boy will forever make me laugh, even twenty feet from a prison farm where all hell could break loose. "Fine. What rhymes with *Ford*? Spell *Lord*," I say.

He does, correctly. Something harder, then. Off in the distance, dogs howl. I ignore 'em and stay in our moment. I pick a new rhyme, this time beginning with *C*.

"Like to tie somebody up? Or a guitar chord?"

"Clyde Barrow, you make me proud."

"Now, that's music to my ears. And speaking of, I get to write our last verse once this is all over with and we get our land."

"Last verse?"

"Of this song. We'll have more if I get my way." He winks, but the darkness tries to steal it from me. It can't. I saw it, maybe 'cause Clyde's expressions are as similar as my own. He peers off to the left again. His hand finds the gun on his lap, and his fingers begin to wrap 'round the stock, then stop. "They're coming back."

Hamilton's the bigger of the two, stockier. It's easy to see who is who, and Hamilton doesn't have that sack of guns anymore. Mullens is all but capering to get on our side of the fence.

I say, "Looks like Mullens is going to live to see another day."

• • •

That day includes taking Hamilton, bright and early, back to Dallas, where he can keep up his twice-a-month routine of driving to Eastham prison to visit Raymond. With a prison term of 266 years for auto theft, armed robbery, and murder, Raymond would've had endless visits ahead of him with his brother. But today will be their last one—at this prison, at least. Lord knows Raymond can easily find himself behind bars again with the flea-brained choices he makes.

This afternoon, though, Hamilton will sit 'cross from Raymond and give him the nod that the guns are in place. Raymond knows where them guns will be, considering he was supposed to plant them in the sewer all those months ago. The Colts and their clips will be there, waiting for Skelley in an ol' inner tube.

Tomorrow, the fellas will bust out, and Clyde's debt to Skelley will be paid. An added bonus, it'll be the first breakout ever at the prison farm. Orchestrated by none other than Clyde Champion Barrow and his lass. Bet ya that'll chap their hides.

As we approach Dallas, I let it all sink in, 'specially what'll come next: An ol' farmhouse with chickens pecking at the dirt out front. Cows out back. Maybe a pig or two, but for slaughtering. Once Blanche gets out of prison, I won't let her name 'em. That is, if she'll forgive me for all I put her through.

I shake the thought away and concentrate on the quiet streets of Dallas. We gamble on any lookie-loos still being asleep and drop off Hamilton outside his duplex on Harrison Street.

That's that, as far as our time in Dallas. It makes it easier we're on the opposite side of city from home, over ten miles from Clyde's parents' house, even farther from my ma's in Cement City. Still, I feel my heart tuggin' in their directions.

In a few hours, my ma will be waking up for church, donning her Sunday best. January in Dallas starts chilly, so she's likely to wrap a shawl 'round her long-sleeve dress. I've got one 'round me. A nice dress, too. 'Cept, I don't got anywhere to wear it. It's been years since I've been to church, something I ain't proud of. But I spend time praying, I do.

Right now I'm praying the escape goes without a hitch. Before I know it, Monday passes without any alarm bells, meaning Skelley retrieved the guns, and after driving all the nearby roads to plan our getaway, we're rolling down that dead-end road again. It's time to see if the good Lord will continue to answer my prayers.

He's certainly making the morning suspenseful. Honest-to-goodness fog rolls off the river, and the sun seems hesitant to join us. I wrap my shawl tightly 'round my shoulders for more reasons than one.

Clyde appears relaxed. I ain't surprised by that. We have a jittery ex-convict in our rear seat, who no doubt knows a thing 'bout Clyde's quick trigger finger. Clyde's calm demeanor will keep Mullens thinking Clyde could snap at any moment.

We don't go as far up the road as before; we don't need to. That was to get Mullens and Hamilton close to the sewer. This time, we wait near a field the inmates should be clearing any minute now to prepare for the spring planting season. Our escapees will come to us. Most likely at a sprint.

"*X* marks the spot," Clyde says. He pulls off the road. I peer though the mist and a thick patch of trees, spotting a clearing along a creek bank. Beyond it, the fence lines the farm's perimeter. "Hold her down, Bonnie."

"Showtime," I say and grab the lapel of Clyde's jacket. I pull him in for a kiss, laced with both excitement to get this here job done and fear this here job could go terribly wrong. "You take care of what's mine, you hear?"

He waggles a brow, then he barks at Mullens to bring him another gun. Clyde puts the Colt in the back of his trousers and reaches for his trusty Browning automatic rifle.

Clyde, in the lead, creates a new entrance into the prison's chain-link fence and cuts through the trees. They take their places, crouching by the creek bank. From their vantage point, they can see the field where the inmates will flood for their morning's work. I cannot. I'm left to wait, to listen, to hope. To pray. It's risky what Clyde's 'bout to do. But the law won't know we're behind it unless they see him, unless he stands tall and spreads out his arms, as if to say: *I'm back, and I did this to you.*

In the past, I'd scooch over to the driver's seat in case Clyde races back, hollering, his arms waving. But with a stiff left knee and a mangled right leg, being the getaway gal is no longer part of my wheelhouse. All I'm left to do is warm my seat.

The cold air carries the sound of nickering horses. I envision the inmates entering the fields with their tools. Up on horses, the guards patrol, looking down their noses at the men. I cringe to think of the butt of a gun that once slammed into Clyde's back, or glanced the crown of his head 'cause of a guard's poor aim.

Overlooking the field, Clyde could easily open fire, using his practiced aim to take down those guards. But he won't. It's not time for him yet.

I wring my hands. I wait. I listen for sounds of the inmates coming our way. That's when Clyde's to spray bullets into the heavens, clearing the way for the escapees, but also pulling the attention to himself.

Metal clinks. Wood splinters. Horses neigh. Inaudible voices pass through the trees. Then, a gunshot.

I grip the door handle. That ain't how it's supposed to go. Only Clyde's to fire. My eyes jump to him. Still crouched. That gunshot wasn't fired at him. But it was aimed at somebody. There's a shift in the air, from a normal morning of chopping wood and clearing the field to chaos. Men shout. There's a second shot. A third closely follows. And a fourth bang. Something's gone terribly wrong.

Stay down, I urge Clyde. *Just come back to me.*

He leaps to his feet.

Clyde sprays bullets, his barrel angled up at the treetops. He screams, "Let's go!" before he stretches out his arms. There he stands, a target. I can't look away, pleading a bullet won't rock his body. He's got a vest on. 'Course he's got that on, but even a single inch of Clyde unprotected is too much for me.

I lay on the horn. Clyde turns, and I throw up my arm, as if to say, *That's enough, you fool.*

It gets Clyde running back to me. Mullens, too, who did little more than cover his head once the firing began. Yesterday, he told me, almost as a braggart, that he'd done eight terms in jail, but for nothin' more than robbery. I smiled back politely.

My smile now for Clyde is genuine. "You don't got any bullets in your body," I call, leaning out the driver-side window.

"No new ones," he corrects, between breaths.

"They coming this way?"

As if on cue, four men run through the trees.

"More lads than I was anticipating," Clyde says under his breath. He opens the car door. "You're going to have a party back there, Mullens." He laughs, but the sound of it dulls. "Where's Skelley?" he shouts to the approaching escapees.

I recognize Raymond, but not the other three. Raymond, mud up to his knees, slows outside the car, towering over Clyde, yet cowering at Clyde's anger. "He ain't coming."

Clyde bangs the hood. "What you mean he ain't coming?"

Raymond raises his hands, one holding his gun, the other an ammunition clip. "Said he wouldn't last on the outside."

Eyes closed, Clyde growls, "Get in."

Two of the men go in the trunk. Raymond and another fella, who introduces himself as Palmer, go into the back with Mullens. Clyde drives, fast, following our planned escape route.

I hold my breath, but for once no one follows us. No one is shooting at us. Farm Number One is done. Done. I let out the breath. By the grace of God, we may've taken three steps forward.

WE'RE ON THE RUN, BUT THAT AIN'T ANYTHING NEW. YET now we're on the run with more heads than ever, with prices on those heads.

Clyde keeps his lips pressed together and his eyes trained on the road as he navigates the turns to get us away from the prison. In time, he demands, "What were those shots back there?"

He won't ask 'bout Skelley again; Clyde will deal with those emotions inside, but I know they're weighing on him. Have to be after that fella was Clyde's motivation for so long.

Palmer says, "Ray dropped his ammunition clip, left me to deal with 'em all on my own while he fumbled 'round in the mud."

"It slipped," Raymond growls. He uses the back of his hand to rub his nose. With the bags under his eyes, I'd wager he hasn't had any opioid-induced sleep in weeks. It shows.

Clyde shakes his head. "Any guards die?"

There are nods.

"Which one?"

"Crowson," Palmer says. "But he had it coming."

Clyde states, "He got me a few times, too."

Nothin' more needs to be said; Palmer's got Clyde's blessing.

I notice a thin line 'cross Palmer's temple. I point at it.

"Got lucky." He smears the blood with his fingertips. "Bullet barely scratched me."

I turn forward in my seat. Ain't even close to the worst I've seen.

Clyde wants a new Ford. He drives for hours, maybe five, stopping along the way for some spending money at a filling station. Then, we leave our two-door coupe in a ravine in Oklahoma and find us a four-door sedan.

We drive, no one in the trunk this leg of our ride. New fellas' names are Henry Methvin and Hilton Bybee. The seven of us ain't going anywhere in particular, which ain't nothin' new for Clyde and me. But we don't want to stand still where someone can happen upon a car of fugitives.

That night, Clyde shoves blankets into the fellas' arms and tells 'em to sleep under the stars. Stretched out in the rear seat, I rest my head on Clyde's shoulder, overtop where a bullet once struck him. My body presses against his, stealing his body heat.

The boys would be smart to cuddle up outside. Those stars ain't going to offer any warmth. But their own beds would, far away from here. And us.

"Clyde," I say. "This car of ours feels too full."

He says, "Ain't nothin' but the two of us." I playfully slap his gut, satisfied with his groan. He closes his eyes, exhales. When he's looking at me again, Clyde doesn't waste another breath before kissing me. "Raid's done." He kisses me again. "It's over. Behind us." A third time. "We'll find us a radio. We'll be hearing our names."

"Think so?"

"Know it. They won't be happy."

This time, I kiss him. "Good."

"We're almost there. Now we only need the money for the land. But, Bonnie, I can't rob alone, and no, it ain't going to be you."

"I wasn't—"

"You were."

I was going to make the suggestion. But it wouldn't have made sense, not with me not being able to walk on my own. It was my eagerness talking, wanting to get us on our land months ago.

Clyde says, "The lads want to rob a few banks to get it done."

I prop myself up. My brow furrows out of fear. "But everyone and their mama will be looking for us."

Clyde shrugs, not 'cause he ain't taking it seriously—I can see it in his eyes—but 'cause he doesn't have another answer for me. He pats his chest for me to lay back down. "It won't be long before it's only the two of us, and, Bonnie, better believe I'm dying for that."

There's a lot I'm dying for, and right now, it's for more of Clyde; it's to ride this high that his past stayed on that prison yard. I slide my hand over his navel, and with a quick tug, Clyde's shirt is free from his trousers. His stomach sucks in. "Why ya want me alone, Clyde?"

He chuckles, deep, and I lose myself in the sound. "You've always had a healthy imagination. I'm sorry I haven't let ya use it much."

"But now?"

Clyde opens his arms, as much as the rear seat will allow, and that boy smirks at me.

I make quick work of his belt and, for a few moments, it's only clanging and Clyde's quick breathing. His skin's hot, hotter as I slide my palm down. Clyde trembles, the quivering of his body passing into mine.

• • •

If anyone heard us last night, they've been wise to keep their mouths shut and grins to themselves. It's likely they've got other things on their minds, like robbing banks. The boys all need the money. Raymond's got people to pay and dope to buy. Mullens has money to collect from Raymond. Hilton Bybee and Joe Palmer were originally put away for murder, and money'll give them boys a better shot at staying out. And Henry Methvin, well, he's a bank robber through and through. I reckon ol' habits die hard.

It's 'cause of Henry's well-known enthusiasm for robbing banks that Clyde asks him to sit out the first one. Hilton Bybee and Raymond go in alone, but they come out with a fella on their heels.

The boys actually laugh as the fella gets in his car and tries to chase us down.

Clyde snorts. "Who's this lad think he is?"

Within two turns, we've lost him, and Clyde puts a thousand-mile jump between us and the bank. *Jumping* isn't anything new for us. But Clyde used to only drive four hundred miles or so from a crime. Now Clyde won't rest 'til we've fled at least double that. And it's as if his body knows how many miles we've gone without him looking at the odometer. I lean over to see how far we've gone and, yep, one thousand and two miles.

This time, we end up in Oklahoma, and the boys have their eye on another bank. All of 'em, 'cept for Mullens. That little man suggests he go gather more clothes and other necessities for us all.

He says, "I'll meet back up with y'all in a few days."

Right. I'll be a monkey's uncle if we ever see that fella again. He didn't get his thousand clams from Raymond, but he got a pocketful. It must be enough. Or rather, he's had enough of the "Bonnie and Clyde" mode of living. That being, living out of an automobile. During the winter. Melting snow to drink. The smell of a campfire always in your hair. Eating straight from tin cans. Wearing multiple layers of clothing, day in and day out, stuffed with newspaper to help keep warm. Never knowing who to trust. Or how close the law actually is.

Clyde tunes in to a battery radio, and we all huddle 'round it. Sure enough, our gang's the talk of the town. At first, Palmer's at the heart of it, having pulled the trigger that took down the guard. But, then, there it is, just as we had hoped.

"No doubt," the radio personality says, "fugitive Clyde Barrow, who's wanted in nearly every state 'cross our country's middle, was behind it all. There he stood, proud as a peacock. Even without her being seen, I'll bet Miss Bonnie Parker was near enough for him to touch."

Clyde and I exchange a smile. It feels mighty fine, knowing we stuck it to the law.

"Colonel Lee Simmons, manager of Eastham prison," the personality goes on, "is said to have promised the dying Major Crowson that he'll resettle accounts. 'Those fellas had their day. We'll have ours,' are the colonel's exact words. Clyde Barrow and his posse embarrassed the colonel and that prison amply. But you heard it here first. The colonel insists Clyde Barrow and Bonnie Parker won't get away with it. The manhunt is—"

Clyde ticks off the radio. "Enough of that."

I meet Clyde's eyes again, and I shrug. It ain't that I'm not startled. Knowing someone's out to get ya will always be unsettling. But hearing the law is after us isn't telling me anything I don't already know.

Some of the fellas don't take it as well. Raymond mouths off to Clyde that we should put a hole in Palmer's back for the colonel's vendetta against us.

"Palmer only added fuel to the fire," Clyde says.

Seconds later, Raymond nods off. It's a telltale sign he's been using morphine. First he's awake, not quite firing on all cylinders but spicy as a pepper. Then, he's asleep, dead to the world.

A few days later, the boys rob again. We jump. The days are long, offering plenty of time to look over our shoulders. Bybee leaves. Now it's just Joe Palmer, Henry Methvin, Raymond, and us. Three fellas too many.

The first day of February, they are at it again, this time in Iowa, I believe. We jump. Palmer takes his cut and—thank you, Lord—off he goes on his own, taking some of the heat with him.

We let things cool down after that, before Clyde, Raymond, and Henry pocket four thousand dollars from another bank job. Our collective cut of the pie is a couple thousand dollars, giving us plenty to celebrate whenever we're alone. Clyde keeps it in a bag, tucked under his seat. It's a nice amount, but we need more to get us off the road for good—before we're found. Clyde taps Pretty Boy Floyd whenever he can by telephone, and we learn the law already picked up Bybee. That ain't encouraging.

"Say," Henry starts one morning, in his usual spot in the rear seat—him on the left, Raymond on the right. "I wouldn't mind if we ended up in Louisiana this time."

Clyde takes a drag from his cigarette. "Why's that?"

I prop my elbow onto the seat's back, cupping my eyes to avoid the sun's glare. I'm just as curious for his response. The boys don't often have suggestions for Clyde.

"My father's got a place there," Henry says. "And it ain't one the law would know 'bout. It ain't under his name."

"It got beds?" Clyde asks. Henry nods. "Tell me which way to go."

Henry does, talking over Raymond's snores. For the first time in a long time, we've got us an actual destination, besides a bank to rob. I know Henry's spooked by Bybee's arrest and is only using us to get to his daddy safely, but everyone needs a helping hand now and again.

The sun's sinking behind the trees by the time we're traveling a long gravel road. Prairie land stretches left and right, front and back. "Just up ahead," Henry says.

I ask, "All this your daddy's?"

Henry nods, and I drink it all in with my eyes. Land, lots of it. Soon the crunch of gravel stops and our tires create their own path through the overgrown lawn.

I say, "Looks like your daddy could use another cow or two to keep this grass down."

And in that tree—the big one, next to a pond—a rope swing would be nifty. I'd put fences lining the drive, telling people which way to go to get to the house. That is, if the law wasn't hunting us and we could entertain visitors.

I smile at the farmhouse. It ain't much, hardly more than a box with a porch out front. But even in the last minutes of daylight, I can see its potential. It ain't nothin' a few shutters and flower boxes can't fix. Maybe a bright red front door.

Off to the right, between two oaks, a chicken coop would fit perfectly. Or maybe the pigpen. The leaves would let through rain, but not much sun, leaving the hogs with lots of mud to keep 'em cool when Louisiana gets over eighty.

"Bonnie," Clyde says, standing at my side of the car.

I startle from my daydream and I ain't exactly sure why, but my cheeks grow hot. Hotter, as Clyde carries me inside to meet Henry's daddy. He resembles Henry a great deal. Dark hair, light eyes, razor-sharp cheekbones, and a mouth that's always on the verge of a smile. Mr. Methvin ain't exactly smiling now, though. Not at Clyde, Raymond, and me, anyway. Only at his boy, who he's got wrapped in a hug. I get the sense Henry's daddy is tolerating our presence, being we brought his boy home.

The farmhouse is bare bones. No plumbing, no electricity. But there's a well outside and a bathtub inside, two things high on my list of priorities. That and, of course, a bed. I know Clyde's got a shotgun within reach, but it feels safe here, the law without the wherewithal to come knocking on this door. So, later, with the campfire washed from my hair, a layer of dirt scrubbed from my skin, and in the arms of the man I love, I let out a contented sigh. Clyde presses his lips to my temple for a kiss, then to my ear and whispers, "Soon."

29

IT'S A PUNCH TO THE GUT TO LEAVE THAT FARMHOUSE BEHIND after only a day. I prop my chin on my gloved hand, resting on the car's open window. There's a chill in the air, and I snuggle deeper into my coat, the fur collar tickling my skin. The sun's warmth on my face is the promise of a new day—and maybe that there's a place like Mr. Methvin's out there for us.

It also ain't a bad thing that only Raymond is left in the back of our car—and at the moment, he doesn't have a word to say. The road we're on is narrow, too thin even for two cars to pass without one pulling off into the brush. Clyde ain't in a hurry, he's minding the dirt road to save us from any flats. I soak in the quiet, close my eyes, and let the wind have its way with my hair.

A drop of rain hits my face, and my eyes pop open. I'm quick to get the window up.

Clyde smirks. "Got ya, did it?"

"Nothin' some powder can't fix."

"Bonnie, there ain't an inch of ya that needs fixing."

That boy. I smile. He returns it, and wowee, I like when he smiles. Clyde almost looks like a younger version of George Raft from *Scarface*. My very own Rinaldo. My very own right-hand man.

The rain comes harder, angry sounding. I'm searching for my tube of lipstick when I, instead, spot two figures up ahead in the road. Clyde's fingers dance over his gun. We ain't moving no more. "Clyde," I say and look more closely through the rain hitting our windshield. "Those are two young'uns."

Two young'uns caught in the cold rain. I motion for Clyde to get the car going again.

"Raymond," I say. "Give me one of those blankets. Use another to cover up your gun." I cover ours. The rest are in the trunk, out of sight. "Clyde, I ain't 'bout to leave those kids to be soaked through."

He lays a hand over his heart. "Wouldn't think of it," he says. "I got no problem giving 'em a ride."

"Good." I pump my arm 'round and 'round 'til the window's down. Clyde stops the car alongside the kids. "Hey there, sweeties." I smile, being careful not to make it too big to scare 'em off. "How 'bout we give you a ride?"

The little girl is a head taller than the boy. Her younger brother, I assume. He's shivering plenty. So is the little girl, who's got her eyes trained on my fur coat. "All right," she says slowly.

I shout over my shoulder, "Raymond, help this li'l fella into the car and get him wrapped up tight." Then to the girl, "How'd you like to join me up front?"

She bites her bottom lip, then pushes her brother toward the back of the car, where Raymond's waiting. I push open my door and pat the seat beside me. "Bet this coat would look mighty good on you. I already got it all warmed up."

I wiggle out of it, and the girl wiggles in.

"Would you look at that," I say. "I was right."

The girl grins and tries to wipe a wet strand of hair from her face, 'cept her arm is nothin' but sleeves. I help her. We're moving again.

"I ain't ever wear anything this nice," the girl says.

"I didn't either when I was your age." I search up ahead at nothin' but road. "Where you two headed?"

Her arm points ahead. "School."

"I always liked school."

I get an eager smile, with a mouth full of teeth, none missing. "Me, too."

"Let me guess, you're 'round ten? Bet you're a great speller by now."

"Twelve," she says, quietly yet proudly. "My brother's ten."

"Ah, I'm a big sister, too. Lots of work, ain't it?" I wink.

That earns me a giggle.

Clyde bumps my shoulder. "Now don't get yourself attached." His head cocks, as if an idea yanks it to one side. "Unless ya want to keep 'em. I reckon the law won't be quick to shoot at us if we've got two kids by our windows."

"Shush now. Don't frighten them," I say. But I got to admit, "She looks a bit like me with that light hair and those blue eyes, wouldn't you say?"

"Bonnie . . ."

I scratch along my collarbone and turn back to the girl. I was only pointing out the similarity, that's all. Right? Before I can say anything more, Raymond says to the boy, "You want to see my baby?"

I scrunch my brows and shift to see him pulling back a layer of the blanket to reveal his machine gun. "Raymond, you put that away, you hear?" The little girl goes sheet white. "It's okay, sweetie, we ain't going to hurt you."

They weren't the best choice of words; I ain't sure she even thought *hurt* was possible 'til I put the idea in her head.

Clyde curses under his breath at Raymond. Then says, "Pretty lass, is there a road by school where I can drive really fast? Wider than this one? With fewer holes?"

The little girl licks her lips, so much indecision dancing 'round her face. Finally, she nods. "My daddy uses it to get to town, the big one."

"That'll do just fine," Clyde says.

"Clyde," I say. "You ain't really thinkin' of . . ." I let my wide eyes say the rest. I hold my breath, not sure what Clyde's planning. Either he's going to stop at the school yard or go flying past it, taking the kids with us. The little girl is snug beside me, and I have a moment of weakness, liking how she fits between me and Clyde.

Clyde stops the car beyond the school yard. The highway's not far off, maybe a few hundred more feet. And I know it's the right thing to do. The girl mentioned her daddy, someone who'd miss this darling child deeply—or at least I would if I were him. I know I miss my lost child, and he or she was barely mine. That ain't right, to tear their family apart, after we've torn so many families apart, to make myself feel whole. Or, in Clyde's mind, to use these children to keep the law from shooting at us.

"Sweetie," I say to the girl. "Why don't you hold on to this jacket for me? But if anyone asks you, you found it. It ain't from a lady and her sweetheart who gave you a ride. Do you understand?"

The girl's eyes flick to Clyde, back to me. She nods.

I reach 'cross her and push open the car door. Before the girl can get out, I touch her arm, holding her still. "And sweetie, I got one more thing I want to ask of you. As long as you live, you won't ever—neither of you—get in another car with someone you don't know. You promise me that." She does, in a mouse-sized voice. I kiss her cheek and say, "Now run along. You've got school."

• • •

It's another punch to the gut to leave those children behind. I remind myself, it's the right thing to do. The non-selfish thing to do. And after all we've put Jones through, it's a sin for even entertaining the idea of taking 'em with us.

As we drive, leaving Louisiana behind, I glance in the sideview mirror, catching Raymond's reflection. I've grown tired of that face, 'specially after his round of show-and-tell, and I imagine that big mole on his forehead to be a bull's-eye.

That bull's-eye only grows larger when he opens his mouth, saying, "Let's swing by Dallas."

Whatever for? I want to ask. That's only the most dangerous place for us to go.

Clyde stares in the rearview mirror, expressionless, 'til Raymond explains, "I want to pick up Mary."

Clyde's eyebrows rise.

My breath hitches. "The four of us, riding together?"

Raymond says, "You two ran with another couple before. I don't see what the big deal is now."

I hold the air in my lungs, but I'm just 'bout out. And, Lord, my brain needs air to process all this.

Mary's name hasn't crossed my mind since the first bank job in April of '32, all of two years ago. I haven't laid eyes on her in even longer. And now Raymond wants to bring her on the run with us? Not only that, but he thinks the two of 'em could be like Buck and Blanche? Can replace Buck and Blanche?

Clyde's fingers tighten, unwind, tighten on the steering wheel. The speedometer ticks to the right. A backcountry bend looms ahead, and I say, "Clyde, honey, slow down," while knowing if anyone could make this turn at this speed, it's him. His gaze flicks down, to my leg, and he eases off the gas.

I light a cigarette, take a drag, then pass it to Clyde. I see it working as his features relax, as his jawline softens. We make the turn, nearly a ninety-degree angle.

"I don't want to hear you bring up my brother again," Clyde says coldly.

"All right, man, all right. I'm sorry. But I think Mary can do us good. She's smart. Savvy. A schemer, I dare say. Just a couple jobs more"—he motions between the two of 'em—"then we'll be on our way. And, come on, man, I haven't seen her since before I was locked up. A man's got needs. I know you know that."

What this fella doesn't know is when to shut his trap. Clyde's annoyance flares and he flicks the tip of his cigarette, a spark flying back toward Raymond, who's wise not to complain.

But I say, "Have you know, I ain't here for Clyde's virile needs." Our needing each other goes both ways, and is more significant than some body to hold.

Raymond's quick to apologize.

As he should; last I heard, Mary's held plenty of bodies to make a buck. I don't know what Raymond wants with a prostitute.

Clyde exhales. "Another set of eyes ain't the worst thing in the world. Bonnie, got a hankering to see Mary again?"

Do I? I shrug. We ended on well enough terms when Doc's closed its doors, but like I said, that was years ago. Years can change people. It's changed me.

The next day, Mary's waiting under the awning of a tattoo parlor on the outskirts of Dallas. Raymond stumbles out of the car, having shot himself with some morphine on the way there, and twirls her 'round.

It'd be sweet, if mixed emotions weren't hitting me from all sides.

Raymond opens the rear door, announcing, "Look what the cat dragged in."

Mary crawls in, a face so caked with makeup it'd take the strength of ten men to scrub it off. Her hair's shorter than I remember, and it looks as if she had a finger curl—too many days ago.

The first time I saw Mary I remember thinking she had *It.* Sex appeal. The way she moved was suggestive. Her clothing was the nines. Not a stand of hair was out of place.

Granted, at the moment, she's crawling 'cross the backseat, her knee catching on her black fur coat, but I can't help thinking, *She's lost the* It.

That doesn't stop her from sitting down with an *oomph* and adjusting her long coat. Raymond reaches into the car, handing her a fur hat, and she fashions it just so, tilted to one side.

"Hello there, Saint Bonnelyn. Clyde."

I feel like I'm seventeen again, meeting Mary for the first time. Cat had my tongue then, and at twenty-three years old, cat's got my tongue now. Mary's got that way 'bout her, where ya intrinsically know it'd be bad to do or say anything to displease her.

"Let's put the cards on the table, shall we?" she says. The tone of her voice ruffles my feathers. "I'm a sporting girl, yeah, and I've been at this racket awhile. Do I like it? Can't say I enjoy the smell or the weight of those men on me. But it's better than eight hours a day—if I could even get the job—standing behind some counter, talking nice to whoever walks up. I'd rather talk nice to men with money to spend, without getting flat-footed or sway-backed from being on my feet all day. I get three times as much money lying flat on my back." She takes Raymond's hand. "My sweetheart knows what I do, and I know what he does." Mary meets my eyes. "And now, we all know, so I don't want to see you looking down your nose at me, Bonnelyn."

I bob my head, prudently. I let the silence stretch, but I realize it's not 'cause I'm intimidated anymore, but 'cause . . . "I'm going to lay the cards out on the table for you, Mary. I ain't the same gal you bossed 'round. I know a little something 'bout surviving, and if you want to ride with us"—I motion between Clyde and me—"I'll look at whoever, however I want." I let that sink in, then add, "And I go by *Bonnie* now."

Clyde puts the car into gear. "Glad that's all settled."

30

WHAT'S NOT SETTLED IS HOW LONG RAYMOND AND MARY are going to be with us. Two more jobs? Three? To get our farm, we need more. We got a good haul the other day, though. Mary's eyes lit up as Clyde and Raymond split the money, each adding to their stashes.

I lay stretched out on a blanket, staring up at the trees. My fingers tap against my stomach. The boys are off hitting somewhere else, something smaller this time. Clyde wants a break from banks, and he's likely to hit a place like an oil station, a meat packing plant, or a Piggly Wiggly grocery store.

Mary went into town to get us food, hopefully at a place Clyde ain't robbing. Town's at least a mile away, and I know she's going to regret walking all that way in her military heels. But I need a break from the gal, so I let her go without any type of fuss. She always seems to be at my hip, and for the life of me, I can't look at her without seeing Blanche, without knowing I ruined Blanche.

I roll onto my side, catching my eye on a rabbit two trees away. I begin to move for the pistol I always keep beneath the blanket, then stop. I don't have it in me to shoot the thing, and Mary's supposed to be bringing back food.

Boy, am I ready to escape this life, once and for all. I know Clyde and me don't exactly have a place to go yet, no land we've claimed as our own, but I need it to be Clyde and me, with no one else riding his coattails. That's what they do. They look at Clyde and see him as someone who's evaded the law for nearly two years now. He must know what he's doing. That must be what they're thinking. So here they are, hiding with us. Robbing with us.

I reckon Clyde uses 'em back, him not all that keen on robbing alone. Ain't like I can help.

An engine roars not far off, and now I got the pistol firmly in my hand. The sound cuts off, and I watch between the trees for any movement. I spot two men—one tall, one shorter, both carrying bags—and I lower my gun.

Raymond calls, "Where's Mary?"

"She went to fetch food forever ago."

Clyde shoots him a look, and it ain't a friendly one.

Raymond's already backpedaling. "I'm going. I'll get her."

Clyde hands him our keys, giving him a warning glare, then drops on the blanket beside me, laying his head 'cross my middle. Our loot's in a large bag beside us, always close by.

He says, "I don't trust that lass."

I stroke his hair. "Why's that? I mean, Mary ain't easy to like, but she's harmless, no?"

"She comes from a rat family. Odell may be my pal, but I've always been careful what I say 'round him. And I can't figure why she's here. Last I heard Mary was part of a ringer house, meaning she had a madam to answer to. Unless she's giving that all up . . ." He shrugs.

"She misses Raymond?"

"Would you miss that lout?"

I laugh.

Clyde turns his head, his cheek resting on my stomach. And there's a hint of fear in his eyes, along with sadness. "I don't like Mary off unsupervised, is all. What if she makes a deal? Bonnie"—he licks his lips—"I haven't wanted to tell you this, but back in Sowers when the law almost got us, that man driving was a family friend of my pa's. So-called friend," he corrects. "He got a car and a fistful of money to let the po-lice know where we'd be. Where I'd be. The rest of you were put at risk 'cause of me."

"The rest of us chose to be there. Clyde, I choose to be here. With you. Whatever that may bring."

He breathes, long and hard. "Say, I got something to show you. Something happier than all this." He produces a newspaper he had tucked in his trousers. "Now, I ain't one to pat my own back."

"Sure you are."

He playfully narrows his eyes. "Go on and give her a read."

I take the paper, not sure what he's getting at. I'm not surprised to see his photo. Since pictures can be wired through telegraph, photos of us appear in any ol' newspaper 'cross the country. But the headline already has me shaking my head, giving me a clue 'bout Clyde's inflated head.

BARROW

That's it. "What is this?"

He's smiling. "Read it, Bonnie. It's a poem some lass sent in."

My country 'cause of thee
Sweet land of misery
Please hear my plea.
The bank's my enemy,
It stole so much from me.

I look up at Clyde. "Why'd they print this?" I'm reading again before he can answer. The writer sweetly goes on 'bout how Clyde's a phantom, evading the police—and thus, providing entertainment at a time when spirits are at their lowest. I can see it; a newspaper cost two cents, or nothin' if picked up off the ground. They're common enough, used plenty to shield the homeless from the cold. We know a thing or two 'bout that.

"The end's where it gets good. Skip there," Clyde says.

When his gun goes rat-tat-tat
My heart goes pitter-pat.

"Come on," I say.

"What?" Clyde's grinning like a fool. "I think she's got talent."

I laugh.

I say, leave the 'bad man' be
But if he's caught,
Bring that Barrow straight to me.

"Wow." I try to hide a smile, but this Barrow pulls it out of me. "Why'd they even publish this?"

"Clearly, it gets a reaction."

"Clearly. Well, sorry, Mabel K. Moore, he's all mine."

"Oh, is Mabel her name? Does it also say where she's from?"

I raise the paper, ready to whack him. "I never should've taught you to read."

"Too late for that, darling, and now—"

A Ford rumbles nearby. "They're back," I deadpan.

And they stay 'round. Always yappin', when they're awake, that is. I can't help averting my eyes when I catch a flash of silver and a dark bottle. As the morphine works in their bodies, their voices grow louder.

Wherever we are, sleeping in the car, resting out under the trees, taking birdbaths from whatever water we're near—I try to quiet 'em.

"Oh, Saint Bonnelyn, who's going to hear us out here?" Mary rubs her fingers together, as if brushing off dirt. "The trees? I don't know why your man can't put you up in a real place. Has he heard of a hotel?"

I grit my teeth and wait for 'em to come down from their high. Then, they sleep—and it's blissfully quiet. Unless we got to move, then they complain if they're jostled awake by a bumpy road. But Clyde insists: If we're dozing on the side of the road and someone drives past, that's it. We need to change locations in case the fella decides to double back. Clyde'll drive two hundred, three hundred miles, 'til I'm sure his eyes are 'bout to bleed, before he pulls over again. After that, he'll sleep all day. If he can, without us having to move again. Being we don't got a pattern. I reckon it makes it harder for the law to guess where we're hiding.

"Clyde," I whisper one night. This time we tucked ourselves in the woods, out of the car, hoping for a full night's sleep. I ain't sure if he's awake or not, stretched out beside me on his back. He's got his eyes closed but his fingers steepled on his stomach. If I didn't know better, that boy's praying. "Clyde."

He opens one eye. "Yes, darling?"

Raymond and Mary are on the other side of our campfire, only the embers glowing. Even now those two feel too nearby. With a bit of a struggle, I pull myself closer to Clyde. The springtime weather's been warmer, but damper, and it's like every drop of moisture cramps up my knee that much more.

"I ain't sure I can take much more of 'em. Mary's been ribbing at me."

He absently plays with the serpent ring he made for me. "She's jealous of you."

"Of me? She don't seem to 'specially enjoy this lifestyle of mine."

"She's jealous you got more waiting for you."

The way he says it, a hint of excitement in his voice, has me propping myself up on my elbow. The moon's full tonight, lighting up the sky and one of his dimples. "Clyde Barrow, is there something you ain't telling me?"

He nods, years dropping from his face. "Found out something this morning when I made some calls. Something good. But I've been holding it close, 'fraid I'll jinx us."

"Clyde, you're going to make me burst!"

He lets out one of those laughs that's all breath. "I live to see you this way, all lit up. Okay," he quickly adds when I drum my fingers on his chest. "Henry Methvin wants to meet back up with us." He holds up a hand to quiet my protests. "But only 'cause he's got land for us."

I sit up. "Land?"

"His daddy's. Ya know, that land you were planning in your head." He winks.

I'm at a loss for words. All this time, land, land, land. It's what we've been working for. And here it is, Henry putting it on a silver platter for us. "Clyde . . ." I palm my mouth.

"I know, Bonnie, I can't quite believe it either. But he says it's ours if we want it."

"Can we afford it?"

"He don't want much for it. Nothin', really. Henry said the house and all that land is too much for his daddy. The deed was handed to him dirt cheap, so he wants to pass it on. Maybe he's hoping for that good Lord of yours to drop some good fortune in his lap for helping us out."

"You think? But what 'bout Henry? He's a wanted man. Ain't his daddy's land a safe haven for him?"

"That's his business, and the lad hasn't given me a reason to question him. My business is giving you what I promised. That is, if you want it?"

"That's a fool's question. When do we leave?"

"We're going to meet up with Henry first. He'll take us there."

"Fine, then, when we doing that?"

Clyde smirks. "Soon."

• • •

I'm giddy. With vigor, I scrub my extra dress in the river. I don't even care my hands are a splotchy red. When's the last time I've been honest-to-goodness giddy? It's got to be when Blanche told me that Clyde was coming for me, when I was locked away in that jail. And now, Clyde's coming through again, making good on his promise to get us out of this life and onto our own land.

I drop my dress and, on my knees, I splash the cold water on my face. It's exhilarating, even as my body shimmies from the blast of coldness.

I don't want to get too ahead of myself, 'cause life has a way of yanking me back, but I can't help continuing my daydream I started days ago as we drove up to our soon-to-be farmhouse. I'll want to bring out my ma, after we make sure it's safe, of course. She can rest her fingers after sewing at the factory for countless years. And Clyde's parents—I wring water from my dress—his parents can finally leave their nightmares from Dallas behind.

I fling my dress in the air, catch it as it comes back down.

"Is that how ya wash clothes without a nice man from the dry cleaners doing it for ya? Maybe I can pay you to do mine," Mary says.

I ain't too big to admit a soft growl rumbles in my throat at both the comment and Mary's presence. I'd keep washing, but I'm done. Instead, I try to stand but the damned grass is slick.

"Looks like ya could use a hand, *Bonnie.*" She puffs on her cigarette, blowing the smoke from the corner of her mouth. "Wouldn't hurt for us to play nice. Let me start by helping you up."

I accept her hand; standing up can be a son of a bitch, a bigger bitch than Mary. I go to let go, hopping ain't anything new to me, but Mary holds on tight. She leads me back to our campsite. Clyde ain't here. But he didn't tell me he was going anywhere, and the car's still here. I look 'round, but all I see is Raymond with his arms behind his head, his ankles crossed, hat over his face.

"Why don't you have a seat," Mary says, "and I can do something nice with your hair."

I pat my head, letting my hand linger there. The dye I darkened it with has long grown out, that being 'bout a year ago. I haven't done up my hair yet today. I usually do, even if it's putting on a hat and fingering some waves into the hair that shows.

"Go on," Mary urges and practically pushes me onto my blanket. "Turn this way," she demands. "The lights better through the trees."

I sigh, but do as she says and let her fuss with my hair. Ain't long before my stomach is hollering at me, coiling itself into knots. This . . . right here . . . someone doing my hair is something Blanche would do. I grab my hat, twisting the crochet fabric between my hands. It's hard to think 'bout Blanche without being hard on myself. But I should be, after all I put her through and where she is now—without the man she loves. I reckon that's something I'm going to pay for, for all of eternity.

Mary shifts on her knees, stopping in front of me. Her tongue sticks out the corner of her mouth as she calculates her next move. She gestures for my hat, and I hand it over.

Up close, under all that makeup, I notice a scar. And another. I search for more, but Mary's eyes flick to mine, and I look away. Makes me wonder, once again, what the past four years have done to Mary. If maybe these marks are from overzealous or unhappy Johns. It'd be easy for Mary to get morphine from her uncle to numb the pain, whatever pain that may be. Easy, too, for Raymond to get hooked on her stash, and also on Mary.

Sad. That's what it is.

"Hey," I say softly. "How's your uncle?"

She doesn't respond, and I search her face. Mary's gaze ain't on my hair, it's overtop my head. I start to move, and Mary snaps back to attention, holding my head in place. Tight, too tightly.

"Mary," I say.

"Sorry, Bonnie, just a li'l more."

"No, what's going on?" The gal ain't much bigger than me—probably only a hundred pounds soaking wet—and I tear out of her grasp. Raymond's hat is on the ground the last place I saw him, sleeping. Now he's at the car, on the driver's side. That right there is peculiar enough. Clyde always drives.

"Raymond." I draw out his name. He's frozen still, his hand under the breast of his jacket. "What ya doing over there? Where's Clyde?"

As if responding to his name, Clyde strides from the trees, his Browning rifle trained on Raymond. Without thinking, without a reason why, I pull my pistol from beneath my blanket and make Mary my target.

"Clyde," I say. "Why we got our guns aimed at these two?"

"Reckon that's a better question for Ray. Bet if he empties his pockets, you'll have your answer."

Mary curses under her breath.

Clyde wags at Raymond with his gun. "Go on now."

By the time he's done, Raymond—nothin' more than a snake—has tossed five stacks of money, wrapped 'round the middle with a band, onto the front seat.

He says, "Clyde, man, let's not do anything rash."

Clyde spits on the ground, and Raymond quiets down.

I brace myself for the gunshot. Ain't anyone 'round to hear, and this is the second time Raymond's double-crossed us, this time skimming from our money. I may hobble over there and do it myself. But Clyde only says to me, "Let's go, Bonnie. This bullet's better served elsewhere. Ray's good enough dead as is."

I bend to grab my blanket, but Clyde says to leave it. "We've got better waiting for us."

Ain't that the truth.

31

A FEW MILES DOWN THE ROAD, CLYDE AND I SHARE A GLANCE and both start laughing. We left those scoundrels high and dry—before they could go and do it to us. That had to be their plan: rob us blind then skedaddle.

Clyde whistles. "Ain't that something?"

"Where were you? Before all that?"

"Off sitting in the woods."

I cock my head.

"I don't trust a dopehead as far as I can throw him, and Ray's a big lad. A broad like Mary is only after money. Had a feeling they were scheming long before she crawled into our backseat. I simply gave 'em the opportunity by making myself scarce."

I try to mimic Clyde's whistle, but I've never been one for whistling. Clyde chuckles. "At least your hair looks pretty." He means to keep our jokes going, but the mention of hair strikes a chord with me. "Hey, now, Bonnie, why's that face of yours going south?"

"I've been thinkin' a lot 'bout Blanche."

"We'll get her back." And I know he doesn't mean out of prison. I twist my lips, not so sure Blanche'll come near us again, 'specially since she'll see Buck every time she sets eyes on Clyde. "Well," he says, "we can try. But first, let's get Methvin. We got us a drive back to Texas."

I don't question why he's there instead of Louisiana. But, like us, I can reckon most fugitives like to roam. A few hundred miles later, Clyde pats Henry on the back. Clyde's mostly cordial with his fellas, but Henry's royalty to us now. I give him my own one-hundred-watt smile and a hug. I didn't think I'd be so happy to welcome one of the fellas back into our car. But here he is, and tomorrow's a fresh start. Tonight, we'll find a side of the road to sleep on 'til someone passes by, then we're off to Louisiana. That ride, if we're hugging the state lines, could eat up a full day.

I wake to the distant sound of church bells, a beautiful sound. Propped against the passenger-side door, my head resting on a rolled-up blanket, I don't bother moving or opening my eyes. I only listen. Clyde's got us on a backcountry road, but I'm surprised we lasted all night and into the morning, which is already warm. I'm glad we slept with the windows down.

My church back in Cement City has a single bell. From the overlapping clings and clangs, this melody is the result of numerous chimes. I wonder if every Sunday they put together such a complex harmony, then I realize it's Easter. March is now behind us, and it's the first of April.

The harmony continues, and I try to memorize it, wishing there were words so I could sing along. I picture Billie smiling.

Ain't long before there's a rumble, a revving. With Texas being so flat, that noise, like the bells, can carry. I open my eyes, certain Clyde will be rousing, too. He's got a sixth sense for the sound of engines. Henry's still asleep in the back. Clyde immediately orients himself. His eyes flash to me, to his rifle, to his rearview mirror, to the key he keeps in place. He's halfway to reaching for the ignition key when he pauses. I twist in my seat, seeing what Clyde hears. Two motorcycles approach over a hill.

I can't help remembering the last time a motorcycle came up behind us.

"Hurry, Clyde, should we go?"

Clyde's knee bobs. "That might turn them onto us if we take off. It's too late now. We'll let 'em pass, then head the way they came."

"Henry," he shouts, and slides his gun along his right leg, hidden out of sight, "look alive. We've got company coming up behind us. Let's hope they go by." He says the last part mostly to himself.

Poor Henry isn't as quick to wake up. He ain't as quick to conceal his gun. Before I know it, I'm sucking in my breath 'cause those motorcyclers are right outside our car, and they aren't going by.

In fact, they're patrolmen with shiny badges on their chests.

From the corner of my eye, I watch, my heart pounding. "They look green," I whisper, leaning closer so Clyde can hear me over all the engines. "Don't even got a hand on their guns. Bet they're peach-fuzz cops."

The one officer knocks on Clyde's door. Clyde stares straight ahead, his fingertips dancing on his gun. He nods, agreeing with me. "Henry," he says between his teeth. Their eyes meet in the rearview mirror. "Let's take 'em."

I've seen Clyde kidnap before. He's likely to throw open his door, startling the officer before shoving a gun in his face. With Henry doing it, too, the patrolmen will be in the back of our car in no time.

'Cept there's a bang. I do a double take, my brain taking precious seconds to catch up. Henry's out of the car, firing. Then Clyde's doing it, too. All that's left is empty bikes.

Clyde ducks his head to get back into our car.

"Shit!" He punches the wheel. "Get in," he calls to Henry.

But I want to kick Henry right back out.

"Hostages," Clyde says, his voice eerily calm. "That's what I meant by take 'em."

Henry grabs clumps of his hair. "Fuck."

That word comes out plenty more. I press the heel of my palms into my eyes, not believing that only minutes ago, I was listening to the melody of church bells, and now it's a string of profanities. When I drop my hands, my eye catches on Clyde's ring, and my breath shudders, knowing this mishap—if ya can even call it that—is a monstrous step back.

The bells are long gone. We're long gone. There wasn't anyone 'round to chase us, a small blessing.

"We can't go to the farm straight away." Clyde talks to himself, barely loud enough for me to hear. I grit my teeth, with nothin' helpful to say, so I sit here, twisting my ill-fated wedding band. "I won't risk it. Can't lead any heat there. Got to get a new car. Got to drive. Dammit to hell."

We pass a sign for FORT WORTH. POPULATION: 106,482.

I slink lower into my seat, feeling the familiar pang of nerves. I search for the false confidence I sometimes get at being another pretty face in a sea of people, but it's hard to come by, knowing that the lives of two patrolmen are draining out of 'em onto a dirt road.

Downtown is a mass of buildings, jutting into the sky at staggering heights. Brick buildings. Stone buildings. Signs for drugstores, theaters, tailors, and the like, snake up buildings and dangle from awnings.

Clyde points at a small red light blinking on and off near an intersection as we pass through. I bet it's flickering 'cause of us. I imagine cops responding to the signal, scurrying for a call box, checking in with their headquarters to get their assignments.

To find us.

Do they know it was us?

Clyde stops at the first Ford V-8 he sees. "Henry," he says. "Follow me out of town."

I straighten in my seat, not wanting Clyde to go anywhere without me. But that boy's seeing red right now, and I ain't going to cross him.

"No," Clyde adds and steps on the gas pedal. "I've a different idea. I used to spend some time over in the stockyards. Lads in those parts keep their heads down. Let's get us a room."

I can't help myself: "A hotel room?"

"I reckon anyone looking for us wouldn't expect it, and Bonnie, look up at those clouds. They look mighty heavy to me."

And fierce. That's reason enough for me to want shelter in something other than our auto.

A streetcar rides beside us for a stretch. A dark-haired boy presses his nose to the window, staring down at me. He waves. He can't be more than five or six, but I've got anxiety firing on all cylinders. I sink lower in my seat and inch my hat down.

"Bonnie, say, name a lass from the pictures."

"Right now?"

"I've an idea."

I scratch my forehead "Joan Crawford."

"And another."

"Other day I read 'bout this li'l gal, Shirley Temple. She got her start at only three. She's 'round five now." Nerves keep me saying, "Ya know, I found my first stage 'round that age. Buster pushed me up there on a Sunday morning, with all the kids taking turns to sing a song. Gal before me sang 'Jesus Loves Me,' but when *my* mouth opened, out came 'He's a Devil In His Own Hometown.'"

I recall a line:

When it comes to women, oh! oh! oh! oh!

He's a devil, he's a devil.

Behind me, Henry smiles, but he doesn't make a sound, probably wanting Clyde to forget he's even there. Clyde shakes his head, but he's clearly amused. "How on earth did you know that honky-tonk song?"

I shrug. "Heard it on the radio."

"Okay, how on earth did that story never come up at supper with your ma?"

"She's still mortified, is my best guess."

Clyde's laugh is deep. Gloriously deep. "All right, my li'l mischief-maker, this should be easy enough for you. You and Henry will check in to the hotel under the names Shirley Crawford and"—he gestures—"give me a big actor."

"James Cagney," I offer.

"You two will check in as Shirley and James Crawford. Ya hear that, Henry?"

"Yes, sir."

That *sir* is comical. Henry can't be more than a year or two younger than me. Double that for Clyde. But Henry knows this extra heat is on us 'cause of him, and more important, that Clyde calls the shots.

"I'll get rid of our Ford," Clyde states, "then I'll stroll in to the hotel through the front door, a thirsty patron, settling closest to the radio at the bar. Bonnie, get the room key. Henry, get her there."

Henry's a few heads taller than Clyde. Despite the fact I'd rather use my arm to whack Henry upside the head, I hold on to his waist. His arm winds 'round me. My free hand has our bag with our measly belongings and loot. He easily carries me at his side, my feet tap-dancing 'cross the floor. To anyone, we're a young married couple attached at the hip, and I got the band on my finger to prove it. Not like anyone will recognize me without a stogie between my lips, that being the only photo of me the papers ever care to print.

The lobby ain't grand, but it's dripping with local flavor. The town's known as the last stop before the Wild West. A cheerful woman behind a desk greets us. I meet her cheer and—presto—there's a room key in Henry's hand.

"Three oh five. You see that, honey? Three oh five happens to be my lucky number."

I say it nice and loud. Over at the bar, Clyde brings a tumbler to his lips and his shoulders slightly bob at my theatrics.

Upstairs, safely behind closed doors, I exhale. Henry excuses himself to use the little boys' room, and I finger open the drapes. To the left, a sign stretches 'cross the dusty brick road, letting us know we're in the stock-yards. To the right, Exchange Avenue meets Main Street, the direction trouble would come from if the law tracks us down.

There ain't many buildings taller than us. It ain't like downtown. Here, the saloons and shops are attached in a long strip of brick, which the rain is currently pummeling. Good thing the men scattering like ants got those big ol' cowboy hats to keep the wet off their heads.

I'm starting to get antsy 'bout Clyde's whereabouts when a knock bangs on the door. Henry's still in the water closet. I slide my pistol out of my skirt, holding it under my chin while I tuck in my blouse again. Arm bent, the pistol goes behind my back. I edge open the door.

Then it's all thumps and heavy breaths as I'm whisked 'cross the room with a hand under each cheek—butt cheeks, that is—and, by sheer momentum, my legs wrap 'round him. Clyde. "You're a madman," I squeal.

"Mad 'bout you, Miss Crawford." He tosses us on one bed, tosses my pistol on the second, and palms my face. "You really are beautiful."

"You really are drunk."

"Not quite, only had one pour. But between us, it don't take much more. I'm simply glad to be anywhere but out there." He nods toward the window, the wind howling beyond. "With you."

Henry emerges from the bathroom.

"And Methvin," Clyde adds, with less enthusiasm. Much less.

• • •

It takes a while for that howling to stop, even longer for the rain. I pull aside the drapes, careful the light doesn't stir Henry. The rain's still coming down. Besides foot traffic and a few cars, all's quiet below. There ain't police running this way. I slump into a chair by the desk and roll my head left to right, right to left.

It's been a few blissful days of running water, electricity, and soft beds. Each morning Clyde brings a paper to me, like he's off doing right now, and we scour the headlines. We haven't been in there, not for the murders of the patrolmen, at least. But last time Clyde saddled up to a bar in the shadows of a saloon, he heard mention on the radio how funerals are being prepared for E. B. Wheeler and H. D. Murphy of the Texas State Highway Patrol.

I tap my fingernails against the wood desk. That ain't something I feel good 'bout. Lousy, actually. So many of Clyde's deaths are out of necessity, but this here was a fool's mistake, a mistake that may mess up our plans to get to our farm after all. Sounds callous to put it that way, but I'm not sure there's another way to frame it.

A key rattles in our lock, and Clyde walks in. He taps a newspaper, folded in half, against his hand.

"What?" I say. "What's it say in there?"

"Am I that obvious?"

"Clyde, I know you inside and out. And right now your outside looks sour. Did you read it?"

"Some of it. Its words are a fair bit larger than that poem the other day."

"Give it here," I say and spread it wide on the desk.

OFFICERS SLAIN BY KILL-CRAZY YOUTH AND HIS MOLL.

"Now that ain't the whole truth. You ain't looking for people to kill."

"Bonnie, darling, if you're already upset, you best stop while you're ahead."

I stare at his face one, two seconds longer, trying to read his expression. I come to the conclusion: defeated.

"Clyde, you ain't giving up, are ya?"

He rubs his lips together. "On our farm, nah. But what they're saying 'bout us here will make it harder for us to get there." He points at the paper, for me to keep reading. I can, I think, only 'cause I know Clyde ain't throwing in the towel.

The first paragraph ain't even 'bout Easter morning. It's a sensational account of the things we've done. Us laughing vindictively as we escape the scene of a crime. Me, described as *always* having a large, black cigar gripped between my teeth. A vivid account of a shopkeeper dying in a pool of his own blood.

"You've never killed a shopkeeper."

"Lads and I took out an operator at a filling station, remember?" He rubs his brow. "While you were locked up. Maybe that's what they mean."

"Did you pull the trigger?"

"Does it matter? The man's dead."

"Clyde."

"It was Ray, as far as I know. I was busy cleaning out their safe when the shot went off."

I keep reading, feeling twitchy, feeling torn. We're called "a pair of human rats." They got my age wrong, saying I'm only nineteen. But they didn't miss how I was married before, and my husband now rots in jail. Somewhere between these half-lies is the truth, and the truth of the matter is we've been the ringleaders behind many gruesome murders.

Finally, the patrolmen on those motorcycles are mentioned. Edward Bryan Wheeler. Only twenty-six. Then Holloway Daniel Murphy. Twenty-two. Murphy's younger than us, and it's, no lie, his first day on the job. These deaths sting like a hornet. Clyde was supposed to drive 'em far away from their precinct then let 'em loose, like we've done before. Instead, they'll be pushing up daisies.

I palm my mouth and say, "No."

There, in black-and-white, is a photo of a young woman in a wedding gown. I saw it when I first spread the paper, but I didn't think it'd be part of this story. Yet it is. Murphy's fiancé wore her unused gown to the funeral. Unused by only eleven days.

Bring my fiancé's killers to justice.

I swallow but nothin' goes down, and I got to look away from her picture before anything comes up. I greedily read, driven by the horror. My stomach knots more at a supposed eyewitness account, which is how the law fingered us for the crimes.

The red-haired dame—guess that's me—*used the sole of her foot to flop the young patrolmen onto his back, cackling at him the whole time. Then, she shot him point blank.*

'Cept I never even got out of the car. That sparks my anger. "That so-called witness is saying I turned him over with my foot. He clearly didn't get a look at me. Did he forget to mention how I hopped on over on one leg? Did I levitate," I say, my voice growing hysterical, "so I could flip him with my one good foot?"

"Bonnie. That's enough. You've had enough." Clyde kneels next to me and grips my face, turning me to him. Before he does, my eyes catch on a phrase.

Dead or alive.

AFTER CALMING ME DOWN, CLYDE'S HANDS RUBBING UP AND down my arms, he shakes Henry awake. We pay up for another twenty-four hours, but leave midday, our heads down, looking guilty as sin. Clyde spots a Ford out front and we're on our way. We trade for another Ford a few miles later. Even in these parts, we can't count on people looking the other way. Not anymore.

Clyde curses, and not for the first time.

Love poems by gals like Mabel K. Moore will become something of the past. Who's going to applaud outlaws portrayed to have zero trace of a soul? How long before they seize their proverbial pitchforks and shout for our escapades to come to an end?

Yet there's one consoling thought: If we make it to the farm tomorrow, how long before they grow tired of searching the papers for "Bonnie and Clyde"?

We won't be in there, for anything factual, at least.

The car's movement has me woozy. I grip the door handle.

Clyde's head ticks toward me. I'm puzzling him; we're barely moving on the rain-soaked roads, but I feel like I need to hold on. I feel the tide turning. No, it ain't turning. Those waters *have* turned. And now they're churning 'round us.

We head north into Oklahoma. Louisiana is southeast. That's the direction I want to go. Henry does, too. "My father's going to think something went wrong if we don't get to the farm soon."

"The land won't up and walk away, will it? We still got a deal, don't we, Henry?"

"Of course. It's just been longer to get there than I thought it would."

Clyde flicks the underside of his hat, lifting the shadow from over his eyes. The look he gives Henry in the rearview mirror is clear.

Whose fault is that?

But he says, "The roads up in these parts are gravel. We're better off here than inching 'cross the south."

"Not the road we're on," I say.

"No," Clyde says evenly. "But we ain't far off. 'Nother few miles."

The mud's so thick I'm afraid we won't make it to the crunch of gravel. And gravel means flat tires. Mud or a flat. What choices.

I bet the water in the field over yonder would come halfway to my knees. Rows of spinach or lettuce leaves—I can't tell which—barely show. The setting sun reflects on the water, making the plants the same reddish tint.

I ask, "What's that saying? Red sky at night . . ."

"Sailor's delight," Clyde answers.

Then, we ain't moving anymore; the mud gets us before we can see if the gravel will give us a flat.

Clyde's door squeaks open, and he circles the car. Henry joins him. I turn in my seat, following whichever way they go. Soon, they've got both hands on the trunk, and I'm rocking forward and back, barely so. Seems their feet keep slipping. I get out of the car, as if my weight will matter much. It doesn't. With one hand sliding down the car, I hobble to help. Each hop is precarious, the mud slick and squishy, but I make it, frowning 'bout our newest ridiculous debacle.

I get to pushing, if what I'm doing with two hands and one leg can be called that. I'm more leaning against the thing—before I slip, both palms and a knee leaving indentations in the mud. Clyde gets me 'round the waist and back to the mud-free passenger seat, where I shake out my hands. "What now?"

He sighs. "I ain't keen on trucking through those fields." He scours the other side of the road. A few buildings and some machinery dot the top of a hill. "An old mining company looks to be that way."

"Clyde," Henry calls. "We've got company coming."

"Law?"

"It's hard to tell."

I peer over the seat, out through the back windshield, and I can't tell either. It ain't like patrolmen get special automobiles, unless you count the P.D. or POLICE that's sometimes painted on the sides.

"Don't see any writing," I say. "But it's getting dark."

Clyde removes his hat, wipes his brow, puts his hat back in place. "Bonnie, hold my Browning in your lap, will ya? Give it here if it looks like I'll need it."

I cradle the rifle like a baby, ready for Clyde to snatch it.

Feels like an eternity before the car rolls up on our left. Clyde's on my side of the road, his left hand on the roof, his right hand dangling by me.

"Stuck?" the driver calls.

"Yeah, got ourselves bogged down," Clyde says.

I angle myself away, giving the passerby a view of my back and not Clyde's gun. But when I glance over my shoulder, the man's standing on his running board, both hands on the roof—and his eyes ain't on me. They're on the seat behind me, where we've got a few guns in plain sight.

Clyde's voice booms, demanding the man's attention. "We could really use another hand." The man's eyes flick to Henry. But Clyde, he scrutinizes. By the way his mouth drops open, but no words come out, it's clear the caper is up. This man knows he's two car widths from the now infamous Clyde Barrow.

Clyde says, "We'll be on our way after that. You go yours, we'll go ours."

Meaning, *We don't have a reason to hurt ya.*

Fumbling, the fella's butt first goes in the mud before he climbs into his driver's seat. We get a clear view of his taillights after that.

"This ain't good," I say.

"If I were a betting man, he'll go straight to the law. He's too spooked not to." Clyde jiggles his fingers, and I hand over his Browning. "Get your pistol, Bonnie."

That's when I realize it's not here to get. My head's been all clouded up. I close my eyes, picturing the dang thing on the hotel bed. "Left it at the stockyards," I say.

"Grab one from the back," Clyde says to me. "Henry, you watch the north. I got the south. Fire at anything that comes our way. Straight off. You don't wait for shots to be fired. You hear?"

Henry nods and trudges through the mud toward the front tire. The boy swallows with each step. Adrenaline drove his trigger finger before. This'll be different for him. It'll be different for Clyde, too. He doesn't like to shoot first but—I suck in air, feeling as if electricity is laced through it—whatever semblance of a moral code Clyde's lived by doesn't matter anymore. It stopped mattering Easter morning.

"Bonnie," Clyde says, "I want you down on the floorboard as small as you'll go."

I don't want to hide down by our trash and road maps. I want to stand by my man. What I realize, though, is that Clyde needs for me to be safe. So, my heart pounds into my thighs, my head rests on my knees, and I pray headlights don't come our way.

Night could fall. The mud could harden. It could happen.

33

I LISTEN FOR ANY INDICATION SOMEONE'S HEADED OUR WAY, but it's quiet. Over time, my pulse ain't racing, but it still lets me know it's there.

So does the sun, though barely.

Henry repositions. The mud squelches.

I tap my foot and cringe at the pricking sensation. A pen, or something sharp, pokes into my rear.

Clyde hollers, "Look alert. Got eyes on someone headed this way."

Suddenly, my pulse is at it again. Knees to my chest, I breathe out so long it's like I'm breathing fire straight into my legs. I ain't sure what Clyde's waiting for. Maybe he's had a change of heart. Then, no, it's like firecrackers go off. My heart flutters, panic seizing me, then it's over. In less than three seconds, a twenty-round clip can release from a gun like Clyde's—and it did.

I pop my head up. Clyde's waving away smoke, crouched down. Maybe thirty yards ahead there's a copper's car.

"Henry!" Clyde sweeps his arm, motioning him over.

The boy's feet look like they're stuck in the mud. He's proven he can handle a gun. Henry was in the pen for armed robbery, after all. But here he is, with both his hands slack at his sides, a gun dangling at the end of one hand, and I reckon he'd be happy to never hold a firearm again.

"Henry," Clyde demands. "Go on and check our handiwork."

The boy starts going.

Clyde says, "Hurry now."

Henry runs, slipping in the muck. Casually, Clyde takes another clip from his pocket. Turns out, he doesn't need it. Into our backseat, Henry leads an officer, with a head wound I need a better look at. A second patrolman is left behind, good as dead. Henry's words, not mine. And I'm reminded again how badly I want out of this world.

With my pistol propped on the back of my seat, I kneel, and keep an eye on . . . "What's your first name?"

"Percy."

Squinting through the darkness of the car, his badge fills in the rest. I keep an eye on Percy Boyd, Police Chief.

The car rocks forward, back, forward once more. Clyde and Henry ain't having better luck this time.

"And yours?"

I sigh. "I think you know my name."

For a man bleeding from his head, his expression is one of a cocky son of a gun. "Bonnie Thornton."

"No," I say reflexively; I expected to hear *Parker*, not *Thornton*, and I glance at my wedding band. "That's nothin' more than my legal name." My gaze dances to my right hand, and my heart sinks to the floorboards. My serpent ring is gone. In the mud? Maybe when I shook off my hands.

I breathe out sharply.

Percy asks, "Everything all right?"

I regrip my gun. "Are *you* all right? I ain't bleeding from the head."

"Bumped it, is all."

I resist the urge to jump from the car and paw through the mud. I overcompensate, staring hard at Percy. His eyelids aren't quite even. One droops lower than the other. His nose is crooked, as if he's broken it before. Looks to be in his thirties.

I say, "You don't look scared."

"I am."

"You don't look it."

"So you've said."

I twist my lips. "Take off your tie."

He does, no questions asked.

"Now," I say, "you move quick or put your hand on me, I'll scream. If I scream, you'll be able to count your last breaths on one hand."

With that, I crawl from the front to the back, no small feat while keeping my gun on the man. "Remember what I said." I discreetly pull up the side of my skirt and tuck the gun underneath, then I wrap Percy's tie 'round his head wound. "Too tight?"

"Nah."

I'm back up front, gun back on Percy. Ain't the smartest thing I've done, making myself vulnerable and all that, but it felt like the right thing to do.

"Got some eyes on us," Clyde calls. "Lots of 'em."

It's as if, all at once, the nearby town has come out to see the results of Clyde's gunfire. Up on the hill by the mine, a group of people loiters, pointing. No doubt, speculating. And coming toward us is a big ol' truck with tires large enough to make me jealous. At gunpoint, Clyde flags down the fella, a farmer.

The situation is giving me the shakes. All we need is for the farmer to think himself a hero or any one of the people up above to liken himself a desperado, and any of us could end up dead.

Like so many times before, it's as if a thought passes from my brain to Clyde's as he hollers, "Folks, a good lad has already died today, and if this here car don't get moving again, more good lads will die. I suggest you keep your feet planted and your consciences clean. And you," he says to the farmer, "get whatever wire you got 'round our bumper."

The only fella who dares to move is the farmer. I light a cigarette, alternating between watching the farmer and the people up on the hill—whispering, pointing, thinking they know the first thing 'bout the road that brought us here.

Thankfully, in no time, the farmer's big tires do the trick and yank us free. Clyde tips his hat and we're gone, the beams from our headlights bouncing.

I've done my fair share of watching our hostages. "Henry," I say, "you watch him." I face forward and tell Clyde, "That's Percy back there."

"Don't be afraid to get some shut-eye, Percy," Clyde says. "We've got some miles to put behind us."

• • •

Clyde isn't lying. He drives all night. It isn't 'til the sun shows its face that I see how red his eyes are. Mine can't look much better. I tried to stay up, to keep him company. Won't lie, though, I dozed off a time or two.

A stop at a filling station or a bump in the road always brought me back.

One time, Clyde chuckled, and I wouldn't put it past him to have aimed for whatever jostled our automobile.

Soon, Clyde pulls over, and we take turns by a tree. He finds us a café after that, and Henry brings back sandwiches and soft drinks. Not the most normal of breakfast foods, but we missed dinner and all of us had a hankering for some chipped beef.

I save the newspaper Henry brought me 'til after I eat, but my eyes keep going to it. I force down my last bite, barely chewing, and toss my sandwich wrapper aside in exchange for details on our latest incident.

"Jesus," I say, "it's a whole spread." I skim, knowing I'll pour over each word later. There's mention of my marriage to Roy again, and more of our lives are exposed this time. Details you'd think nobody would care 'bout. My daddy dying when I was young. Clyde chopping off his toes in prison. The poems I left behind at Oak Ridge. Our crash into the dry riverbed. Buck's death. I got to close my eyes after that and count to ten. With photos of Raymond and Joe Palmer, in connection with the prison farm breakout, I'm relieved Buck's face ain't staring back at me. There's the photo of Clyde and me, though, where I playfully pointed a gun at him. Hard to believe, and also accept, all that's happened since then.

"They're calling us partners in love and crime," I say to Clyde.

He flips a hand. "Now, that ain't half bad. Better than being called a pair of human rats like last time."

"This time, too." I growl. "And there's that photo of me with the cigar again."

"Bonnie, darling, why do you let that get to you?"

"'Cause, Clyde, and Percy you listen, too. You tell 'em, Percy, that it ain't true. You tell 'em that nice girls don't smoke cigars." I look back at our hostage. "That ain't the start of a smile I see on your face?"

Percy says, "Funny that's what you'd like to refute in all you're reading."

Clyde laughs. "He's got a point."

I cross my arms. Sure, I know it doesn't make full sense, but that cigar may be the only absolute thing I can hang my hat on as being untrue.

I read on. "Henry, you're in here."

He starts to speak, then has to clear his throat. "I'd rather not hear any more 'bout that morning."

I twist my lips. Me, too. Then, I come to last night. The dead fella's name was Cal, a widower and father of seven. He'd been a contractor 'til he lost it all when the depression hit him square in the face, so he took a job as an elected constable.

We've been known, Clyde 'specially, to cover all lawmen in the same blanket. The law, who shook him down to wear him down, who staged fights to get him fingered, who brutalized him in a prison yard, who looked the other way when footsteps followed him into a dark corner. Who shot at our families.

All those faces became the same, became one.

But constables, like Cal, aren't professional lawmen. They're only doing it for the fifteen bucks a week, which ain't even a lot for a family Cal's size.

I fold the newspaper, tapping it with my finger; ain't feeling good in my gut.

Clyde asks me, "What's eating ya?"

"Fella from last night was a constable."

He clucks. "Percy." Clyde pauses, wipes his mouth. "Sorry 'bout the old man."

Clyde ain't big on apologies, and despite today's weather being as good as it comes, a dark cloud might as well hover over us. We ended a marriage a mere eleven days before it began. And now we took down someone else who's a product of these here depression days. That man didn't deserve to die that way. Buck didn't deserve it. Blanche shouldn't be in jail. None of this, not a single bit, would've made my daddy proud.

But so much of what they're saying 'bout us ain't true, either. We ain't out to get people. My daddy would understand that, too.

I search by my feet 'til I find a pen, and in the margin, I get out my guilt and fears the best way I know how, a poem. This one, I decide, will be the story of Bonnie and Clyde.

THERE'S SOMETHING MAGICAL 'BOUT WORDS FILLING A PAGE, a photograph of sorts, capturing moments of time. Now those words pour out of me 'til I have a poem that's nearly a hundred lines long and the margins of the newspaper are filled.

After all that's happened, the last lines feel inevitable.

Some day they'll go down together
they'll bury them side by side.
To few it'll be grief,
to the law a relief
but it's death for Bonnie and Clyde.

These last lines will haunt me.

I set my poem aside and rest my head against the window. I crack it open for air. A building reads FT. SCOTT LAW, and I open a road map to get a sense of where we are. I find us, up in Kansas, and trace my finger back to where we began in Oklahoma. If I got the spot correct, we couldn't have gone more than sixty or seventy miles north, but Clyde drove us 'round all of God's kingdom to get us here.

He pulls over and retrieves a spare shirt from the trunk. Clyde's only got a few, but the one Percy's wearing is stiff with blood from where he sliced open his head while dodging Clyde's bullets.

"Out ya go." Clyde hands Percy the shirt. "Wish I could say it's been a pleasure."

Stubble coats the bottom half of Percy's face. "Likewise."

And that's that. It's back to only Clyde, Henry, and me.

We're runnin' again, and I bite my bottom lip, my finger following our path on the map, 'til we start heading south—toward the farm?

My poem's dark with my regrets bringing me down and the walls closing in, but here we are, still alive and free. I still have a sliver of hope, like the last slice of the moon before it all goes dark, that we'll get out of this with air in our lungs.

With a quick yank on the steering wheel, Clyde pulls us over again. "Henry, this is where we part ways."

"What?" he says. Both Henry and I sit up straighter. He surveys 'round us. A bus stop ain't more than ten paces ahead. Farther off, the start of a small town.

"Clyde, I know I messed up, but I thought—"

"For now. That land won't do Bonnie and me any good if the law tracks us there. We'll meet you there in a month. Make it a month and a half, whatever that Sunday is." Clyde reaches into his breast pocket and pulls out a few bills, offers them to Henry. "How's that sound?"

Henry licks his lips, nods, and—once again—that's that.

Instead of going into town, Clyde turns us 'round, finding a different way on the backcountry roads. I relax into my seat, as relaxed as I can be out here on the road, where there's always the threat of the bogeyman leaping out to surprise us.

"And then there were two," I say softly. Clyde takes my hand. I can't help asking, "Where we going now?"

One side of Clyde's mouth turns up. "To the farm, of course." He laughs. "Bonnie, you should see that reaction of yours."

"You mean my confusion? You just got done telling Henry we wouldn't see him 'til next month."

"And we won't, but I want to be on our land."

"You don't trust him anymore?"

"Ain't many people I trust now. Present company excluded. Luck's gotten us plenty far. Farther than it should've. 'Bout time we slow down and use what's between our ears. It's back to the woods."

"The woods?" I groan.

Clyde runs his finger down my nose, right over the creases I've put there while scrunching in dismay. "Aye, but the woods on our very own land."

• • •

Clyde starts using his noggin right away. We steal cars, one after another, not far from the last. It's a different pattern, but a clear pattern in the direction we're headed. Which, of course, ain't the direction we're actually headed.

But we also don't want to lead the law way up north then sneak way down south. So we create a path of stolen cars to Fort Smith, that being a central location between all our normal haunts: Texas, Oklahoma, Arkansas, Louisiana, Kansas, and Missouri.

From there, we change our plates to one unscrewed from a junkyard and jump the three hundred or so miles to Sailes, Louisiana.

One hand on my belly, I feel like singing. But I won't; we ain't out of the woods just yet. In fact, we wait for nightfall and roll into the woods that line our soon-to-be acreage. Clyde doesn't dare start a fire, but it's warm enough where snuggling up with each other will do.

"Did we really do it?" I ask.

"Just 'bout. I'm going to sneak over to the house now and again to see if I spot anything funny. If not, we'll meet Henry and make all of this ours for keeps."

On my side, I nuzzle into Clyde's neck. "I can't even imagine."

But that's a lie. Sleeping with both eyes closed, being clean on a regular basis, not fearing flat tires or lookie-loos. Not escaping one ambush after another.

I can easily imagine all of that. Lord knows I already figured where the pigpen will go. My fingers twitch at getting inside the farmhouse. I'm lying on my right hand. I shift, pulling it out, showing Clyde my ring-less finger.

"I lost our snake somewhere back in that mud. This ol' thing," I say of Roy's band, "represents all the bad from before. But your ring . . . *our* ring," I correct, "has always given me hope of our future. It's lousy it's gone."

"Bonnie, you don't need a ring to prove the existence of a future for us." He puts my left hand over his heart. "You can feel it whenever you want."

I sigh, one where the breath comes out of a smile, and I slide our hands onto my tummy. "You can feel it here, too, or at least I think so. I only realized this morning as I was thinking through all that's happened in the past few months."

"You ain't serious?"

I nod, vigorously. "We're going to have that family, Clyde."

He's quick to say, "Let's try for another." Clyde switches our positions, his hazel eyes gleaming down at me.

"I don't think it works that way when we already got one cooking."

"Never hurts to try, darling."

• • •

I wake with that familiar stiffness in my back from snoozing on the ground, but also with a smile. Then panic. Clyde ain't here. Hasn't been for a while, his body heat gone. I frantically pat the ground where he should be, as if that'll do a dang thing. When I spot a note, scribbled on some old trash, I simper at my own theatrics.

Back soon.

It's the first I've seen Clyde's handwriting, a wild realization after all we've been through. All the letters he sent from Eastham were typed, now I know by someone else. Maybe Skelley. There are only eight letters in his note, but there's an intimacy in being the first to know that Clyde loops his two *o*'s together.

I've a big smile for him when he returns. He withdraws a journal, saying, "Picked this up for you. Drove an hour each way 'cause I didn't want anyone recognizing me 'round here. But I see you scribbling on scraps and I wanted you to have a home for your words."

I patiently wait for him to stop yapping, then plant one on him.

I start by recopying my poem, giving it the name "The Trail's End." I snort at some of the stuff I've written, revising here and there, but I keep most of it the same, even the ending. This here captured a moment in time, and I think those moments should be preserved, even when the future takes an uphill climb.

Like how, the next day, the newspaper I'm reading puts a smile on my face.

"Nice girls don't smoke cigars," said Miss Bonnie Parker, companion to fugitive and murderer Clyde Barrow.

Percy came through.

Over the next few weeks, I continue to keep an eye on the headlines. Unfortunately, it's not as redeeming. There's gossip 'bout a lurid love affair with Raymond, 'bout the banks we're accused of robbing but didn't, and even how the media mocks the law for not being able to bring one smallish man and his even tinier woman to justice. Then Raymond's name pops up again, this time 'cause he found himself back in the pen.

Clyde ha-ha's at that, then says, "I'd like to write a letter to Henry Ford."

"The car manufacturer?"

"The very one. I reckon I owe him some gratitude."

I tear Clyde a clean sheet of paper and let him go at it.

Dear Sir:—

I smirk. "Ya don't need both the colon and the dash."

"Too late now."

Clyde gushes to Mr. Ford 'bout what a dandy car Ford makes, how he drives 'em exclusively, praising the automobile's sustained speed and performance.

Ford has got every other car skinned and even if my business hasn't been strictly legal it don't hurt anything to tell you what a fine car you got in the V8.

He signs it,

Yours truly,
Clyde Champion Barrow

The next day, we mail it. It becomes normal for us to leave our woods and drive for a hundred miles in any ol' direction before returning at the end of the day. Clyde says it'll give folks less chances to spot our Ford on the farmland, along with giving us an opportunity to see if anyone trails us to the farm. I counter how it gives others the opening to discover us here, with all our coming and going.

I ain't sure there is an ideal scenario of what we should be doing or how we should be acting, besides making a go at an honest life. That's what we do, Clyde keeping his sticky fingers to himself. Of course, that means we don't have any money coming in, but sleeping in our car or in the dirt means not having to pay four dollars a day to snooze at a tourist camp, and with only the two of us, we can make do with a loaf of bread for eight cents and a jar of apple butter for ten.

Our biggest expense is gas at ten cents a gallon. With Clyde sometimes lugging us for upward three hundred miles in a round trip, that easily costs us two dollars a day. Over sixty dollars by the time we'll settle on our farm.

Guess that figure doesn't seem so grand when we spent nearly half of the same amount on a Remington typewriter for me. And for Clyde, a fifty-dollar saxophone.

"You can play this thing?" I ask Clyde after he puts it in the trunk next to my typewriter. I waited in the car when he went in, not wanting to draw attention to us by having to hobble.

"Been a while. Bet it'll be like riding a bike."

One of those is seven bucks, and I'm tempted to ask for one, but we don't got a place to put it yet. Soon we will, in only a couple more days, when we're set to meet Henry at the house. Over those days, we fill our trunk with a tablecloth, costing a dollar five; bedsheets, seventy-four cents; bath towels at thirty cents each; a gas lantern, five sixty-nine; and a few wool blankets at a dollar a pop.

I keep adding it all up, almost obsessively, afraid our money will run out and Clyde'll have to rob. It won't, not for a while at least; our stash is over a grand. That's most folks' salary for a year, if you've got yourself a decent job. Like a schoolteacher. A college professor makes even more, more than double that. An actress—geez—she could keep rollin' that amount higher and higher, all relative to how popular her films become.

Those were once my aspirations, and I'll admit a touch of "what could've been" scratches my throat, but that life with eyes on me—either at the front of a classroom or by a camera—is for a different gal. This gal doesn't want to be seen, 'cept by Clyde.

Sunday morning, he's carrying me with an arm under my knees and another 'round my back. Clyde doesn't have any hands to hold a gun, and we're trying to show Henry some good faith, so the gun we do have is in my right hand, under a spare shirt in my lap. Through the trees is our soon-to-be farmhouse.

"I haven't seen anyone at the house the times I checked." Clyde sidesteps a fallen branch. "Henry's daddy must've already moved on. An apartment in Arcadia is what Henry mentioned. Ain't more than a few miles from here."

"He get a job?"

"Not sure."

Clyde hesitates at the last tree, listening, watching. "Henry's car ain't here yet. Unless he parked farther down."

We creep into the clearing. I don't like that we're creeping.

"Think it'll ever stop," I whisper, "people caring 'bout us?"

He clucks. "Not sure they should. I had my reasons for what I've done, but it doesn't make it right. You, Bonnie . . . you never shot a soul, though."

"I shot *at* folks."

"Who are living to talk 'bout it. That matters. I'm glad it's you and not me who's growing our bairn." At the porch, Clyde raps a step with his foot. The step'll hold. It's anyone inside he's testing. I squeeze the gun. "Should've left you two behind."

I ignore him; I'm nervous enough without Clyde worrying 'bout me and our baby. "Are you sorry you killed people, Clyde?"

He climbs the steps, painstakingly slow. "I'm sorry it came to that, in all but one case. Now, quiet." His eyes dart 'round, peering through the windows, over his shoulder, out over the yard. Clyde dips, lowering us and his hand to doorknob level.

"It ain't locked," he whispers, almost to himself.

He kicks the door open. In my mind, the door's creak could make a nest of birds take flight. But inside the house, it's as quiet as a lamb. I close my eyes to listen, to hope we ain't the lambs on the way to slaughter.

Light casts in through the windows, motes drifting in the sun's rays. The farmhouse is sparse, just as I remembered it, most everything crafted from wood. A table, some chairs, a wall of shelving. The last will be perfect to collect books. It's been too long since I've tucked my legs under me and read for hours, without looking over the page 'cause a sound stirs me out of the novel's world.

Clyde sets me down by the door, and it's understood by his wide eyes I'm to stay right here. 'Cept first he grabs me by either hip and scoots me to the left so I'm not in the open doorway. I hold the gun against my outer thigh; it ready, yet hidden.

Clyde pulls his own pistol from the band of his pants and pokes his head into the kitchen at the back of the house, which is hardly more than a stove. Then he walks down the long hall, kicking open doors, four rooms in all by the sound of it. I wonder if, years from now, we could turn the smallest of those rooms into a washroom, if plumbing ever comes out this far. Electricity, too.

Fortunately, by now, I know a thing or two 'bout not having either of those. I shift my weight, putting more on my mangled side, and I realize I don't feel as wobbly.

"Bonnie."

I nearly topple over. "Heavens, Henry, you scared me."

"Didn't mean to give ya the jeepers-creepers."

I laugh, then call, "Clyde, Henry's here."

He strides out, trying to appear causal-like with his gun not fully gripped at his side. But I know Clyde, I know he rivals Jesse James with the quickness he could sling a gun.

"There you are, lad." Clyde grins. "Sense any heat on your way out to these parts?"

"None my way."

Clyde nods. "Well, let's get this done. What ya need from us to even up?"

Henry holds up his hand. On a ring dangling from his finger is a key. "You'll need this and that should do it from me."

"No payment?"

"My father said he don't want your money. He's got a deed for ya, says it's up to you how to get your name on it."

Clyde nods. I'd put money on Clyde getting in touch with Pretty Boy Floyd to "legally" change our names. That ain't something I ever thought 'bout, but what's it matter to me if a paper has something on it other than my own name? Buster's real name is Hubert, after all. Billie's is Billie Jean, but we ain't ever use the whole thing. Maybe officially, I'll go by Elizabeth, my middle name.

And unofficially, I'm Bonnie. To all those reading the papers, I'm half of "Bonnie and Clyde," who after twenty-seven months of outrunning the law, secretly got a place to call our own. My daddy was a bricklayer, so he never had a reason to step onto a farm, but he'd like it here. He would've.

Now with the key in Clyde's hand, Henry looks ready to be on his way, all his weight on his heels. "Where will you go?" I ask him. "Somewhere safe, I hope?"

"I've got someone looking out for me," he says. His weight's so far back, he may fall right over.

Clyde nods. "I'm glad for that."

Henry takes a step back, out on the porch. "Should be on my way." He's down our steps in a flash, striding to an old pickup truck. "My father said Wednesday works if ya want to get that deed."

My voice is singsong as I say, "Wednesday it is."

Clyde wraps his arm 'round my shoulder as the blue truck, mostly rusted, thumps over the grass toward the gravel road. He snorts. "Methvin won't make it far in that beater."

"It's no Ford," I say cheekily.

In response, Clyde's got me dangling over his shoulder, and he's barreling through the house to the main bedroom. I've never had a dress come off so quickly. Before I know it, I'm on my back, shoes still on.

Then, Clyde takes his time, his eyes scouring all of me. I kick off one shoe, then the other, my skin practically begging to be touched by this boy. But first, I think, *freeze*.

The lust in his eyes, the fullness of his bottom lip, the way a strand of hair falls free. How I fist my hands into the sheets in anticipation. I want to remember Clyde—and us—this way, always.

He lowers himself on top of me in our new bedroom, in our new house, in our new life, and my heart may burst with happiness and relief.

OUR FIRST NIGHT, CLYDE RUNS DOWN THE HALL IN HIS BARE feet and out onto the porch. He comes back pressing on his eyes and with a mouthful of how he thought he heard something. Monday night, he does it a second time.

Tuesday night, though, we sleep straight. I wake, splayed out like a child, on a bed fitted with the sheets we purchased the other day. In days, ever since Clyde got us an armful of food from a nearby café, we haven't ventured beyond the necessities of the water pump and the outbuilding. We've been content to spend our time within our four walls. I sat by the windows, daydreaming, but most of my hours have been spent in Clyde's arms. It's almost as if the last few years of runnin' caught up with us all at once, and all we could manage was laying 'round.

Not today, though. Today we get ourselves clean, put on fresh clothes—a red dress with matching shoes for me—and get our butts into our car. We've got a deed waiting for us.

Before he turns the key in the ignition, Clyde chuckles to himself and loosens his tie. "I'm a farmer now, no need for this ol' thing." With that, he drapes it over the rearview mirror. "But," he says, "Bonnie, pull up your dress and stretch out your leg."

I raise a brow.

A dimple pops out. "I ain't being fresh, though the thought's crossing my mind now."

Slowly, 'cause I ain't sure what this boy's up to, I do as he says, even if I struggle on account of the lack of room.

Clyde goes and presses a revolver against my inner thigh. He tapes it there, wrapping the white adhesive 'round and 'round.

I'm shaking my head. "What'd you do that for?"

"I don't want Mr. Methvin seeing me with a gun. Good faith, like with Henry. But I'd like you to have one close by."

I frown. "If we're going to put all of this behind us, we should start acting like it's behind us."

"We will, as soon as I've got that deed in my hand."

I smile at that and put on sunglasses. My arm dangles out the car. The air feels good as we get going; the day's sure to be a hot one. I turn my hand forward and back, letting the breeze dance over my skin. "Say, when we going to get word to our families?"

"Before the bairn comes," Clyde says. "I'd like Billie out here to help with that. Both mas, too."

My smile grows. "I like that you've thought 'bout that."

"I've been thinkin' 'bout other stuff, too."

"Like?" I prod.

"Like the last verse of our song. Don't got that guitar yet, but I imagined the chords and how it all could go."

"Like?"

We transition from the grass to the gravel. The main road—and by main I mean backcountry—ain't too far off now, 'round a bend and over a hill. We're tucked back far, real far, with only a rusted mailbox with COLE written on its side marking the start of our drive. And with the trees on either side, even that could easily be missed.

Clyde clears his throat, all dramatic-like, and my heart swells. "Thought the first line could go something like, *There'll be a time, this day, tomorrow or the one after . . . Where they stand up, chin out, ready to say their wrongs.*"

Already, I imagine a dark melody, even more so when he sings, *"Death'll see his chance, his moment, cackling with laughter . . . And they'll say, here we are, shouting it out, singing their song . . . Of love and loss and ups and downs, a life with one eye open . . . Ohh"*—he draws out the word, his hazel eyes leaving the road to lock on mine, then dropping to my belly—*"Oh, oh, oh, don't be a fool, these footsteps ain't for you."*

He swallows, and in a soft voice, I say, "I ain't sure if that's beautiful or horrifying. Do you think they're going to find us, Clyde? That why you sang that?"

"All I know is, I've got a lot to answer for, either in this life or the next. But the life that got us here"—Clyde licks his lips—"I wouldn't wish it on anybody. It ain't one for our li'l one to follow."

I shake my head, knowing I'll wish on every falling star I see that things are different from here on out. We turn onto that so-called main road and Clyde takes my hand. "But, Bonnie, I've said it before and I'll sing it again . . . *How the story ends, no one knows . . . But one thing's clear, you'll see . . . Bonnie and Clyde, meant to be, alive and free.*" He smiles. "I don't see any prison bars 'round us. There won't ever be."

"Nope."

Clyde laughs at my confidence. It's there, even if I do worry what the future will bring. I know it won't be behind bars, though; Clyde would never let it come to that.

That means we can keep on living, so close to having the deed in our hands that'll officially make this life ours. Clyde's words, even morbid with his mention of death, are a hell of a lot more positive than how I ended my poem.

I pull my journal from beneath my seat, wanting to read my poem to not only retrace how we got here, but also chase away my final words: *but it's death for Bonnie and Clyde.*

Someday. But for now, we found our way out.

"Sun is bright, ain't she?" Clyde slides on sunglasses as we bump 'round a bend. "Well, I'll be," he says.

"What's that?"

"If I ain't mistaken, that's the same truck that barely made it down our drive."

Up ahead, off to the side of the road, I snort at the blue truck Henry borrowed from his daddy. Now it's tilted to one side.

I say, "Flat tire."

"Looks that way. Don't see Mr. Methvin, though," Clyde says under his breath.

I shrug, figuring the old man slipped into the woods to find some shade.

"Something ain't right," Clyde says.

While searching for Mr. Methvin in the tree line, I blindly reach for my makeup kit, intent on powdering my nose. I say, "Honey, quit being paranoid. We did it. We're not runnin' no more." The sun flashes against something silver. "And I for one—"

Am a goddamn fool.

I see it, barely, as if my mind's conjuring the scene from a memory. But this is the here and now, and a row of men wait with guns, crouched amidst the undergrowth. I let out a cry, clawing at my skirt, trying to get to the gun Clyde taped there. He yanks his foot off the pedal. Neither will do us any good.

We lock eyes. His, mine, they both say one thing: *It's too late for us.*

He cries, "Bonnie."

I breathe, "Clyde."

AUTHOR'S NOTE

Bonnie and Clyde were killed in an ambush on May 23, 1934. Bonnie was twenty-three, and Clyde was twenty-five. When the shooting stopped, it's said that both were shot more than fifty times. After the infamous Eastham breakout, Colonel Lee Simmons made good on his word, meeting with Frank Hamer, a retired Texas Ranger, and telling him, "I want you to put Clyde and Bonnie 'on the spot' and then shoot everyone in sight." It's in part because of Henry Methvin and his father, who researchers say Clyde was purchasing land from, that Hamer and his team knew where to find Bonnie and Clyde that Wednesday morning. In exchange for Henry's pardon from the state of Texas, the Methvins agreed to deliver Bonnie and Clyde to the authorities. In the 1934 footage of their funerals, the voiceover claims Bonnie was the only woman ever to be shot down by officers of the law.

I'm often asked what inspired me to write a story about Bonnie and Clyde. My curiosity stemmed from wondering what made this duo tick and become so accepting of a life of crime, especially Bonnie, who came from a wholesome upbringing. While emotionally and morally difficult to write, I wanted to tell the story through Bonnie's eyes, speculating on her thoughts, reactions, motivations, and remorse. W. D. Jones, who I refer to simply as Jones, is quoted as saying Bonnie never fired a gun at anybody. Others say she did, but historians tend to agree that Bonnie was never responsible for any deaths during their twenty-seven-month crime spree. Clyde is a different story, some saying he was responsible for at least six of the thirteen victims of the Barrow Gang.

Often, the media and films have presented Bonnie as someone who sought celebrity above all else, and while I found instances of Bonnie adoring films, liking to sing, and enjoying the spotlight, I didn't get an overwhelming sense that Bonnie's motivation was fame. Bonnie's desire to be someone is speckled throughout this novel and its prequel, *Becoming Bonnie,* but I didn't make it a central theme. Instead, I concentrated mainly on Bonnie's dreams, which evolve with her experiences, and also her desire to remain with Clyde during their life on the lam.

To bring their crime spree to life, the events, people, and general timeline within this novel are inspired by real life. Any historical inaccuracies are my own, as storytelling was my main objective, and also due to the fact that there are various accounts of Bonnie and Clyde's life of crime. The Eastham breakout is one such example, where I found varying accounts from James Mullen, the Dallas Police Department, and various Bonnie and Clyde experts.

Bonnie's pregnancy is another element that has been debated. I chose to side with the researchers who believed Bonnie was with child when she was slain during the ambush. In order to heighten that moment, I speculated the possibility of Bonnie being pregnant prior to that moment. While Bonnie did fall into a coma and became handicapped after Clyde crashed into a dry riverbed, it's my fictional addition that she also miscarried.

Another fictionalized element is Clyde's close partnership with Pretty Boy Floyd. There is documentation of Clyde contacting him in hopes of them working a job together, but Pretty Boy Floyd has been quoted as saying he didn't want to get mixed up with "those Texas screwballs." I chose to embellish this connection as a plausible resource for information. However, Clyde was involved with Pretty Boy Floyd's brother, staying with him and recuperating at his home after the Sower's ambush, where Bonnie and Clyde were both shot after a family friend betrayed them.

As far as the fates of the other characters within this book, W. D. Jones was arrested only a few weeks after leaving Bonnie and Clyde. He was paroled after six years. After the Eastham breakout, Raymond Hamilton and Joe Palmer were recaptured separately. Later, they escaped again, further embarrassing Simmons. They were recaptured again and both died in the electric chair. Raymond's brother, Floyd Hamilton, initially received two years for harboring Bonnie and Clyde. After continuing his career of crime, he ultimately spent twenty years at Alcatraz. While Henry Methvin was pardoned for previous crimes, he ultimately was convicted due to the death of Cal Campbell, a murder that occurred after the pardon agreement was in place. Eventually, Methvin was released. An unknown person, knowing Methvin informed on Bonnie and Clyde, knocked him unconscious and left him on a railroad track, where he was cut in half.

Blanche Barrow received a ten-year sentence. She underwent a number of operations to save her injured eye, but none of them was successful. After six years, Blanche was released and went on to remarry. At the age of seventy-seven, she died from cancer. Much of Blanche's character in the novel is fictionalized, as her storyline greatly affected Bonnie's storyline in the prequel, *Becoming Bonnie*. Blanche, and Bonnie and Clyde's crime spree in general, is also greatly fictionalized in the 1967 film, where Blanche was depicted as an over-the-top preacher's daughter. In real life, her father was a logger and farmer. On occasion, he acted as a lay minister.

Billie Parker is quoted as saying about her sister and Clyde, "The kids led a rough life, and they wouldn't want anyone—then or now—to follow in their footsteps." In Bonnie's last poem, written a month before their final ambush, she wrote:

Some day they'll go down together
they'll bury them side by side.
To few it'll be grief,
to the law a relief
but it's death for Bonnie and Clyde.

Bonnie never received her last wishes, as she and Clyde were not buried side by side. And while I gave Bonnie a happy ending within the final chapter, I ultimately had to take it away.

Within my novel, the poems written by Bonnie are her own words. The poem by Blanche was written by the real-life Blanche. The poem submitted to a newspaper by Mabel K. Moore was inspired by a poem submitted to a Dallas newspaper by Myrtle J. Potter. The song lyrics are my own.

For nonfiction accounts of Bonnie and Clyde's escapades, I'd recommend Blanche Barrow's memoir, edited by John Neal Phillips, and also *Go Down Together* by Jeff Guinn. If you, like me, were curious what made a wholesome girl like Bonnie Parker turn to a life of crime, I've explored Bonnie and Clyde's possible backgrounds, beginning in 1927, in the prequel *Becoming Bonnie,* the untold story of Bonnie before Clyde.

TURN THE PAGE FOR A SNEAK PEEK OF

JENNI L. WALSH'S

BECOMING BONNIE

1

BUT I, BEING POOR, HAVE ONLY MY DREAMS.

Hands in my hair, I look over the words I wrote on the Mason jar atop my bureau. I snigger, almost as if I'm antagonizing the sentiment. One day I won't be poor with dreams. I'll have money *and* dreams.

I drop my hair and swallow a growl, never able to get my stubborn curls quite right.

My little sister carefully sets her pillow down, tugs at the corner to give it shape, the final touch to making her bed. "Stop messing with it."

"Easy for you to say. The humidity ain't playing games with your hair."

And Little Billie's hair is down. Smooth and straight. Mine is pinned back into a low bun. Modest and practical.

Little Billie chuckles. "Well, I'm going before Mama hollers at me. Church starts in twenty minutes, and you know she's got to watch everyone come in."

I shake my head; that woman always has her nose to the ground. Little Billie scoots out of our bedroom, and I get back to taming my flyaways and scan my bureau for my favorite stud earrings, one of our few family heirlooms. Footsteps in the hall quicken my fingers. I slide in another hairpin, jabbing my skull. "I'm coming, Ma!"

A deep cough.

I turn to find my boyfriend taking up much of the doorway. He's got his broad shoulders and tall frame to thank for that.

I smile, saying, "Oh, it's only you."

Roy's own smile doesn't quite form. "Yes, it's only me."

I wave him off, a strand falling out of place. Roy being 'round ain't nothin' new, but on a Sunday morning . . . That gets my heart bumping with intrigue. "What ya doing here so early? The birds are barely chirpin'."

"It ain't so early. Got us less than twenty minutes 'til—"

"I know."

"Thought I could walk you to church," Roy says.

"Is that so?" My curiosity builds, 'specially with how this boy is shifting his weight from side to side. He's up to something. And I ain't one to be kept in the dark. Fingers busy with my hair, I motion with my elbow and arch a brow. "That for me?"

Roy glances down at an envelope in his hand, as if he forgot he was even holding it. He moves it behind his back. "It can wait. There's actually something else—"

I'm across the room in a heartbeat, tugging on his arm. "Oh no it can't."

On the envelope, "Final Notice" stares back at me in bold letters. The sender is our electric company. Any excitement is gone.

"I'm sorry, Bonnelyn," Roy says. "Caught my eye on it in the bushes out front."

My arms fall to my sides, and I stare unblinking at the envelope, not sure how something so small, so light, could mean something so big, so heavy, for our family. "I didn't know my ma hadn't been paying this."

Roy pushes the envelope, facedown, onto my bureau. "I can help pay—"

"Thanks, but we'll figure it out." I sigh at my hair, at our unpaid bill, at the fact I'm watching my sister after church instead of putting in hours at the diner. Fortunately, my brother's pulling a double at the cement plant. Ma will be at the factory all afternoon. But will it be enough?

I move in front of the wall mirror to distract myself. Seeing my hand-me-down blouse ain't helping. I peek at Roy, hoping I don't find pity on his face. There he goes again, throwing his weight from foot to foot. And, sure, that boy is sweet as pie, but I know he ain't antsy thinkin' my lights are suddenly going to go off.

"Everything okay, Roy?"

"Yeah."

That *yeah* ain't so convincing.

"You almost done here?" he asks. Roy shifts the old Mason jar to the side, holds up the earring I'd been looking for.

I nod—to the earring, not to being done—and he brings it to me. Despite how this morning is turning out, I smile, liking that Roy knew what I was looking for without me having to tell him.

"Ready now?" he says.

I slide another pin into my hair. "Why's everyone rushing me?"

Roy swallows, and if I had five clams to bet, I'd bet he's nervous 'bout something. He edges closer to my bureau. He shakes the Mason jar, the pieces of paper rustling inside. "When did you write this on the outside?"

But I, being poor, have only my dreams.

I avert my eyes, being those words weren't meant for Roy's. "Not too long ago."

"Ya know, Bonnelyn, you won't always be poor. I'll make sure of that."

"I know I won't." I add a final pin to my hair. "*I'll* make sure of that."

"So why'd you write it?"

"I didn't. William Butler Yeats did."

Roy shoves his hands in his pockets. "You know what I mean."

I shrug and stare at my reflection. "It inspires me, wanting to be more than that line. And I will. I'll put a white picket fence in front of my house to prove it."

"*Your* house?"

I turn away from the mirror to face him. His voice sounded off. Too high. But Roy ain't looking at me. He's staring at the wall above my head. "Our house," I correct, a pang of guilt stabbing me in the belly 'cause I didn't say *our* to begin with. "That jar is full of our dreams, after all."

Really, it's full of doodles, scribbled on whatever paper Roy had on hand. Napkins. Ripped corners of his textbook pages. The top flap of a cereal box. He shoved the first scrap of paper in my hand when we were only knee-high to a grasshopper: quick little drawings of me and him in front of the Eiffel Tower, riding horses with dogs running 'round our feet, holding hands by the Gulf's crashing waves.

Our dreams. Plenty of 'em. Big and small. Whimsical and sweet.

But this here is the twenties. Women can vote; women are equals, wanting to make a name for themselves. I'm no exception. Sure, I'll bring those doodles to life with Roy, but I would've added my own sketches to the jar if I could draw. Standing at the front of my very own classroom. At a bank counter, depositing my payroll checks. Shaking hands with a salesman, purchasing my first car.

Call it selfish, call it whatever ya like, but after struggling for money all my life, *my* dreams have always come before *ours*.

Still, I link our hands. "I'm ready to go."

• • •

"Hallelujah!"

The congregation mimics my pastor's booming voice. The women flick their fans faster with excitement. Pastor Frank shuffles to the right, then to the left, sixty-some eyes following his every movement. From the choir pews off to the side, I watch his mesmerized flock hang on his every word, myself included. My ma is amidst the familiar faces. She prefers to use Daddy's brown hat to cool herself, holding on to him even after he's been gone all these years. I can't say I blame her.

"Amen!" we chime.

Pastor Frank nods at me, and I move from the choir box to the piano. I bring my hands down, and the first chords of "Onward, Christian Soldiers" roar to life. Every Sunday, I sit on this here bench, press my fingers into the keys, and let the Lord's words roll off my tongue. Ma says Daddy would be proud, too. I sure hope that's true.

It's another reason why I'll make something of myself. In our small town or in a big city, it doesn't matter much, but Bonnelyn Parker is going to be somebody. Wherever life takes me, whatever final notice stands in my way, my daddy will look down on me and smile, knowing I ain't struggling, I'm thriving. I'm more than poor.

I push my voice louder, raise my chin, and sing the hymn's last note, letting it vibrate with the piano's final chord.

The congregation shouts praises to the Lord as Pastor Frank clasps his hands together and tells us all to, "Go and spread His word."

Voices break out, everyone beating their gums at once. I slip off the bench, weave through the crowd. A few people are always louder than the rest. Mrs. Davis is having a potluck lunch. Mr. Miller's best horse is sick. He spent his early morning hours in his barn, from the looks of his dirty overalls.

Ma's got more pride than a lion and makes certain we're dressed to the nines, even if our nine is really only a five. Still, my older brother's vest and slacks are his Sunday best. And even though we've got secondhand clothes, my sister's and my white blouses are neatly tucked into our skirts. We may be pretending to look the part, but our family always gets by. We find a way, just like we'll make sure that electric bill gets paid. Though I don't like how Ma let this bill get so late.

I rush through the church's double doors, sucking in fresh air, and shield my eyes from the sun. A laugh slips out. There's my brother, playing keep-away from my little sister with one of her once-white shoes. Buster tosses the shoe to Roy. Roy fumbles it. No surprise there, but part of me wonders if his nerves from earlier are sticking 'round. On the way to church, he wouldn't let me get a word in, going on nonstop 'bout the weather. I reckon the summer of 1927 is hot, real hot, but not worth all his fuss.

"Little Billie, those boys picking on you?" I call, skipping down the church steps, keeping my eyes on Roy.

He takes immediate notice of me, missing my brother's next throw. "Say, Bonnelyn." Roy wipes his hairline. "I was hoping to do this before church, but you were having trouble with your . . ." He gestures toward his own hair, then stops, wisely thinkin' better of it. "I've a surprise for you."

"A surprise? Why didn't you tell me so? I could've hurried."

He also wisely doesn't comment on my earlier irritation at being hurried.

"Follow me?" Roy asks, his brown eyes hopeful.

"Not today, lover boy," Buster cuts in. "Bonn's watching Billie."

Billie hops toward me on one foot, her voice bouncing as she proclaims how she's eleven and doesn't need to be babysat no more. I bend to pick up her lost shoe, letting out a long sigh. Roy sighs too. But Roy also looks like a puppy that's been kicked.

"Will the surprise take long?" I ask him. "Buster doesn't need to be at work for another two hours."

"Actually an hour," my brother says. "But Roy here probably only needs a few minutes, tops." He winks, and Roy playfully charges him.

My cheeks flush, and not 'cause Roy and I have done *that*. Roy hasn't even looked at me in a way that would lead to *that*.

"Let's go." I bounce on my toes and push Roy down the dirt-packed street, then realize I don't know where I'm going and let Roy lead. Buster's laughter trails us.

We go over one block, passing my house, nestled between the cemetery and the library. An old picket fence that Ma's been harping on my brother to paint for ages stretches 'cross the front.

Cement City is barely more than an intersection, and there ain't much farther to go; just the cement plant, a few farms, and the river. Then there are the railroad tracks, separating us from Dallas.

I glance up at Roy, confused, when we stop at a home just past the library.

He motions toward the house, his sweaty hand taking mine with his. He swallows, his Adam's apple bobbing.

"What is it?" I ask him. "Why're we here?"

"My father said they are going to tear down this old shack."

With its crooked shutters, chipped paint, caved-in roof, I can understand why. No one's lived here for years, and Ma doesn't go a day without complaining 'bout its drab looks and how it's bad for our little town.

I nod in agreement.

"But," he says, "I've been squirreling away my pennies, and I've enough to save her."

A cool heat rushes me, but I'm not sure how that's possible. I wipe a strand of hair from my face. "You're buying this here house?"

"I am," he says, his Adam's apple bouncing again. "For you and me.

Our house." Roy keeps talking before I can get a word—or thought—in. "Bonnelyn . . ." He trails off, digs into his pocket. "Here's another one for your jar."

My eyes light up, recognizing one of Roy's infamous black-and-white doodles.

It's our church.

It's Roy.

It's me, in a puffy dress.

I look up from the doodle. It's Roy no longer standing in front of me but down on one knee.

"Bonnelyn Elizabeth Parker," he says, "I'm fixin' to take you down the middle aisle."

I knit my brows. "Are you proposing?"

"Well I ain't down here to tie my shoe."

I'd laugh, but I'm stunned. Marriage? With Roy? I swallow and stare at the drawing, his lovely, heartfelt drawing.

Sure, marrying Roy has always been in the cards. *But* . . . I'm not sure I'm ready yet. Some people wait 'til their twenties to get married, in today's day and age, giving 'em plenty of time to make their own mark.

Roy taps the underside of my chin, forcing my gaze away from his doodle and down to him.

"I . . . um . . . I'm flattered Roy. I am. But we're only seventeen—"

"Not now." He stands slowly and palms my cheek that's probably as flushed as his own. "We've got some growing up to do first. I know you got dreams for yourself."

I sigh, in a good way. Hearing him acknowledge my goals relaxes me. Those jitterbugs change a smidge to butterflies. "You really want to marry me?"

"I do, Bonn." Roy leans down, quite the feat to my five-foot-nothin' height, and presses his lips lightly to mine. "When we're good and ready. You tell me when, and that'll be it. We'll create a life together. How does that sound?"

I smile, even while my chest rises from a shaky breath. I curse my nerves for dulling my excitement. My boyfriend declaring he's ready to build a life with me shouldn't give me the heebie-jeebies. It doesn't, I decide.

"We'll finish school," Roy says.

I force my smile wider.

"I'll get a good-paying job as a reporter," he goes on. "You can become a teacher, like you've always wanted. You can lead the drama club, be onstage, do pageants with our little girls."

Now my grin is genuine. "We're going to have little girls?"

"Of course. A little fella, too. 'Til then, I'll fix this house up. She'll be spiffy when I'm done with her, white picket fence and everything."

"You think?"

"I know it." He dips to my eye level. "You're happy, right?"

Am I *happy*? I roll those five letters 'round my head. Yes, I've been stuck on Roy for ages. He made me happy when we were seven and he picked me dandelions, when we were ten and he stopped Buster from making me kiss a frog, when we were thirteen and he patched up my knee after I fell off my bike. The memories keep on coming, and I don't want that happiness to stop. His proposal caught me off guard, that's all. But, yes, we'll make something of ourselves, and we'll do it together.

I lean onto my tiptoes and peck his lips with a kiss. "Roy Thornton, I'd be honored to be your wife one day."

He hoots, swooping his arms under me. Before I know it, I'm cradled against his chest, and we're swinging in a circle.

I scream, but it's playful. "You better not drop me, you clumsy fool."

He answers me with a kiss on the side of my head, and then another and another, as he carries me toward my ma's house.

Freeze, I think. I don't want the secure way he holds me, the way the air catches my skirt, the hope for what's to come, to stop, ever.